Lisa Langley was suffocating. Being buried alive. Swallowed by the darkness.

Cold terror clutched her in its grip. The wooden box imprisoning her was so small, her arms and legs touched the sides. She tried to scream, but her throat was so dry and parched that the sound died.

Tears mingled with the sweat on her cheeks, streaming into her hair and down her neck. What kind of maniac buried a woman alive?

The same kind that robbed you of your life the last few days.

William White. The man she'd dated off and on for the past six months.

The man otherwise known as the Grave Digger.

IN A
HEARTBEAT

RITA HERRON

HQN™

ISBN: 0-7394-6355-1

IN A HEARTBEAT

Other titles by Rita Herron sure to keep you up at night

A Breath Away
Mysterious Circumstances
The Man from Falcon Ridge
Midnight Disclosures
Undercover Avenger
A Warrior's Mission
The Cradle Mission
Memories of Megan
Silent Surrender
Saving His Son
Forgotten Lullaby
Her Eyewitness
Send Me a Hero

And don't forget to watch for Rita's next romantic suspense

Last Kiss Goodbye

Sending chills down your spine summer 2006!

To Allison Lyons—for our first big book together.
Thanks for all your suggestions and patience.
Hope we celebrate many more together!

PROLOGUE

LISA LANGLEY COULDN'T breathe.

Heat engulfed her, and perspiration trickled down her brow and neck, the cloying air filled with the scent of decay, blood and foul body odors.

Her captor's smell.

Her own.

She was suffocating. Being buried alive. Swallowed by the darkness.

Cold terror clutched her in its grip. The wooden box imprisoning her was so small her arms and legs touched the sides. An insect crawled along her chin, nipping at her skin, biting at the flesh. She tried to scream, but her throat was so dry and parched that the sound died.

Tears mingled with the sweat on her cheeks, streaming into her hair and down her neck. What kind of maniac buried a woman alive?

The same kind that robbed you of your life the last few days.

William White. The man she'd dated off and on for the past six months.

How could she not have known what kind of monster he was?

She trembled as the terrifying memories rushed back—the first day the suspicions had crept into her mind. The subtle nuances that William possessed a violent streak. His morbid fascination with the articles in the paper describing the murders.

The odd look in his eyes when the press named him the "Grave Digger."

Above her, a shovel scraped the ground. Dirt splattered the top of the box. Rocks and debris pinged on top of her. The shovel again. More dirt. Over and over. The eerie drone of his voice humming an old hymn faded in and out as he worked.

The past few days had been a living nightmare. He'd heard her call the police. Had known she'd figured out his identity. Had known that the FBI was coming for him.

There was nothing else he could do, he'd told her—except treat her as he had his other victims.

She'd thought each day she would die. But each time, when he'd finally left her, bruised and hurting, she'd managed to will herself to survive. Because she'd thought she might be rescued. That Agent Brad Booker would make good on his promise to protect her.

Particles of dirt pinged off the mound above her again, the sound growing faint as she imagined him finishing her grave.

And then the silence.

It frightened her the most.

He had gone. Was never coming back. Her body convulsed with fear. She was hidden beneath the ground, locked in the endless quiet.

No one would ever find her.

She tried to raise her hand, to roll sideways so she could push at the lid. Her right hand was broken, throbbing with pain, but she dragged her left one to her side, twisted enough to turn slightly, and clawed at the top. Her nails broke into jagged layers, and her fingers were bloody and raw, with splinters jabbing her skin.

He had nailed the top shut. And laughed as she'd begged him to stop.

A few grains of sand sifted through the cracks, pelting her face. She blinked at the dust. Tasted dirt.

It was so dark. If only she had a light.

But night had fallen outside when he'd laid her in her casket.

She pushed and scraped until her fingers grew numb. In spite of the unbearable heat, chills cascaded through her as death closed in. Then, slowly, peace washed over her as she reconciled herself to the fact that she was going to die.

The life she'd dreamed about flashed into her mind—a beautiful white wedding dress. Getting married on a warm, sandy beach with the breeze fluttering the palm leaves and the ocean lapping against the shore. Moonlight shimmered off the sand as they exchanged vows, while her father stood in the distance, smiling proudly.

Then she and her husband were making love beneath the open trees. Promising to hold each other forever.

And later, a baby boy lay nestled in her arms. A little girl danced toward her.

A little girl she could buy a birthstone ring for, just as her mother had for her. Once she'd outgrown it, she'd made it into a necklace. But William had stolen that, too. Had ripped it from her throat and thrown it to the ground. It was lost forever. Just like her dreams.

Too weak to scream, she felt the sob that erupted from her throat die in the dusty abyss of her prison.

The hopes of that life, of a family, faded with it as she closed her eyes and floated into the darkness.

SHE HAD TO BE ALIVE.

The tires of Special Agent Brad Booker's sedan screeched on the wet asphalt as he veered onto the narrow dirt road leading around the old farmhouse. It was pitch-dark, a cloudy moonless night. He'd reached "Death Valley." At least that was the nickname the locals had dubbed it after several people had died in the valley.

Now he knew why it had been dubbed the gruesome name.

The grass and trees all looked brittle and frail from the drought, the outbuildings run-down and dilapidated, the lack of life a sign that it was deserted. He'd heard rumors about the area. That the soil wasn't fertile. That plants and animals couldn't thrive here. That families didn't, either.

He threw the car into Park, jumped out, grabbed a

flashlight and shovel from the trunk and took off running. Behind him two other cars raced up and parked. One his partner, Ethan Manning. The other a squad car from the local Buford police.

His heart pounded as he tore through the dark, wooded area searching for ground that had been freshly turned. Limbs cracked and branches splintered beneath his boots. It had been over twenty minutes since Brad had received the call from the reporter.

The call describing the spot where Lisa Langley was buried.

Jesus.

Brad had promised to protect her.

But he'd failed.

Behind him, the men's voices sounded as each decided which direction to go. It was so damn dark they could barely see their own feet, the towering oaks and pines like a jungle that blocked out any light. They parted, the locals with the police dogs allowing the hounds to lead. Brad wove behind them to the right, shining his flashlight over the dry ground, ignoring the buzz of insects and threat of snakes as he raced through the briars and brambles. A voice inside his head whispered to him that it was too late.

Just as it had been for the other four victims.

Another voice ordered him to fight the panic.

But the air in the box wouldn't last long—if the oppressive summer heat didn't cause Lisa to have heatstroke first. And then the bugs would feast on her body.

He banished the image and forged on.

It seemed like hours, but only a few minutes passed before one of the police tracking dogs suddenly howled.

"Over here!" the officer yelled. "I think we've got something."

Brad spun around and raced toward him. Seconds later, he spotted the mound of dirt. The single white rose lying on top.

The Grave Digger's signature.

"Damn it!" His heart clutched painfully as he imagined Lisa Langley down below. Terrified. Dying.

Or dead already.

He loosened the knot in his tie, then jammed the shovel into the ground, swiping at the perspiration on his face with the back of his shirtsleeve. Manning and the locals followed, digging with a frenzy. Dirt and rocks flew over their shoulders as they worked. Sweat poured down Brad's face, the sound of the shovels and the men's labored breathing filling the humid air.

Finally, the shovel hit something hard. A wooden box. Just like the others.

His heart pounding, he dug faster, raking away the layers of soil until they uncovered the top of the box.

"Give me a crowbar and some light!" Brad shouted.

Ethan knelt beside him, shoved the tool into his hand. Brad attacked the box while the locals shone flashlights on the dark hole.

The wood broke and splintered. Brad clawed it open. His throat jammed with emotions. Fury. Rage. Guilt.

Lisa Langley. Such a beautiful young girl. Left naked and dirty. Bruised and beaten. Her fingers were bloody from trying to dig her way out. Her eyes were closed.

Her body so still.

"Too late," one of the locals said.

"Shit," the other one muttered.

"No!" He couldn't accept it.

Even though he never went to church, wasn't sure he was even a believer, a prayer rolled through his head as he reached inside and lifted her out. She was so limp. Heavy. Cold. He spread her across his lap, then immediately began CPR.

Ethan ran to the car and brought back blankets, draped them over her body, then felt for a pulse.

Gazes locked, the two men paused, paralyzed, for just a second.

Brad continued CPR, muttering under his breath. "Come on, damn it, Lisa, breathe! Don't you dare die on me."

Time lapsed into an eternity as they waited. Finally her chest rose slightly.

Ethan made a choked sound. "Jesus Christ, she's alive." He jumped into motion, punching at his cell phone. "Where the hell's that ambulance? Get it here ASAP—our vic is breathing!"

Brad sent a thank-you to heaven, then lowered his head and wrapped the blankets more securely around her, rocking her back and forth. "Come on, Lisa, stay with me, sweetheart," he whispered. "Help is on the way." He shook her face gently, trying to rouse her into consciousness, but she was in shock. He wrapped the blankets tighter, hugging her closer to warm her. Somehow, if she lived, he'd make it all up to her.

And when he found the bastard who'd done this to her, he'd make him pay with his life.

CHAPTER ONE

Four years later

"THE GRAVE DIGGER IS BACK."

Special Agent Brad Booker stared at the crime scene in shock, the detective's voice mimicking his own thoughts. The Grave Digger case—this whole scenario reeked of it.

That first one had almost cost him his career, his entire life.

His mind ticked over the similarities. Four years ago, the final victim, Lisa Langley, had been found on another moonless night. It had been dark and so damn hot the heat had literally robbed his breath. As if the thought of her missing hadn't already done so.

Just like the other victims, he'd found her in a rural, deserted wooded area. Rotting vegetation and overgrown bushes marred the trail. Yet they had plowed through and found the grave tucked into the midst of Death Valley.

Except today, there was no white rose on the grave. This killer was making his own statement. Adding his personal signature with the gold cross dangling around the woman's neck. But what was the significance?

Hopefully, Joann Worthy's battered body would give them some answers. The stench of blood, decay and death permeated the air. Crime scene technicians combed the woods with flashlights, searching for evidence in the inky night. Insects buzzed noisily. Cameras flashed, capturing all angles of the woman's lifeless body and her burial spot. The medical examiner was busy logging details of injuries and determining the cause of death. A rookie Buford cop named Surges turned green as he spotted the already decaying body, and ran toward the bushes.

Brad stood rooted to the spot, sweat coating his neck and trickling down his back. An image of Lisa's grave four years ago flashed back. Digging furiously in the heat of the night. Praying she was alive. Knowing it was his fault if she didn't survive.

Barely resuscitating her.

And then the trial. Watching Lisa face her attacker. Listening to the gruesome details describing what the man had done to her. Then seeing the man finally locked away.

Another local, Gunther, sidled up to him. "You sure it's not the same man? Maybe that first Grave Digger got out of jail."

"Impossible." Brad swiped at the gnats swarming around his face. "William White died in jail nine months ago, of a massive head injury from a prison fight. I identified his body myself." In fact, he had flown directly to the facility the minute he'd heard of White's demise. Had wanted to make sure for himself the sadistic psycho was really gone. That he could never escape and hurt another woman again.

Especially Lisa.

Then Brad had driven to the mountain cabin she'd rented near Ellijay in North Georgia to deliver the news himself. To see the relief on her face.

To find out if the ghosts still haunted her.

He'd somehow known they would, that she'd never fully escape them. And when he'd realized that he reminded her of the worst time of her life, he'd forced himself to leave. But he'd never forgotten her. Never stopped blaming himself.

Never stopped admiring her courage or...imagining that things could have been different if she'd never been a victim.

But a personal relationship with Lisa Langley was a pipe dream, especially a short-term one, which was all a jaded man like him had to offer. He knew nothing about love. Commitment. Families.

Dealing with a traumatized victim.

His own mother had thrown him out as a kid, discarded him like day-old meat. His bitter childhood had nearly turned him into the type of men he chased today. And there were times even now when he thought he might cross the line. Times when he'd come so close that he'd nearly tripped and fallen over to the dark side.

He had actually done so in the past.

The night he'd finally gotten his hands on William White, that killer instinct in him had emerged again.

Sweet, blissful relief to have caught the man had filled him, just as the rage and injustice of what White had done to his victims had made Brad nearly take the man's life. Because Brad Booker was a man without mercy.

And White had seen that wrath.

Brad had no regrets. He would have enjoyed watching the killer die.

Forcing himself back to the present, he glanced at the victim's body as the M.E. rolled her over. Bile rose in his throat. When they'd found her, Lisa's lower back had been covered in welts in much the same way. Thank God she was safe now.

And keeping her safe continued to be part of the job. No one knew where she was. The new name she'd assumed.

And he intended to keep it that way.

But this poor woman…it was too late.

"Can you believe this?" His partner, Ethan Manning, strode up, notepad in hand, rubbing at the sweat on his neck. "We were in a drought back then, too, a real scorching heat wave."

Brad nodded. "And the killer always left the body in an isolated place." The proximity to his own cabin on the lake seemed eerie, too coincidental. He didn't like coincidences.

"Wooden box was nailed shut with the same kind of

nails," Ethan said. "And he chops off the victim's hair. Brutalizes them. Even calls a reporter to gloat."

Brad grimaced. "But this time he left a cross instead of a rose."

"What's that all about?" Ethan asked.

"Maybe some indication that he's a religious freak." Brad scoffed at the idea. "Any sign of rape?"

The one thing Lisa had been spared. Thank God. Apparently White had been impotent.

"Can't tell yet, but I'll let you know," the M.E. said. "He cuts the fingernails off to get rid of trace evidence."

If the woman had been raped, then the copycat was deviating slightly from the first killer's MO. Still, there were so many similarities. "How could this copycat know every last detail?"

"The papers carried the trial," Ethan suggested. "And he could have read the transcript of Lisa's testimony."

Brad's gut clenched. Every word of that agonizing testimony had been seared into his brain.

"Or hell, he probably bragged about it in prison," Ethan said. "You know how these sickos are. White was a sociopath."

Brad nodded. Right, the bastard had no conscience.

Brad almost understood. He'd been forced to get into perps' heads too many times. Had seen their handiwork. Had witnessed their unspeakable acts.

Had begun to think he might be tainted himself from the violence. Not knowing his daddy or the genetic pool he'd come from triggered disturbing questions in the dark hours of the night.

The M.E. lifted a maggot from inside the box and bagged it. July 1, the dead of summer, and the Atlanta temperature soared near a hundred, making the heat in the box even more suffocating.

The poor woman. How long had she been kept down there before her killer had called? Brad turned toward Gunther, the local officer. "She the one you've been looking for?"

"Matches the sketch," he said, tight-mouthed. "I'll phone the family to meet us at the morgue and verify her identity."

Brad grimaced. One of the worst parts of the job. Telling the victim's family.

He still remembered Dr. Langley's reaction when he'd phoned to relay the news that they'd found Lisa. Alive. Only the man hadn't reacted as he'd expected.

"We'll question the other inmates where White was imprisoned," Ethan said.

Brad mumbled agreement. "And I want to talk to that reporter."

"I'll get someone on the lumber supply companies," Ethan said. "He may be building these boxes himself, like White did. Maybe we can get a jump on where he bought the wood."

Surges staggered up, wiping at his mouth. "Sorry."

"Don't sweat it, kid. You'll get used to it," Brad said. "Just start canvassing those cabins around the lake."

Surges nodded, and Brad contemplated different possibilities—such as what if White hadn't been operating alone years ago?

Sometimes serial killers worked in pairs….

The hairs on his neck tingled. They'd explored that angle during the original trial, but had never found any evidence to support it. But they could have been wrong.

Ethan moved up to his side. "Are you going to tell Lisa?"

Brad jerked his head toward his partner and swallowed hard. He'd never confided his feelings for White's final victim, but Ethan had sensed the attraction. That Brad had nearly lost perspective.

But Lisa hated him. Would barely even look him in the eye.

How could he blame her? He'd hounded her for information on her boyfriend for weeks, accused her of covering for the man, even suggested White had used her, that she was a fool if she didn't know the truth.

Then, when she'd finally phoned him to admit her suspicions, he'd promised to protect her. But White had gotten to Lisa first. The week that followed had been hell for Brad.

But nothing compared to the ordeal Lisa had endured. Seven days and nights of pure torture.

Ethan cleared his throat. "Booker?"

"No, not yet. I don't want to alarm her."

"You think that's wise? Maybe she remembered something during the last four years that might help us. Like the place where White kept her. Or a second man."

Brad nodded, feeling resigned, while they both tried to focus on the details regarding this other woman.

But as things wound down, and he strode back to his

car, a sense of foreboding followed him. Could he ask Lisa to relive those nightmarish details again? To tap into her subconscious, where she'd repressed some of the horror?

Of course you can. You're the man without mercy. You can do whatever it takes to get the job done.

His stomach knotted as another thought struck him. If this psycho was copying White's crimes to a tee, would he go after Lisa just as the last madman had?

FOUR YEARS LATER, and Lisa still checked over her shoulder everywhere she went. She sighed, determined not to obsess over the past as she drove around the small north-Georgia mountain road toward Ellijay. But this particular stretch of road, barren and practically uninhabited, with acres of woods, always gave her the willies.

Lush green grass, wildflowers, rolling hills and valleys filled with groves of apple trees all swished past, the scenery so picturesque she almost wanted to stop and take a photo. To venture into the woods off the side of the road to pick some flowers.

Yet a sliver of unease raced up her spine as she glanced into the shadowy groves. It was too isolated. The shadows held danger. The trees created a canopy of hidden secrets. The leaves shading the sun painted the forest in darkness.

And another drought had rippled across the South. A water shortage had caused the grass to wilt, the flowers to die, the heat to kill. Just as it had when the Grave Digger had struck.

She sped up, anxious to pass the area and enter the

small town, where everyone was friendly. She'd purposely left Atlanta after her ordeal because in every crowd she'd seen a potential attacker. In every dark alley, a psycho waiting to grab her. In every smile from a man, an invitation for trouble.

Would she ever get over her paranoia that someone would attack her again? That becoming involved with a man would end in danger?

William is dead, she reminded herself for the hundredth time that week, as she turned into the day care parking lot. *He's never coming back.*

And you have a new life.

Or did she?

How could she really have a life if she continued to be afraid of her own shadow? If she held herself back from friendships, from involving herself in the community because she didn't want to become a victim again?

No, it had to be this way. She was just trying to survive.

Now, she was safe. She'd changed her last name from Langley to Long. She'd rented a small cabin on top of a rolling hill with apple trees surrounding it. She could see anyone approaching from miles around.

No one in Ellijay knew her true identity, or what had happened to her four years ago.

She intended to keep it that way.

Didn't want the pitying looks. The curious questions. The suspicious eyes wondering if she was crazy. The condemning ones that screamed she was to blame for her own assault. And for those other women's. If only she'd been smarter, come forward sooner....

Just as her father had thought. Oh, he hadn't come right out and said it, but she saw it in his eyes. The disappointment. The shock that she was no longer daddy's perfect little princess. His conviction that she was playing into the victim role.

But she had been fighting it on a daily basis.

She parked, then climbed out of her Toyota. Instantly, heat suffused her, and her feet crunched the dry blades of grass of the lawn. Glancing around quickly, she noticed a tall, broad-shouldered man with wavy hair standing on the corner. He was watching her with hooded eyes.

Chilled by the realization, she hurried into the Love 'N Play Day Care, where she'd worked the last four summers. Thanks to Special Agent Brad Booker, who'd helped her relocate, she'd secured a teaching job at the local elementary school, and supplemented her income by working at the day camps in the summer. She waved good morning to the director, Luanne Roaker, who was talking to a parent in her office, and rushed to her classroom to set up for the activities.

Teaching preschoolers wasn't the career she'd chosen before the attack, and certainly not the career her father wanted for her, but her priorities had changed drastically when she'd been pulled from that grave. Of course, Dr. Liam Langley, prestigious surgeon, didn't understand that. First he'd wanted her to be the society wife, marry a doctor, serve on the volunteer committees as her mother had done when she was alive. When Lisa had mentioned a career instead, he'd suggested she follow in his footsteps and become a doctor.

When she'd chosen teaching, and relocated, he'd been furious.

But she liked working with the children—they were so innocent.

Just as she'd been once.

Never again.

Since the attack, she'd lost her sense of trust, given up on her dreams of marriage and a family. The kids she taught filled that void. They gave her the love she needed, their innocence a precious commodity, offering her hope that one day she'd be normal.

Free of the nightmares that haunted her.

Thirty minutes later, after she'd greeted each of her students with a hug and given Ruby Bailey, her assistant, instructions for setting up the daily art activity, she gathered the group into a circle for their morning share time.

"Miss Lisa," four-year-old Jamie said in a low voice. "I had a bad dream last night."

Lisa patted the little girl's back, grateful she'd finally opened up to share. For the first three weeks in her class, she'd barely spoken. "Tell us about it, Jamie."

The other children waved their hands, anxious to speak.

"I had a bad dream wast night, too," exclaimed Sandy, a towheaded girl who hadn't learned to say her *L*s.

"I have bad dreams all the time," Louis yelled. "But my mama says they're not real."

"They are too real," Jamie mumbled.

"Mine was about spiders," Sandy said. "Icky spiders with a miwwion-triwwion wegs."

"I dreamed about being a princess," Peggy said.

"I wants to be Spiderman for Halloween," Davie Putnam said.

"Halloween's not for a long time," Billy Lackey shouted.

"Let's let Jamie finish first, then the rest of us can share," Lisa said, gently steering them back on track. "Jamie, Louis is right, dreams aren't real, but sometimes they feel real, don't they?"

Sandy scrunched her nose. "The spiders felt reawl. Wike they were crawwing on me."

Lisa squeezed Sandy's hand. "I'm sorry, sweetie. I don't like spiders, either." She turned back to Jamie. "Is that how you felt, Jamie? Like the monster was right there with you?"

Jamie bobbed her head up and down, her lower lip trembling. Sandy scooted over and put her arm around Jamie. "It's awright."

Probably a remnant of her own therapy, but Lisa had learned that if she allowed the children to express their anxiety first thing in the morning, their entire day went smoother. "Tell us the rest of the nightmare, Jamie. Sometimes if you talk about your bad dreams, they go away."

"There was a big ugly monster hiding under my bed." Jamie's eyes widened. "He had green hair and black teeth and scales all over his body!"

"Eww." Several kids shrieked, while Roddy Owens, a big kid with a devilish streak, mocked them.

"Scaredy-cats. Scaredy-cats."

Lisa lifted a warning hand. "Roddy, we don't make fun of others for how they feel."

The voice of the therapist she'd seen after the attack echoed in her head. *Emotions aren't always rational. You simply have to learn to control your reactions.*

"What happened next, Jamie?" Lisa asked.

"He grabbed my feet, and he dragged me under the bed." Jamie wrapped her arms around her waist. "It was so dark. I don't like the dark."

Lisa hugged her. "A lot of people are afraid of the dark, honey. Maybe you could ask your parents to get you a night-light. I sleep with one myself."

"You do?" Jamie said. A few of the children seemed surprised, then others piped in.

"I gots a night-light," Kelly Ames claimed. "It's a Cinderella one."

"I got one shaped like a spaceship," Ernie Walker squealed. "With sparkly colors on it."

Lisa relaxed as the children shared, the morning racing by as they broke into groups for play activities. Finger painting was on the agenda for the day, so she tied an apron around her front to protect her clothing. Art was her favorite activity, and although Ruby sometimes complained of the mess, Lisa loved it. The kids could express themselves and their creativity while having fun and learning how to mix colors.

By one o'clock, when the class left for home, she was exhausted, but her spirits were high as she studied the colorful, bright pictures the children had painted. She and Ruby tacked them on the bulletin board.

Ruby laughed good-naturedly. "Wow, we have everything from bugs to barrettes."

Lisa smiled at Sandy's rendition of spiders, although Jamie's interpretation of her monster disturbed her. Could that monster be real? Maybe a parent abusing her?

Or was she overreacting? Letting her own distrust of men make her suspicious?

"Ruby, do you know anything about Jamie's family?"

Ruby frowned. "Just that her mother died last year."

That's right. Lisa remembered the single parent status from her file, although Jamie never spoke of it. "What about her father?"

"He's a contractor, works long hours, but I hear he's very loving. He's a deacon at the church."

Hmm. Maybe the monster wasn't her father. Maybe a manifestation of Jamie's fear of being alone, of losing her mother.

Lisa's heart squeezed. She'd lost her own mother when she was about Jamie's age. She'd make it a point to pay extra attention to the little girl.

After all, Jamie was only five. She should have childish fears.

But Lisa should be conquering hers.

NEARLY A WEEK HAD PASSED since they'd discovered the first victim of the copycat Grave Digger.

A week that had brought them no closer to finding the killer.

A week of thinking about Lisa Langley and wondering if she was all right.

Sure, Brad had the locals check on her. Physically, she was fine.

But was she really healing? Moving on with her life?

From his reports, she seemed to be. So why was he so damn nervous? Why had he been unable to sleep for the past six nights, wondering if she'd heard the news of the Atlanta woman's abduction and death? If for some reason this new killer would come after her.

He knew for a fact that she didn't read the paper anymore, that she rarely watched the news. That the least criminal behavior triggered her paranoia, when she was struggling so hard to recover.

But what if she had heard and was frightened? Lying in bed wondering why he hadn't been the one to inform her a copycat had left White's signature?

Would Lisa call him if she knew?

He'd left his number, told her countless times to phone him if she needed him.

Had hoped that she might so he could hear that soft, sultry voice of hers.

God, you're sick. As if you'd have something to offer.

You're Brad Booker, a bastard child. A man who's seen the most abysmal side of life. A man who's killed without blinking twice.

A man who should have protected her but let her down.

The clock chimed midnight, the hours ticking by a constant reminder that another victim might be taken any minute. That this case was a chance for him to redeem himself in the eyes of his superiors. He'd been walking a tightrope ever since the White disaster. And this time he had to toe the line. Prove the hard-edged agent was still in control. Methodical. Able to compartmentalize. Stay detached.

Reeling with frustration, he climbed from bed, wiped at the perspiration on his neck and opened the French doors of his cabin, aching for the quiet lull of the lake outside. The heat blasted him, though, insects swarming on the patio, being fried by the insect zapper he'd hung from the railing. He watched them dive toward it, circle the light, be drawn to its brightness. Then he heard the sizzle as they met their death.

Just as he would ruthlessly take down the killer.

As he'd done before.

What would Lisa think if she knew about his past?

He shook off the thoughts. The case was all that mattered.

The first Grave Digger, White, had chosen all brunettes. That is, until Lisa. But Lisa's abduction had been about revenge. Silencing her for reporting him to the police. Not the same motive as the others.

The first victims had fit the same profile, had all been grad students in their twenties. Brunettes just like White's mother.

Grave Digger #2 had started with a brunette, too, although she wasn't a student. She was a professional. Would this new guy deviate even more from the pattern as time progressed?

The mangy mutt that hung around the lake stood near the woods, his skittish gaze connecting with Brad's. The poor dog looked more like a lone wolf in the shadows, his gray coat matted and nasty. He had obviously been abused and would hardly come near Brad, which was fine with him. He didn't want or need anyone depending on him.

Still, from time to time he left food and water on the porch so the damn dog wouldn't starve.

He'd forgotten tonight. The dog hadn't.

Of course, the animal looked as if he'd expected it would come to this. That Brad would let him down.

Grumbling beneath his breath, Brad went to the kitchen, retrieved the dog food, then brought it to the back porch, filled the bowl and put clean cold water in another. His cell phone trilled, and he tensed, his hand hesitating before he shoved the dog food bag inside and grabbed the phone off the end table. Just as he feared, Ethan's number appeared. He clicked in. "Yeah?"

"He has another victim," his partner said, deadpan. "That reporter, Nettleton, called it in."

Brad shut the French doors, yanking on his jeans and a shirt. "I'm sure Nettleton's eating up the story just like the first GD case."

"Yeah, and Booker, you're not going to like it."

He was reaching for his gun, but froze, clenching the phone with a white-knuckled grip. "Lisa Langley?"

"No, Mindy Faulkner."

God, no. Brad staggered backward, a sick feeling in his stomach. He'd met Mindy when he'd questioned her at the hospital after White had died. She was an E.R. nurse, but she hadn't been on duty that night. He'd dated Mindy a few times after White's trial. Had thought by sating himself with another female he'd forget this insane lust toward Lisa.

It hadn't worked.

But Jesus, he didn't want Mindy dead or suffering, either.

His gut clenched as he jammed his gun in his holster and rushed to his car, the reality of his job returning, reminding him of another reason he didn't get involved with women. Being close to him put them in danger.

Was the killer someone he knew? What if he'd chosen Mindy because of him?

HER SHRILL CRIES shattered the peace he craved, the screeching sound echoing off the concrete walls and boomeranging through the ventilation.

She had been crying all night.

Scratching at the walls. Beating on the floor. Howling like an animal.

As if she thought someone might hear.

A deep laugh rumbled in his chest. If she only knew that her attempts were wasted. Futile. That she was so far away from another house that no one would ever know she was here. Not unless he wanted them to....

A sharp pain splintered through his head, and he gripped his temple, doubling over, rocking back and forth to stem the mind-numbing intensity.

What was wrong with him?

He'd been sick before, had his share of medical problems and doctors, but he'd never had headaches before. Never felt this excruciating agony.

Yet he was emboldened by the pain. Empowered just knowing that life and death were both only a heartbeat away.

The air in his lungs grew tight, and he wailed in anguish, the blinding fury that drove him erupting as he tore down the steps. He stumbled. Hit the edge. Grabbed the rail for security.

Another shrill scream pierced the air, reverberating through his head, slicing into his skull as if knives were carving into his brain matter, digging through the frontal lobe and picking at his cerebrum.

He cursed, bile rising in his throat as another scream rent the air. She wouldn't shut up.

Not unless he made her.

The pain in his head intensified, throbbing relentlessly. He grabbed his skull, sweat pouring off his body as a dizzy spell nearly overtook him. It was so damn hot he needed a drink of water. It was almost as if the heat had sucked the life from him, clouded his brain, dried out all his senses.

A litany of curse words flew from his tongue, vile and loathing comments on mankind in general, especially women. He hated his weakness.

Didn't she know that he couldn't take it? That he needed rest. Quiet. Time for the medication to settle.

That without it, she wouldn't live another minute. That it was all her fault he'd been sick.

A cool darkness bathed the interior downstairs. Shadowy streaks of cobwebs dangled in the black corner. Rage seared through him as he spotted her lying on the floor, begging. Her blond hair spilled around her bare shoulders, her breasts lay waiting, supple and distended, her legs curled toward her belly to conceal her secrets.

"Please let me go," she whimpered.

He staggered and flattened his hands on the wall, then watched her through the bars of her prison. Her face was milky-white, void of color, her eyes two red-rimmed, swollen cages holding small, listless green orbs. Perspiration coated her entire body.

"Lisa?"

"No… Please let me go."

Tiny black-and-white lights flashed intermittently like shadowy dots, frozen in front of his eyes. Remnants of memories exploded into his consciousness. Memories that seemed foreign. Memories of another woman coming toward him. Beating him nearly to death. The cries of a terrorized child following. The pain in his chest.

A small dark room, so small he could barely move. Blood seeping down his arms. The smell of urine. A man's voice echoed loud and threatening. "You don't deserve to live."

Then he was someplace else. In the dirt, dying. No, a hospital.

A nurse's face rose above him from the grave.

Angelic. Making promises. She was there to save him. The smile faded.

Then she was gone. The pain returned. The lights dulling. The sound of the woman's voice crying.

"Please, please let me go. I'm not Lisa."

He reached out and unlocked the door, the key jangling

against the metal as she shrank into the corner like a child. Simpering. Feeble. Weak. A coward.

She'd done nothing but beg and try to bargain with him.

No, she wasn't Lisa. Lisa was innocent. Sweet. Caring. Even during the trial, she'd been perfect.

Exactly the kind of woman he wanted.

And in good time he would have her.

For now, though, he'd have to satisfy himself with this woman. Mindy.

"Come here, sweetheart." He lowered his voice. Turned on the charm. "I won't hurt you. Let me make it all better."

She whimpered, the sound clanging through the chamber of endless dark walls. Silky hair streamed around her shoulders in a tangled puddle as she lifted her head. Her eyes resembled two black pools of terror. Her naked body protested as his gaze raked over it. Nipples jutted out. Flesh quivered. Goose bumps skated up her veiny, overheated skin. Lithe long legs curled tighter to her chest to hide her treasure.

His laugh tore through the putrid air. Then he curled his fingers around her bony arm and dragged her toward him.

CHAPTER TWO

HE WAS CHOKING HER. Dragging her across the floor. Embedding his hands in her hair, yanking it from the scalp.

"You shouldn't have told, Lisa. You should have kept quiet."

She gritted her teeth, refusing to beg for freedom. How could she have been such a fool? Four women had died because she'd worn blinders.

Maybe it was her turn.

He tossed her body against the cold concrete, and she spotted a wooden box. Dear God.

A coffin. Just her size. He had planned this out. Had built it just for her.

A protest died on her lips as his hand connected with her cheek. She flew backward, her head striking the cement wall. Stars danced and twirled in front of her eyes. The scent of blood assaulted her. Other fetid odors followed.

Then she passed out.

When she awakened, she was lying inside the box. Her limbs ached, felt heavy, as if they'd been weighted down. Heat clawed at her skin, robbing her of air. She looked into his eyes, begging, pleading for mercy. But he had the eyes of a devil, as if the fiery heat had eaten away his soul.

Then he dropped the lid on top of her, shutting out the light. She sucked in air, felt sweat stream down her face into her hair.

The hammer slammed against the wood. He was nailing it shut.

She tried to scream, but her throat was so raw and dry that her voice died.

A sob welled inside her. He couldn't do this. She was only twenty-five. She had so much to live for.

A job. Maybe another man and a child.

She tried to turn, but the wooden walls scraped her sides.

Then the song began. His grating voice whispered its eerie drone, "Just a rose will do...."

LISA CRIED OUT, her heart pounding. The room spun as she jerked upright.

Perspiration trickled down her forehead. She gripped the sheets with clammy hands, searching the darkness. The curtain fluttered in the sultry breeze from the window. The scent of honeysuckle drifted through the opening. The smell of grass followed, and heat lightning flashed across the sky.

Had she left the window open?

She normally locked everything securely at night.

Panicked, she threw her legs over the side of the bed and listened for an intruder.

The wind whistled. A tree limb scraped the glass

pane. Shadows hung outside like bony hands, clawing at her in the pre-dawn light.

She flipped on the light, but it flickered and went off. Her breath rattled out, tense in the night. Had she lost power, or had someone disconnected the electricity?

She searched for the baseball bat she kept under the bed. Wished she'd gotten up enough nerve to buy a gun.

A squeaking sound splintered the quiet, and her breath rushed out. She clenched the wooden bat and tiptoed toward the bedroom door. From the doorway, she could see the small bath, den and galley-style kitchen. She'd purposely chosen the open plan because there was no place for an intruder to hide. She hesitated at the door, peered through the black emptiness. The light she kept burning in the den had been extinguished, too.

A shadow floated across the window.

Someone was outside.

BY 8:00 A.M., Brad stood in the midst of the stifling hot task force room the FBI had designated for the Grave Digger #2 case, and drew a line across the whiteboard to indicate the time the second victim, Mindy Faulkner, had been reported missing. So far, the task force consisted of himself and Ethan, two local Atlanta detectives, Anderson and Bentley, Captain Rosberg, and two Buford cops, Officers Gunther and Surges, who'd been on the scene when they'd found the first victim. They were expecting a profiler from Quantico at some point, but she hadn't yet arrived.

Outside, horns honked from the heavy morning traffic,

sirens wailed as the ambulances rushed to Crawford Long and Grady Hospitals and a construction crew from a neighboring building cluttered the background with noise. Rush hour was in full swing, the commuters slogging through the downtown maze from the inter-states, while locals hit Atlanta's subway system, MARTA, and Georgia Tech and Georgia State students dragged themselves from coffee houses to their first class.

The temperature was already soaring in the high nineties. Warnings to parents not to leave their children or pets in a car alone, along with talk of heatstroke among the elderly, filled the news, the drought another reminder that Mindy wouldn't last long if they didn't find her soon.

Brad gestured toward a roll-away map and pierced it with different colored push pins indicating where the first victim, thirty-one-year-old Joann Worthy, had dis-appeared, then where her body had been found.

"Okay, what do we have so far?" he asked.

Officer Gunther raised a thumb, the sweat stains beneath his armpits growing. The city air-conditioning must be on overload because the system in the building wasn't working, and they were all melting in the swel-tering temperatures, suit jackets tossed aside and sleeves rolled up for relief, although none seemed forthcoming. "We canvassed the lake area, interviewed the neighbors within a five-mile radius of where the body was found. No one saw or heard anything suspicious."

Brad grimaced. Just like the first time. "Do we have the M.E.'s report or word from forensics yet?"

"Nothing definite from forensics," Ethan said. "Preliminary autopsy shows multiple contusions to the body, lacerations on hands, wrists, blunt force trauma to the head, signs that the perp attempted to sexually assault the woman, although he didn't rape her."

"He's varying from White then," Brad said. "But if he failed at rape, he may be impotent, as White was."

"It probably adds to his agitation," Ethan added.

A chorus of mumblings rushed out in agreement.

"We looked for a connection between Worthy and White, but so far, we haven't found one," Brad said. "Mindy worked at the hospital where White died, but she wasn't on duty the night he was admitted."

Ethan spoke up next. "I'll interview White's old cell mate, Curtis Thigs. He was released on parole a few days ago. Then maybe I'll talk to some of the other inmates."

"Good luck," Detective Bentley said with a chuckle.

Brad shot them a menacing look. Nothing about this case was funny. "We need to cross-check for other parolees recently released, mental patients as well."

"I'm on it," Captain Rosberg said.

"Any leads on the lumber for the coffin?" Brad asked.

"We're still checking it out," Detective Anderson said. "It may take awhile. Construction crews in and around Atlanta are too many to count."

"Make it a priority." Brad gestured toward his partner. "How about the first vic—a boyfriend in the picture?"

Ethan shook his head. "According to her roommate, she hasn't been seriously involved with anyone for some time."

"He's choosing them at random?" Captain Rosberg asked.

"Maybe." Brad still didn't know what to think. White had chosen all coeds. Joann Worthy had been a computer consultant. "Where was the Worthy woman last seen?"

"A sushi bar around the corner from her apartment." Ethan consulted his notes. "No, wait, after that, she went into a dance club called Johnny Q's on Marietta Street."

"And no one saw a man with her?" Brad asked.

"Two guys hit on her, but she brushed them off," Ethan added. "Got a description. We're following up. Last the bartender saw, she stepped outside for a cab."

"The cab companies?"

"We've shown her picture. No one remembers picking her up."

Shit. A dead end.

Ethan rapped his knuckles on the wooden table. "We'll keep looking into her activities and friendships, though, see what we can find."

"How about our latest missing woman...Mindy Faulkner?" He nearly choked on the name.

"Thirty, slender, dirty-blond hair, five-four, one hundred and ten pounds, blue eyes," Captain Rosberg stated.

"He varied again. Joann Worthy was a brunette," Brad said. "Mindy's a blonde."

Everyone nodded and made a note of the detail.

"According to a nurse at First Peachtree Hospital where she works as an R.N., she left the hospital yesterday afternoon around three," Rosberg continued. "None of her coworkers have seen her since. And her landlord says she didn't show up at her apartment after work or last night."

"So, we've got several hours unaccounted for," Detective Bentley said. "He could have picked her up anywhere."

Brad nodded. "Let's get busy. The first GD kept each victim seven days and nights. This copycat held his first victim for only three. The clock is ticking."

The group dispersed, each officer heading out to his assigned part of the investigation.

Ethan's boots hit the floor. "You think there's a significance to the time period he's holding them?"

Brad twisted his mouth in thought. "Yeah. White said God made the world in seven days and nights. This guy leaves a cross, keeps his vics three days. If he's following White's twisted logic, maybe the resurrection of the Grave Digger is symbolic of Jesus coming back to life."

Ethan cursed. "On the third day, he rose from the dead."

Brad nodded. "And Mindy's paying for it."

Ethan gave him an odd look, almost sympathetic, although neither man did sympathetic. "I know you're beating yourself up over this, Booker."

Of course his partner would see through him. Hadn't Ethan's own family been killed two years ago? It had turned *him* into a hard-ass, one who took too many risks sometimes.

Brad cursed. "Mindy might die because she knew me. And the first body was dumped near my house. He's taunting me, shoving the blasted case in my face."

"We'll find her," Ethan said, although Brad knew the words were lip service. There were no guarantees. And so far, no concrete leads.

"I've made a list of all the men I've crossed in the past five years," Brad said. "I'm running their names to see if anyone might be on parole or have connections nearby."

"Good plan." Ethan shrugged into his jacket. "Have you thought about talking to Lisa Langley?"

"Hell yeah, I've considered it." Brad threw down his pen and scrubbed his hands over the back of his neck. "But I can't put her in jeopardy again."

Ethan jammed a cigarette into his mouth, but didn't light it. He'd been trying to quit smoking for months, but kept falling back on the habit in times of stress. Not that their job wasn't always stressful. "I know you don't like it, and neither do I, but we have to do everything we can to save this girl."

As if Brad didn't know that.

But bringing Lisa out of hiding to do so didn't seem like the smartest idea. Besides, he wasn't sure she could help.

Or maybe he was losing his edge again. His perspective.

Because Brad Booker, man with no mercy, had found a heart when he'd heard Lisa's tale of horrors. And when he'd pulled her from that grave and held her, he'd felt a personal connection.

He couldn't afford to have a heart. Not with Mindy's life on the line.

"You're right." He loosened his tie, cleared this throat, swallowed back bile. "I won't tell Lisa on the phone. I have to see her in person." He owed her that much.

Ethan nodded. "Keep in touch. I'll call you after I talk to White's cell mate."

Brad pocketed his cell phone. The last thing in the world he wanted to do was track down Lisa and inform her that another Grave Digger was haunting the city, or make her relive the nightmare of her attack.

But he had to save Mindy's life. And if Lisa remembered anything new that might help, he needed to talk to her.

LISA MUST HAVE IMAGINED the shadow. Still, she couldn't fall back to sleep, so she sat in the rocking chair for hours, staring at the window.

Early morning, the shadow reappeared. Footsteps clattered outside.

Lisa reached for the phone to dial 911 when a knock sounded at the door. She nearly jumped out of her skin.

For a few seconds, she could barely move, the fear she'd grappled with for the past four years paralyzing her. Then sanity returned, and she dragged in huge gulping breaths, trying to calm herself. A serial killer wouldn't announce himself at the door.

Only hers had four years ago. She'd actually been dating him and hadn't known it....

Besides, how had the window gotten open? And why had she lost power when it hadn't been storming?

The knock jolted her again, and she raced to her bedroom, yanked on a full-length cotton robe and belted it, then pushed her disheveled hair from her face as she hurried to the door.

She rarely had visitors. Mrs. Simmerson from across the valley occasionally stopped by with home-made goods, and occasionally Ruby dropped by for a visit, but never this early in the morning. Someone had rented the cabin about a half mile down the road, but she hadn't met him yet. She didn't intend to, either.

"Miss Long, it's your new neighbor. Name's Aiden Henderson."

She tensed at the sound of the man's voice. It was deep. Scratchy. A smoker's voice. "What do you want and how do you know my name?"

"The real estate agent told me." He cleared his throat. "I...the power went off, so I thought I'd check and see if it was just my place or everyone else's."

He could see hers was off, too, couldn't he?

"My phone isn't connected yet," he continued. "Or else I'd call it in."

She stood on tiptoe and looked through the peephole. The entire mountain and valley were dark. "I'll call in the power loss. Someone probably had an accident and hit a transformer."

"Probably." A tense second followed but he didn't leave. A sliver of early morning sunlight illuminated him enough for her to see what he looked like. He had light brown, wavy hair, was probably in his late thirties and wore jeans and a black T-shirt with boots. A scar marred his lower arm, making her wonder if he'd been in an accident. He was big, too, almost six feet, at least two hundred and thirty pounds.

William had been shorter and a mere one-eighty, but he'd crushed her like a matchstick doll.

And something about this man seemed familiar. But she couldn't think where she might have met him. Then it hit her. "I saw you in town, didn't I?"

"I think so. At least I recognize your car," Aiden replied. "But you looked like you were in a hurry so I didn't introduce myself."

She shivered and rubbed her hands up and down her arms. Had he been following her?

"I received some of your mail in my box yesterday." He indicated a couple of envelopes with a beefy hand, and she froze, wondering if it was a trick to lure her to let him inside.

"You can just slide them beneath the door."

He fidgeted, then stooped and did as she'd requested. "Thanks."

"And here's your paper."

"Just leave it on the porch."

He stuffed wide hands into his jean pockets. "You don't happen to have any coffee brewed, do you? I forgot to buy some when I went to the store."

So he'd been grocery shopping. "No. Listen, I really need to go. I'm late for work."

"Oh." Disappointment laced his voice, and he peered toward the window. Then a smile tilted his mouth. "Well, if you need anything, I'm right down the road. Since we're neighbors, I'm sure we'll be seeing a lot of each other."

She doubted it. "All right, thanks."

"I put my number on one of the envelopes." He shrugged, a frown pulling at his lips. "Listen, the newspaper mentioned that a woman had been murdered in Atlanta and another one abducted. You being single, living alone, you ought to be careful. We're not that far from the city."

Lisa froze, her nails digging into the wooden door. How did he know she was single?

A breeze fluttered the trees, rattling the windowpane, and she shivered, grateful when he finally ducked his head and loped down the porch steps. She slid to the window and watched as he disappeared down the dirt road. But his words rushed back to haunt her.

A woman had been murdered in Atlanta. Another woman was missing.

A wave of pure panic overcame her, making her body tremble.

William White is dead. You're safe.

But curiosity won out, and she jerked open the door and grabbed the paper. The headlines startled her into shock: The Grave Digger Returns!

Her chest in a spasm, Lisa staggered to the couch, sank onto the fabric and dropped her head between her knees to keep from passing out. No, William was dead. Brad had told her so himself.

It was impossible that he was back.

Her stomach rolled as she lifted her head and skimmed the article. A copycat. He'd killed one woman so far. But the MO was the same. He'd buried the woman alive. And he'd taken a second victim already. Special Agent Brad Booker was working the case.

Her sense of peace shattered. She clutched her throat, the suffocating feeling returning.

Brad Booker's face materialized in her mind. Handsome, sharp, chiseled features framed a visage that revealed no emotion. He had an almost stoic smile. And cold, whiskey-colored eyes that remained detached most of the time.

He had dragged her from that dark grave with his bare hands. Had been kind to her during the trial. A Rock of Gibraltar.

Yet he'd kept his distance since.

Because he had seen the woman William White had turned her into. Had known what a fool she was for not realizing the truth sooner.

Humiliation flushed her face as she remembered waking in the ambulance, naked and dirty, then looking into Brad's anxious eyes and seeing the horror of what had happened to her mirrored back.

Brad Booker had seen her shame. He would always look at her with pity.

As William White's final victim.

Still, sometimes in the heat of the night, when loneliness held her in its icy clutches and her past haunted her, she wished that things could have been different.

She hated William White. He'd stolen something from her that day, something she'd never get back....

As BRAD DROVE TOWARD Ellijay, the city traffic gave way to winding country roads, lush green farmland, sparsely populated areas dotted with clapboard houses and trailer parks, then rolling hills and mountains. Apple orchards filled the countryside, advertisements for the apple houses painted across barns and on homemade signs. The buzzing traffic sounds faded to a purr, the pace slowing as he put more and more distance between himself and the city.

But the two-hour trek passed in a tense blur, the beauty of the countryside diminishing as the heat wave sucked the life from the flowers and trees, turning green grass and leaves a dull brown.

A deadly kind of brown that reminded Brad of the Grave Digger and the grisly details of his crimes. No wonder Lisa liked living in the mountains. After enduring the grueling months of the trial and media publicity, she must find the serenity of the country-side, the fresh clean air and small-town atmosphere therapeutic.

Before he'd left the office today, he'd reviewed the transcripts of Lisa's trial, searching for clues that might lead to where the Grave Digger could be holding Mindy. But at the time of the trial, Lisa could only describe the place as dark, cold, a small prison built in a fortress. Maybe a basement, an old warehouse, an abandoned building in the country.

It could have been anywhere. White had beaten Lisa unconscious before he'd stuffed her into that box, put it in the back of his SUV and driven her to an isolated patch of woods between Cumming and Dawsonville.

Then he'd dug her grave. He was calculating. Sadistic. Showed no remorse.

He'd known just the right amount of time it would take for the victims to die, exactly how long they could breathe underground before they expired, and had timed his phone calls so the police had arrived too late each time.

Except for Lisa.

Had the man miscalculated? Or had he found a sudden moment of conscience, changed his mind and decided to let Lisa live? Or had Lisa been stronger than he'd realized, able to hold on to life longer?

White hadn't broken once during the interrogation. He'd been cool. Unemotional. Exhibited sociopathic behavior.

Even during his prison confinement, White had never revealed his secret hiding place, the reason he'd started his crime spree, or admitted to a second party helping him. According to the prison psychologist, White had been abused as a child. Then he'd suffered a head injury when he was a teenager that had caused him to experience a psychotic break in his twenties.

The sun nearly blinded Brad as he wove through the small town of Ellijay. Midmorning, Lisa would be at work at the Love 'N Play Day Care. He passed several small storefronts, an antiques shop, a small, old-fashioned diner, an ice cream parlor and bookstore, along with the town library, courthouse and police station. A beauty shop, an arts and crafts store that sold handmade items on consignment, and a bridal boutique occupied one corner. About a block from the center of town, an old white house had been converted into a day care. A white picket fence decorated with colorful wooden cartoon characters, including a life-size Mickey and Minnie Mouse, encircled the center. Ancient oaks and pines flanked the property, offering privacy and shading the outdoor playground, although the earth looked parched, the ferns and flowers drooping with heat. Squeals and laughter floated through the air as dozens of children built imaginary castles and roads in the sandbox, played on the jungle gym and monkey bars and pushed each other on the swings.

He frowned. These kids were innocent.

Was that the reason Lisa had chosen to work with children? To return to that time and place before she'd known the ugliness that existed?

Had he ever been that young and innocent himself? No.

Pushing aside his own bitter memories, he scanned the area for Lisa. When he didn't see her outside, he strode up to the front door of the day care and went inside. A plump receptionist with dark curly hair and a gap between her front teeth sat at a desk, the director's office to the right.

"Welcome to Love 'N Play. I'm Deidre, what can I do for you, sir?"

"I'm here to see Lisa Long."

"Do you have a child in her classroom, Mr....?"

"Brad Booker." He didn't want to alarm her or reveal he was FBI. "No...um, but I'm considering moving to Ellijay and enrolling my child."

She pasted on a friendly smile, revealing dimples. "Well, she's in class right now. But the kids are going to be dismissed in a few minutes, if you could wait."

"Yes, that would be fine."

"You can watch the class through the window if you want." Deidre gestured to the hallway, toward a glass partition on the upper half of one wall. "Lisa's an excellent teacher and day camp worker, one of our most loving helpers. The kids just adore her."

He was certain they did. The sight of the small children stirred unease in his gut as he peered through the glass. He'd never attended preschool, had never been around kids much, either, and he felt out of place.

Music chimed through the room, and the boys and girls danced in a circle, waving bright, colorful scarves, twirling and giggling, some bumping into one another and tumbling to the floor with laughter. Lisa stood in their midst, waving a purple scarf around her head, swaying and laughing with them. She stooped and picked up a tiny girl, then twirled her around until the child giggled. Suddenly a chorus of other voices begging for the same treatment broke out. Lisa laughed and, one by one, gave each of the kids an adoring grin and followed suit, her skirt swirling around her.

Brad's chest tightened. She looked so damn happy, carefree even. So different from the traumatic woman during the months of the trial that he wanted to freeze-frame the image and leave her undisturbed by this latest horror.

Knowing she couldn't see him, though, he took an

extra few minutes to study her. Her heart-shaped face had always seemed so delicate and pale, yet now a slight tan gave her a healthy glow, and her hair seemed shinier, blonder, with natural highlights. Her too-thin body seemed rounder and more sexy, her arms more muscular, as if she might have been exercising or working out in the yard.

Today, she wore a simple white cotton blouse with gathers up the middle, accentuating her curves, along with a denim skirt that swirled around her ankles. Dainty sandals on her feet revealed long narrow toes with red-painted toenails.

His body stirred with desire....

He'd known that beneath the battered woman there was a beauty. But he hadn't imagined how sexy and tempting she'd be when that traumatized look faded, and she actually smiled.

The few times he'd visited since the trial, he'd noted the wariness reflected in her big blue eyes. Had known that seeing him was a reminder of the worst time of her life. Another reason he'd stayed away.

She suddenly glanced up and spotted him. He felt like a voyeur for spying on her, but hadn't been able to resist. Once again, as he feared, the smile froze on her face, the light in her eyes diminishing rapidly.

He fisted his hands by his sides, hating to shatter her happiness. But he had no choice.

Another woman's life was hanging in the balance.

THE MINUTE LISA HAD READ the paper this morning, she'd known Special Agent Brad Booker would visit today.

Her stomach clenched as their gazes met. For a moment, she thought his whiskey-colored eyes flickered with emotions. Regret. Need. Loneliness. Maybe even… attraction.

But the look disappeared so quickly she was certain she'd imagined it. In fact, his jaw snapped rigidly tight, indicating his mind was on one thing and one thing only—this latest case. He was all FBI.

But during the trial, when he'd sat by her side, she'd sensed the bottled-up rage that simmered below the surface of the tight-lipped, hard-edged agent persona. She felt that rage teetering on the verge of exploding now.

"What is it, Lisa?" Ruby asked. "Honey, you look as if you've seen a ghost."

She had. The ghost of a past she'd left behind. "I…" Jamie and Peggy tugged at her skirt, and she jerked her attention back to the children. "Time to collect our scarves," she said, adding a light tone to her voice to hide the turmoil riddling her. "Dance over to the box and put them inside. Then get your backpacks ready to go home."

The kids ran toward the cubbyholes and grabbed their bags, then Ruby gathered them into a circle to hand out the day's artwork, butterflies they'd created from clothespins and tissue paper. Finally, Lisa lined them up in the hallway for car pool, hugging each one goodbye before Ruby connected them with their ride.

Hoping to stall as long as possible, Lisa hurried into the room and began straightening up.

Ruby gathered the art supplies. "Go on and speak with that man, I'll finish up here. You shouldn't keep him waiting."

Lisa bit back the truth, hating to lie to her friend. But Ruby was a born mother and would worry to death if she knew the facts about Lisa's past. She'd been trying to build a new life here, to escape the pitying looks and questions. She couldn't let the ugliness from her past color her new world.

Only now Special Agent Brad Booker had shown up at her workplace, threatening that tiny bit of peace. Because he was here to talk about his investigation. The Grave Digger. The past one. And the present.

He had to look for a connection. On some level, she understood that, but she didn't like it. And another part of her, the feminine part, resented the fact that work was the only reason a man like Brad would visit her.

"Go on, scoot." Ruby whisked a hand toward her, and Lisa relented, retrieved her purse and walked into the hall.

Brad approached her, his broad shoulders squared, his face devoid of expression. He didn't immediately speak, seemed to understand that she needed time to process his appearance.

Just as she remembered, his skin seemed naturally bronzed and his short clipped hair was as black as coal, as if somewhere in his past he had Italian ancestry. God, he was an intimidating man, handsome as sin but rock-hard, with unforgiving eyes.

He was undeniably the sexiest man she'd ever seen. She remembered rousing in his arms after he'd pulled her from the grave, and had felt an instant connection to him. With Brad, she'd never been afraid.

At least not physically. But emotionally…he scared her to death. He made her want to feel again. To take a chance.

But discussing the Grave Digger was something she couldn't handle.

Besides, he had demons haunting him that were every bit as awful as hers. Demons she knew he'd never talk about, just as she didn't about her own.

"I knew you'd come," she said, when he started to speak. "But we're not going to visit here. Let's go to the coffee shop."

He gave a clipped nod, his gaze scrutinizing her. She wondered if she had glue on her clothes, or if he was simply remembering the way she'd looked during the trial, the way she sometimes still saw herself. Her hand automatically went to her neck to feel for the amethyst that her mother had given her, but then she remembered it was gone. William had stripped it off, just as he'd stripped her soul.

The old familiar humiliation crawled back up her spine. When Brad found her, her entire body had been black-and-blue with bruises, her cheeks, nose and lips purple and swollen, her eyes red-rimmed and bloodshot from lack of sleep and crying, her long blond hair chopped in ragged tufts from where William had sawed it off like a savage.

So ugly.

She jerked her gaze in front of her to keep from covering her face and hiding at the memory. She'd thought she'd cried out all her pain four years ago.

It was amazing how quickly it resurfaced.

They walked along the sidewalk, down the block, the light summer breeze fluttering the trees, whipping her denim skirt around her ankles, and bringing the faint aroma of Brad's cologne, some masculine woodsy scent that she still remembered from the ambulance ride. She'd been grasping for a lifeline that night, latching on to anything positive to will herself to stay alive. His scent had been one of them.

His low, soothing, husky voice another. The feel of his hands, the third. The connection had been so potent that sometimes in the night when she was alone she swore she could still feel his fingers stroking her palm.

Pots of geraniums, marigolds and impatiens filled the window boxes and planters in front of the stores, adding color, although the normally cheerful signs of summer that usually lightened her moods did nothing to alleviate her anxiety today. In fact, they only reminded her that even when beautiful things flourished, ugly ones might be festering below the surface.

Five minutes later, they scooted into a booth at Daisy's Diner, the small local hangout, where food and gossip were a daily ritual. They both ordered coffee, although Lisa dumped sweetener in hers, then added a cube of ice to cool it, and cradled her cup in her hands. Anything to stall, to keep her from reaching for Brad and begging him to make this nightmare go away.

Brad's dark gaze skated over her, relentlessly calm, haunted. "You said you knew why I was here?"

Lisa nodded, unable to look into his eyes, his face,

to see the pity. She felt him watching her, studying her as he had through the trial, as if she were a fragile piece of glass that might shatter any second. Wondering if he should call a shrink. Would she be able to hold it together long enough to testify?

The case had all hinged on her. He had been relentless in pushing her for details...details she'd tried so hard to forget.

Lisa shivered. "He's...he's back, isn't he?"

Brad reached out to touch her hand, then pulled away as if he shouldn't. "No, it's not William, Lisa," he said in that gravelly voice that made her wish she wasn't so weak, that she had the courage to look him in the eye and admit her attraction. "He is dead, just like I told you."

"Then a copycat killer?" she said quietly.

"I'm afraid so. We found the first victim a few days ago."

Anger simmered in his voice. Yet the protective tone underlying it also aroused something deep inside her. Something she hadn't thought about in ages. She had clung to Brad's promise while William had tormented her. Knowing that he was out there looking for her, that he wouldn't give up, had kept her alive.

"He's kidnapped another woman now. Her name is Mindy Faulkner."

Lisa closed her eyes. Hearing the woman's name made it more painful. Made *her* real. How did Brad do his job? "I'm sorry, Brad...."

He reached out again, and this time covered her hand

with his own. Lisa tensed, savoring the comfort, the warmth of his skin. He had wide palms, soft but slightly callused. Long fingers, blunt nails. She'd memorized those in the ambulance, as well.

How many times had she lain in bed at night, aching for someone to hold her? Thinking about those hands? His strong arms. Wanting him to touch her. Soothe her. Stir some life back into her endlessly listless body.

If only she'd met him before she'd met William White. Before he'd tainted her....

Brad cleared his throat, ran a finger over her palm. "I hate to ask you to do this, Lisa, but I need your help."

She sighed, disappointment mushrooming inside. Had she really hoped he'd come because he wanted to see her?

"How can I help you, Brad? I don't know this woman or anything about this copycat man." *Not like I did last time.*

Guilt flared in his eyes. Damn it, she didn't want his guilt or pity.

"It's been four years, Lisa," he said in a low voice. "Except for the length of time the killer keeps the victims, and the fact that he leaves a cross instead of a rose with each one, this guy is copying the original crimes to a tee. He's either read the trial transcripts, talked to White or he was a second party to the first crimes. Maybe there's something you've remembered during the last four years that might help us."

"No..." Lisa shook her head, denial mounting.

"There's nothing more to tell…you know everything. And there wasn't a second man."

"You might have repressed his memory. Maybe he was there in the shadows, just watching, or maybe—"

"No." She fidgeted with the coffee cup, took a sip, pushed it away, disgusted. Maybe she hadn't remembered everything that had happened. But God, she didn't want to… And Brad couldn't ask that of her. He'd seen what White had done to her. The horrid pictures. The brutal details.

"Maybe something about the place he held you," Brad insisted in an even voice. "White never revealed the location during the interrogation or his prison stay."

Lisa stared into his cold eyes. How could he do this to her? Ask her to remember. To revisit that evil tunnel of darkness. "I can't do this, Brad. Please, stop it."

Suddenly shaking all over, she jumped up and ran outside. Heat suffused her, the sun scalding her as she ran toward the day care parking lot and the safety of her car. Dust flew up from her sandals, and she nearly stumbled over a crack in the sidewalk, but she forged on, her stomach heaving as she grabbed the car door, swung it open and collapsed inside.

A minute later, Brad stood beside the car, holding open the door, towering over her. "Listen, Lisa." A muscle ticked in his jaw as if he was angry, but anguish laced his voice. "This woman…I know her. She…we dated." His voice dropped a decibel, riddled with fear, more guilt. "I can't let her die."

A shudder overtook her. Brad had met someone. Had

fallen in love. And like a foolish girl, Lisa had harbored hope that one day he might see her as someone other than a victim.

She chewed on her lip, fighting to steady her breathing. Four years ago, Brad Booker had been her savior. She wouldn't be alive now if it weren't for him. How could she possibly turn him down?

Tears blinded her as she righted herself. She trembled, feeling blistering hot and freezing cold at the same time. It had taken every ounce of courage she possessed to move on with her life, to try to forget the horrible things William had done to her.

If she traveled down that road again, willing up memories, reliving it, she might not survive a second time....

CHAPTER THREE

BRAD GRIPPED HIS HANDS by his sides as Lisa drove away. He had the sinking feeling that he'd screwed up in some major way. Maybe he had been insensitive. Coldhearted. A bastard.

Even cruel to have come here.

He'd seen Lisa fidget, and remembered her tears over the lost amethyst that her mother had given her. It had been the only thing she'd had left of her, and White had torn it from her just as he'd torn her clothes. Brad would never forget the day Lisa had told him. Her mother had given her the ring on her fourth birthday, and explained that amethyst had been worn by royalty in the fifteenth century and was supposed to control evil.

But the amethyst, made into a necklace, certainly hadn't done its job with White.

All day Brad's imagination had pummeled him with horrid images of what Mindy was enduring. He'd had to ask for Lisa's help. Details from Lisa's trial, the inhumane treatment, then Joann Worthy's bruised face passed through his mind. He leaned against the car, heat beating down on his back.

The ritualistic behavior of other serial killers compounded his worries. Sometimes they changed MOs. Their depravity escalated. Who knew what this new guy was capable of? If he'd only gotten started...

Mindy was a nice woman, a nurse with a bright smile and kind heart. She helped others selflessly, had tried to be the woman he desired.

But Brad hadn't had his head in the game.

Because another woman occupied his mind.

Now the case dominated his mind. Not Lisa Langley in particular, he told himself. He'd simply found a soft spot for a victim. Had felt guilty over his part in not preventing the abduction.

And hell, he'd be lying if he didn't admit he'd imagined holding her, kissing her, taking her beneath the sheets and proving to her that every man wasn't a sadistic animal. He'd fantasized about making slow, easy love to her until he put a smile on her face that would wipe out the sorrow White had left there.

But that meant nothing. A sexual attraction, that's all it was. No emotional attachments.

Brad Booker didn't need anyone. Didn't want to get involved. Couldn't allow himself to.

He brushed at the dust coating his slacks, climbed in his sedan and cranked the engine, grateful for the blast of the air conditioner. An old-timer stopped by his pickup truck and studied him, his wife shifting a foam container of leftovers in her hands as she, too, peered at him. The diner probably served as a boiling pot for

gossip. Brad supposed they didn't see too many strangers in town. They were automatically suspicious.

Had they overheard his conversation with Lisa in the
diner? Were they Lisa's friends, trying to protect her?

If so, he should be happy she'd found solace in these
north Georgia mountains. Friends in the small town.

And one day she might find a lover.

He pinched the bridge of his nose, ignoring the stab
of unease at the idea as he debated over what to do.
Drive back to Atlanta? Spend the night?

What good would staying do?

He had work to do to find Mindy. And Lisa knew how
to contact him.

But she obviously thought he was a bastard. And he
had been. Otherwise, Mindy might not be in danger.

And Lisa wouldn't have run from him as if he was
the devil himself.

LISA WANTED TO RUN AWAY.

Again.

She clenched the steering wheel with a steel grip and
guided the car through town toward her cabin, trying to
plan a route of escape. But where would she go this
time? And how far would she have to run to escape the
demons? Would she need to change her name again?
Get a different type of job?

The bitter memories of the days and nights of her
captivity rolled through her head. Day one—the blind-
fold. The tauntings. The darkness. The unbearable heat.
The stench of blood and decay. Day two—his evil touch.

The beating. The sick mind games. The constant fear pressing in her belly. Day three—the box beneath his bed. The sounds of his breathing. The claustrophobia. The hints of what he wanted....

Day four—the hunger. The dry, parched throat from pleading with him for water. The dreams of dying just to escape.

Gasping for air, she hit the power button to roll down her window and gripped her stomach, fighting nausea. A breeze rushed in, hot air filling the car. Dark clouds floated across the sky, obliterating the sun, but the weather forecast had predicted no rain. Yet the green-tipped mountaintops rose in front of her, the open pastures and farmland offering a sanctuary. Cows grazed in the fields, lazily gathering around a watering hole. A farmer in overalls was riding his tractor. An elderly woman in a bonnet stood with a hoe, examining her vegetable garden, a plump yellow squash in one hand. So picturesque. Safe. A perfect place to grow old and raise a family.

She thought she'd escaped the ugliness when she'd moved here. But in a heartbeat, one quick flash of time, Brad Booker had brought it all back.

She hated him for it.

Yet she ached to turn the car around and seek solace in his arms.

Blinking to clear the tears and regain control, she forced herself to concentrate on the beauty surrounding her. In the fall, when the apple trees were heavily laden, their fruits spilling to the ground, she gathered the

Granny Smith apples and baked dozens of pies. Last year, she'd canned and frozen at least a bushel, had made homemade applesauce, apple butter and jelly. She'd savored the tart tastes, the miracles of nature.

How could that nature include humans so depraved that they fed on the weaker at heart?

Humans like William. And now this latest sick man.

How did Brad Booker continue to do his job without the atrocities of it eating at his soul?

She was still shaking when she sped up the driveway to her cabin, the serenity she normally experienced at the sight of her log home lost in the emotions warring within her.

Brad had suffered the atrocities—she'd seen it in his eyes. Heard it in his voice.

And there were the recriminations.

He was blaming himself now for this woman's disappearance. As she'd once suspected he might have blamed himself for her abduction.

But it hadn't been his fault. Just as it wasn't this time.

Brad was the good guy.

William had been psychotic. And she had been a fool for not believing Brad the first time he'd hinted that her old boyfriend was trouble.

Her emotions in a tailspin, she glanced down the valley at the cabin where the stranger had just moved in. He'd been lurking outside her place this morning. Who was he really? What did she know about him?

Panicking, she threw open the car door and bolted up the graveled drive toward the house. Warm sunshine splintered through the dark clouds, the afternoon heat engulfing her as she opened the door and slipped inside. She slammed the door and locked it, then leaned against the wooden frame, trembling. She was safe. No one had followed her. She could hide out here forever.

The quiet seemed eerie around her.

Then the truth assaulted her. She'd chosen this cabin because it was at the top of the hill, away from strangers, from the town, so no one would bother her. Yet the location had isolated her from others to the point of preventing her from making friends.

Because she had wanted it that way.

The kitchen cupboard in the corner, filled with dozens of jars of apple butter and jelly she'd canned, mocked her. Dozens of jars—but she lived alone. All alone.

She had no one to share them with. Wouldn't allow anyone close enough to even consider offering a dinner invitation.

She dropped onto the sofa and heaved for air, the realization that she'd locked herself away in a self-imposed prison filtering through the haze. William had taken everything from her the day he'd kidnapped her. Had stolen her innocence. Her trust in men. Her dreams of the future.

She glanced around at the bookcase, the sofa table. Empty. Only a few pictures of family. No boyfriend. No hopes of ever having one.

Only a framed photograph of her mother, and a picture of her father, sat on the table, one she'd clipped from the newspaper. He looked austere. Imposing. But he'd actually smiled, obviously primed because the article declared him a brilliant surgeon.

He never smiled at her now. Since the trial, she was no longer daddy's little girl. Although they occasionally spoke on the phone, conversations remained brief to prevent any tracing so she could remain hidden. Of course, they had argued long before William had entered her life. Her father's goals for her had been different from her own. He wanted her to be a social star, she wanted none of the limelight.

And she'd hated it even more when all the publicity about the trial had focused on her.

Sure, she'd told herself she was healing.

But this morning's headlines, seeing Brad Booker again, knowing another woman was suffering as she had—the fear, the paranoia, the anger all came crashing back.

How could she say that she was happy here when she refused to open the door to a neighbor? When the least little shadow or sound sent her skittering into near cardiac arrest?

When she would choose to run and hide rather than help another woman escape the horrors she had experienced? What kind of coward was she?

And how much more was she going to allow William to take from her?

BRAD KILLED THE ENGINE. Although he needed to work the case, he wasn't quite ready to head back to Atlanta. He phoned Ethan for an update, but they were still chasing leads. They desperately needed to find out where the killer had taken Mindy.

Had Lisa remembered something that might help?

How do you know this guy is using the same place to hide his victims? He could be anywhere.

His stomach growled, adding to his irritation. He might as well grab something to eat before he faced the two-hour drive. The waitress glared at him as he entered the café, as if she'd seen Lisa running out, and wondered what he'd done to her. Great. Now everyone in Ellijay would probably think he was a bad guy.

Hell, who was he kidding? They'd be right. He'd just thrown Lisa back into her nightmarish past.

Besides, he couldn't show the locals his credentials without revealing Lisa's identity, something he'd sworn not to do.

The diner was rustic, with knotty pine walls and plank flooring. Photographs of antique cars and local scenery hung along one wall, and a collection of antique farming tools filled a case in the corner. Checkered tablecloths and fresh daisies on each table gave the restaurant a homey feel, the smells of homemade vegetable soup and pies wafting through the air.

He ordered a bowl of Brunswick stew and a glass of sweet iced tea, his gaze automatically scrutinizing each patron. Mostly old-timers. Three women wearing outdated Sunday dresses gathered at a round table eating coconut cream pie and sipping coffee. Two farmers conversed over the blue plate lunch special—meat loaf, green beans and mashed potatoes with gravy. A handful of teenagers stuffed into a booth laughed over their milkshakes and burgers. A real southern small town.

Everyone appeared friendly, seemed to know one another. A safe place to raise a family. Nothing like the city, where psychos could hide among the masses.

Yet was Lisa really safe here?

Not if there had been an accomplice, or if this latest killer came looking for her.

Brad finished the stew, paid the bill and headed back to his car, knowing the clock was ticking. He was just about to leave when his cell phone rang. He winced, then checked the display, bracing himself for bad news from his partner.

A private number showed up, instead. "Brad Booker."

"It's Lisa."

He closed his eyes, his gut knotting at the sound of her strained voice. "Are you all right?"

A long sigh escaped her, heartfelt and labored but resigned. "Yes. Where are you?"

One hand tightened around the steering wheel. "Getting ready to leave town."

"To go back to Atlanta?"

"Yes."

A breathy quiver followed his reply, then she whispered, "I…I'm sorry, Brad."

He scraped a hand through his hair, the sweat-coated strands sticking to his fingers. God, why was she apologizing? She had every right to hate him. "Don't, Lisa, it's all right. I shouldn't have come—"

"No," she said, her voice stronger, "you obviously

care about this woman, she's missing... I...I'll help you if I can."

He heard her insinuations. She thought he and Mindy were involved. He should correct her. But why bother? He did care about saving Mindy. And he couldn't get involved with Lisa.

"Do you want me to come by?" he asked quietly. "We can talk."

A heartbeat passed, pulsing into a tension-filled minute. "No."

He chewed the inside of his cheek and fiddled with the radio. "All right. Call me if you need anything."

"Wait." She hesitated again, then said, "I mean yes. Come over...."

He scrubbed a hand over his face at the sound of the waver in her voice. She'd been crying. "Are you at the cabin?"

"Yes."

He cranked the engine and shifted into gear. "I'll be there in a few minutes."

He disconnected the phone and sped away from town, battling his own emotions. The reason he'd almost screwed up so badly before. He couldn't repeat that mistake a second time. Mindy's life was at stake.

But Lisa's soft anguished voice taunted him as he climbed the mountain.

SHE WAS IN THE BOX AGAIN. *She couldn't breathe. The darkness was closing around her, choking her....*

Lisa caught her head between her hands, rocking

herself back and forth, tears falling as the trembling continued.

The wooden edges brushed her sides. Held her captive.

It was dark. Hot. So hot the air felt like a furnace. And she was suffocating, her throat muscles clawing at the air for a breath.

Then she was cold. Chilled and aching. Shaking uncontrollably.

He had left her there all day. Hidden away as if she didn't exist. Her cries had done nothing but elicit rage that he unleashed on her.

Her battered body was too numb to move now. Or maybe it was the cramped position in the box. She'd long ago lost track of the time. Had she been here hours? Days?

The panic that streaked through her wouldn't dissipate. It ate at her, chewed at her nerve endings relentlessly. The air felt stifling. How much more of it was there?

She closed her eyes, willed herself to drift away. To another place. To another time when life existed. When sounds meant something other than his sinister laugh or her own terrified cries.

The front door creaked open. The floor squeaked like cheap linoleum. A muttered curse reverberated through the room, and she knew he'd entered. Could smell the sweat and stench of his body. His boots scraped against the side of the bed as he sat down and kicked them off.

She froze, praying he would have mercy and release her. Or at least end the torture and kill her tonight.

The box springs protested as he stretched out on top

of the bed. The mattress sagged, pressing into the box with his weight. Then he began to move. Slowly at first. The screech, screech of the bed was redundant, grew faster, the mattress sagged deeper and harder against her box. His breathing became erratic.

A sob caught in her throat as she realized what he was doing.

The mattress dipped and squeaked again, the noise intensifying, the movements more rapid as his breathing grew more and more excited. Finally a bellow. Pain? Pleasure? Rage?

Then he jumped off the bed, cursing loudly. She felt the box moving, being jerked, dragged from beneath the bed.

But instead of opening it, he was hammering it shut, tighter…pounding, pounding, pounding….

"LISA!"

It took her several seconds to realize that she had lapsed back into her nightmares. Even when she was awake they haunted her.

It took her another minute to realize the pounding was real. Someone was knocking at the door.

She hugged her arms around herself, panicking. Had the killer found her?

"Lisa! It's Brad. Let me in, or I'm going to bust down this door."

Jerking back to reality, she fidgeted with her hands, then finally willed her legs to be strong enough to stand. Brad's voice broke through the haze again, and she rushed to the door, nearly stumbling over the braided rug on the floor and knocking a magazine off the end table in her haste. She'd phoned him only a few minutes ago, told him to come over. But then she'd sat down, started remembering….

"Lisa!"

"Just a minute." She fumbled with the door lock, her hands shaking. Finally, she unfastened the lock and chain, then opened the door.

He stalked in, his dark eyes stormy. "For God's sake, are you all right? You scared the hell out of me when you didn't answer!"

Then his gaze met hers, and he must have read the truth in her eyes, because he reached out for her. She fell into his arms, clutched at his shirt and let him hold her.

TIME PASSED IN A BLUR of nonreality. He had lost time before. Had awakened with only a hazy memory of where he'd been or what he'd done. And it was happening again….

It had to be the medication.

He opened his eyes, his stomach convulsing as pain rifled through his temple. The dull throb became more incessant as it filtered through the rest of his body. He felt so damn weak. Just like before. But he'd been given a second chance at life.

It wasn't supposed to be this way, though. Dark. Painful. Dreary.

He was supposed to be happy. Full of life. A strong, virile man. Able to do things he hadn't done in a long time.

Fading sunlight fluttered through the blinds, slicing

diagonal rays across the room. He rolled to his side to block it out, then stared in shock at his hands.

They were bruised. Dirty. Covered in blood.

Dried blood. Dark. Crimson. Crusty.

Blood also stained his shirt and pants. Red clay caked his fingernails and his boots. Scratches marred his hands and arms, as if he'd been pawed by an animal. His shirt was torn, the rip revealing more deep gashes on his chest. And he was sweating profusely.

What the hell was happening to him?

His head reeling, he turned sideways, swung his legs over the side of the bed and swayed, dizzy. Grabbing the edge of the mattress to keep from falling, he held himself steady while the room settled. More sweat coated his body and ran down his neck and back. The stench of some foul odor assaulted him. Swamp water. A sewer maybe.

He scanned the room, questions ticking in his head as he read the hands of the clock: 6:00 p.m.

The last thing he remembered was walking out the door twenty-four hours ago.

With unsteady hands, he reached for his pills and choked one down. Were the dark images that had slipped into his dreams real, or had he'd imagined them?

The blood on his hands indicated that he hadn't simply dreamt of vile acts, but that he'd performed them. That he had enjoyed them. That she had deserved it.

That tonight he would lose time again, that he would fade into the abyss of darkness where a monster's soul stole his body, that he would continue to do so until someone stopped him.

But they would have to catch him first.

And that was not an option.

CHAPTER FOUR

BRAD TRIED TO STEADY his raging heart as he held Lisa, but the familiar fear that had gripped him four years ago returned with a vengeance. When she hadn't immediately answered the door, he'd nearly gone out of his mind with worry. And now, feeling her in his arms again, her chest rising and falling as she gulped in air, her slender frame trembling against him, the scent of her feminine shampoo invading his senses, he was helpless to do anything but stroke her silky hair and mutter non-sensical words.

Damn it. He had to get a grip. His career depended on it. And so did Mindy's life.

Slowly, forcing his brain back into professional mode, he eased away, studying her as he would a stranger.

Except Lisa wasn't a stranger.

Her face had lost the rosy color and bright smile she'd worn at the day care when she'd danced with the children, the change a stark reminder that he'd resurrected the painful memories that she'd tried so hard to bury.

"Brad…I'm sorry. For a moment everything rushed back."

Anger ripped through him. "You don't have to apologize, Lisa. For God's sake, I know I'm the last person you want to see."

She dropped her hands from his shirt, backed away, hugging her arms around her waist as if he'd called it right, and she had no idea what she'd been doing. Long lashes fluttered over pale cheeks that now looked drawn with worry.

"Are you all right?" he asked, knowing good and well she wasn't.

"Yes, I'm fine." The same valiant look she'd managed to wear during the trial slid back on her face.

He shuffled, dragged a hand through the short strands of his hair. It was a mistake for him to have come here.

"Sit down," she said quietly. "I'll get some coffee."

He gave her a clipped nod, forcing detachment into his expression as she hurried away from him to the adjoining kitchen. Figuring she needed time to assimilate, and he needed it to regain his bearings, he turned and surveyed her small cabin. He'd been here maybe a half-dozen times over the past four years, and the homey atmosphere never ceased to amaze him. Yet her new home felt more impersonal.

Lisa didn't keep clutter or knickknacks, no small ceramic kitty cats or collections as she had in her other apartment. To break the awkwardness when he'd first visited her here, he'd asked about that, but she'd turned sheepish and merely shrugged. He'd finally decided that she didn't want the space to feel cramped—a remnant of her traumatic days in the box where White had locked her. She needed open spaces, room to breathe....

After growing up in a foster home and sharing a room with other orphans, he understood about feeling crowded.

The den was a tasteful smattering of blue and yellow, with a soft plump denim couch, throw pillows and an oversize chair in yellow-and-blue plaid. A few magazines, mostly educational and arts and crafts ones, were stacked neatly on the pine coffee table. A photo of Lisa in her mother's lap graced the end table, another five-by-seven of her and her father at her high school graduation beside it. Lisa looked so young and happy, full of dreams for the future. But her father...Brad had never quite gotten a good reading on Liam Langley. Not during the questioning when she was missing, or during the trial afterward. He wondered if the two of them stayed in contact.

He noticed a small clay cup on the bookshelf, misshapen and painted bright orange. It seemed out of place, until he realized one of Lisa's students had crafted the cup. Beside it stood four framed photos, each one a group shot of the kindergarten classes she'd taught since moving to Ellijay. Several childlike drawings also decorated her refrigerator. Maybe adding these touches was a sign she had begun to heal, to let others into her life.

Even if they were children....

Lisa approached him, carrying a tray with two mugs, creamer and sugar, and a pot of coffee. The temptation to reach out and help her taunted him, but he sensed her skittishness and refrained, vowing to be patient. She filled a thick clay mug for him. So she remembered his preference for black. Was that all she remembered about him?

She dropped an ice cube in her own to cool it, and he almost smiled. He hadn't forgotten her small habit. Just as he'd never forget anything else about her.

Her gaze finally shot upward and met his, and he grimaced at the wariness darkening her eyes. Yes, she obviously remembered more—his promise to her that he'd protect her. His failure to do so. That it was his fault she'd spent days being beaten and tormented by William White.

And when she looked away, a blinding clarity that he'd never wanted to face sank in—she would never forget that he was at fault, or forgive him.

LISA CRADLED HER MUG to her like a lifeline. "Tell me about this woman that's missing, your girlfriend."

Brad's gaze shot down to the coffee in his cup, his jaw tight. "She's thirty years old, a nurse at First Peachtree Hospital in Atlanta."

"How did you meet her?" Lisa asked, then silently chastised herself. Hearing the details of Brad's personal relationship was none of her business and would drive home the fact that she hadn't had one in years. And that the last relationship had gone horribly wrong....

"At the hospital," he said, seeming nonplussed by her question. "When I went to talk to the doctors after White died."

Lisa gasped. "She knew William?"

He shook his head. "No, she wasn't on duty the night he was hospitalized."

"Oh, my goodness." Lisa gasped again. "Are you sure the same man kidnapped her and that woman, Joann Worthy?"

Brad nodded. "He's calling the reporter White used to deliver his messages, Wayne Nettleton."

"Why him?" Lisa asked.

"He must have enjoyed the way Nettleton sensationalized the story about White. White admitted he chose Nettleton because of his propensity for printing gruesome details."

His gaze met hers as if to study her reaction. Lisa sipped her coffee in an attempt not to reveal her surprise or disgust. Wayne Nettleton was a sleaze.

"We've questioned him just like before, but so far, he's clean," Brad said. "He has an alibi for the nights both women were reported missing, although it's shaky."

"Where was Mindy when she was abducted?" Lisa asked, trying desperately not to picture the scene in her mind.

"She left the hospital when her shift ended, around three. Caught the MARTA train. She doesn't have a car. Never showed up at her apartment that night. Police have questioned neighbors and no one saw anything."

"Does she have family?" Lisa asked softly.

"No."

Lisa's heart ached for her. If they found her, she'd need a support group to recover. Then again, Lisa's own father hadn't exactly been Mr. Mom after the attack. Not that he ever had been. After her mother's death, he'd closed himself off, thrown himself into work. She'd tried to get his attention by being the perfect child.

But she hadn't been perfect.

And he'd seen all those flaws at William's trial.

"We found the first woman in the woods near Lake Lanier," he said quietly. "I don't know if you read the entire article, but he buried her in the woods surrounding the lake by my cabin."

Lisa set her cup down with a clatter. "Brad...you think this is personal?"

He shrugged, but the bitterness that suddenly darkened his whiskey eyes to brown confirmed the answer. "He's throwing it right in my face. How can it not be?"

"Don't do that." Lisa automatically reached for his hand, then drew back at Brad's rigid posture. "This isn't your fault, Brad."

Just like it wasn't when I got attacked.

He shot her a closed look, daring her to argue, then downed his coffee with one big gulp. "Let's stick with the case. I'm running a check on everyone I've had contact with the past five years. Maybe something will turn up there."

"And I suppose the police are questioning her friends and neighbors."

"Yeah, just like they did Joann Worthy's. But if this killer sticks to the same time frame as he did with Joann, Mindy has only a couple of days at best."

Lisa moaned quietly. Was Mindy suffering now?

Wishing her abductor would go ahead and kill her, as Lisa had wished with William? Or was Mindy holding on, clinging to life, praying Brad would find a way to save her?

"We've set up a stakeout in the wooded area where Joann's body was found," Brad continued. "But I don't expect him to choose the same burial spot twice."

Lisa shivered.

"I'm sorry, Lisa, I didn't mean to resurrect the memory of your experience."

"Forget it." She quickly dismissed his apology, although the image of her own grave flashed in her head like a still photograph that had been framed in her memory forever. "Do you have any suspects in mind?"

"My partner's gone to question White's old cell mate. He was paroled a few days ago."

Lisa's hand tightened around her mug at the implications. William's cell mate was free. Knew William's secrets. Even where he might have held her and the other women.

He might be copying William's crimes.

And if he did, would he choose her as one of his victims?

The appearance of her new neighbor suddenly resurfaced, and her suspicions mounted. "Brad, I'm sure I'm being paranoid, but this morning a strange man came to my door."

Brad's head jerked up. "What happened?"

Lisa explained about the visit. "He said his name was Aiden Henderson."

Brad jotted that down. "I'll definitely check him out."

Lisa fidgeted. "Like I said, I'm probably being paranoid. But he brought me the paper and specifically mentioned the story about the missing woman."

Brad frowned. "It could be a coincidence."

Or maybe he'd known William, and he'd come here looking for her, only pretending to be a neighbor.

BRAD SAW THE WHEELS turning in Lisa's mind. She knew that a copycat killer meant danger for her.

"Lisa—"

Her phone jangled, and she startled, hitting the table with her knee and sloshing coffee onto the tray. Her gaze flew to him, and he maintained a guarded expression, not yielding to the voices in his head urging him to reach out and calm her. She grabbed a napkin to blot up the mess, but the phone trilled again, and her fingers were trembling, so he took the napkin from her.

"Let me clean it up while you answer that."

She swallowed, hesitating another second, then stood and checked the caller ID. With a pinched look between her brows, she retrieved the handset. "Hello, Dad."

Brad poured himself another cup of coffee, stood and paced to the window in the kitchen to offer her privacy, although his body was wound as tight as a spring. He had a feeling he knew the reason Liam Langley had phoned.

And he would not be happy with Brad's visit with his daughter.

Langley hadn't held back his opinion of Brad or minced words to soften the blow four years ago.

Not that he'd blamed him.

In fact, Langley had discovered Brad's checkered past, the man he'd almost killed as a teenager, and threatened to tell Lisa. Brad had had to walk away. He hadn't wanted Lisa to remember him as a teenage killer.

"I'm fine, Dad," he heard her say. "No, really." She paused and twisted the phone cord in her hand. "Yes, I've heard about the copycat." Another pause. "No, I'm not coming back to Atlanta right now. Dad…" Irritation laced her voice. "Listen, I have a visitor, let me call you back."

Another long paused followed, and Brad imagined Dr. Langley grilling her over the identity of her guest. Finally she replied in a low whisper, "Yes, it's Special Agent Booker."

She glanced up at him in apology, and he shrugged, although his gut clenched. He didn't know why the man's opinion of him rattled him, but it did.

"Dad, no—"

Lisa sighed audibly, gave Brad a helpless look and held the phone away from her. "He wants to talk to you."

Brad nodded, not surprised, then crossed the small kitchen-den combination in three strides and took the handset. "Dr. Langley, Booker here."

"You son of a bitch, what the hell are you doing there?"

"I came to check on Lisa. I do that from time to time."

"I warned you to stay away from my daughter," Langley snapped. "You are not fit to be in the same room with her."

Brad grimaced. He didn't need reminding that he wasn't good enough for Lisa.

"I had to see her," he said in a low voice.

"I saw the story about that poor woman, Joann Worthy, in the paper," Langley said. "For God's sake, Mindy Faulkner works at the same hospital I do. The police have crawled all over the place asking questions. They even questioned *me*."

Brad silently grimaced. "I'm sorry, sir, but they're simply doing their jobs. I assume you realize we're dealing with a copycat killer."

"And my daughter is in danger again." Langley's voice rose a decibel. "That's why you're there, isn't it?"

"Not exactly," Brad said.

"What do you mean? You haven't been seeing her, have you?" Langley hissed in distrust. "I thought we settled that issue four years ago."

That issue? Although Brad knew Langley was right, he still balked at his attitude. "No, this is not a personal visit." But not because he didn't want it to be.

"Then what is it? You think she might know something to help you now, so you want to dredge up the past. I won't let you do that to her, Booker."

"I don't like upsetting her either, sir, but we have to do everything possible to stop this maniac."

"But how could Lisa possibly help you? She told you everything at that blasted trial."

"We think this man might have known White. Maybe he was a cell mate or buddy, someone who White confided in. He might know where White took his victims—"

"My daughter has a name, goddamn you," Langley snarled. "Use it."

Brad cleared his throat, his own patience teetering on a thin line. "You don't need to remind me," he said in a warning voice. "But if this copycat is taking his victims to the same place White used, it would help if we could find that building, and Lisa might know where it is."

"Like I said, my daughter has been through enough, Booker. If she's buried that memory, it's for a good reason. Now I don't want her involved in this at all." He heaved a breath. "In fact, I tried to talk her into coming here to stay. If not, I'll hire a bodyguard for her."

"Dr. Langley, I don't know if that's necessary now—"

"If he's a copycat, following White, why *wouldn't* he come after Lisa? As you pointed out when you forced her to testify, she's White's only surviving victim. For all we know she may be the reason this psycho started up again."

Brad clenched his jaw, unable to argue the point. It was, perhaps in reality, the very reason he had driven here himself. "I swear, Dr. Langley, I will protect her this time."

"You expect me to trust you with Lisa's safety?" Langley shouted. "You sure as hell didn't protect her the first time."

"I know that." Anger mounted within Brad. Every day he wrestled with the guilt that ate at him. It was like a sore that wouldn't heal. But he angled his head away from Lisa, refusing to upset her any more than necessary. "If this lunatic comes after Lisa, he won't get her. I'll give my life before I'll let that happen."

"Your life won't be worth anything if he succeeds," Langley said. "Because if one hair on my daughter's head is harmed again, I'll kill you with my bare hands."

LIAM LANGLEY STARED at his perfectly manicured hands. The hands of a surgeon. A man who saved lives.

A man who had failed to protect his daughter.

Gripping his desk with a shaky sigh, he forced the rage that had eaten at him for four long years at bay, rage that had only slightly dissipated with White's death.

Anxious now that the police might make some connection between him and Mindy and the night White had died, he accessed the only file that could condemn him and deleted the information, then fed the printout on his desk into the shredder.

He should have destroyed the papers a long time ago, but no one had asked any questions at the time.

Now, with Mindy missing and this copycat killer dredging up the past, he couldn't be too cautious.

He had carefully constructed his career, had built his reputation on a genius IQ and refined surgical techniques, always acutely attuned to the latest cutting edge procedures.

Nothing would destroy the name he had built.

But he'd had to take action against White.

Lisa's bruised body and anguished voice floated back in the dark recesses of his mind. That trial…no, the abduction had changed things for him. Had given him a different perspective on human life.

People claimed that doctors shouldn't play God. He

usually agreed. But the opportunity had presented itself for revenge, and he'd craved it.

White had deserved the fate that had been bestowed on him.

Liam refused to feel an ounce of guilt for it whatsoever.

"I CAN'T BELIEVE my father's reacting this way, Brad," Lisa said. "I haven't spoken to him in months, and now he wants to call and boss me around like I'm a child."

Brad adopted a smile, although it was tight. "Your father is just worried about you, Lisa. I can't blame him for that. If I were in his shoes, I'd feel the same way."

He meant if he really cared for her. She struggled to stave off the hurt his comment triggered.

And her father's attitude toward Brad disturbed her. He'd bad-mouthed the agent after the trial, insisted Brad was no better than a criminal himself. They'd argued about Brad more than once, creating a wedge between them. But she couldn't tell Brad. "I still refuse to stay with him," Lisa said.

"It might not be a bad idea," Brad stated. "His place is secure. He wants to hire a bodyguard."

"No." Lisa spun away, desperately grappling for control. "You don't understand…it hasn't been the same with us, not since…the kidnapping."

The silence stretched taut between them, reverberating with the harsh truth.

"I'm sorry, Lisa."

She closed her eyes, letting his deep voice wash over her, soothe her as she had all those days during the trial.

Funny how Brad hadn't been doting, had barely said anything specific, but his presence and quiet air of command had grounded her, given her comfort, hope for normalcy one day. And here in Ellijay, she'd thought she'd found it.

Gathering her strength, she turned back to face him. "I'm happy here, Brad. I like teaching, the mountains. I won't allow another crazy person to rob me again."

"Then help me, Lisa. I don't want you or any other woman to suffer at this copycat's hands."

Willing her courage to sustain her, she nodded and moved back to the sofa. Her nerves still on edge, she picked up the small needlepoint pillow and crushed it in her hands. "All right. But I'm warning you, I still don't remember where William kept me."

Brad's steadfast gaze didn't waver. "Maybe if we talk through everything one more time, you might remember something new. If not the place, maybe a friend of William's, a neighbor, an old roommate, someone who White might have confided in."

"Okay," Lisa said, grim but determined, "where do you want me to start?"

Brad hesitated. "At the beginning. When you first met White."

She inhaled sharply, averting her gaze as the memories flooded her. "I was enrolled at Georgia State. I had seen William around campus. He played intramural hockey, said he was interested in sports medicine. We hung out at the Library—"

"The student library?"

"No, the Library, on Marietta Street. You know—the local hangout bar for college students. They serve drinks, play recorded music."

"That's right, now I remember us discussing the place."

"One night he approached our table. I was sitting with two girls in my study group when he started talking to all of us, and he seemed...nice." Lisa hesitated, remembering his act changing so abruptly.

"He fooled a lot of people, Lisa."

She gave a wan smile, but shook her head as if she still blamed herself for not seeing through him.

"You two started seeing each other then?"

She nodded. "We didn't really date exactly, just met at the bar, hung out at basketball games, attended a couple of concerts together." She paused, struggling to recall the progression of their romance. Why she'd been attracted to William, when now just the thought of him made her skin crawl. When she'd taken off her blinders and first suspected that he had a dark side.

"Like I told you before, we saw each other for about six months. The last few weeks he changed. He was moody, charming one minute, then secretive the next. And he exploded a couple of times when I questioned why he was late."

"But he never hit you before the abduction?"

Lisa shook her head, studying the stitching on the pillow, avoiding looking at him. "He raised his hand one time, but I shrank back, and when he looked at me and saw what he was about to do, something snapped, and he left the room. I didn't hear from him for a week that time."

"Then he sent flowers?"

She nodded, swallowing hard. "He showed up with a single white rose every day that week."

Brad said nothing, and Lisa continued. "One night he made a big production about wanting us to be together. But then…when I finally decided we should…that I would…" She halted, uncomfortable.

"When you agreed to sleep with him, he couldn't perform." Brad filled in for her in a flat voice.

Lisa chewed the inside of her cheek and nodded, unable to face him. How could she have wanted to sleep with a monster? "He got so frustrated, then he…blamed me." She closed her eyes, his humiliating accusations reverberating in her head.

Brad folded his hand over hers, stroked her palm gently. "You know it wasn't your fault, Lisa."

A labored sigh flowed from her lips, although she still felt ugly inside from the comments. "Yes. The therapist I saw after the abduction…we worked through it. But at the time…"

"You tried to make it up to him," Brad said flatly.

"Yes." That one word was filled with pain and the heartbreaking ache of shame. "Then he left," Lisa said in a low voice. "I didn't see him for another week."

"And when he returned?"

"He was his flirty, charming self. He started with the roses all over again. Said he wanted to take it slow, make up for the time before."

"And you tried again?"

Lisa stood, squashing the pillow in her arms as she

walked to the window and glanced outside. Dusk had settled, the purples and oranges of the sky streaking through the window, making the majestic mountains outside as picturesque as a postcard.

But her memories were a sharp contrast, as if someone had taken a paintbrush and swirled charcoal-black paint across the bright colors of the horizon.

"I was a fool. By the third time, I realized that he had problems. That's when I tried to pull away."

"But he didn't want to let you go."

"No, he said that wasn't an option, that he loved me. *Only me.*" She shuddered. "That night…I heard something sinister in his voice. Something dark, something that scared me."

Later that evening, she'd discovered the nail clippings William had kept, clippings from each victim covered in blood and dirt.

And then she'd realized he was a serial killer….

LISA'S WORDS SOUNDED hollow, the courage it took for her to repeat the story taking its toll. Her face had paled, her posture wavering as if the burden of memory was too heavy to carry. He wanted to wrap her in his arms and erase the horror forever. But her father's words trilled in his head and he kept himself in check. Liam Langley knew about Brad's past.

Things *he* didn't want Lisa to know.

Still, Brad wanted to keep her safe. He wanted to return to the city and leave her with the beauty of the mountains, apple trees and glorious sunsets still intact, unmarred by the darkness of the past and his failure as her protector.

But Mindy might be staring at her grave right now. Or inside it.

"He's a sociopath," Brad said, resorting to the psychiatrist's diagnosis of White after his arrest. "He suffered from a psychotic break triggered by years of abuse. Lisa, you couldn't have known that, because he didn't want you to know."

She looked at him then, with a lost expression, as if the memory had been stirred from the dark cauldron that held her most painful secrets. "I should have caught on sooner. That one time he had scratches on his face and blood on his clothes…"

"You had no reason at the time not to buy his story of a mugging."

Shadows streaked through the window, hovering around her bleak gaze. "Maybe I knew and didn't want to admit it," she said softly.

"No." Brad crossed the room, willed her to stop picking at the threads of her guilt just as she was ripping the threads of the pillow's stitching. "When you sensed he was dangerous, you did call, Lisa. That took courage."

"But it was too late." Raw anguish tightened her voice. "I could have saved those other women if I'd had my eyes wide open. And dear God, how could I have even thought I cared about a person like him? How could I ever have considered sleeping with him?"

"Lisa, stop it," Brad snapped. He couldn't allow her to blame herself, not now. "Every single one of those women were fooled by him. They got into his car willingly. There were no forced entries, no abductions at gunpoint."

"No, all that came later."

Silence stretched between them, as explosive as shattering glass on hot pavement.

"Let's focus on details," he said, trying to draw her away from the guilt. Hers and his. "You never met White's brother?"

"No. He told me he didn't have any siblings."

"Birth records prove he did. But White claimed he hadn't seen his brother since he was a teenager. And his mother has been dead for years."

"Do you think his brother is the copycat killer?" Lisa asked.

"I don't know. Prison records indicate that a man named Clyde White logged in to visit William a few months back. He might have kidnapped Mindy to get back at me."

"Then he might want revenge on me, too," Lisa said, her voice quivering. "But what about Joann? Did you know her?"

Brad shook his head. "No. And so far, we haven't determined a connection between her and Mindy, or her and White." He paced across the room. "We've issued an APB for the brother. He's one possibility, but right now we have to explore all the alternatives."

She inhaled sharply. "What other alternatives?"

"Did White have any male friends that hung with him or with the two of you, a roommate or guy he played sports with, maybe?"

Lisa closed her eyes as if thinking back. "There was one man...I think his name was Vernon. He was kind of an odd guy, really thin, not very sociable. He tagged along behind William."

"You didn't mention him before," Brad said.

Lisa frowned. "I didn't think it was important. Besides, he sort of disappeared after William and I started dating. In fact, I don't remember seeing him the last four months William and I dated."

"What was his last name?"

Lisa rubbed her temple. "Uh, Vernon...Handle. No, Hanks. I think he liked photography. He always had a camera around his neck. Said he liked to take candid shots. Maybe photography or journalism was his major."

Brad jotted the name in his notepad. "Do you know what happened to him?"

"No. I assumed he hooked on to someone else when William blew him off."

"I'll check him out. Did he ever talk to you? Make a play for you, anything like that?"

Lisa shook her head. "No, he acted uncomfortable around girls, had sort of a pocked face, as if he'd had problems with acne when he was younger. William said he didn't want him latching on to him."

"He cramped his style?" Brad said in disgust.

She swallowed, dropping her hand to the pillow again. "I guess so."

"But what if William was lying? Or what if this guy followed William, maybe stalked the women, too?"

Lisa's eyes widened in horror. "You mean, he might have w…watched?"

Brad shrugged, sickened by the possibility, but a second party might explain the copycat. This guy Vernon was a loser, nerd, shy around girls, got his rocks off watching William work the women. Maybe he had followed White and discovered his secrets… It wouldn't have been the first time a serial killer had an accomplice. Or he might have accidentally stumbled on White beating the women or burying them, and blackmailed him into letting him watch. Perverted, but possible.

Now that White was dead, Vernon's own psychosis could have progressed to the point that he was emulating his mentor's crimes, craving the power—learning the thrill of killing himself.

Then again, if Hanks had followed White and discovered what he was up to with the women, and he'd disappeared, who was to say that White hadn't killed him and hidden or buried his body someplace else?

Brad's phone trilled, and he checked the number. His partner.

"Booker. What's up, Ethan?"

"I'm in Valdosta. Talked to White's cell mate's wife, Chartrese. She's got a new man in her life."

"What about Curtis?"

"Claims she hasn't seen Thigs. Apparently he didn't come home when he was released. And he hasn't reported to his parole officer, either."

Shit. Thigs had lived with White, might know all his secrets. And he was missing.

Now they had at least three suspects who were close to White. All of whom were nowhere to be found.

Just like Mindy.

Thank God, none of them knew where Lisa was right now. The hairs on the back of Brad's arms stood on end, a bad feeling pinching his gut.

Or did they?

LISA, LISA, I know where you are now....

Vernon Hanks closed his eyes and pictured her beautiful face in his mind. Perspiration trickled along his jaw as the tepid air blew in from his open bedroom window. He'd been searching for her for four years.

And now he'd finally found her.

Only he'd temporarily stolen a new name and lied to her today when he'd met her.

Excitement pinged through him, pumping adrenaline through his veins. Unable to sleep, he rose, scratching at the sprinkling of hair on his belly as he strode through the room, unlocked the door to his chamber of secret pleasures, and gazed at the photos he'd collected and taped on the corkboard walls. Photos of Lisa when she'd first come to Georgia State.

She had been so young and vibrant. That yellow-blond hair fanned around her innocent, heart-shaped face as the fall winds tossed the strands from side to side. She had a little pug nose that had probably begged to be tweaked as a child and a chin that tipped up slightly. And her high cheekbones and smile loved the camera.

His gaze skated sideways to a photo of her in her

dorm room, sitting cross-legged with her hair in pigtails, looking about twelve years old. She'd been munching on a slice of cheese pizza—he knew because he had delivered the damn thing. Then there was one of her at an ice cream shop licking a mint chocolate chip ice-cream cone. The cutoffs she wore revealed long, shapely legs that he had dreamed about in his sleep. He'd followed her that day, watched with envy as her tongue had flicked out and caught the melting ice cream and sucked it into her mouth. That night, he'd had his first dreams of her, wet dreams filled with images of that tongue working on him, of him melting in her hands.

In the next candid shot, she wore a simple white cotton bra and panties. He'd snapped it when she wasn't looking, one day when he'd sneaked into the dorm and hidden in the girls' bathroom. Then he'd watched with ecstasy as she'd stripped and climbed into the shower.

His body hardened at the sight of her small breasts in the photo, his memories conjuring wet dreams again—the dainty pink-tipped nipples jutting out for him, the subtle curve of her spine and belly, the thatch of pale blond curls surrounding her heat. The heat he had longed to touch…

But she had fallen for William White.

And ignored Vernon. Just like the others.

He had wanted to feel sorry for those women when he'd seen the photos in the paper. When he'd read about the way William had ended it with them.

William, his mentor.

His friend.

The man who had tried to kill him.

But Lisa was the one he loved. The one White shouldn't have taken. Because she should have been his.

He traced a finger over the latest addition to his collection—the photo he'd snapped this morning when he'd seen her walking into the day care. She'd stolen his heart all over again, had robbed his breath. She was so close now, only a heartbeat away.

And soon she would know exactly how he felt about her.

CHAPTER FIVE

BRAD GLANCED AT LISA to see how she was holding up. She seemed to have gathered her composure, but she looked fragile. Terrifying memories of the attack still lay buried beneath the surface, hidden in the multiple layers of her calm.

What if his visit caused them to surface into full-fledged nightmares again? Would he destroy any progress she'd made in recovery here in the mountains?

"Booker, you still there?" Ethan asked.

Brad shook himself. "Yeah. Does Thigs's wife have any idea where he might have gone?"

Ethan sighed. "No. And she wasn't very cooperative. Said she sent him divorce papers the week before he was released, that she doesn't want to see his sorry ass back."

"So Thigs could be pissed right now. And we both know how he vents his anger."

"On women," Ethan said. "But you'd think his wife would be the first one he'd want to see."

"Yeah, you'd think." Brad tapped his fingers on the end of the handset. "Can you arrange for the locals to place a tail? He might show up—"

"Already done, partner."

"Good. I guess I'll see you back in Atlanta then."

"Whoa," Ethan said. "Not so fast. Have you learned anything from Lisa Langley?"

Brad shared their conversation about White's brother, Vernon Hanks and the mysterious neighbor.

"Listen, Valdosta's only a couple of hairs from Augusta, where White grew up. I'll swing over there and see what I can dig up on the brother."

"Good idea." Brad gave a cursory glance at the clock and frowned. "No word from anyone on Mindy yet?"

A second's hesitation passed in strained silence, answering his question, the images of Mindy struggling for her life flashing into his head.

"Sorry, not yet."

Brad silently cursed. *Not yet* meant that at least that reporter, Nettleton, hadn't called to inform them of her burial spot.

A drop of sweat rolled down his forehead.

Maybe they still had time….

TIME WAS RUNNING OUT for Mindy Faulkner.

Wayne Nettleton skimmed the front page article he'd written today, his face exuding the smile of a genius wordsmith, a man who knew how to use language to paint a picture as vivid as the photograph of the burial spot where they'd found Joann Worthy's lifeless body. Albeit a grim picture, but then again, that was the cold face of murder. The very stuff that sold papers.

The Grave Digger Returns! read the headline, forcing

the endless stories of drought and water shortages to the second page.

A tingle of elation splintered through him at his good fortune. Then again, man made his own fortune, didn't he? His own success. A man who sat on his lazy, slovenly butt all day shouldn't reap the rewards of success and fame—only hard work, careful planning and proper timing could do that.

And of course a great sensationalistic, sadistic serial killer.

He laughed out loud.

Nettleton had all the necessary elements on his side right now, all in the palm of his open hand, ready for him to mold and shape like clay, just as he had the last time. All he had to do was fill in the colors, the shades of gray and black and white, the details that would horrify the public, and perhaps raise the stakes again by offering up the only surviving victim of the first Grave Digger. Lisa Langley. Her pretty, sweet face with those angelic eyes had been good for publicity before. They would be again.

Ahh, but life was grand.

The first Grave Digger serial killer cases had made Nettleton's name. But the last three years his career had stalled, and his health had gone downhill. The heart attack. Lots of tests. Surgery. Medication.

Now he was back.

His career needed rejuvenation, though, and the rebirth of the Grave Digger would serve the purpose. Especially if he brought Lisa Langley out of hiding.

He flipped through the scrapbook chronicling the

first case and stared at Dr. Liam Langley's photo. He was standing on the courtroom steps, his arm around his daughter, murder in his eyes.

The asshole doctor wouldn't like this new story. No, he'd hate to see his poor little girl dragged into the proverbial murk of another sinister madman's plan. Yet the public had eaten up Lisa's innocence, her pleas that she'd had no idea White had been a monster until he'd unleashed that dark side on her.

Even that stupid Agent Booker had fallen for her guileless act, as if he'd had his nose jammed in her crotch too long to see the truth—that she'd gotten what she deserved for being so stupid.

And now another woman was in trouble. This one had screwed Booker, then turned up missing.

The next victim of Grave Digger #2.

If Booker wasn't careful, he might find himself on the wrong side of the interrogation table.

Releasing a wry chuckle, Nettleton carefully pressed the fake beard onto his chin, then around his jaws, smiling at the disguise as he combed his dark hair away from his forehead. He had some homework to do on the Faulkner woman before he could finish his story.

If they found her body, saw that she, too, had been buried alive, as had Joann, his story would already be written and ready to go to print. Reporting was, after all, just a game. A game to be played by the masters. A game to be manipulated if need be. A game he intended to win at all costs.

A game that would once again glorify his name and put him in the limelight.

"LISA, I KNOW WHAT dredging up all these bad memories has cost you," Brad said.

Lisa rose, gathered the tray and moved to the kitchen, unable to sit any longer. The small room closed around her, the suffocating summer heat another reminder of her ordeal in that vulgar wooden box. "If it helps you find your girlfriend Mindy, it's okay."

"No, it's not." Brad followed her. "But I appreciate your help."

She nodded, forcing an image of Brad and Mindy together into her head as she turned to face him. Through the window behind him, she noticed that the sun had set long ago. The summer temperature would be cooling only slightly, though, and Mindy might be locked underground, just as Lisa had been, fighting for every breath. "I just hope you find her…in time."

A muscle ticked low in his jaw. "I need to make some more phone calls and then get online. Do you mind?"

Lisa shook her head, startling as a rumble of thunder rolled in from the hills. "No, but I thought you'd be in a hurry to return to Atlanta."

His gaze locked with hers, the masculine scent of his aftershave filling up the tiny kitchen. His five-o'clock shadow had grown thick, adding to his rough-edged hellion image, and he'd shed his jacket, the holster holding his gun a glaring reminder that he had killed before, and would do so again. "There are a dozen cops working from the city. I want to research this Vernon Hanks, and find out about Aiden Henderson," Brad said. "My partner's checking out White's brother's hometown, and we've issued an APB for White's old cell mate, Curtis Thigs." He scrubbed a hand through his hair, spiking the dark ends. "Locals are searching for Mindy, and we've got a tail on another old boyfriend." He shrugged. "Let's talk about the place where you were held…maybe after dinner."

A frisson of alarm bolted through her, her uneasiness mounting. "You're staying for dinner?"

"If you don't mind." He shrugged. "Or I'll take you out if you want."

Lisa shook her head. "No. I like to cook. It keeps me busy." *Helps my frazzled nerves,* she wanted to say, but didn't. "Besides, no one here knows about my past. They're bound to ask questions."

His lips flattened into a thin line. "Right. I guess I stirred enough gossip by my visit at the day care. And people saw us at the coffee shop."

She nodded. "It'd be best not to be seen together again. I'll simply tell everyone you were an old family friend, that you were just driving through town."

He almost looked offended, but then his guarded expression returned, and he flipped open his phone and punched in some numbers. He asked for a man named Rosberg, then disappeared out the door and returned with a laptop. His hair was damp from perspiration, his shirt dotted with moisture.

He still looked sexy as hell.

But he was only here because of the Grave Digger's return.

And she was just a tool to help him find the woman he loved—Mindy.

BRAD CONSIDERED correcting Lisa's interpretation of his relationship with Mindy, but once again refrained. What purpose would it serve?

Lisa would never see him as anything but the man who'd asked her to testify against White, then nearly let her die.

And Mindy's life might depend on him keeping his objectivity.

"Do you have any word on Mindy?" He squeezed his fingers across the bridge of his nose to stem the headache developing behind his eyes.

"I'm afraid not," Captain Rosberg said. "The tail is still on the last man she dated, Terry Bitterton, but Bitterton stayed home all day, then signed into the hospital at three. He claims he and Mindy only went out twice for drinks after their nursing shift ended."

"Did you get a read on him? Does he seem upset about her disappearance?"

"More worried that we think he's a suspect. According to him, they were just friends."

"He could be lying. Or maybe he wanted more than friendship," Brad said.

"We'll see," Rosberg replied shortly. "How about you? Has this visit to the Langley woman paid off?"

Brad shot a glance at Lisa, his chest tightening at the sight of her in the kitchen. Steam rose from the stove, the homey atmosphere and cramped quarters making him uncomfortable. Lisa stirred spaghetti sauce, the smell so enticing his stomach growled and his mouth watered. Although her back was to him, he'd watched with admiration as she carefully cut fresh tomatoes, garlic and other ingredients and added them to the pot. She'd prepared a salad and had removed from the freezer a loaf of bread that appeared homemade. The scene looked so domestic that for a moment he'd felt as if he should leave, that he didn't belong here.

Another part of him savored the delicious smells and cozy cabin. He could easily imagine a fire in the stone fireplace in winter, he and Lisa curled beside the flames with a picnic and bottle of wine—

"Booker?"

Brad cleared his throat, wondering where that ridiculous image had originated. He'd never had a romantic picnic with anyone, and wasn't about to start dreaming of one now. "She remembered a man named Vernon Hanks who used to hang around White. He disappeared a couple of months after they met. I'm going to search the national database now to see if I can find anything on him."

"Hmm, maybe it is a lead," Rosberg said, and Brad realized that the man had been skeptical about his reasons for rushing to see Lisa.

"I'm also investigating everyone I might have ticked off in the last few months in case this guy kidnapped Mindy to seek revenge on me," Brad said. He filled Rosberg in on his conversation with Ethan, as well as Lisa's new neighbor, then promised he'd check back in. Rosberg agreed to do the same, then Brad hung up and accessed his computer.

A few minutes later, he'd learned a few things about

Hanks, but nothing important. Certainly not where he was now. Damn.

Could Hanks be the killer?

Brad had told Rosberg, Ethan and himself that he wanted to drive here to tap into Lisa's memory, but deep down in his gut, he'd had a more selfish reason for coming—he'd needed reassurance that she was safe. The fear that gripped him when he thought of Mindy at the mercy of another madman was horrific, but nothing compared to the terror that had seized him when he thought the man might track down Lisa.

She thought he was driving back to Atlanta after dinner.

How would she react when he broke the news that he had no intention of leaving her alone tonight?

Not when a copycat killer was on the loose and her life might be in jeopardy.

LISA HAD NEVER entertained a man for dinner at the mountain cabin. The sheer presence of Brad had resurrected old fears, yet at the same time, his masculine energy radiating through the room triggered her awareness of how much she'd missed having a man in her life. Of having someone to share a simple home-cooked dinner with. Someone besides Ruby. The older woman was a great friend and she loved her to death, but a female friend wasn't the same as having a male in the house.

Her nerves on edge, Lisa nearly chopped off the tip of her thumb with the knife as she began slicing the homemade bread. She hadn't realized she'd shrieked out loud until Brad appeared beside her. Blood trickled from her thumb, and he grabbed a napkin and wrapped it around the wound.

"Are you okay?" His eyes searched hers, deep, probing, silently referring to the emotional state, not just the cut.

She nodded. "It's not that deep."

Not like William's bruises.

The tension rattled between them, the sweltering heat making it worse.

"You'd better clean that cut," Brad said in a husky voice.

She nodded, lifted the napkin, turned on the faucet and ran cold water over her finger.

"Where are your Band-Aids?" Brad asked.

She gestured toward a small cabinet above the stove, and he opened the door, retrieved the box, then ripped one open with his teeth. Her body tingled as he gently took her hand in his, wrapped the bandage around the tip of her finger and secured it.

"Thank you." She couldn't drag her gaze from his wide, blunt fingers. Fingers that could pull a trigger and end a life, but which had been so gentle she imagined them running across her face. Then to her cheeks, her neck, and lower, down to her breasts...

He was standing so close to her she inhaled his scent again, felt his breath on her hand as he checked the bandage. "You're welcome."

Heat climbed her neck, then he swallowed, and released her finger.

"Dinner's ready." A sudden breeze rattled the windows, mimicking the roaring of her heartbeat as she backed away. How was she going to feel when he left tonight? Bereft? Lonely?

"It smells delicious," Brad said, filling the awkward silence. "I can't tell you how long it's been since I've eaten a home-cooked meal."

Lisa smiled, although it took every ounce of effort she could muster to make it look natural. "I hope you like it."

"Spaghetti's my favorite dinner."

She'd remembered that but refrained from comment. "I…there's wine if you'd like a glass."

"One glass," he said with a shrug, then uncorked a bottle and poured them each some merlot.

She ran her finger along the stem of the goblet to calm herself, while he tore into the food as if he needed to occupy his hands. Or maybe he hadn't eaten in days.

"Did you find out anything when you were on the phone?"

He shook his head no, then paused and sipped the wine. "You said Hanks disappeared a few months after you met White. According to the college, he dropped out then. There's no sign of him returning to school or trans-ferring to another university." Brad finished by relaying what little he'd learned from his partner and Rosberg.

"Where did you learn to cook?" he asked suddenly.

Lisa paused with her fork in midair, grateful he'd

changed the subject. And what a relief to have a normal conversation.

"From my nana." She smiled at the memory. "She was my father's mother, a short, wiry lady with soft gray hair and big green eyes. She stayed with us for a while after my mom died, when I was four." She scooped up a bite of spaghetti and chewed it thoughtfully. "My father was working all the time, building his practice, was on call. But Nana loved to try new recipes, so I spent hours in the kitchen with her." She sipped her wine, lost in the memory. "One year we made ten different kinds of Christmas cookies for a cookie swap. I've never eaten so many chocolate chips in all my life."

A slow smile spread across his face. "You sound very fond of her."

Her smile slipped slightly, and she swirled the wine in her glass, looking pensive. "I was, but she died a few years back. I still miss her, although it's been a long time."

He dropped his gaze back to his food and tore off another hunk of bread. "It must have been hard losing her."

She shrugged. "It was. But I have good memories of her. They'll last a lifetime."

His gaze swung upward, and she read something in his eyes. An apology for making her relive the bad ones earlier.

She sighed tiredly. All they'd ever done was talk about her. "What about you? Where's your family?"

"I don't have any," he said simply.

Lisa swallowed. "I'm sorry. What happened?"

He dug his fork around his plate, swirling spaghetti between his spoon and fork. "My mother gave me up when I was little." He shrugged as if the admission didn't bother him, although the flicker of unease in his eyes warned her that he didn't intend to continue the discussion.

"Why didn't she keep you?" Lisa pressed.

"Her boyfriend hated having a kid around. He talked with his fists. She did what he wanted."

Lisa swallowed, horrified at the thought. "Then who raised you?"

"Foster homes," he said in a clipped voice.

"I…hope they were good to you." Sensing deep pain hidden inside, Lisa ached to reach out and touch his hand.

But Brad turned close-lipped, wolfed down the rest of his dinner with a vengeance, then rose and cleared his plate without speaking again. "Thank you, that was great."

She'd managed to eat most of her food, she realized as she carried her own plate to the sink.

"There's apple pie." She gestured toward the counter.

"God, Lisa," he said in a husky voice, "you'll spoil me."

She wouldn't mind that, she thought. After all, he looked lost, like a little boy who'd never been spoiled or loved. How could a mother just abandon a child like that? And what about his real father?

She refrained from asking, though. She hadn't gotten

involved with anyone since William, and she couldn't start now. Not with someone as hard and cut off as Brad.

Especially when he was in love with another woman.

BRAD HAD NO IDEA why he'd confided that tidbit about his past, but now that Lisa knew he'd grown up in the system, he couldn't quite look at her. He'd see pity, questions, maybe even disdain, just as he had when he was a kid at school and the others had called him a bastard, a homeless child.

Just as he had when his mother's boyfriend had beaten him senseless and called him a bad seed. Brad had grown up determined to show them just how bad he could be. And he had been for a while....

"I'll clean these up, then we can talk," Lisa said. "But I'm warning you, Brad, I still don't remember much about the place William kept me."

He nodded, hating to press the topic but it was necessary. Manners insisted he offer to help with the dishes, too, but sharing domestic chores with Lisa gave him an odd feeling. His foster mother had yelled at him when he didn't do things her way, so he'd learned to hang back, stay out of the way, do what he did best.

Cause trouble back then.

Now, it was work.

So he hit the research again while she cleaned up, biding his time until she was ready to talk.

He skimmed his list, a total of five criminals who might hold a grudge against him, then analyzed and sorted the data. That was his trademark—compartmentalize. Concentrate on the things he could control. Focus on the case.

The first three names he checked confirmed that the perps were still in jail. The last two proved to be more worrisome, although he finally discovered that Wendel Mendez had been extradited to Brazil, then sentenced to life in prison.

Mendez was not the Grave Digger.

The last name on his list took him longer to locate, but he finally tracked Vrenny Lopez down and learned he had been released on parole four months ago. But he'd been picked up ten days before on a parole viola- tion and was now in jail in Denver pending new charges of robbery.

Next, Brad punched in the name Aiden Henderson. He checked the DMV records, police database, and learned the man had been a religion major at Georgia, had taught high school in Cartersville and had no prior records. Nothing to be alarmed about. Nothing that stuck out.

The clang of pots and pans being stored jerked him from his reverie, then Lisa slid down beside him at the table.

"Any luck?"

"No. All the criminals on my list who might want revenge against me are accounted for." He relayed the information about Aiden Henderson.

Lisa chewed her bottom lip, looking slightly relieved. "I've been trying to think about the place William held me, Brad." She twined her hands together on the table, then stared at them. Her nails had been manicured, painted a pale pink. So feminine and soft. Just like Lisa.

But the frown on her face tightened with the ugly memories.

"It's just like I told you before," she said in an oddly disconnected voice, as if she was talking about something that had happened to a stranger. "I was unconscious a lot of the time. When I did wake up, it was dark. A small cramped room with a cement floor, like a basement."

"No windows?"

"No."

"Did you smell anything unusual?"

"Just mold and…blood. Urine."

From his prior victims. "What about sounds? Did you ever hear anything?"

"Besides his mindless ranting?" Lisa asked, then recoiled as if she shouldn't have let the bitterness seep out.

"Maybe cars as if you were near a highway? Horns from an eighteen-wheeler? A boat from a lake, or a train maybe?"

A startled expression flashed in Lisa's eyes. "A train?" She pressed her fingers into her temples. "I'm not sure. Maybe. If so, it was far away, but there might have been a whistle. I only heard it once or twice. In fact, I'd forgotten about it. I guess I thought I'd imagined it, that it was just the ringing in my ears from when he'd hit me."

Brad grimaced. Those bruises on her face and body had driven him to nearly take White's life.

They were also the reason he'd almost gotten suspended afterward.

This case was his chance to save his career—the only thing he had to live for.

He checked his watch with another grimace. If the killer kept to his schedule, Mindy had less than twenty-four hours to live.

He couldn't let her die or survive with her death on his conscience.

CHAPTER SIX

LISA WATCHED OVER BRAD'S shoulder as he retrieved a map on his laptop outlining the area surrounding "Death Valley." He entered data requesting a scan for any towns or communities within a hundred mile radius, zoning in on those with railroad crossings or train stations, and waited for the computer program to feed him the information.

A few seconds later, he'd pinpointed five different places north of Atlanta and had alerted the locals to search the locations.

"They'll find something, Brad," Lisa said. "Maybe tonight."

God, he hoped so. "The problem is manpower," he said. "Some of the locals in those small towns only have a sheriff, and maybe a deputy at best."

"At least they know where to look in their home-towns," she said.

She massaged her temple again, and Brad frowned. "Headache?"

"Just tired." From all the stress. Of thinking about William. Of seeing Brad again. Of knowing he saw her as a victim, not a woman.

It was time for him to leave….

"I know you're eager to get back to Atlanta," Lisa said. "Do you want me to make some coffee for the road?"

An odd flicker glimmered in his eyes, then his jaw tightened perceptibly. What else did he want to ask her?

"I'm not going anywhere tonight, Lisa."

Her breath caught. "What do you mean?"

"I'm not leaving you alone," he said in a husky voice. "If I drive back to Atlanta, you go with me."

She gaped at him, too stunned to reply. If Brad wasn't going back tonight, did he intend to stay here with her?

IT WAS GOING TO BE a sleepless night.

Brad had braced himself for an argument from Lisa, and when she had argued, he hadn't known quite what to say, so he'd resorted to his brusque manner, which he realized had appeared as pure insolence and male high-handedness. That attitude had driven her to her bedroom for the night. Alone. Which was exactly what he wanted.

The fact that she'd closed the door told him she'd accepted the circumstances. But she didn't like him invading her cabin, much less her peace of mind.

Still, she'd conjured up enough strength to answer his questions, to revisit a path riddled with ghosts, a path no woman should have to travel the first time, much less the second or third.

But he had promised her father he'd protect her, and more importantly he'd promised himself. And he would do so with his life.

He scrolled through the computer database, searching for information on similar crimes, researching two other men who had grudges against him, then scanned for more information on White and anyone he'd associated with in college or his past life.

Mindy. The images bled into his concentration. Her locked in a wooden box fighting for her life. Had the killer decided to bury her tonight in the middle of the drought, where the heat was suffocating and the bugs would feast on her? If so, how much air would she have? Would she be conscious when he put her in the ground?

Brad dropped his head forward, battling the horrific thoughts and images. He had to or they would paralyze him. Body tight with tension, he rose and paced to the kitchen window and stared outside. A dozen apple trees filled the backyard, the lush green hills illuminated by streaks of a gray sky that promised rain but hadn't delivered. In the fall, the fruit would weigh down the branches of the trees, the overripe ones falling to the ground. That is, unless the drought killed the crops.

And if they survived, the apple houses would be loaded with MacIntosh and Granny Smith apples, red and golden delicious ones along with other products—smoked trout and apple butter, apple bread, apple fritters and fresh cold apple cider. He imaged Lisa picking a basketful, peeling and slicing them, then coating them with sugar and baking them into pies, just like the one that sat on the counter.

He'd never in his life had someone bake him a damn pie.

The mere thought unearthed a strange surge of emotion inside him.

He forced it at bay, calling on the anger, the isolation, the cool detachment that he thrived upon to block out the ridiculous thoughts. When this case ended and Lisa was safe, he'd go back to the streets of Atlanta, back to hunting down crazed killers and lunatics. And Lisa would be left safe at home with those pies.

There was no place in her life for a man like him.

Knowing he might receive a call any minute, a lead, he forced himself to lie down on the sofa, although his broad body hung off the side and his feet dangled over the end. Any rest he could get would be welcome tomorrow, he told himself.

Then, hopefully, he'd find her and put this second Grave Digger in jail. Then Lisa could return to her haven here in the mountains, and he could resume his own life.

But sleep never came; instead, images of Lisa in bed alone aroused him. And when he banished those, an image of Mindy clawing at the ground from her burial spot tormented him the rest of the night.

LISA STUMBLED TOWARD the bathroom the next morning, her white cotton gown clinging to her legs in the morning heat. Still blurry-eyed, she bumped into a solid wall of chest. "Oops."

Two strong hands caught her in the bathroom doorway, the fingers gently gripping her bare arms. She inhaled, instantly aware Brad was half-naked. He wore only a towel knotted around his waist. His chest still gleamed with moisture from his shower, and the terry cloth did nothing to hide the morning erection that strained against the fabric.

"Sorry. I hope you don't mind that I went first," he said in a thick voice.

She sucked in a sharp breath, then glanced up at the water droplets clinging to his black hair. His eyes were a smoky hue this morning, and they skated over her with an intensity that made her stomach quiver. The rest of her body tingled in response, her gown unable to conceal the hardening of her nipples.

He swallowed, his Adam's apple bobbing up and down, then cleared his throat. "How did you sleep, Lisa?"

Sleep. Who had slept? "Fine. You?"

He shrugged, heightening her awareness of the massive width of his shoulders. She'd never seen Brad in anything but a suit, and the sight of him so...nearly naked completely stole her speech as well as her rational mind. His chest was bronzed, sprinkled with dark hair, his nipples a dark brownish color, his arms muscled and tanned. The five-o'clock shadow had disappeared with his shave, and the scent of a menthol aftershave invaded her senses.

"I...um, need to go to the bathroom," she muttered, then felt herself blush at the statement. "I mean shower."

A lopsided smile tilted the corner of his mouth. "Okay, I'll start some coffee."

"Thanks." Remembering his impudence the night before, she suddenly felt ridiculous for indulging herself in a moment's fantasy. She was making a fool of herself over a federal agent who only saw her as part of an ugly investigation. "Brad...did you hear anything last night?"

Any sexual friction that she might have imagined disappeared immediately. "No."

She gave him an apologetic look, then nodded and dashed into the shower to escape his probing eyes. All night she'd tossed and turned, her sleep encumbered by nightmares of William and the ordeal he'd forced her to go through. Occasionally, she'd jerk awake and try to concentrate on positive thoughts.

But the bedclothes sliding against her sweat-soaked skin made her think of Brad, and she'd imagined his hands and lips replacing the sheets, gliding over her bare arms and legs in a sensual journey that stirred a restless, unsated need within her. Heat rippled through her in waves, the thirst for his touch palpable.

She splashed water on her face, then glanced in the mirror, shocked to see her cheeks flushed from hunger and her nipples visible beneath the gown. In the early morning light, Brad had to have noticed.

What had he thought?

Did he still see her as a victim or could he possibly see her as a desirable woman?

Inhaling to calm herself, she stripped off her gown and stared at herself in the mirror. For the past four years, she hadn't been able to do this, because *she* had seen herself as that victim. In the photos from the attack, every inch of her body had been black-and-blue, bloody, bruised. Brad had found her that way. Had sat in the court and viewed the pictures again with the jury.

Now, on the surface those bruises had faded. Her

skin had always been naturally pale, but the long walks in the apple orchards in the summer sun had given her a slight tan, a healthy glow. Her breasts weren't large, but they were firm, round, her stomach concave, her body lean and muscled.

The image of the photos flashed for a brief second again, and she blinked, then forced herself to really see the woman who stood before her now. She was stronger. Tougher for the ordeal she'd endured.

But was she completely healed through and through, or did those bruises still underlie her every action? Would they keep her from giving herself to a man if the occasion arose?

If Brad ever expressed interest…

BRAD'S BODY WAS STRUNG tight as he threw together breakfast. He should have waited on Lisa, but after touching her, feeling her so close to him, seeing her naked body silhouetted in that gown in the early morning sunlight, he had to do something to keep occupied.

Did she have any idea how beautiful she was? How much she aroused him?

He scraped the scrambled eggs onto two plates, grabbed the bread from the toaster and spread apple jelly on it—homemade, no doubt—reminding himself that this domestic, cozy morning scene was not a part of his life.

And it never would be.

Playing bodyguard was not like playing house. Or having a real live-in lover.

Neither of which he would be any good at.

"You're a bad boy," his mother had said. "We don't want you anymore."

"I wish we could place you," the social worker had said. "But you just don't fit in any of these families. They want nice boys."

His phone jangled, at the same time a knock sounded at the door. He tossed on a shirt although he didn't have time to button it, and went to answer both.

"Yeah, Booker."

"Ethan."

"Did you find anything on White's brother?"

"No, no one in town has seen or heard from him in years." Ethan paused and the knock at the door sounded again. Brad checked out the window, wondering who in the hell came to Lisa's at this time of day. A short round woman he'd seen at the day care stood on the doorstep with something in her hand that looked suspiciously like homemade bread. He felt as if he'd been dropped onto the set of an *Ed* rerun.

"Hang on, Ethan," he said. "There's someone here, let me get Lisa."

Ethan mumbled okay, and Brad kept the phone to his ear as he crossed the room, then rapped his knuckles on the bathroom door. "Lisa, you've got company."

The door flew open, and she emerged in a terry-cloth robe that covered her from neck to toe. Thank God. He didn't need any more distractions.

"Who is it?" she whispered.

He shrugged. "A friend of yours from the day care."

She flattened her hands against her cheeks, which were still rosy from the steamy shower. "Ruby. I'll get rid of her."

He nodded, then turned back to Ethan. "Did you find out anything? Some place White's brother might have gone? Did he keep in touch with anyone in town?"

"No. Not much of a trail there, but get this—I checked with the warden at the prison, and six months ago, White had a visitor."

Brad's adrenaline pumped up a notch. "His brother again?"

"That's the way the man signed in." Ethan sighed, his voice rising with excitement. "And he visited White a couple of other times, too. Booker, you're not going to believe it, but his last visit was the day White died."

"OH, MY GOODNESS." Ruby gave Brad the once-over, then smiled at Lisa and fanned her face. Thankfully, Brad had his back to her and was deep in concentration. "I didn't mean to interrupt," Ruby tittered. "I had no idea you had company, dear."

Lisa flushed. Ruby had to have noticed the strange car in the driveway, but her inquisitive nature had gotten the best of her. "It's fine, I was just getting dressed for work. I'm sure Brad will be leaving soon, too."

Too late she realized she should have said that he'd just stopped by, although Ruby would hardly believe that at 7:00 a.m.

Brad clicked his cell phone closed and turned to face them, clearly uncomfortable. But his expression softened slightly at the sight of the older woman.

Lisa had no idea how to explain his presence. "Um, Ruby, this Brad Booker—"

"I'm an old friend of Lisa's from Atlanta." He extended his hand and shook Ruby's. "It's a pleasure to meet you, ma'am."

Ruby patted her neatly coiffed curls and grinned. "Well, Mr. Booker, I hope you'll enjoy your visit in Ellijay."

"He's not staying," Lisa said.

"Actually, Lisa's accompanying me back to Atlanta," Brad announced at the same time.

Ruby's gaze drifted between them. "Goodness. How long will you be gone, Lisa?"

Lisa gave Brad a warning look. "I…I haven't exactly agreed to go to Atlanta."

Ruby glanced back at Brad, but his expression remained stoic. Sensing the tension, Ruby babbled on. "Well, I just wanted to drop off this banana bread. But I see you've eaten, so I'll leave it for later and let you two hash this out." She paused, then tottered to the door. "You want me to see if Mary can cover for you today?"

"No." Lisa gave Brad a warning glare. "I'll be there." She followed her assistant to the exit, ignoring Ruby's whisper of encouragement to take some time off and pursue the man—Ruby was a relentless flirt herself— then closed the door and turned to Brad, hands on her hips. "I can't believe you told her that."

"I have to go back to work on the case, and I'm not leaving you here alone."

"But, Brad…" A panicky feeling tightened her chest. "I'm perfectly safe. No one knows I'm here."

"You're not safe until this copycat killer is caught, Lisa. Now, if you don't trust me as your bodyguard, I'll assign another agent to take the job, or you can call your father and let him hire a private service." He moved nearer, so close she could see the flare of temper in his eyes. "What is it going to be?"

Lisa stared at him, determined not to let him railroad her. She liked her independence, had lost too much of herself four years ago. But the dark fervor in Brad's eyes shook her to the core. He'd already made up his mind. There would be no arguing.

And she'd sensed the underlying hesitation in his question. If she didn't trust him…? Good Lord, she trusted him with her life.

It was her heart she was worried about losing this time.

The phone jangled, cutting into the silence stretching between them, and Lisa startled, then gaped at the handset as if it was a foreign object. Needing a reprieve from Brad's unsettling gaze, she picked up the phone.

Heavy breathing filled the line, then a low murmur. "Hello, Lisa."

She tensed at the man's voice. "Who is this?"

"You stole my heart four years ago, Lisa," he said in an almost singsongy voice. "And I'm coming back for it."

Then the phone clicked into silence.

BRAD WAS STILL WAITING on Lisa to answer him, his heart thumping more rapidly the longer she hesitated. Did she trust him? Did she want another agent assigned to her?

Then she paled and leaned against the chair, her face crumpling as she held the phone midair. Something was wrong.

"What is it, Lisa? Who was that?"

"I don't know." Her gaze swung toward him, the fear in her eyes sending a sharp jolt through his system.

He jerked the phone to his ear but heard the dial tone blaring, then punched star sixty-nine for the call back number. The result showed out of area. Meanwhile, Lisa slumped onto the sofa, hugging her arms around her and rocking back and forth, a dazed look in her eyes.

"Lisa?" His instincts roaring to life, he slid down beside her and gently placed a hand on her back, stroking, massaging. "What's wrong?"

She slowly angled her head toward him. "It was a man. He…said I stole his heart four years ago, and that he's coming back for it."

"Damn it." Brad ground his teeth, biting back the litany of profanity on the tip of his tongue. "What else?"

She shook her head, looking confused. "That's it." A frown creased her brow. "I don't understand…what did he mean? And who would call me and say something like that?"

Brad had a terrible feeling that he did know, but he hated to panic her. "Is your phone number listed?"

"No. You know it isn't."

"Right." He'd help set her up here. "Who in town has your number?"

"Just Ruby and the people I work with."

"None of the parents you teach?"

"No. We don't give out our home numbers."

Another possibility struck him. "Have you dated anyone since you moved here?"

He braced himself in case she answered yes. After all, he wanted her to be happy, to move on.

She dropped her gaze to her hands, her voice a low, thready whisper. "No. There's never been anyone."

"How about someone who might have asked? Anybody you turned down?"

She took a moment longer answering, then looked into his eyes. "No." Another frown drew her brows together. "What's going on, Brad?"

"I don't know, but I'm damn sure going to find out."

VERNON COULDN'T STEADY his breathing as he dropped the phone in its cradle. Simply hearing the sound of Lisa's voice had made him hard, caused a burning ache to roll through him that he hadn't felt in years.

Not since his surgery.

But he was back again. Alive. Ready to confront the world and be the man who captured Lisa's heart, just as she had captured his so long ago.

Granted, William White had torn them apart. He'd caused Lisa to be wary of men; Vernon could see that in her eyes now. And he hated it. He'd also heard it in her voice when he'd knocked on her door, and it had about near killed him.

He rubbed a hand over his groin, then his sex, feeling the heat rising and churning, about to explode. But he wouldn't relieve himself.

No. Only bad boys did that. And he wasn't a bad boy. Not like the men his mama had entertained. He had talked to the Lord. Turned himself around.

He would wait. Hold back for Lisa. And when he held her in his arms, he'd show her how gentle a real man could be. How he could make her tingle and light up with fire by running his hands all over her body.

He knew how to please a woman. Not like William White, who'd pretended to be a great lover but who couldn't keep it up long enough to satisfy a woman. William was a selfish man. He never thought about the lady's pleasure, only his own.

Sick, sadistic animal.

Vernon's chest puffed up with pride. He wasn't like White. He was smart, cunning. And now with the surgery, he was even halfway attractive. More importantly, he cared about Lisa's needs. Enough to be patient.

Enough to love her the way God intended.

He had learned so much about White over the past four years, too. White had gotten what he deserved for hurting Lisa.

Vernon adjusted himself inside his pants, lifted the weights he used to strengthen and build his muscles, then struggled to work through the routine his physical therapist had suggested. Biceps curls. Overhead lifts. Squats and thrusts.

When Lisa had known him, he had been weak. Just a scrawny boy.

Now he was well developed and muscled. A man.

The very reason she hadn't recognized him when she'd looked through her peephole.

He dropped the weight to the mat, heaving in disgust. Lord, he hated to think of Lisa hiding out there, alone, frightened.

Deciding he should slow things down after making that phone call, but unable to stop his obsession, he dragged on a T-shirt, then stepped onto the porch of the little clapboard house he'd rented. Dry, dead leaves crunched below his feet, the brittle pieces fluttering off into the dirt. Seconds later, he stalked through the woods that separated their properties, his breath erupting in hot puffs as he climbed the incline for a view of her cabin. The tall oaks and pines shivered in the breeze around him, the shadows of the leaves and needles dancing on the ground, catching his eye. For a second, he was lost in their patterns, seeing animal shapes and faces and even parts of bodies in the designs. A hand. A finger. A leg. All mutilated.

No, he had to banish the dark thoughts.

The sound of a door opening slapped him back to attention, and he pushed through the bushes, staying well hidden but watching for a glimpse of his beloved. He wouldn't approach her now. Wouldn't spook her. Especially when he hadn't bothered to clean himself up. He wanted to smell good and look his best when he met her face-to-face.

But he had to sneak a peak at her now, see her face when the sunlight hit that golden hair. Watch as she tried to figure out who her admirer might be. Was she smiling now? Dreaming of who her secret caller was? Thinking about how she could finagle a meeting?

His heart suddenly clenched, dropping into a painful rhythm as she stepped onto the wooden porch. Lisa wasn't alone.

A tall, big-shouldered man with dark hair and expensive sunglasses exited the cabin with her. He wore a fancy pin-striped dark suit and one of those red power ties, and his shoes looked as if they'd been spit polished.

Fury raged inside Vernon as he zeroed in on the man's face. That son of a bitch Special Agent Brad Booker. Vernon had seen photos of him with Lisa after her attack. Had read the articles. Booker had saved Lisa from death, then coaxed her to testify.

Vernon should thank him for that. And actually, Booker had led him to Lisa. Unknowingly, of course.

But he wouldn't thank him for anything. Because in those photos, just like now, he recognized that primal instinct of man that only another male could understand.

Booker wanted Lisa for himself.

Was that the reason he was here now?

No! A scream built in Vernon's throat, nearly sending him to his knees. It was *his* turn to be with Lisa. She couldn't be interested in that agent. Vernon had gone through so much to make himself presentable to her, to be the man she wanted.

And sweet Jesus, it had taken him three and a half years to track her down.

Booker slid a hand to the back of Lisa's waist, then leaned close to say something to her, and the rage inside Vernon erupted into hot lava floating through his veins. Booker was not going to take Lisa away from him like White had.

No. Vernon had been a weakling back then, a boy without enough balls to stand up for himself. But not this time.

He picked up a tiny branch, crunched it in his hands. Bark cut into his skin and blood dripped to the ground.

Booker would go down if he had to. Because Lisa belonged to him.

Vernon pressed a bloody hand to his heart, the thud, thud, thud accelerating as he imagined her naked beneath him. Him thrusting inside her tight sheath. Over and over.

Yes. The pinwheels of a plan began spinning into place in his mind, and he felt comforted. Calmer. More assured. He'd looked for Lisa forever.

Now she was only a heartbeat away. And soon she would be his.

CHAPTER SEVEN

"CALL RUBY." Brad reached for the phone. "You're not going to work. You're staying with me."

"But Brad—"

He pushed the handset toward her, but she resisted. "I don't like it any more than you do, Lisa, but we have to treat that phone call as a threat."

Lisa's bottom lip quivered. "Maybe it was just a prank."

Brad jammed the phone into her hand. He hated like hell to scare her, but if it was the only way to keep her safe, then he'd damn well do it. "Lisa, you remember what it was like when White kidnapped you, when he put you in that grave—"

"I can't believe you would ask me that. How could I ever forget?" Lisa's voice cracked with emotions. "I think about it every day. Every night when I close my eyes…I remember him touching me. The stench of his body odor. The box closing around me."

God, her voice sounded anguished. Hollow.

Brad felt like the lowest. But he couldn't retract his comment—if Lisa had to be scared into accepting his protection, then so be it. "That's the very reason we aren't going to take a chance on this second guy coming after you and succeeding this time."

She shook her head, the pain in her eyes tearing at him. "But I'm tired of running," she admitted, her voice small. "I thought I was healing, Brad, recovering from the kidnapping, but…" She hesitated, gestured around her. "I've been hiding out instead."

"No, you've been building a life." Brad's heart clenched, but he spoke with conviction. "You have a beautiful place here in the mountains. Pictures of the children on the refrigerator." He gentled his tone. "And I saw you at the day care. The kids adore you, and so does the staff. You look stronger now, happy. At least you did until I arrived." He reached out, stroked her arms. "I want you to have all that, to live your life without ever being afraid again." *Even if that means I'm not in your life.*

Lisa nodded slowly. "But maybe this copycat isn't after me at all."

He couldn't dismiss the man's choice of words: *You've stolen my heart. I'm coming back for it.* It had been a warning. "We can't ignore that phone call, Lisa. It's too much of a coincidence."

Her expression turned grave. Resigned. As if she'd lost the battle she'd been fighting for four years. As if she'd known she would the minute he'd shown up in town.

But at least she was still fighting.

Then again, going with him was half the problem. He'd let her down before.

He wouldn't do so this time.

Lisa punched in the day care number and spoke with Ruby, her voice stilted. When she hung up, she retreated to the bedroom to pack a bag. He phoned Ethan for an update and left a message. His phone jangled as soon as he disconnected from Ethan's voice mail.

"Special Agent Booker?"

"Yes."

"This is Sheriff Theo Hallwater in Woodstock. I sent my deputy out looking around. There's an abandoned house nearby that we're going to ride out and check. My deputy said he saw a suspicious car out there earlier. He ran the plate, but the car was stolen."

Brad's pulse accelerated. "Give me the location, and I'll meet you there."

The sheriff recited directions, and Brad jotted them down, then met Lisa at her bedroom door and took her bag. "Come on, there's an old abandoned building in Woodstock we're going to check out."

"You think Mindy might be there?" Lisa asked.

God, he hoped so. "I don't know, but the sheriff is suspicious. It's worth a shot." They hurried to his car, and he started the engine. As he veered onto the highway, he tried to remain optimistic that they'd find Mindy and the killer at this building.

But his gut warned him that Mindy was already dead.

"I HOPE MINDY'S NOT DEAD." Anne, a young redheaded nurse, with startling hazel eyes, looked up at Wayne Nettleton, tears glistening on the fringes of her lashes.

"I know. Mindy's a great girl," a chubby nurse with

bifocals added in a worried voice. "God knows we've been blessed to have her. We've all been sick about her disappearance here at First Peachtree."

Wayne's chin itched beneath the fake beard, but he fought the impulse to scratch it for fear the danged thing might slip and reveal his disguise. Not that he'd actually needed one to question the hospital staff, but he'd just left a seedy area where he'd questioned a few of the homeless, and had wanted to fit in. If they'd known he was a reporter, they'd probably have run. He'd learned long ago if he blended into the crowd, he'd glean more information.

He had shed the ratty clothes before entering the hospital, and was pretending to be a relative of Mindy's, an uncle who'd rushed to Atlanta out of concern for his missing niece. He'd played the sympathy card when he'd first arrived, forcing a couple of tears from his eyelids. That had done the trick. The nurses were eating out of his hand now, really to spill their guts.

Besides, when people learned that the Grave Digger was calling him personally, they tended to look at him as if he was the killer.

"She enjoyed working at the hospital," Nettleton continued.

"Yes, she loves nursing," the redhead said. "She always keeps her head in emergencies."

Wayne nodded, smiling at the chubby one, Doretha. She was as round as she was tall, with soft folds around her neck and a chin that reminded him of a chipmunk. But he'd tease her, flirt, whatever was necessary to keep her talking. "Mindy has a spontaneous side to her, too," Wayne said. "And she's so pretty."

"Lord, yes, that she is," Doretha said with a twinkle in her eye. "She likes to have fun. And let me tell you, more than one man's head turned around here when she walked past."

Anne tapped her fingernails on her clipboard. "I thought she was getting serious about a guy awhile back, but they ended things suddenly."

"That FBI agent, Brad Booker," Doretha said with a head bob. "He was a looker, but he was too brooding for Mindy. And Lord knows, the hours the man kept. He'd never be around to help raise babies with her."

"She still had it bad for him," Anne murmured. "But she thought he was in love with someone else."

Wayne made a mental note to add Booker's involvement with Mindy to his article. He'd like to question Booker now, too. See his reaction. Although if he did, he might arouse more suspicion on himself… Not a good idea.

Doretha snickered. "It didn't take her long to find someone else."

"Was she seeing anyone in particular?" Wayne asked, keeping his tone level.

Doretha and Anne traded skeptical looks. "Well," Doretha finally said. "She dated one of the male nurses a few times. And…I saw her leave with Dr. Langley twice."

Wayne's eyebrows shot up. "She socialized with Lisa Langley's father?"

Anne gave Doretha an odd look. "I don't think so,"

Anne said. "They worked together, but date—no. He's quite a bit older."

As if that mattered, Nettleton thought.

"I saw them arguing in the hall a couple of weeks ago," Doretha added. "But it must not have been important because they went to lunch the next day."

Wayne frowned and pressed a thumb to his chin to stem the goddamn itch. "Was there anyone who disliked Mindy? Someone who'd want to hurt her?"

Anne scrunched her nose in thought while Doretha's pudgy cheeks ballooned outward. "Not that I know of," Anne finally said.

"Everyone loved her," Doretha added.

Which meant these women knew nothing. Wayne had been an investigative reporter too long not to realize that the lack of a connection between the victims complicated the police's case even more. But there was a connection… The police just hadn't figured it out yet.

He pasted on another look of concern. "I'd like to talk to Dr. Langley," he said. "Can you page him for me?"

Doretha checked the schedule. "He should be out of surgery by now. I'll see if I can find him." She batted her eyelashes at Wayne, and he offered her a solicitous look.

"Thank you, I appreciate it."

Doretha showed him to the vending machine, and he grabbed a cup of coffee while he waited. But ten minutes later, she returned to the waiting area. "I'm sorry, Mr. Faulkner, but Dr. Langley has already gone for the day."

He cursed silently, but thanked her and accepted the

business card she handed him, smiling at her scrawled phone number.

"If you need anything while you're in town," Doretha said, "feel free to call. Our thoughts and prayers are with you for Mindy's safe return."

"Thank you so much." Aiming for sincerity, he tucked the card in his pocket, knowing good and well he wouldn't call this woman, not unless he needed more information.

Deciding a quick visit to Dr. Langley's home might spruce up his story, he headed toward the elevator. The fact that Langley's daughter was the final victim of the first Grave Digger, that Langley worked with Mindy Faulkner, and that Booker had dated her was too much of a coincidence to ignore. More spice for his article.

And what about Lisa Langley? She'd disappeared after the trial four years ago. Did she know about this copycat killer?

Maybe Langley was with her now. And maybe Langley would lead him to Lisa. An interview with daddy's little princess would certainly raise even more hype about the story.

LISA STARED OUT the window at the passing scenery as Brad drove down the mountain through Resaca and several other small towns, the dismal gray sky overhead mimicking her mood. Rolling farmland and small, quaint towns passed, reminding her of the contrast to Atlanta with its skyscrapers, heavy traffic, endless milling people and sea of anonymous faces.

She tried to think about the kids at day camp, about the art activities they were doing, the innocent little faces, the smiles and laughter, the tears over trivial things like stubbed toes or frustration over not being able to tie their shoes. The friendly people in town, the small diner where everyone knew everyone else, the homemade banana bread Ruby had brought.

The things she'd miss in Atlanta.

She'd felt safe in Ellijay, surrounded by the jutting mountain ridges, fresh air, apple houses and normally clear blue skies.

Now, she felt anything but safe.

Exactly the way Mindy must be feeling. No, Mindy's terror was much more real right now. She was probably being brutalized, tormented, her throat dry from lack of water, her body slowly dying, just as the flowers and grass were wilting from the drought.

And then the terror of being buried alive….

The familiar burn returned to Lisa's throat, sending chills cascading down her arms and neck, and she opened the window for air.

Brad remained sullen, brooding, his eyes trained on the road, his hands clenched tightly around the steering wheel. She ached to comfort him, to assure him they'd find his girlfriend alive, but how could she make a promise like that when she had no idea if it would come true, when she had no control over the situation?

"I'm sorry, Lisa," Brad murmured in a low voice. "I know you'd rather be anywhere but with me."

She glanced at his taut face and saw the anguish in

his expression. Had he felt this way, been tormented, when he'd searched for her that night?

His gaze cut toward her, and her breath caught. He had. She saw it in the flash of pain and remorse in his eyes. The same sense of helplessness she felt now.

Only he had dated Mindy. Their relationship was more personal.

"I want to tell you we'll find her," she said in a strained voice. "I…pray we do, Brad."

His mouth worked from side to side. "I know you do, and I…appreciate you helping."

"I haven't done anything," Lisa said.

A strained lapse of silence followed. "Yes, you have," he said in a low voice. "You faced the past to help Mindy."

Had she? Or had she done it for Brad?

Or maybe for herself. It was time she confronted her fears. Perhaps if she helped save Mindy, she could forgive herself for the other women. Forget the helplessness and anger that had nearly driven her crazy those first few months after her own abduction and rescue.

He turned his gaze back to the curve ahead. Traffic slowed, an eighteen-wheeler shifting into low gear, the car in front of them riding its brakes. Someone slammed on a horn and a chorus followed.

"I could drop you at the police station before we meet that sheriff," he offered.

Lisa spotted the railroad crossing up ahead, and her stomach knotted. "No, don't waste time. You need to hurry."

His breath hissed out as the car bounced, then flew

over the railroad tracks. He turned onto a dirt road, then followed it for about three or four miles to a boulder where a mailbox sat at an odd angle, as if it had recently been plowed over and jammed back in the ground.

Brad spun onto the narrow dirt drive, the car bouncing over the gravel and earth, hitting potholes and spewing dust in its wake. Brittle bushes and weeds nearly as tall as the car door scraped the sides of the car, and limbs clawed at the window.

Through the cloud of trees and weeds, Lisa spotted an old clapboard house in a small clearing. An ancient washing machine and sofa sat on the rotting front porch. A beagle loped down the steps, then stopped and cocked its head before dropping back to the ground to chew on a half-gnawed bone.

The sheriff's car was parked to the side, a rusted Chevelle on an incline, facing down the hill behind the house.

Brad stopped his vehicle and gestured for her to stay in it. He locked the door, but left the key inside. "If there's trouble, don't wait. Get the hell out of here."

She frowned, and worried her bottom lip, jiggling her leg up and down while he drew his gun and slowly approached the house. A second later, a barrel-chested man in a sheriff's uniform appeared. Brad followed him inside the house, and Lisa fisted her hands, her leg bouncing faster as she waited.

The house was quiet. No signs of life.

Did that mean they were too late? That Mindy was dead inside, or buried somewhere on the property?

THE STENCH OF DRUGS and chemicals heated the summer air as Brad entered the wooden house, the sight in front of him giving him a jolt of surprise. Marijuana plants filled one entire back room, visible from the small living area, and a meth lab had been set up in the other.

Drug paraphernalia littered the wooden floor and threadbare furniture, along with empty pizza boxes, beer cans and a crack pipe.

He frowned in disgust and disappointment. "This isn't our killer's place."

The sheriff shook his head. "I doubt it, too. We found a couple of teenagers here when we arrived. They stole the car. We have them in custody already. We don't need the likes of this in our town."

No town needed it, Brad started to say, although drugs, drug dealers and meth labs seemed to be cropping up in the rural areas by the dozens.

"Did your boys look around?" Brad asked.

"We checked the storage shed out back. Nothing but rusted farm tools. And we found supplies in the car. As you can tell, the only crop these boys are growing is weed."

Brad nodded. The scenario was all wrong for the Grave Digger, even a copycat. Although he preferred the rural areas, and the woods, and it was possible that he might choose a place near this cabin for burial, if he sensed a drug house, he wouldn't want to be close to it for fear of calling attention to himself.

"I'm going to look around."

The sheriff nodded. "Suit yourself."

Brad's chest felt heavy as he headed outside. Lisa was

waiting in the hot car, so he went straight to her and opened the door. "It's just a meth lab," he said wearily. "The sheriff found a couple of kids here when he arrived."

"No Mindy?"

He shook his head. "I'm going to walk around out back, but I don't think this is our place."

Brad started to close the door, but his cell phone rang. He quickly flipped it open. "Booker here."

"Special Agent Booker, this is Wayne Nettleton of the *Atlanta Daily*."

Brad sucked in a breath. Nettleton, the Grave Digger's contact. "I'm listening."

"I just got a call about the Faulkner woman."

That was odd; before, the killer had phoned in the middle of the night. He was varying his pattern again.

"Where do we look?" Brad bowed his head and listened while Nettleton rattled off the address. Seconds later, Brad jumped in the car and tore way, racing toward Buford.

If Mindy was buried where Nettleton said she was, once again the copycat had chosen a location near Brad's very own home to leave her body.

LISA HAD THOUGHT the tension couldn't get worse, but as they approached Buford, every bone and muscle in her body ached with anxiety. And every minute was filled with the pulsing agony of wondering what they might find. When she'd heard Brad phone his partner, then the local police in Buford, she'd wanted to offer encouragement. But she couldn't deliver false platitudes or promises. Brad lived with the grim reality of death and violence every day, of knowing the depravities of mankind. He had even killed when necessary. When she'd asked him about other cases during her trial, he'd clammed up and refused to talk. But she'd heard hints that he had a reputation as a man without a conscience.

Yet he had never been anything but tender and understanding with her.

She thought about her father, too. The distance that existed between them. Thanks to Wayne Nettleton's coverage in the *Atlanta Daily,* along with a few other reporters hell-bent on depicting every gory detail of the Grave Digger's sadistic crimes, her father must have been eaten up inside, going out of his mind with worry.

Then again, Liam Langley was normally an emotionless man. He had bottled any feelings he'd once had after her mother died, and rarely revealed them to Lisa. After Brad had saved her, her father had shut down even more, keeping his distance, as if being close to her shamed him.

Her father had also blamed Brad. From her hospital bed, she'd heard him yelling at him. He'd accused Brad of incompetence. But Brad had done everything in his power to save her.

She had been the fool to trust William White.

She wouldn't make that mistake again. For that very reason, she'd cut herself off from all men.

Except for Brad. Occasionally, his face, his voice, had slipped into her mind, taunting her with what-ifs, teasing her with fantasies of a life that might have been, but never would be.

Had Brad blamed himself when she'd been kidnapped, as he was blaming himself now?

The next few minutes, she gripped the console as he manipulated the turns, curves and traffic lights. He flipped on a siren and raced through Buford to the winding road leading to the lake.

"How did you make it through that night?" Brad asked in a voice thick with emotion. Worry? Concern?

Lisa licked her lips and placed her hand over his, aching for him, for Mindy and for herself, for all they had lost at the hands of a madman. "I kept telling myself that you would come," she said simply.

His mouth twisted sideways, pain darkening his smoky eyes. "I was almost too late."

"But you saved me, Brad," Lisa said softly. "If it weren't for you, I wouldn't be here now."

His gaze shot to hers, questions and guilt shadowing his face. "I..." He shook his head, but didn't finish his sentence. She didn't have to ask why.

He was wondering if he would be too late now, if Mindy had assured herself he'd come, if death would cheat him this time.

They finally reached the turnoff for the property, and a police siren chimed in with theirs. Brad dovetailed into the turn behind the officer, and followed him down a twisted dirt road that led to a more deserted part of the lake, an area not yet overrun by cabins and new lake homes. Another police car was already parked near the edge of the woods.

Brad braked to a stop. "You can stay in the car."

"No." Lisa touched his arm. "I'm going with you."

He swung his head toward her. "No, Lisa…you don't need to see this."

Her fingers closed around his wrist. "I've lived it before, Brad. I know exactly what to expect."

He hesitated, but she reached for the door handle. "Come on, we're wasting time."

Glad she'd worn sneakers and jeans, she followed behind him as they entered the woods. Ahead she heard voices and saw shadows flutter between the trees. The sound of men giving orders broke the quiet.

When they reached the clearing, Lisa froze, bracing herself for the worst. Brad placed a hand in front of her to prevent her from going any farther, but in the clearing ahead, she saw a mound of freshly turned earth.

Then two policemen lifted a wooden box from the ground.

CHAPTER EIGHT

INSECTS BUZZED and nipped at Brad's neck and face, feasting on his sweaty skin. He barely noticed. Instead, he raced ahead and began helping the officers pry open the wooden box. Dunbar, the crime scene tech, had quickly photographed the area before they'd lifted the coffin from the ground, and was snapping pictures of the surrounding area. The soft sounds of lake water slapping the bank filled the tension-laden air, the calls of crickets and frogs mingling with the low whine of a motorboat echoing in the distance. The murky gray of nightfall and death loomed ahead, dismal and omnipotent.

Following police orders, Lisa stood in the distance, away from the grave site. Time lapsed into a warped slow motion for Brad that spiraled into what felt like eternity, although in reality, only seconds passed until they tore off the lid.

He held his breath, hoping Mindy would still be alive.

But the second the top was lifted, his hopes disintegrated. Mindy was dead. Even though darkness shrouded the woods, he noted the bruises on her naked body. The insects that sucked at his own flesh had already dug into hers. And a gold cross identical to the one they'd found on Joann Worthy dangled around her neck.

His first instinct was to leave the scene, to close his eyes to the horror, but he was a primary on the task force investigating the crime. Still, he leaned against the tree, had to take a minute to let the dizziness pass.

Inhaling sharply, he balled his hands into fists by his sides, his nails digging into his skin. What kind of sick monster got his pleasure pounding on defenseless women, then leaving a religious symbol as if he had the power to decide who lived and who died? Did he see himself as some kind of God?

White certainly had. And now there was another....

Frustration radiated in waves of heat from Brad's body. He was so damn tired. And when he caught this one, there would always be another and another and another.

He couldn't save them all.

He hadn't realized he'd staggered sideways until he felt Lisa's hand grip his arm. "I'm so sorry, Brad."

He swallowed hard at her low whisper, glancing at her but not really seeing anything for a minute. "You shouldn't be here. She died because she knew me," he said with a groan. Like an out-of-focus camera distorting images, Lisa's face swam in front of him, her features blurring and slipping in and out of his vision. He blinked several times, then pressed his fingers to the bridge of his nose and massaged until the dizziness subsided. But the pain and shock of seeing Mindy brutalized and dead would stay with him forever.

"Jesus, he did a number on her," Detective Anderson muttered.

"Looks like she died of asphyxiation," Captain Rosberg said.

"Cut her fingernails just like the first victim," Detective Anderson added.

"Her name is Mindy," Brad stated, remembering Liam Langley's bitter words about using the victim's name.

"I realize you knew this woman, so take a minute, Booker." Captain Rosberg slanted him a sympathetic look, unusual for the hard-ass cop.

Surges, the young rookie who'd thrown up the night they'd found Joann Worthy, clutched his stomach, his face turning ashen.

Detective Anderson shook his head. "Surges, for God's sake, you don't know the vic. You have to get a grip. Do you want to make it as a cop?"

"Hell, yes, it's the only thing I've ever wanted to do."

"Then you can't go puking every time you see a corpse," Rosberg barked. "Toughen up, be a man."

Surges swiped at the sweat droplets on his upper lip and nodded, a determined expression tightening his mouth.

Brad's own anger kicked in.

Lisa inched closer to him, her breath shaky, and he suddenly pulled himself out of his shock. She looked pale, haunted.

He reached for her. He had to take care of the crime scene and her. "God, Lisa, I shouldn't have brought you here. Are you all right?"

Anguish darkened her eyes, the shadows of night

playing along her face and painting it in heavy gray lines. "I survived, Brad. I'm just…s-sorry she didn't."

Brad's breaths caught in his throat at her selfless-ness. But Lisa's hands felt icy-cold. The whites of her eyes were too bright, her pupils dilated. "Let me walk you back to the car. You don't need to watch the in-vestigation."

"No." She gripped his arm. "I'm okay. I want to be here for you."

He narrowed his eyes, trying to discern whether she was simply being brave or if she was really okay, but she squared her shoulders. "Please, Brad. I promise not to get in the way."

He reluctantly nodded, although her hands still felt like ice cubes and the trembling of her lower lip belied her words. He ached for her, for Mindy…felt like such a failure that he'd let them both down. And he'd never be able to make it up to Mindy.

But Lisa was here, alive, well, and he intended to keep her that way.

"At least sit down. You look exhausted." Thankful Rosberg had given him a moment's reprieve, he guided her over to a large rock jutting from the ground, and coaxed her to sit there. In spite of the sultry heat, she was shaking, the warmth not returning to her hands. Afraid she might go into shock, he rushed to the car, returned with a blanket and wrapped it around her shoulders.

"If you need anything, just let me know." He gently brushed the hair from her eyes. "You promise?"

She nodded and caught his hand. He squeezed hers

in return, then released it. Seeing Mindy's dead body, knowing that anyone who associated with him, anyone he got involved with, might be put in danger because of his job, only hardened his resolve to keep his distance from Lisa. She would be safer if she never saw him again.

Resigned, weighed down by guilt, he joined the other detectives at the crime scene. He had to resume authority. For Mindy's sake, he had to make sure every piece of evidence was collected.

She had died because of him. And he intended to find her killer and make sure he faced the consequences.

Dunbar was studying the body, while other techs combed the wooded area. The rustle of trees and brush made him snap his head around, and Brad grimaced. Wayne Nettleton. The reporter practically dived through the thicket, notepad and camera in hand. Brad scowled. He'd half expected Nettleton to be there when they arrived.

Then again, if he was guilty, maybe he'd purposely waited so he wouldn't incriminate himself.

Captain Rosberg immediately stepped up, flanked by Detectives Anderson and Bentley. "What are you doing here?" Rosberg asked.

Nettleton's inexorable gaze traveled over the grave, swung to Brad, then to Lisa. Brad clenched his fists, prepared to keep him away from her.

"The killer called me so I could write the story," Nettleton muttered.

Brad frowned. Could he possibly have staged a copycat killing in a ruse to get his career back on track?

THE SIGHT OF Wayne Nettleton snapping photos sent Lisa back mentally and emotionally into a state of frenzy that she had run from and thought she'd escaped.

The scraggly haired reporter with long, gangly legs and arms and a nose too big for his face, had harassed her during William's trial. He'd painted her as an imbecile for not realizing she'd been dating a serial killer, had suggested that she'd deserved to be attacked because she'd worn blinders and let four other women die.

Worse, he seemed to care more about sensationalizing the events of the crimes and the victims' histories, pointing out each and every indiscretion the women had made, as if they had been victimized because of their own faults, than he did finding the killer.

She had despised the man.

And her father had looked at her as if those allegations were true. Had made her feel as if she'd embarrassed him, the esteemed surgeon, in front of his prestigious friends. Early on, Lisa had learned that embarrassing him before his colleagues was unforgivable.

And she had committed the cardinal sin when she'd gone public with her testimony against William White.

Had her father really expected her to just sit quietly by? The therapist had advised her to testify, had claimed it would help her heal. But facing him on the stand still hadn't been enough to erase the damage he'd inflicted.

"Nettleton, you don't belong here," Brad said in a harsh voice.

The reporter snapped another picture, ignoring him.

"You forget that the killer is calling *me*. He's doing that for a reason."

"Just like White did?"

"I'm sure he read the series I wrote on the first Grave Digger." Nettleton grinned, revealing a row of crooked front teeth, and Lisa shivered, remembering him turning that vacuous smile on her.

Brad sneered, his disdain for Nettleton obvious. "And he's copying him, so why not call you again?"

"Exactly," Nettleton said in a smug tone.

"Your career hasn't fared so well the last four years, has it, Nettleton?" Brad asked.

The man scratched his collar with two fingers. "I've had some health issues."

"And that story you embellished about the mayor didn't hurt your reputation at the *Atlanta Daily?*"

Nettleton's smile turned to sullen insolence, but he recovered quickly, spinning toward Lisa. "It's good to see you again, Miss Langley. You've actually made my job so much easier."

Brad lurched forward as if he might pounce on Nettleton, but Lisa stood her ground. "I hope I can help find the killer."

Nettleton's smile lapsed into a hearty chuckle, the sound eerie, as if it had floated across the lake and boomeranged back. "Ahh, the innocent virginal princess returns to assist the feds in saving more damsels in distress?"

Lisa's insides churned. "At least I'm sincere in wanting to help. You're just here to make a name."

"And you're going to help me do it," Nettleton said.

Brad jerked him by the collar. "Unless you have more information to give us, something the killer said that might hint as to his identity, Nettleton, then I want you out of here. This is a crime scene, and I don't want it compromised."

"I have every right to be here," Nettleton argued.

Captain Rosberg strode up beside Brad. "Do you have more information for us, Nettleton?"

The reporter ground his teeth. "Not yet, but I will."

"What does that mean?" Brad asked.

"When he kills his next victim," Nettleton said with cocky assurance. "You'll want me to call you then, won't you?"

Lisa glared at him, detesting every fiber of his being.

"If you know something and you don't come forward," Rosberg said, "you will be charged with accessory to murder."

"Or murder itself," Brad interjected, "if you're responsible for the crimes."

"Listen to him," Rosberg said. "In fact, I just learned you visited White in jail."

Brad's gaze swung to Rosberg's. Brad hadn't heard about Nettleton's visits, but he wasn't surprised. Nettleton would do anything for a story.

"I have an alibi for both murders," Nettleton said.

"Then where were you last night?" Rosberg asked.

Nettleton frowned. "Chasing a lead. And you know good and goddamn well that my sources are confidential."

"So is this investigation," Brad said. "Now either

leave or these officers will escort you away from the premises in handcuffs."

Nettleton glared at him, then stormed off in a cloud of anger.

Lisa studied the phantom figures created by the shadows of the pine needles where he disappeared, forcing herself not to look at Mindy Faulkner in the hard wooden box. But she couldn't shake the memory of being buried underground or the fear that this killer might attack her. Might try to kill her again.

She didn't know if she'd have the courage to survive a second time.

The medical examiner arrived, followed by a crime scene unit, and Brad filled Dunbar in on the details. The next few hours dragged by in a horrific blur of voices that broke through the parapet she'd constructed to protect her mind from the details.

The wooden box the woman lay in resembled the one that had been her own coffin. As with her, the length and width had been custom designed to fit her body, allowing her no room to maneuver inside. There were claw marks on the inner walls where Mindy had tried to scratch her way out, just as there had been with Lisa. Her fingers had bled, were raw.

The killer must be insane to have committed such vile, inhuman acts. On the other hand, that kind of detail took planning and time as well as foresight, meaning that he was smart, cunning, clever.

And he had not chosen the women at random.

These kidnappings and murders were well-thought-out, premeditated murders. Each victim was chosen for a reason, her casket sculpted specifically for her.

Lisa tried to remember what the criminal profiler had said during William's trial. White had been severely abused as a child. Had suffered a psychotic break from head trauma when he was a teen. He was a true sociopath.

Evidence revealed White had prior instances of violence when he was a child. He'd tortured animals, had killed his own cat in a sadistic way, cut off body parts, then buried it while it was still alive.

He'd been practicing for adulthood, for more heinous crimes.

A shudder coursed through her, and she tried to drown out the sounds of Brad's agents and medical examiner as they discussed Mindy's body and searched the area. The CSI tech took her shoe print, and Brad explained that they had to eliminate hers from the others found at the scene.

The smell of death and blood wafted toward her, along with some rotting vegetation.

She gripped her hands into fists, angry for Mindy Faulkner. Who could have done this to her?

William's missing brother? Vernon Hanks, the young student who had dogged William?

Or…another possibility entered her mind. Brad had insinuated that Wayne Nettleton might know more than he was telling. He had certainly researched William's MO, knew every gory, distinctive detail of the past crimes. Was it possible that he'd staged these killings just to do a follow-up story? The idea seemed preposterous, but when she'd looked into Nettleton's devious eyes earlier, and at the trial, she'd sensed that the man had no morals or scruples.

He had thrived on magnifying the painful details of the attacks—anything to sell a story and build his name. And he had known exactly where to find the bodies.

He hadn't acted especially surprised to see her, either, simply pleased. It was as if he'd known where she was all along. Or maybe he'd driven her out of hiding with these murders, then followed Brad to her cabin, knowing she would come to the grave site.

Was that part of his sick game—to make her relive the horror all over again?

NETTLETON STOOD BENEATH the thicket of trees bordering the crime scene, his clothes sticking to him, the hum of mosquitoes buzzing in his ears. But he couldn't tear himself away. He had to see the body. The reaction of the cops. The expression on Lisa Langley's face when she mentally revisited the grave.

Elation stole through him at the sight. Agent Booker was reacting just as he'd expected. He was shaken to hell, mad as a hornet and worried sick about Dr. Langley's little princess.

The other cops stumbled around, logging details, studying the ground, searching for footprints, their feeble attempts at trying to catch this killer almost comical. The Grave Digger was too smart for them.

In fact, he anticipated the cops' every move. And he stayed one step ahead of them all the time.

Because he was a master at the game.

Nettleton's gaze fixed on Lisa Langley as he snapped a photo, remembering her as the little girl who'd been Miss Magnolia when she was a child. The young woman who'd single-handedly survived the first serial killer, who had testified and sent White to jail. The courageous woman who'd stolen the hearts of strangers everywhere with her beautiful blond hair and those stunning blue eyes. Eyes that held sadness and secrets.

The truth about how it felt to be locked inside that box.

She had refused to grant him an interview. Had denied him the right to tell her personal story.

But one day he would get her alone, and she would tell him everything about her emotional journey. Exactly what it felt like when the killer had touched her. How the heat had nearly driven her insane. How the claustrophobia had mounted.

How it had felt to witness the top of that coffin being nailed down, shutting her into the darkness.

And what her final thoughts had been when she'd closed her eyes and given in to death.

He couldn't wait for that day to arrive....

CHAPTER NINE

BRAD WAS STILL REELING from Nettleton's comments as he watched the crime scene techs collect samples and search for trace evidence. He'd heard Dunbar was new with CSU, but he was supposedly a stickler for details. If there was any trace evidence to be found, he would find it, and pass it on to the task force via the lab.

Brad tried to suppress thoughts of Mindy and the last time he'd seen her, the night he'd ended their short relationship. Her long hair had been swept up in a French twist, with sparkly clips holding it in place. Silver dangling earrings had dropped to her bare shoulders, her scoop-necked red dress revealing just enough cleavage to tempt him to take her to bed one more time.

After all, the sex had been good. Not great, but good.

And he hadn't had a woman in a damn long time. Because every time he'd tried to make love to someone, he'd seen Lisa Langley's face in his mind. Other men fantasized about strange women, hookers and movie stars during sex, and he had once done that without thinking twice. A warm willing body was all that he'd wanted.

But that was before Lisa.

Not that he'd ever slept with her.

But he had wanted to. So many times.

Mindy had cried the night he'd ended it, had actually claimed she'd thought they might find something special together. But his heart hadn't been in it. Hell, at one time he wouldn't have even thought he had a heart.

But he did, and it belonged somewhere else—a place that was forbidden.

To a person he could never have.

Now, poor Mindy's long hair had been whacked off in a choppy style. The tears had dried on her face along with blood and dirt. Bugs had already infiltrated the wooden coffin and had eaten at her hands and arms. And the stench of body fluids and decay swirled around him, made worse by the insufferable heat.

He tried to compartmentalize. To evade thoughts of Mindy's final hours in the box. But the dark eerie images drew him anyway. Her desperately clawing to get out. Fear racing through her. The terror of being trapped underground, the air slipping away.

He'd heard Lisa's vivid descriptions. Her low voice still echoed at night in his dreams, her words a picture that had been permanently etched in his mind.

The nausea rose again in his stomach. Stomping back his own emotions to remain professional, he glanced at the rookie cop to see how he was holding up. Officer Surges had composed himself and was measuring the depth of the grave, although his face was still a pasty-white as he climbed in, recorded his findings, then watched Mindy's body being placed in a body bag. Dunbar was searching for tire tracks, comparing each to the emergency and police vehicles.

"She's been here several hours," the medical examiner finally said. "Estimated time of death is midnight."

"He probably buried her sometime earlier," Brad said, "then waited until this afternoon to call it in, to give himself plenty of time to escape."

"Clipped her nails just like before," Rosberg added. "Wonder if he kept them like White did."

Brad shifted on the balls of his feet and swatted at a gnat. "He must be driving a truck, a big SUV or station wagon, or he couldn't haul the coffin out here." He glanced at Rosberg. "I'll get someone to start working that angle. Run a DMV check on the suspects we have so far."

"You're talking about White's brother and his cell mate?" Rosberg asked.

"Yeah, and Vernon Hanks." Brad loosened the knot at his tie, the heat and stench getting to him. "Nettleton drives a Yukon, doesn't he?"

"Yeah, says he needs it for his camera equipment."

"How convenient," Brad said wryly. "Maybe he has other uses for it, too."

Rosberg slanted a curious look his way. "You like Nettleton for this?"

"He's as good a suspect as any we have." Brad glanced back at Lisa for the fiftieth time to make sure she was okay. "Let's put a tail on him. He's an arrogant asshole. I want that cocky smile wiped off his face."

Rosberg rubbed a hand over his stomach, reached

inside his pocket and took out a roll of antacids, then popped one into his mouth. "You're not contemplating a personal vendetta, are you?"

Brad arched a brow. "It's a criminal investigation. We have every reason to suspect Nettleton." He explained about the phone call Lisa had received.

"You think our copycat may try to kidnap her?"

A chill slid down Brad's spine. "It's possible. But this time, we're going to catch the bastard first."

IT WAS LATE IN THE NIGHT by the time the crime techs finished. Brad and Lisa drove to his cabin in silence, fatigue and anxiety intensified by the humid air in the car. Brad cut the engine when they arrived, and Lisa opened her eyes. She'd rested her head against the headrest, but she hadn't been able to fall asleep.

She wondered if either one of them would rest tonight. A mangy looking dog with wiry brown hair and an awkward gait loped from the forest and stared at the car as they parked. Lisa clutched the door handle, wondering if the animal was friendly or if it would attack. "Is that your dog?"

Brad squinted through the darkness. His eyes looked bloodshot, his face strained. "No. But I leave him food sometimes."

"Does he have a name?"

"Beauregard."

Lisa relaxed and studied the poor animal's posture. Fatigue lined his features. "Who named him that?"

"I did, after a homeless man I once knew."

"Someone you arrested?"

Brad hesitated. "No, this old guy I shacked up with once."

Lisa's mouth parted slightly. "You lived on the streets?"

He angled his head toward her, looking bone-tired. "It was a long time ago."

But the memory still lingered in the far corners of his mind, just as ghosts did her own. "Maybe when this is over, you can tell me about it."

He shook his head. "When this is over, you're going back to Ellijay, to your kids and your nice life."

Lisa latched on to that thought, although for some reason the idea of leaving Brad bothered her. He seemed different tonight. Less intimidating. Even vulnerable, maybe.

The mutt watched Brad as he exited the car, hungry for affection. Lisa opened her car door and started to climb out, but Brad came around to help her before she could drag herself from the soft leather seat. Exhaustion tugged at her limbs, but the dog loped up to her, and she knelt and petted him. "There, there, boy, I know it's hot out here. We'll bring you some water."

Brad opened the door and retrieved a bowl of cold water, then set it outside.

"Aren't you going to let him in?" Lisa asked.

"No." Brad gestured for her to come inside. "I don't have time for a dog."

"But he looks so lonely. Didn't you have a pet growing up?"

He gave her an odd look. "My foster parents said they

didn't get money for taking in unwanted strays. Animals, that is."

She frowned, her heart hurting for him. How could a person say something so cruel to a child?

She wanted to talk more, ask more questions, but his closed expression cut her off. The small den held a hodgepodge of old furniture. A brown leather sofa and a recliner in beige-and-brown plaid faced a TV. Newspapers littered an oak coffee table and a cream-colored rug partially covered the wood floor. A state-of-the-art computer system occupied one corner, that one item symbolizing Brad's priorities.

"There are two bedrooms. The guest room is small," he said as if in apology. "You can sleep in my room."

"No. The guest room's fine." Not his room, with his scent and clothes inside. Too much temptation for her aching heart. Brad was grieving for another woman tonight. It wouldn't be right.

"Do you want something to drink or eat before you turn in?" Brad asked.

Lisa shook her head. Her head throbbed, and she had lost all appetite after seeing Mindy's dead body.

That could have been her four years ago. She hadn't been able to shake the realization that it still might be if she wasn't careful.

BRAD SHOWED LISA to the bedroom, his hands knotted by his sides, the urge to touch her a palpable throb.

God, he was selfish. Mindy Faulkner lay dead in the morgue, and all he could think about right now was the fact that it could have been Lisa. That he wanted to hold her so badly he was almost shaking with need.

He cursed silently. He was losing his edge. Letting his personal feelings affect his job. Just as he had four years ago.

And for a minute, she'd made him feel guilty about that mangy dog. As if he needed something else to take care of. Besides, he didn't want to get attached to the animal. It was better that way for both of them.

"We have to share the bath," he said in a low voice, remembering that morning when he'd used Lisa's shower, and shampoo, then shared breakfast with her. And just yesterday he'd watched her dance with those children.

He wanted to spin the clock back to that moment, block out all the ugliness. To haul Lisa in his arms and hold her forever. To make love to her until the darkness faded.

"Thanks, Brad," she said softly. She hesitated, looked up at him, and he almost reached for her. But in spite of the heat stirring his body to life, he held on to his resolve and said goodnight.

Lisa closed the door behind her, and Brad sighed, fighting the possessive feeling that overcame him when he was around her, struggling with his insatiable desire. He couldn't have Lisa. Neither could he sate his need for her by taking her to bed.

Because he'd inevitably have to walk away from her, and if he slept with her, he wasn't sure he'd be able to do that.

Images of Mindy bombarded him as he splashed cold water on his face. Knowing sleep wouldn't come yet, and feeling bad for the damn dog, he set out food, grabbed his boxing gloves and headed down to the big oak tree by the lake where he'd hung his punching bag.

Five minutes later, he pounded the bag, venting his frustrations. Hard solid jabs with his left and right. He swung his leg up and karate kicked the center a few times, then threw punch after punch, harder, faster, each time more forceful, the images of Mindy at the morgue fueling his temper. Sweat drenched his chest and ran down his back, and he tugged off the shirt and tossed it onto a tree stump, then swiped at his forehead with his arm and began again. With every slam to the bag, he imagined catching the sick bastard and taking him down.

He continued the grueling beating, relentless, unscathed by the blood that seeped from the boxing gloves and the tremors that rocked through him.

Finally, when his legs buckled beneath him, he dropped to the ground on another stump, threw off the gloves and let the blood drip from his fingers. Oblivious to the pain, he lowered his head onto his hands, closed his eyes and gave in to the anguish and exhaustion.

LISA HAD TOSSED and turned, but sleep had eluded her. When she'd heard the door close and realized Brad had gone outside, she climbed from bed and followed him down the trail. The summer heat was stifling, but a slight breeze from the lake rippled the water, splashing gently against the rocky embankment. Sensing he wanted to be alone, she'd stood beneath the shadows of the hardwoods and watched as he'd pummeled the punching bag until his hands were bloody and sweat coated his muscled back.

Seeing Mindy's body being lifted from the grave had resurrected horrific memories for her. And she sensed Brad's anguish.

But the case also made her feel lucky to be alive.

A sliver of guilt assaulted her for the thought, but she banished it, reminding herself that she had been given a second chance, and she *should* appreciate life, should make the most of her time. After all, life could be given or taken away in a heartbeat.

But tonight wasn't about her. She ached for Brad. Saw what he was going through, and wanted to offer him comfort the way he had comforted her four years ago on that long ride to the hospital.

The blood droplets trickled from his hands onto the ground, but he seemed oblivious. She hurried back to the cabin, grabbed a damp cloth and rushed down the path to him again.

When she neared, she paused to study him, debating whether to intrude on his private moment. Finally, sensing that he'd exhausted his anger, she tiptoed toward him. Thunder rumbled above. Twigs snapped beneath her feet, cutting into the silence, and a frog chirped and leaped across the ground in front of her. She was sure Brad would turn around at any second and order her to leave him alone. But he was so lost in emotions and grief for Mindy that he didn't notice until she stood by his side. His head was lowered onto his hands, the sculpted muscles in his arms bunched tight, his bronzed skin slick with a fine coating of perspiration.

He didn't look at her, but his body stiffened.

Touched by the depth of his pain, she slowly reached out and placed a hand on his shoulder, then stroked his back gently. He didn't move for a second, simply sat still and silent, the brooding loner who didn't need anyone, the savior who fought for justice even when it might cost him his life.

"Brad…"

"Go back to bed, Lisa."

"No." She moved closer, slid her other hand to his back, massaged the knot in his neck. "I'm so sorry. Tell me how to help you."

He cleared his throat. "You can't."

"Let me try," she whispered. She slowly moved in front of him, knelt and wrapped the damp cloth around his hands, absorbing the blood. "I know you're hurting. I know you loved Mindy, and I wish I could bring her back, that I could replace her—"

"Don't say that." He lurched up and gripped her hands, the volatile emotions in his eyes so wild that she stepped back from him, afraid she'd crossed the line.

"I…I can't stand to see you like this," she whispered.

"You don't get it, do you, Lisa?" He released her, flung his hands above his head. "I am sorry Mindy's dead, but that's my job and guilt talking. I wasn't in love with her. It wasn't like that. We only dated a couple of times."

Lisa staggered backward. "What?"

"I said I wasn't in love with her." He rammed a hand

through his hair. "I almost wish I had been. She was so upset when I told her that I didn't want to see her anymore, maybe I pushed her into going out with someone else. Maybe the killer."

Lisa's heart fluttered in shock. "What are you talking about?"

"She wanted us to be together," he said, pacing now like a madman. "But I didn't. I…I couldn't be with her."

"But…I thought…" She searched her brain for the exact words, then forged on when she couldn't find them. "It does matter. You're hurting for her now."

"It's my fault she was kidnapped, my fault she's dead," he said in an agonized voice. "Don't you see? I didn't protect her, just like I didn't protect you."

Lisa stumbled closer to him, his words wrenching her heart. Thunder rumbled again, the trees closing around her, but she couldn't let Brad suffer alone. So she did the only thing she knew to do. She slid her arms around his body and hugged him.

His body went ramrod stiff, his hands dropped to his sides. Rejection stung her nerve endings, but then, as if his will faded completely, he suddenly lifted his arms and dragged her closer to him. She felt the fine sweat from his skin sear through her camisole, felt his muscles tighten and constrict as he clenched her harder, felt his breath on her neck as he lowered his head against her. She tried to pretend that they were simply two people who'd found one another in the loneliness of the night, to forget that the only reason he was holding her was because they'd both seen a dead woman tonight.

Brad had always thought he was a pillar of strength. He had survived abuse. Foster homes. The streets as a teen. And then after…

But when Lisa wrapped her arms around him, he completely lost the battle for control. Through the thin material of her satin camisole, he felt her soft curves pressed against him, felt the stiff peaks of her nipples jutting out, teasing his chest, and his body hardened with need and desire. He held her tightly, his body quaking from wanting to drag her inside his cabin, strip her naked and bury himself inside her.

Finally unable to grasp the ironclad will that had kept him from touching her before, he lifted his head. The pure, unselfish innocence and kindness in her eyes tore at his soul. The flicker of desire that flashed briefly took his breath away.

That slight flicker was all it took. He had wanted her for so long he couldn't remember not wanting her.

"Lisa—"

"Shh." She pressed a finger to his lips. A finger that tasted like sweetness and taunted him with desire.

A growl erupted low in his throat, and he forgot how to fight. Instead, he lowered his head and pressed his lips gently against hers. One taste only whetted his appetite, stirred his hunger, and he deepened the kiss, tracing her lips with his tongue, nibbling at her mouth, urging her to open to him. And when she did, he moaned and ran his hands through her silky hair, pressed her closer, so close his erection strained inside his pants and pulsed between them. The need grew within him like a thirst that couldn't be quenched, and he melded his lips over hers again, this time more bold, sucking on her lower lip and delving inside her mouth with his tongue. She returned the kiss with the fervor of a newfound lover ready to explore, and the sultriness of a woman who wanted more. He wanted to give her everything.

He wound one strand of hair around his fingers, then lifted her head back and trailed hot, wild kisses along her neck, nibbling at her sensitive flesh until a tiny moan floated from her lips. Then he dipped his head lower and flicked his tongue along the soft curve of her breasts. Hunger roared through him as she clutched his arms and offered him access. Emboldened by her throaty sounds, he closed his mouth over one nipple, lifting his fingers to caress the other one.

But suddenly he saw his bloody hand cupping her breasts, leaving traces of crimson, dirt and sweat on her white camisole, and he gasped in disgust and yanked himself away.

"Brad?" Her voice sounded small. Lost. Her breathing feathered out in small spurts that mocked the tormented rasp of his own.

"I'm sorry," he growled. "That…was wrong."

Knowing he was a bastard for muddying her beautiful body with his bloody hands, he forced himself to look up at her like a man. But what could he say? That he was sorry for wanting her?

He was…but only because he couldn't be the man she deserved.

"Go inside, Lisa," he mumbled. "Get some rest."

Hurt and confusion flickered in her eyes for a brief second, but he told himself he'd imagined it. She'd only meant to comfort him.

He had taken more.

She turned and fled up the path to his cabin, dry leaves crunching beneath her feet as she ran, his bloody handprints a reminder that he'd dirtied her with his touch.

She didn't belong in his world.

And he could never leave it.

"THANK YOU, MA'AM. I'll take really good care of the cabin." Vernon tugged the cuffs of his long-sleeved shirt down to hide the scratches on his arm as he handed the gray-haired lady cash for the rent.

"I hope you enjoy your stay here on Lake Lanier, Mr. Henderson," she said. "It's hot in the summer, but the lake's a good cooling-off spot when it's not too crowded."

He nodded, anxious to get away from the old biddy. She'd asked too many questions, had been too inquisitive, as if she'd known he'd given her a fake name.

"I'm sure I'll manage just fine." He loped down the walkway, then climbed into his pickup truck, revved the engine and drove to the bungalow on Pine Nut Drive, adrenaline surging through him. He'd been lucky so far. Finding Booker's cabin hadn't been hard.

Finding one near it had been more of a challenge.

But the summer rental season was in full swing, and he'd hit pay dirt. In fact, he could see Booker's cabin from the one he'd rented, could sit on the back porch and probably hear Booker and Lisa talking.

The idea that she'd left town with the federal agent irked him to no end. The possibility that she'd spend the night in his cabin troubled him more. But the thought of her sleeping in the man's bed was driving him out of his ever-loving mind.

No…Lisa wouldn't have jumped into this man's bed. Not his sweet, innocent Lisa.

Still, if it weren't for the agent and this new copycat case, he might not have found her at all. And he'd been searching for three-and-a-half long years.

He parked the truck, the engine rattling as he turned it off, then grabbed his Bible and his duffel bag and jogged inside. The rooms were sparse, cheap beach furniture filling the space, along with pictures of sailboats and seashores that covered the salmon-colored wall. The owners had even put little fish-shaped soaps in the bathroom. The stupid decorations made him want to barf.

He cradled the tiny soaps in his hand, ready to toss them out, then forced himself to stop. Lisa would probably like those silly fish soaps.

If they were going to be together, he had to please her, not just himself. Loving someone meant making sacrifices. Compromising. Then he'd teach her how to please him. Turn her into the kind of wife he wanted. One who'd obey him. Get on her hands and knees if he ordered.

He straightened the soaps back into place, imagining Lisa's smile.

Seconds later, he slipped out the door to watch the

house. Booker would have to leave sometime. And when he did, Vernon would get a glimpse of Lisa.

But he'd have to be patient. Not push her like White had.

Still, he felt so antsy he was almost randy. She was so close, had no idea he was right next door, that he was watching her every move, only biding his time until he could lay her down beside him and tell her how he felt. Place a ring on her finger. Bind her to him forever.

Then they'd make up for lost time....

He'd bathe her with his tongue. Make her beg for his touch.

He pictured her on her knees, licking and sucking him, and he groaned. She'd be humble, succumb to his wishes. Give him her body, mind and soul.

And no one would tear them apart.

If they tried, he'd kill them.

CHAPTER TEN

GUILT FOR TOUCHING Lisa gnawed at Brad—he couldn't have her. He knew it now just as he'd known it four years ago. So why couldn't he shake this burning need to do so?

Only he hadn't just touched her, he'd pawed at her like a wild animal.

For God's sake, he'd nearly taken her outside by the lake, with sweat and blood dripping from his body. The memory of his grimy red paw prints on her camisole made him sick to his stomach. He'd had to shower the minute he came in, scrub the vile anger from his skin.

Unable to sleep, he studied the files on the victims from the original Grave Digger investigation, then all the notes on Joann Worthy's case, including family members and neighbors who'd been questioned, along with the notes they had gathered on Mindy. As he skimmed the information on Vernon Hanks, he plugged in the data and discovered that Hanks had a half sister. Apparently, Vernon's mother had been married before she hooked up with Vernon's father. The girl's last name was Gunner. He searched further, and finally found an address. South Atlanta. Hmm, he'd question her, see if she knew where her half brother might be.

Something niggled at the back of his mind, some detail that he was sure was important, and he dialed Rosberg. If they all met and hashed everything out, maybe someone would stumble on something. "Let's have a meeting of the task force this morning."

Rosberg agreed. "I'll call everyone, and we'll meet at six."

Brad hung up, then went to check on Lisa. He gently eased open the door and saw her lying on her side, her blond hair tangled around her face. Although the air-conditioning was working, the room still felt warm, and she'd obviously wrestled the sheet off in her sleep. She'd also changed from the bloody camisole and tap pants to a nightshirt that had ridden up her thighs, revealing beautiful slender legs that he imagined wrapped around him. A tiny mole at the top of her leg drew his eye, and he swallowed hard, itching to tuck the sheet back over her, to smooth the hair from her face and kiss the soft skin of her neck again.

She moaned, and he froze. Even in her sleep, it was obvious the old nightmares disturbed her. And they would continue to do so until he caught this latest killer.

Driven by determination, he closed the door and backed away, deciding not to wake her. No one, especially the killer, knew where she was, so she would be safe at his cabin while he met with the task force. He'd let her rest, and see if he could solve this case so she could go back to Ellijay to the fresh air, the mountains and apple trees, to the children she taught.

Then he could put her out of his mind forever.

IT WAS 6:00 A.M.

He rolled over and stared at the clock in confusion, then rubbed his eyes to clear his vision. But dirt stung his eyeballs and his eyes watered, streaking the dry, crusted earth into muddy rivers. Sweating and disoriented, his head rolling as if it had been jackhammered until he'd passed out, he dragged himself off the sofa and practically crawled to the bathroom. Bile rose in his belly at the sight of the blood and mud on his hands. He flipped on the light, then blinked at the blinding pain that knifed through his head. The stench of body odors clung to him. His own.

Someone else's.

What the hell had happened? Had he been attacked? Beaten and knocked unconscious?

He closed his eyes, the room rocking back and forth as if he was on a ship in the middle of a storm. Finally the rocking slowed, and he blinked the room into focus. He was still wearing his clothes, at least his pants, although his shirt lay on the floor, tattered and caked in more blood, dirt and leaves. And there were definitely fresh claw marks on his belly, arms and chest. He stared at them in abnegation.

He'd had scars before. Lived with them for years. First, the early childhood days where he hadn't quite done things right. That locked closet.

Then the fights he'd had in school. The kids picking on him.

He'd sworn he'd grow up to be something better. Forceful. Maybe a cop.

Then the war wounds. Scars born from serving his country. From the malevolence of cheating death on a daily basis.

But he remembered how he'd gotten each and every one of those scars.

The bloody fingerprints and dirt smeared on his torso and face—those he didn't recall receiving. But they stung like hell and carried the scent of a woman.

It had happened before. Once. A few days ago.

Like a bad dream, brief glimpses of moments traipsed through his mind, then receded as if they had happened in another lifetime. He turned on the shower, stripped off the remainder of his clothes, then forced himself into the spray.

He had to wash away the blood, the tears, the fingerprints… Then, just like his memory, they would disappear forever.

LIAM LANGLEY STUDIED the morning paper, his muscles knotting with tension as he read the story of the Grave Digger's return. Last night he'd let his mind travel into the danger zone, and he'd questioned everything he'd done the past few months. Had wondered if it had all been worth it.

But White was dead. He'd seen his body himself, had examined it in the morgue. That dead body had given him pleasure.

The only time he'd actually been excited over a lost life.

He had no regrets. White had deserved to die for hurting Lisa. The taste of revenge lingered on Liam's tongue as he remembered the long grueling days she'd been missing. He removed her childhood photo from his pocket and studied it. The frilly pink dress. The precious amethyst her mother had given her.

The blue blue eyes. The sweet innocence. He could still see her as that petite child, following behind her mother in the garden. Then as his pretty little princess, when she'd been crowned Miss Magnolia. She hadn't wanted the attention. Had shied away from the crowds. But he'd known she was special. Had imagined her debutante party. Pictured her hosting events by his side.

But White had destroyed that future.

Liam folded his wallet and stuck it back in his pocket, inhaling to force his anger at bay as his assistant, Gioni Kerr, slipped into his office.

"Your coffee, Dr. Langley."

She had been with him for the past twenty years and knew him inside and out.

"Anything else you need this morning before your appointments?"

God, yes, he needed this whole copycat killer thing to go away. Gioni of all people knew the reason why.

He gestured toward the photo of the grave. "Mindy Faulkner was found dead last night."

Gioni's soft face paled. "That's…just awful. She was so young."

He muttered agreement, and she eased behind him

and began to massage his shoulders, working her nimble fingers deep into the knots at the base of his neck. "I know how difficult this has to be on you, Liam, but everything's going to be all right."

He dropped his head forward, grateful for her undying support. He hadn't remarried since his wife's death, had simply plunged into work as his lifeline. But Gioni had always been supportive. Her encouraging smile, her efficient manner, her attentiveness to his every need kept him sane. She was attractive, too, with wavy brown hair, clear green eyes and luscious breasts that filled a man's hands and begged for his touch. Gioni would be a good wife if he wanted one. Hell, she'd been hinting at it for ten years. She would agree to marriage in a heartbeat.

Just as she would protect his alibi if he needed her to.

"I don't know what I'd do without you," he said, wishing he truly loved her the way she did him. But he'd never loved anyone but his wife and his job.

And Lisa.

Then she'd been abducted, and he'd changed.

Once, all he'd wanted was to save lives. But after White had taken Lisa, he'd suddenly wanted to take one. That thirst for revenge had driven him over the edge. Put unspeakable thoughts in his head. Thoughts that had caused him to cross the line.

"White deserved exactly what he got," Gioni said in a low voice. "And Mindy…she must have been in the wrong place at the wrong time."

He hesitated, the air in his lungs tight. "You don't think it has anything to do with…us? With what I did."

She tilted her head sideways, sympathy in her eyes. "No. I understand why you...made the choices you did." Her hands rubbed deeper, moved around to his chest. "One...decision can't erase the countless miracles you've accomplished over the years, Liam."

Her soothing words and touch calmed his worry. He *had* helped hundreds of people. Even more so since White had died. "Thank you, Gioni. I don't know what I'd do without you."

"You never have to worry about my devotion, Liam. I'm here for you. Always." She kissed his neck.

He smiled, hearing her silent declaration—that she would keep his secret until the day she died. What had he done to garner such loyalty?

She circled around the desk, knelt in front of him, unfastened the buttons on his shirt and parted the fabric. Cool air from the air conditioner brushed his chest. A spark of hunger flashed in her eyes, and his body reacted, semen already beading on the tip of his penis. She sank her hands into his chest hair and rubbed deliberately slow circles around his nipples. He threw his head back and moaned, but she caught the sound with her mouth and kissed him. His erection strained toward her. Seconds later, she trailed more kisses down his belly, then lower, swirling her tongue up and down and around his navel until he thought he'd go out of his mind.

The sound of his zipper rasped in the quiet, along with his own labored breathing as her fingers worked magic over his body, and her mouth dipped lower. He dug his hands into her hair and pulled her toward him, then her lips found his hard length and closed around him. His sex surged with pleasure, pulsing and throbbing as she sucked him.

Sensations ripped through him, and within seconds his release was imminent. But just before she could bring him to a fiery climax, he jerked her up, flipped her around, tore down her panties and rammed himself inside her.

She groaned and grabbed the desk edge, leaning over to offer him deeper access, her plump breasts swaying. Low moans erupted from her throat as he gripped her hips and pumped inside her. Seconds later, she cried out his name, her body spasming and quivering as he thrust inside her again and again. As her wet juices flowed around him, and her muscles clenched his cock tighter, he allowed his own release to spill into her.

The phone trilled before he could straighten her clothes, the apology ready on his lips as she turned to him. But the smile in her eyes suggested he needn't bother, that he could have her anytime, anywhere, any way he wanted.

"I'll get the phone." Quickly discarding her panties in his trash can, she smoothed down her skirt, the smile she gave him as she left his office as sultry as when she'd entered. All he had to do was ask for sex with her. Hell, he didn't even have to ask.

He reached inside his pocket for his handkerchief, still shaking inside from the physical release, but already wanting more. Hell, he probably wouldn't make it to lunch, not with Gioni strutting around pantyless.

But his gaze fell back on the photo of White, and Gioni's words rang in his head: "White deserved exactly what he got."

No, Liam had wanted to retaliate. White had deserved a much harsher fate.

He should have had to suffer longer, should have been denied medical treatment, as he'd denied Lisa and those other women. He should have been left to rot in a thin wooden box below the ground, should have felt the maggots nibbling at his skin, the air growing thicker, more stale, the metallic odor of his own fear and blood his companion as he slid into the bowels of a hellish death.

Controlling his rage, Liam removed the newspaper clipping he'd kept of White's funeral and stared at it, determined not to let one ounce of remorse intrude on the satisfaction he'd gleaned from the man's death.

Or his interlude with Gioni.

But now another photo plagued his mind. Mindy Faulkner's.

In the dark hours before dawn, she had been pulled from a brown box in the ground just as Lisa had been.

Mindy was dead.

It would be only a matter of time before the questions turned back to him. And if his secrets were revealed…

He shuddered, unable to contemplate that possibility.

IT WAS THE TWELFTH DAY of the drought. Heat infused the building where the task force met, making everyone cranky. There was no relief in sight for the water shortage, just as there was none for the detectives and agents.

Brad braced himself for the meeting, battling help-less rage at the sight of the crime scene photos spread across the table. The harsh light of morning only accen-tuated the brutality of the beating Mindy had taken, the purple-and-blue bruises on her body darker, more prom-inent beneath the fluorescent lighting.

Ethan approached him first. "Man, I'm sorry about Mindy."

"Yeah, me, too," Brad mumbled. "I keep wondering if the Grave Digger chose her because of me."

Ethan's hollow, cold mask remained tacked in place, but a muscle in his jaw twitched, and Brad knew his comment had hit home. He opened his mouth to say more, but Ethan's clipped shake of his head warned him not to tread on the past. Rosberg and the others lum-bered in, all grabbing coffee and doughnuts as they found places around the table. The young rookie was missing, making Brad wonder if he'd already been fired.

A woman entered next, petite with blondish-auburn hair and big brown eyes, sort of a blond Diane Keaton. The dark blue suit she wore molded over curves that oth-erwise would have been seductive, but the tight bun and aloof air surrounding her spoke FBI.

"Gentlemen, this is Karen Slater," Rosberg said. "She's a criminal profiler for the Bureau. I've asked her here to consult with us."

The detectives nodded and muttered greetings. Gunther gave her a look of pure male adoration, while Ethan's sar-castic snarl indicated he didn't think they needed help from a woman, no matter how impressive her credentials.

Brad kept his mind open. Pride forgotten, he'd take help from anywhere possible if they could stop this maniac.

Brad rapped on the table. "All right. Let's do a short recap on what we have to date."

Detective Bentley began. "So far, none of the property owners around the lake saw anything last night."

"Any luck on the wood that he's building the coffins with?" Rosberg asked.

Officer Gunther shook his head. "No significant orders placed at the hardware stores nearby. We noted two purchases that might be our perp, but both were paid for in cash. I tracked them down, but they didn't pan out. One man was redoing his deck, the other built a storage shed."

"How about leads on where he might have bought the necklaces?" Brad asked.

Detective Bentley spoke up. "I found identical ones in two different local mall stores, but no one recalls anything odd about the buyers. A couple were credit card purchases, and I traced those. The first cross was bought by a woman as a gift for her daughter, the second one a father purchased for his teenager." He paused. "I also found the same crosses on eBay. I'm trying to track them down, but need more time. Several church groups have also ordered the necklaces by the dozens as graduation gifts, and gifts for confirmation services."

"Jesus." Rosberg dabbed his handkerchief over his forehead, already sweating.

Ethan jammed his hands in his pockets. "I talked to Chartrese, Curtis Thigs's wife, but she hasn't seen him."

He paused. "He'll turn up at her place sooner or later, though, and we'll catch him when he does."

Rosberg glanced at Brad. "Any other suspects?"

Brad cleared his throat. "I'm still trying to track down Vernon Hanks. From everything I found, he disappeared from school four years ago, right after the first Grave Digger victim was kidnapped. He hasn't resurfaced."

"Any family?" Rosberg asked.

Brad shrugged. "He has a half sister. I'm going to talk to her later."

Brad gestured toward Special Agent Slater and said, "You have the floor."

She nodded, all business. "As you probably know, most serial killers are Caucasian men in their early twenties. Our guy could be a little older, maybe early thirties. He has a past history of violence, was probably abused as a child or bullied. Anyway, he's intelligent, but he never fit in." She paused, tapped her pen on the file. "Preliminary reports show that he has copied White's crimes to a tee, except that he did try to engage in sex with the vics. White was impotent. This guy may be also. Most rape cases are about control. Like White, this copycat definitely wanted to exert power over his victims. White had rage because he couldn't perform."

"And this guy?" Rosberg asked.

"The same thing. He tried to have sex with them but failed. Maybe his impotency is a new problem, and he doesn't know how to deal with it."

"I don't see how this helps us," Ethan said in a surly voice.

"Knowing how he ticks, his motivation, may assist you in pinpointing where he'd take his victims." She paused, consulted her notes, unfazed by Ethan's attitude. "One other observation we need to consider—this man likes power. He likes to punish. He's emulating White because he saw White wield that power, and admired him." She twisted her mouth in thought. "Like I said before, he's intelligent, meaning he may hold a job where he can exert that control. He could be a doctor with a godlike complex, a judge, maybe even a cop. Either that or he's tried to attain one of these jobs and failed, probably because of his inability to fit in socially."

The men in the room rustled uncomfortably. "That's a pretty broad spectrum," Ethan said skeptically.

She aimed a wry gaze at Brad's partner. "Bring me more, and I can tell you more. But one thing is for certain. Mindy Faulkner won't be his last victim. Now that he's gotten a taste for killing, he's likely to escalate. Until Lisa Langley, White chose all brunettes, because his abusive mother was a brunette. We all know he kidnapped Lisa Langley to silence her. Our current perp is not particular to hair color, meaning he hates all women."

"Great," Ethan said. "That narrows it down."

"Like I said, bring me more. Then we'll see a pattern emerge, or he'll make a mistake and we'll catch him."

Brad spoke up, "We'll compose profiles on our current suspects. I'll search the databases for cop-wannabes who flunked," Rosberg said. "Maybe look at the pre-med programs, too."

Agent Slater nodded. "Good idea."

"We have locals searching all areas near railroad tracks or stations," Brad said. "Especially the abandoned buildings near where we found the two graves."

"I still think we need to focus on finding a connection between the two victims," Ethan stated. "Mindy Faulkner worked at the same hospital where White died. That has to mean something."

"But she wasn't on duty the night White was brought into the E.R.," Detective Bentley argued.

"Maybe he didn't know that," Ethan said.

"Hey, wasn't that Langley girl's father one of the doctors on duty that night?" Rosberg asked. "Didn't he operate on White?"

"He was on duty," Brad said. "But an E.R. doctor treated White, not Langley." That niggling started in Brad's head again, and he flipped through the pages of notes on Joann Worthy. Operating on a hunch, he made a phone call. Seconds later, he rapped on the table. "I think I found something. Joann Worthy was called for jury duty the same week White's jury was selected."

The gaping mouths told him he had been right—this was significant.

"She served on his trial?" Rosberg asked in an incredulous voice. "How the hell did we miss that?"

Brad held up a hand, urging them to listen. "That's just it, she didn't. She was excused due to illness."

A chorus of mumblings echoed around the room.

"Don't you see?" Brad said. "If someone had access to that jury list, they might not have known that she was excused. They might have thought she helped convict White."

"Christ." Rosberg waved a hand. "We need to warn the other jurors."

"If he wants revenge on everyone who put White in jail, we have to consider the prosecuting attorney, the judge, everyone involved," Brad added.

"Especially the females," Agent Slater said. "Remember his rage is directed toward the women who wronged him."

"I'll put out the word," Rosberg declared. "But we have to handle this delicately. We don't want to cause a panic."

"Panic—hell, these people have a right to know they're in danger," Ethan snapped.

Brad's gut clenched. And Lisa would definitely be on that list.

In fact, she'd be at the very top.

THE CURTAINS FLUTTERED, a tiny sliver of sunlight from the window illuminating Lisa's face as she lay sleeping on her side. Vernon forced his breathing to a shallow, inaudible pitch, although tamping down the heightened adrenaline pumping through his bloodstream was impossible. Her blond hair seemed like white silk streaming across the pillow, her lips like ripe berries. They were parted slightly, looked so soft, supple. Her satin nightshirt had slipped open at the top, offering a tantalizing glimpse of the pale creamy flesh of her breasts, the soft mounds that would swell with his loving caresses, the dusky-rose nipples that would tighten when his mouth closed over them.

He was so near. Only a hairbreadth away from touching her. All he had to do was reach out, let his fingers dance toward her body, and he would feel that satiny smooth skin.

She twisted slightly, rolled to her back, sighed as if she might wake. He took a tentative step backward to hide in the shadows in case she opened her eyes. Instead, she made a whimpering sound, and a frown marred her delicate features. Then she drew her mouth into a pinched line and cried out as if demons were chasing her in her sleep.

He froze, immobile. Breathless. Hurting for her. Knowing he had to wait.

White had taken the slate of innocence that comprised Lisa's very soul and painted it with ugly tawdry lines. Lines that couldn't be erased, except over time.

And the fact that he would have the honor of making those black marks disappear had been given to him by God. The words of his master rose from the depths of his soul to remind him of that day.

On the third day, he arose from the dead and sitteth at the right hand of the Father Almighty... Yes, Jesus had saved him.

Like a miracle, Vernon had been given a second chance. A second chance at life. A second chance with the woman he loved. Everything would fall into place in due time.

He simply had to be patient.

Inhaling to fortify his resolve, he moved silently toward the night table beside her bed, then slowly reached out and touched her hair.

He would take it slowly. And one day, when she was

ready, she'd realize he could destroy those demons for her forever.

And that she could never escape him.

SHE WAS IN THAT COFFIN again. Darkness covered her like a thundercloud, only it was blacker, sucking the life from her and tossing her into a cold vacuum of nothingness. Dirt pinged onto her coffin, the sound fading and growing hollow as the mound above her grew, and she sank lower, deeper into the cavernous belly of the ground.

Then there was silence. A long deafening silence that stretched into an eternity. She screamed and clawed at the box, ripping at the wood with her fingernails until blood seeped from her fingers. She pushed and pulled at the top, dug into the edges of the sides, trying desperately to find an opening, but the heavy lid wouldn't budge. Despair weighed her down just as pounds of dirt weighted down the coffin lid.

Panic seized her, launching her into a dizzying spell of grief, then she collapsed, unconscious. But a few seconds later, she dragged herself from the well of death with a new resolve. She had to get out. Save herself. She couldn't let William win.

Then she heard footsteps. Someone yelling.

No, the voice was in her dreams. She had floated into the unknown again. Was dying. There was no escape. She squeezed her eyes shut, seeing her father's face in her mind. She was daddy's little girl. Her mother's face drifted into the fog. She was happy, smiling. She and her father were dancing in the yard.

Tears dripped down her father's cheeks as he placed roses on her grave. One of the church ladies sang, "Just a rose will do."

What seemed like a lifetime later, cool air brushed her cheeks. Suddenly she was being lifted from her grave. Someone was knocking at the box. Tearing off the lid. Warm hands closed over her body, shaking her. Lifting her. Holding her.

A husky voice pleaded with her not to let go, to come back.

LISA JERKED AWAKE, sat up and threw aside the suffocating covers. Trembling, she stared into the darkness, a fog of heat swirling around her. Where was she?

It took her several minutes to acclimate herself. She was in Brad Booker's bedroom. She'd been dreaming about her abduction. Had woken up in a blinding cold sweat, rubbing at her neck where the amethyst had once been. But it was gone forever, just as her mother was. And so was William. Brad had seen his dead body himself.

But another killer had taken his place.

Cool air from the ceiling fan stirred around her, brushing her face, reminding her of the voice against her cheek four years ago. Brad's voice.

Then the curtains fluttered against the wood frame of the windowsill, and her stomach clenched.

Someone was in the room.

She could smell his presence. Hear the rasp of his uneven breathing he tried so hard to hide.

CHAPTER ELEVEN

TERROR MOMENTARILY immobilized Lisa, but in the split second the emotion hit her, she fought back. She refused to let panic trap her.

Last time she'd done that, she'd almost died.

She was stronger this time.

She reached for the phone on the nightstand, praying she could dial 911 before the man attacked. The shadow shifted suddenly; the sound of clothing rustled in the quiet. She closed her fingers around the receiver, rolled sideways and dropped to the floor. But instead of lunging for her, he bolted into the den. The front door screeched open, then slapped shut.

Gasping for air, she searched the shadows as she punched in numbers. Not 911, but Brad's cell phone. She had to hear his voice.

One ring. Two. She closed her eyes, one ear listening for sounds that the man had returned. A frog croaked in the distance. The dog howled. The wind swished the curtain against the windowsill. The rumbling of a motor sounded somewhere from the road.

Another ring.

"Booker here." A pause. "Lisa?"

"Brad," Lisa whispered, "there…there was someone in the cabin."

"What?" His breath rushed out. "Are you all right? Is he still there?"

"I'm not sure. He ran into the den and I think he went outside."

Brad cursed. "Lock the bedroom door. I'll be right there."

ANXIETY SQUEEZED the oxygen from Brad's lungs. He had left Lisa at his place, alone. How had the copycat killer known?

The reality of what could happen to her hit him in the gut as he glanced at the crime scene photos spread on the conference table.

"What's wrong?" Ethan asked.

"An intruder was just at my place, in the bedroom where Lisa was sleeping." Brad dialed the Buford cops and ordered a patrol car sent to his cabin, then snapped his phone shut. "I have to go."

"You think he made a move?" Rosberg asked.

"I don't know, but get a CSI unit there immediately to dust for fingerprints. If the son of a bitch was in my place, I want to know who he was and how he found Lisa."

"Maybe he's been tailing you," Agent Slater suggested.

Brad jerked his gaze to her, the realization that she might be right leaving an acrid taste in his mouth.

Worse, if someone had tailed him, he hadn't even noticed.

What kind of agent did that make him? A washed-up failure....

"This could be our break," Captain Rosberg said.

"Another mistake," Ethan commented.

Excitement zinged through the room, although Brad's nerves were too close to the edge to think about the total ramifications. All he knew was that Lisa was in danger, and he had to get to her fast.

Ethan raced behind him as Brad sprinted for the door. Seconds later, he tore through the streets of Atlanta, honking his horn and yelling at everyone in sight to move out of the way. A fender-bender on I-85 sent him into fits, and when he barreled around that, siren wailing, and saw the traffic backed up for miles on Peachtree Parkway, he thought he'd lose his mind.

"Call her back. See if she answers," Brad barked.

Ethan punched in Brad's home number, but the phone rang and no one picked up. Brad cursed and checked the clock. Anything could happen. He had a good half hour drive.

"Jesus, if he got to her..." Brad couldn't finish the sentence.

"She was all right when she called, wasn't she?" Ethan asked.

Brad swallowed, then took the right shoulder of the freeway, flying past the stalled traffic. "Call the locals, see if they've arrived."

Once again, Ethan nodded and followed instructions, his voice clipped. "A unit is almost there."

"What's the damn holdup?" Brad swerved around an SUV covered in Praise Jesus stickers.

"They had a three-car pileup near the lake," his partner said. "But they're trying to get a unit to your cabin now."

"Goddamn locals," Brad bellowed. "They think a traffic problem is the same as a serial killing."

"Settle down, buddy," Ethan said in an even voice. "The traffic accident has fatalities. And we don't know for sure that the intruder was the serial killer. It is summer. He might just be some drunken partier wandering in from the lake looking for a place to crash."

Brad shot him a lethal glance. "You don't believe that and neither do I."

Ethan grimaced, and Brad gripped the steering wheel tighter, the next few minutes stretching into an eternity. Finally he exited and sped toward the lake. He'd purposely chosen the site because it was secluded. Set apart from others, just the way he liked. No nosy neighbors. No one interfering in his business. No one close by to rob him of his privacy.

Another reason he'd thought Lisa would be safe there.

But an isolated cabin also meant that she was alone with no help anywhere in sight. No one to turn to. No one to call. Nowhere to run.

And no safe place to hide.

Curtis Thigs hated hiding out.

But damn it, he didn't want to be dragged back in to the cops and questioned for murder. No sirree, he'd been that route, served his time, and he was done with it. He'd die before he'd go back in the pen.

The blazing sun beat down on his skin, blistering hot, as if he'd been lit by a torch. Good God, he'd missed the outdoors, the sunshine, but he hadn't missed this unbearable heat. Chartrese's apartment might be in the low-rent district, but at least she had some fucking air-conditioning. Not like the shitty oven of a cell where he'd spent the last few years.

He removed a paper clip from his pocket, inserted it into the keyhole of Chartrese's apartment, then jimmied the door open and slipped inside. The smell of her Chanel perfume glided toward him, giving him a hard-on the size of a rock, and he smiled and walked straight to the bedroom. Chartrese was not a morning person. Liked to sleep till noon or later.

He had awakened her like this so many times before. Crawled into her bed and taken her for a ride before she'd barely had time to open her eyes.

Seconds later, he froze, his chest expanding as he watched her snuggle the pillow to her cheek and roll over. She'd dyed her brown hair fire-engine red, but the long daring tresses suited her. Without makeup, in the bright sunlight, she looked almost innocent.

A bark of laughter rumbled in his chest at the thought. He stopped to savor the blast of the air-conditioner for a moment, then inched closer, taking in the scattered clothing on the floor, a black demi-cup bra and lacy panties she'd discarded because she always slept in the buff. The covers rode down, and her 38-D breasts spilled over as she arched and stretched her back.

Sweat beaded on his skin and trickled along his jaw. His body throbbed with the need to take her. It had been so damn long he thought he might burst.

Then she opened her eyes. It took her a second before his face registered. "Curtis?"

"I'm back, baby."

She swallowed, licked her lips. "You got the papers I sent?"

He nodded. "That's why I'm here."

Her eyebrow rose a fraction. "You signed them?"

"I came to make you change your mind." She started to protest, but he placed a finger to her lips and halted her reply. In one deft movement, he discarded his clothes. She inhaled sharply, moved to roll off the bed, but he pushed her back down, inhaling the scent of her fear as well as sex. She watched, instantly mesmerized as he'd known she would be, when he shucked his jeans and underwear. Sure, he had a few new scars. A long one down his chest. Two jagged ones on his belly. The one on his side where he'd sold that kidney.

Prison did a number on a man. But as far as he was concerned, his battle scars made him more virile.

And the scars couldn't detract from the size of his sex.

"You've been lifting weights?" she said in a sultry voice.

He nodded. "Man has to be strong to defend himself." And he planned to do that right now with her. In fact, his body was one of his best weapons. The past few months, he'd worked out day and night and had muscles that belonged on a bodybuilder.

He jerked the covers away from her, exposing the rest of her naked body for his hungry eyes. She hesitated only a fraction of a second before desire tightened her face, then she opened her legs wider as if in invitation. He licked his lips and toyed with the dark curls at the juncture of her thighs, wondering how he'd gone so long without a woman.

He wanted to make it last, to savor the sex, but she was already wet and willing, and he was throbbing. What the hell—he'd take it slow next time.

With a groan deep in his throat, he crawled onto the bed and straddled her. He didn't bother with a kiss, just sank his rigid cock into her tight sheath, kneaded her breasts in his hands as he began to thrust inside her. She raised her hips and met him, rotating her body to take him in deeper, her guttural cries of pleasure ripping his own from his chest. A minute later, he came, his body quaking with the strength of his release. She joined him, bellowing his name and clutching his back until he finally collapsed on top of her.

His breathing rushed in and out, sweat coating his body, and he rolled over and looked at her, wiped a drop of perspiration from her forehead with his finger.

"This doesn't change anything," Chartrese said. "I told you I'm leaving you."

"Nobody leaves Curtis Thigs, baby." His steely gaze trapped her just as his hands manacled her wrists above her head. "Now, why don't you fix me something to eat before we go a second time. Some of your biscuits and gravy would be great."

She yanked at his arm, and he released her, then slapped her butt. She simply laughed, and sauntered toward the footboard, breasts swaying, his love juices still dotting her belly as she dragged on a thin cotton robe. "Breakfast, then you go. The police are looking for you, Curtis, and I don't aim to get in the middle of it."

He cursed. "They talking about that copycat killer?"

She nodded, a frisson of fear darkening her eyes. "Why are they questioning you, Curtis?"

He laughed, glad she was afraid. "Because White was my cell mate. He told me all his secrets."

She tightened the robe around her with a shiver. "You didn't kill that Worthy woman, did you?"

He laughed again. When the headlines about that copycat killer hit the stands, he'd known the police would come knocking at his door.

But he ignored her question, stalked to the bathroom, used the facilities, then loped toward the kitchen, still naked. He wanted to punish her now. Make her worry. Sweat. Wonder just how far he would go.

"Answer me, Curtis," Chartrese said as she removed eggs and milk from the refrigerator.

"What do you think, baby? That I got out of the pen and took to killing?"

Her chin quivered slightly, and he grinned. She deserved to be scared. After all, the bitch had sent him fucking divorce papers in prison instead of showing up for a conjugal visit.

Nobody walked away from Curtis Thigs. Especially not his woman.

White and he had shared that feeling.

Their quiet conversations late at night ran through his head as he filled a mug with coffee.

The last four years, he'd lived vicariously through White's mutterings about what he'd done to those women. What he would do to Lisa Langley when he escaped.

The details of White's fantasies had been etched into Curtis's mind with grueling clarity. He'd craved the excitement of the kill.

What would Chartrese do if he dug a hole and put her in it?

If she didn't straighten up, she'd find out. After all, it would serve her right for embarrassing him in front of his buddies in the joint.

A HAZY SCATTERING of dust motes floated in the gray light like tiny white ghosts against the dark, inky room. Lisa flipped on the lamp to make certain the intruder was gone, then locked the door and closed the window. Heart still pounding, she searched the room for a weapon, but found nothing, so she grabbed a can of aerosol deodorizer from the bathroom and poised it in front of her in case the man returned. His scent still lingered. She could almost feel his fingers touching her skin, closing around her neck.

But she refused to let fear paralyze her. If he came back, she'd fight for her life.

A siren suddenly wailed in the distance, and she

forced herself to take even breaths to steady her nerves. Her gaze was glued to the clock as the seconds ticked by.

Outside, tires screeched to a stop. Car doors slammed shut. Voices broke through the haze of her shock. The bedroom window faced the back, so she couldn't see if it was Brad or a local cop, but at least someone had arrived.

Seconds later, Brad pounded on the door. "It's me, Lisa. Open up!"

She pitched forward and unlocked the door. He jerked it open, then gripped her by her arms. "Are you all right?"

She nodded, but foolish tears sprang to her eyes, and he hauled her up against him. She fell against his chest.

"Shh, it's all right."

"I'm sorry. I was so scared," she whispered.

"I'm here now. You're safe." He stroked her back in slow circles, his voice low and husky as he murmured nonsensical words of comfort. Her tears soaked his shirt, the terror that had clutched at her slowly dissipating, although reality kept it close enough to remind her that she hadn't imagined the intruder.

Or the fact that the copycat killer was on the prowl again, stalking and taking women's lives.

Another man's voice broke through her hushed cries. Special Agent Ethan Manning, Brad's partner. She'd met him four years ago at her trial. "I've checked the perimeter, Booker. He's gone," Manning said.

Embarrassed, Lisa pulled away, drying her eyes with the back of her hand. Brad glanced at his partner, but curved an arm around her waist and led her to the sofa. "Tell me exactly what happened, Lisa."

He continued to stroke her back as she relayed her dream. "When I woke up, he was standing over me," she whispered. "He…reached out as if he was going to touch me, then…I jerked away and he ran."

A frown creased Brad's brow. "He ran? He didn't attack you?"

Lisa shook her head, realizing the man's behavior had been odd. "No, I grabbed the phone and rolled off the bed to call 911. He flew out the bedroom door, then outside. I heard the front door bang shut behind him."

"Did you get a look at the guy's face?" Agent Manning asked.

"No. It was too dark, and he was in the shadows." She hesitated for a second, thinking. "I smelled him first…."

"What kind of smell?" Brad asked.

"Some kind of menthol aftershave," she said. "It seemed familiar."

Brad and his partner exchanged curious looks. "Where did you recognize it from?" Brad asked.

"I'm not sure." Lisa twisted her fingers in her lap, the sickening odor familiar.

"Did Vernon Hanks wear that brand?" Agent Manning asked.

Lisa bit her lip and glanced at Brad, denial mounting. "No…William did." She suddenly gripped Brad's hands. "You don't think he could still be alive, do you, Brad?"

BRAD CLASPED LISA'S HANDS between his own. "Lisa, I told you before, I saw White's body myself. I went to the morgue just to make sure he was dead." *And that you were safe.*

The sound of another siren cut through the tension, the local police car roaring up.

Ethan cleared his throat and stood. "I'll meet them outside."

Brad nodded, then realized Lisa still wasn't dressed. She seemed to realize it at the same time, and her face flushed. "Let me put on some clothes."

He squeezed her hands, not quite ready to release her, but knowing he had to. "I'll be in the other room."

The rookie, Surges, and another officer, named Tandem, walked into the den. "Sorry it took us so long," Surges said.

Brad glared at the men, cutting them off. "An intruder broke in. I want this place dusted for fingerprints, anything you can find. I need to know who it was."

Surges lifted a piece of paper toward Brad. "I found this outside. It looks as if it was stuck on the door, but the wind blew it to the ground.

Brad unfolded the paper and grimaced.

Dear Lisa,
    I have never stopped loving you.
    I am coming back for you soon.
    Then we'll be together
    forever....

There was no signature.
Brad hissed in disgust, but his cell phone rang before

he could ask more questions. He checked the number. Shit. Nettleton.

He walked to the window and stared out at the gray, mottled clouds rolling over the lake as he answered it. For days it had looked like rain, but the sky never delivered. It was almost as if God was taunting them with false promises, holding it back to make them suffer. "Agent Booker."

"Booker, this is Wayne Nettleton—"

"I know," Brad snapped. "What the hell do you want?"

"He has another woman. A girl named Darcy Mae Richards."

DARCY MAE RICHARDS tried to open her eyes, but the maze of colors swirling in front of her made her dizzy. She blinked rapidly, then licked the corner of her lips, the cotton mouth from the drugs her assailant had given her gluing them together.

Where in the hell was she? And where had her attacker gone?

She listened, shivering at the sound of his voice. Was he on the phone? Or had he left the TV on?

The room spun and twirled like a merry-go-round, and she reached for the wall to steady herself, but her arms felt heavy and leaden and she could barely move. She was too nauseous to sit up.

Perspiration trickled down her cheeks. The heat was so unbearable that it felt as if the sun was beating her with its rays. But even though she was sweating like the dickens, an icy chill engulfed her.

What was he going to do to her?

She squeezed her eyes shut, although a mosquito buzzed close by, and something tickled her arm. Oh, God. It was a bug. Or a spider. Crawling up her skin. Inhaling a deep breath to steady herself, she opened her eyes again, trying to blink away the dizzying mirage of colors, but just as she did, the sound of a man's eerie voice droned above her.

"Just a rose will do…."

It was an old religious hymn her granny Richards used to sing, one her family had sung at Granny's funeral.

The same one that first Grave Digger killer had sung to his victims. She'd read about it in the paper the day before.

The night before drifted back in painful bursts of terror. Leaving that bar. Feeling woozy. Wondering if she was coming down with something, or if someone had slipped her that date rape drug. She'd known she had to get home fast, so she'd staggered to her car. Tried to get her cell phone and call her boyfriend to pick her up.

Then something had slammed against the back of her skull.

No wonder her head throbbed like hell.

She wiggled her fingers and tried to move again, but when her fingers connected with wood, pure horror flashed through her as realization dawned.

The sound of the voice, the singing, the wooden box…

She was trapped inside her own coffin.

She opened her mouth and screamed, blinding tears

mingling with the sweat coating her cheeks. "Help me! Someone help me!"

But the effect of the drugs and dehydration had dried her vocal cords and robbed her voice of any power. She tried again, this time the weakness overcoming her as nausea rippled through her. She was going to die. Be buried alive.

Just like the other girls.

And her family would sing "Just a Rose Will Do" over her grave just as the killer was now.

Panic bubbled inside her, more hot tears spilling over. Why her? Why now?

Darcy Mae Richards had always been a good girl. She listened to her mama. Didn't go out at night by herself. Studied hard. Made good grades. Worked as a nurse.

And she was kind to the patients. Waited on them hand and foot. Carried their bedpans and helped 'em bathe, and she didn't do it begrudgingly like some of the others who were burned out. No, she tried to be understanding and compassionate, put herself in the patient's place.

She even went to church. Hadn't missed a Sunday in years.

She had only gone to that bar to meet a girlfriend and plan a party for her fiancé's birthday. She and Dennis were going to be married in a church wedding in the fall. The fall when it was cool, and the leaves all changed to reds, oranges and yellows, brightening the sky, and a breeze would lift her veil and feather cool air along her cheeks. Cool air she desperately needed now. Just as she needed water.

She was drowning in sweat. Heat was slowly sucking the life from her. And the bugs…there were more of them. Clawing at her arms and legs. Nibbling on her flesh.

The rest of the evening rolled back with vivid clarity. Her screaming when she'd awakened, tied to some ramshackle bed. Her struggling to escape when he'd laughed at her cries.

Her futile attempt to appeal to his conscience through prayer.

Dear God. He'd laughed at her tears. Told her no amount of praying was going to get her out of this one.

She'd tried all night, but this maniac had no emotions. When she'd mentioned the Lord, he'd actually proclaimed that he understood and believed.

Because he had risen from the dead just as Jesus had.

Except the devil possessed his body.

CHAPTER TWELVE

BRAD CURSED, then dropped his head and pinched the bridge of his nose with his fingers. "When did you get the call?"

"About five minutes ago."

"Did he say where the girl was?"

Nettleton hesitated. "No."

"Listen, Nettleton, if you're holding back, you'll be sorry."

The reporter cleared his throat. "He thanked me for running the pictures of Mindy Faulkner and Joann Worthy in the paper."

"Sick bastard. He likes the attention, and you're giving it to him." Brad glanced at the bedroom door, dreading telling Lisa.

"If it wasn't me, it would be another reporter," Nettleton said. "And he chose me because White did."

The verdict was still out on that. "Did he say anything else?" Brad asked. "Did you trace the call?"

"No, and no. He's probably using those throwaway cells." Nettleton paused.

"That's what we've figured," Brad admitted. In fact,

the FBI had a tracker on Nettleton's phone, but so far they'd failed to learn anything new.

"Do you know who this woman is?" Nettleton asked.

"You mean you don't?" Brad headed to the desk to consult his files.

"She's not one of the jurors who convicted him," Nettleton said, proving he did know, that he was testing Brad. "Joann Worthy was called for jury duty that week, but she—"

"Got sick and was dismissed," Brad finished. "We figured out the connection this morning and already have officers trying to locate and warn all the jurors, the judge and attorneys associated with the case."

"So how does this Richards woman fit in?"

Brad scratched his chin. It didn't make sense. Just when they thought they recognized a pattern, this guy had broken it. "I don't know yet, but we'll figure it out. Let me know if you hear anything else."

He hung up without bothering to wait for a reply, then found Ethan overseeing the officers. Surges was dusting his front door, while Gunther worked the kitchen. Lisa reappeared, wearing a pair of denim shorts and a cotton T-shirt. Her hair still looked mussed, but she'd thrown it up in a ponytail. Coupled with the fact that she wore no makeup, she looked impossibly young and vulnerable.

Brad's insides churned. "Bad news."

Lisa folded her arms across her stomach. "He has another woman?"

Brad hesitated.

"Who is it?" Lisa asked.

"A woman named Darcy Mae Richards," Brad said. "That was Nettleton on the phone. He just received the call."

"Is she another juror?" Lisa asked.

"No. She was a nurse like Mindy, but she worked at St. Jude's, not First Peachtree."

Which didn't make sense. White had never been taken to St. Jude's. He'd died at First Peachtree where Langley worked.

LISA'S HAND FLUTTERED to her cheek. "We have to do something, Brad. We have to stop him."

Brad asked Ethan to call the agent tailing Nettleton, then lifted his own hand, indicating the note Surges had found. "He left this on the door outside."

Lisa's complexion turned a pasty white. "Oh, my God. He *was* here." She shook her head slowly, searching Brad's face. "But I don't understand. Why didn't he attack me instead of running out?"

"He's obviously playing some kind of sick game," Brad said. "Taunting you. Us."

"He wants me to watch him kill these women, like before. To feel guilty," Lisa whispered.

Brad shrugged. "Don't let him win by thinking that, Lisa. This isn't your fault."

"Maybe I should make a plea on TV," she suggested. "You could use me as bait to lure him—"

"No." Brad gripped her arms, gently shaking her. "Don't even think about doing a foolish thing like that, much less suggest it."

"But this is my fault," she insisted. "I let William kill four women before, and now this guy is punishing me by doing it again."

Brad took a deep breath and lowered his voice. "He's killing these women because he's psychotic, Lisa, because he likes the power and enjoys the game. You're only a small part of the game. If it wasn't you, he would have chosen another woman." He rubbed her arms, hating that he couldn't make this nightmare go away. "We'll catch the sicko, I promise."

"Booker," Ethan interjected. "The guy tailing Nettleton lost him for a while last night."

"Shit."

"And I just talked to Rosberg. A local officer in Atlanta thinks he may have a lead on Curtis Thigs."

"Good. Any news on White's brother?"

"Not yet."

Brad's pulse kicked up a notch. "You take Thigs. I'll check out Hanks's half sister. And put someone else on Nettleton."

Ethan nodded and headed to the door.

"I'm going with you," Lisa said.

Brad considered leaving her with Surges and Gunther, but decided against it. He didn't trust anyone with her safety but himself. He just hoped that Hanks's sister knew where Vernon was hiding out.

And they could find him before this Richards woman ended up like Joann Worthy and Mindy.

AN OVERWHELMING SENSE of helplessness engulfed Lisa as the scenery passed. Suburban subdivisions were scattered along the road, as well as restaurants, strip shopping centers and a new elementary school, a sign that Atlanta's growth continued even farther north. The rural areas and farmland were being bought to house crops of cookie-cutter houses instead of corn and wheat fields.

Brad's expression remained an iron mask of control, but the fine lines around his eyes indicated fatigue. He hadn't slept at all the night before. Had protected her. Had been tracking down leads.

And back in his cabin, he had come running to her aid the minute she'd called.

On some level, she realized she was simply part of the case to him. On another…she couldn't help but be moved by his chivalrous behavior. By the touch of concern she'd heard in his voice when he'd calmed her. By the sliver of excitement she felt when he touched her.

She wanted him to see her as something besides a victim.

Yet how could she do that when she was linked to this new serial killer? When he was taking lives, killing women using the same method as William?

"You look exhausted," she said softly. "You have to rest sometime, Brad."

"When this bastard is caught," he said in a low voice.

"Why do you keep working these cases?" She rubbed her hands together. In spite of the ninety-degree heat outside, they still felt chilled.

"It's my job," he said, as if he'd never questioned the reason he'd decided to be an agent.

"But one after the other, the murders, deaths, the violence…doesn't it wear on you?"

His gaze fell on her again, this time lingering, softening even. "Sometimes."

A quiet recognition dawned in the tension-filled minute that existed between them. Did he mean her case had disturbed him, or that she had?

As if he feared he'd revealed too much, he turned back to the road.

"I…admire your courage," she said softly. "You save lives. And you never think about yourself, your own safety."

"Don't make me out to be some hero, Lisa." He rammed his hand through his hair. "I'm not. If I was, I'd have stopped this maniac before he snatched another victim."

She shook her head. "That's not true, Brad. You've done everything humanly possible to catch him." Sensing the underlying guilt and anguish behind his comment, she realized he wasn't unaffected by the cases or detached as he appeared. He simply masked those emotions to finish the job.

Or maybe he cared too much. Maybe that's what drove him.

She wondered again about his past, his childhood, and wanted to know more. To completely understand what made Brad tick. To soothe away the hurtful words of his foster parents and his own mother.

"He's manipulating us both," she commented instead. "He knows you're a fighter, Brad, that you're tough, and that you won't give up until the end, just like you didn't give up on me. And you did arrest William." She traced a finger over his hands where they were clenched tightly around the steering wheel. "You won in the end, Brad. You will again."

"But we can't allow another woman to die," he said in a gruff voice.

She squeezed the knotted muscle in his shoulder. He raised his hand and slid it over hers, then pulled it down beside him and held it in his lap. The warmth of his pants and body heated her, the tender way he enveloped her palm touching emotions deep inside her. She felt a connection with Brad that she'd never experienced with another man. Had felt it the day he'd rescued her from the grave. She'd missed that connection these last four years.

As they entered Norcross, she studied the small town, her hand still linked with Brad's. The town was quaint, charming. Wooden and brick houses, several of them two-stories with big old-fashioned porches, boasted well-tended yards filled with impatiens, begonias, azaleas and magnolia trees. In spite of the drought, the lawns looked manicured, the houses freshly painted, the atmosphere reminiscent of a Norman Rockwell painting.

A sign for new homes pointed toward a street lined with antebellum reproductions that resembled a picture from *Gone with the Wind*. Railroad tracks lay at the heart of the town, with freight trains and Amtrak still using the system. A restaurant called The Station, complete with an outdoor covered patio, overlooked the tracks. The rest of the square consisted of two Italian restaurants, an art gallery, a pub and a hair salon. A mom-and-pop hardware store with Radio Flyer red wagons in the front window drew her eye, and she smiled. Across the tracks, a park complete with a playground for children held several young mothers with baby strollers and toddlers, and a couple of fathers with their children and dogs. They were enjoying the day, oblivious to the bitter violence that threatened their peace. With a pang of longing, Lisa remembered the kids she taught in Ellijay.

This was a beautiful little town to raise a family. Except for the apple trees, she might be in the mountain town she loved so much.

Brad spotted the side street and turned onto it, and Lisa noted the homes were closer together, less cared for, with weeds choking the grass, and wilted flowers. Finally, Brad parked at a blue frame house with red shutters. The paint was peeling as if the sun had blistered it, and a small row of marigolds bordering the front lawn needed watering. The grass had started to turn brown from the relentless heat as well, but a tricycle and plastic pool sat in the yard, as if the child who played with them offered hope for a better life.

"This is it," Brad said as he cut the engine.

Lisa reached for the door handle. "I just hope Vernon's sister can tell us where he is."

"I TOLD YOU I don't know where Vernon is."

Brad fixed his intimidating stare on Jobeth Hanks

Gunner, trying to read between the lines to determine if she was lying. She'd acted stunned when she'd opened the door and found him and Lisa on her doorstep, but she'd recovered quickly and invited them in, had even offered them iced tea and lemonade. A three-year-old boy named Freddy lay sleeping on a lumpy looking sofa in front of a swirling fan that did little to alleviate the stifling humidity.

"Why do you want to see him now?" Jobeth knotted her hands around the skirt of a faded sundress that hung off her bony frame.

"You've heard about the Grave Digger copycat crimes?" Brad asked.

Her eyes widened, age lines scattering along her young face as if she was ten years older than her birth certificate said. "Oh, my gosh. You don't think Vernon had something to do with the murders, do you?" She glanced feverishly at Lisa. "You're the woman who was buried alive, aren't you? The one who testified in that first trial?"

Lisa nodded, her lips pressing together in a thin line. "Please, Jobeth, if you know anything about Vernon, you have to tell us."

"Why?" The woman squared her shoulders. "So you can arrest my brother for something he didn't do?" Anger hardened her weak voice. "I can tell you one thing—Vernon may have had his problems, but he ain't no murderer. He couldn't hurt a fly."

"When was the last time you saw him?" Brad asked, ignoring her comment.

She folded her freckled hands together. "Well, reckon it's been awhile. But he calls every now and then."

"Where does he call from?" Brad asked.

"Mostly pay phones. He moved around a lot this last four years. Had some hard times."

"What kind of hard times?" Brad asked, struggling to hold on to his patience.

"He…he had an accident about four years ago. Got scarred up pretty bad. Took off after that, hid out for a while."

"His face was scarred?" Lisa asked.

"Yeah. But I never saw him after he was released from the hospital," she said. "I felt bad for him, though. He was always self-conscious, you know. Shy. Thought he didn't fit in."

Brad nodded. He would have been even more so after an accident. "Did he have a job?"

"He picked up work here and there. I believe he applied for EMT school, but they turned him down."

Hanks definitely fit the profile of the killer. "Did you know that he followed White around before White was incarcerated?"

She cut her gaze toward her son, and appeared deep in thought for a moment, as if exposing information about her brother posed an internal hurdle she wasn't ready to cross.

"Please, Jobeth, two more women have been murdered," Lisa exclaimed, "and this killer has kidnapped another one. You have to help us."

An odd look flashed on Jobeth's face, as if Lisa's plea

had pushed her over that hurdle. "Yeah, I knew," she admitted. "Just like I knew he was obsessed with you."

Lisa paled slightly, but recovered quickly and sipped her tea as if urging Jobeth to finish.

"When White first went to jail," she continued, "Vernon used to visit him."

Brad swallowed. White could have bragged to him about the crimes. "Did Vernon confide anything about their conversations? Maybe the place where he kept the women before he killed them?"

She shook her head. "Didn't tell me that, and I didn't ask. But he treated White like he was somebody to look up to."

"Like a mentor?"

Jobeth shrugged.

"What else did he say?" Brad prompted.

"Well, he mentioned that White had a plan. That he talked about faking his death so he could escape the pen."

Perspiration exploded on Brad's neck. Was it possible that White *had* faked his death? Had he somehow managed to escape alive?

LISA TWIRLED HER FORK in her salad, trying to eat a few bites at the restaurant on the railroad tracks where they'd stopped after leaving Vernon's sister's house. But the children's laughter that echoed from the park reminded her she had left her teaching job to return to the past— a past she thought she'd fled.

All because of William White.

But she hadn't really fled the past, not even in Ellijay.

She'd simply coasted through each day, living vicariously through the other families she saw, without any real hope of having one of her own.

She desperately wanted a family, wanted it all. Once this copycat killer was caught…

She glanced at Brad again, the familiar stirring of desire in her belly warming her. She had been attracted to him during the trial, but she'd been so needy, so vulnerable, so…ugly.

She wasn't that woman anymore. She'd gained strength from her ordeal with William, and would fight for a real life this time.

The memory of Brad's kiss burned through her brain, resurrecting a dream she hadn't even realized she'd acknowledged—that Brad was the man she was meant to be with.

That she was falling in love with him for the second time in her life.

William White's face flashed into her mind. The look of rage in his black eyes when he'd discovered she'd confessed to Brad her suspicions. He had the cold, calculating eyes of a killer.

What if this Grave Digger wasn't a copycat?

Brad had been quiet and brooding since they'd left Jobeth's house. "I know I asked you this once before, but, Brad…do you think it's possible that William faked his death?"

His hesitation made her stomach quiver. He finished his burger, then wiped his mouth and tossed his napkin onto the table. "I saw White with my own eyes, Lisa. Hell, I read the autopsy report. He *was* dead."

She nodded, struggling to accept his answer.

"But I'm going to request an exhumation of White's body just to verify it."

She reached for her water with a trembling hand. "So you do think it's possible that he's alive?"

"No. Hell, Lisa, faking a death isn't easy. He'd need help. Someone to doctor his death certificate, switch his body." He dropped his head forward, then looked back up at her. "I know what I saw, and what the doctors told me. Hell, I think White was even an organ donor."

Lisa flinched. His logic made sense, but Jobeth's comment disturbed her. And she'd smelled William in her cabin.

It also seemed odd that William would be an organ donor. Did the recipients know they'd received organs from a killer?

Brad's cell phone rang, slicing into the tension. "Booker."

"Anything new?" Ethan asked.

Brad reiterated their conversation with Jobeth Hanks Gunner. "I'm requesting White's body be exhumed. Hell, maybe he can tell us something from the grave."

Ethan muttered a curse of agreement.

"And I'll check out the hospitals for info on this accident Hanks supposedly had," Brad continued. "See if he had plastic surgery of some kind. Maybe that'll lead somewhere. At least give us a current picture of what he looks like."

"Good. I'm tailing Chartrese to see if she hooks up with Curtis Thigs. But listen, Brad, I just talked to Rosberg. He has a lead on White's brother."

"You got a name and address?"

"Yeah, River Glen subdivision, Duluth. A woman named Haddie Clemens. Think she was married to him at one time."

"I'll run by there." Brad jotted down the address. "Let me know if you find Thigs."

He hung up, and Lisa twisted the napkin in her lap as she waited. "What's this about William's brother?"

Brad grunted, removed a credit card and paid their bill. "We may have a lead on him."

"It's odd that he never showed up at the trial."

"He visited him a few times in jail." Brad shrugged. "Maybe they renewed their brotherly bond."

Lisa fought a shudder. "Do you think he's anything like William?"

"I don't know, but we'll find out."

In fact, if White's brother knew everything about the first Grave Digger, he might be emulating his brother's crimes for revenge, or to continue the family legacy....

DARKNESS CLOAKED Wayne Nettleton's cramped room, the fading sunlight a welcome relief to the relentless heat and badgering rays of the scalding sun. His skull throbbed as if the skin was too tight, and caused dark spots to explode behind his eyes. Pinpoints of tiny white

lights burst through the darkness, swimming like fire-
flies scattering in the black night.

He blinked and swallowed his blood pressure medicine, then massaged his temple, forcing himself to shut
out the pain as he studied the photos of Darcy Mae
Richards. She was young, only twenty-four, with dirty-
blond hair and a small pointed chin. Although there was
nothing extraordinary about her appearance, no specific
feature that was striking on its own, the package all fit
together nicely.

Her photograph would be all over the *Atlanta Daily*
the next morning, right above his byline.

Her parents were probably hysterical by now, the
prayers and tears rolling. Police had been dispatched to
canvass the bar and local establishments bordering it,
but so far, no one had seen anything.

A sense of excitement skated through him. His career
was definitely on the mend, just as his heart had been
for the past few months. He swallowed another capsule
for his headache and glanced at the clock. He had
blacked out, lost time again last night.

The pounding in his head had been so intense he'd
downed a triple dosage of painkillers and passed out.
When he'd awakened, he'd had dirt on his hands.

Dirt and blood.

He'd been standing over Mindy Faulkner's grave.

The pictures he'd taken hung on the matte board
above his desk, along with the ones of Joann Worthy's
grave. He skimmed the other photos, organizing them,
then tacked them on the wall, the arrangement a chron-

ological story of the sequence of events that had led to each woman's demise. He collected photos of the bars where they'd visited before being abducted, their homes, the jury room and courthouse where William White's trial had taken place, their bruised and brutalized bodies in the grave and others that the cops would wonder how he'd gotten. A morbid sense of curiosity had always driven him in his job, but this obsession with gruesome murders, with White and his victims, had become more personal. The interviews he'd conducted during White's stay in prison filled him with hopes for a book one day. Maybe he'd even land a big movie deal.

The resurgence of White's crimes would add to the hype. These photos would appall the masses, but up the sales to a blockbuster hit.

And that would mean fame and fortune for him.

A flash of Darcy Mae's pale face in his mind made his pulse sing. He envisioned her begging for her life, screaming not to die, crying hysterically as she spotted the wooden box crafted for her, and realized its intent.

Another flash, and he saw her in the grave, clawing at the wooden coffin. Heat suffocated her.

There was no way out for her now.

Her fate had been sealed, just as his had the day of his heart attack.

He'd realized the value of timing. If he wanted to achieve the fame he craved, he had to act. Sacrifices had to be made. The fastest way for him to achieve his dreams was to break another major story.

The Grave Digger had to be reborn, and the police had to be challenged. And others would lose their lives.

But this time Booker wouldn't crack the case.

He would.

Then he'd win a Pulitzer, and be famous forever.

CHAPTER THIRTEEN

THREE DAYS SINCE Darcy Mae's kidnapping. Brad rammed a hand through his hair. If they didn't find her, it was the day she would die.

The clock ticked away the hours, the minutes, until Brad feared she would be taking her final breath.

The police still had no idea where to look for her.

He had attempted for two days to question White's brother's former wife, but hadn't been able to contact her. This morning, he'd finally found someone at the house.

He squinted through the blinding rays of the sun as he drove toward Duluth. Lisa remained quiet, almost pensive by his side. The morning temperature had already climbed to nearly a hundred. The heat was draining the air-conditioning inside his vehicle, making the leather seats and steering wheel fiery to the touch. Dried grass and wilted flowers begged for moisture, but the latest water restriction had been posted, and it wasn't pretty. The ban was more extensive—no watering, not even the odd-even day schedule that had been in effect for the past few weeks.

What was happening to Darcy Mae Richards now?

Was she sweltering in the heat? Had the killer brutalized her by now? Or had he already placed her in the ground, leaving her to suffocate?

Brad wiped at the sweat, swallowing back the images while he forced himself to climb into the killer's head. As their profiler, Special Agent Karen Slater, had said, understanding the perp's mind helped find the killer.

But the way this guy had varied his pattern kept throwing Brad off.

He mentally ticked over the details for the thousandth time, hoping to jog some new clue. The victims of the first GD had been brunettes, up until the time he'd taken Lisa. Kidnapping and killing her had been about revenge, keeping her silent, while the others fed his need for control.

Now, the victim's hair color was anyone's guess. According to Agent Slater, that meant that his hatred had grown to encompass all women.

There were other differences, too. First, a woman who might have been on the jury that convicted White, but who hadn't actually served. Then a nurse from the hospital where he'd died. And now a nurse from a different hospital.

If the killer believed Joann Worthy had sat on the jury that convicted him, his motivation made sense. And if he thought Mindy had been in the E.R. or on duty the night White died, Brad could understand that as well.

But where the hell did Darcy Mae Richards fit in?

Lisa sighed and leaned against the palm of her hand. "If William's brother wanted revenge, why wait four years instead of assuming his identity and crime spree when he was first incarcerated?"

Brad shrugged. "That's a good question. Maybe White's death triggered his desire to carry on his legend."

"But if they were close, why didn't the brother show up at the funeral?"

"Another good point. Maybe this visit will tell us more." Either that or it was a wild-goose chase. But they had to exhaust every possible lead.

He punched in Rosberg's number to check on the exhumation of White's body. The captain assured him it would go through, and that the coroner was set to work the minute he received the body. He'd already requested dental records to confirm the ID.

Brad guided the car through Duluth, another quaint town, this one with a theater on the corner of Highway 120, a salvage store in the heart of downtown, and boasting handmade signs in purple and white advertising the Wildcats, the high school football team, which had a longtime rivalry with Norcross. On Pleasant Hill Road, a shopping mall had been built, along with strip shopping centers, car dealerships, a farmer's market and a supersize Wal-Mart.

Duluth had once been a railway hub, with tracks still running through the center.

It was a chilling reminder that the killer might be lurking in one of these homely little towns, hiding out unnoticed in some abandoned house or building.

"Have the police checked for empty houses here and in Norcross?" Lisa asked.

Brad nodded and turned into an older subdivision. Neatly kept lawns strewn with children's toys, sandboxes and swing sets told of young children and a basketball court in one corner held two teenage boys shooting hoops.

Brad parked the car and they climbed out, heat sizzling from the sidewalk. When he knocked on the door, footsteps sounded inside, then a small, frail lady with white hair appeared in the doorway, leaning on a cane.

Brad frowned. "I'm looking for Haddie Clemens."

"That's me."

He must have misunderstood. "I'm sorry, I...was told you were married to a man named White once."

"No, Clyde," the woman said with a wry chuckle. "That was my daughter's husband. Hang on." She wobbled to the staircase and yelled upstairs. "Zizi, there's some folks here to see you. Get yourself down here now."

A minute later, a haggard looking woman with ratty brown hair and mismatched clothes shuffled down the steps. She needed serious dental work, and wore a pair of out-of-date Coke bottle glasses. "Who're you?"

Brad introduced himself and Lisa.

Zizi's bloodshot eyes widened, looking even more distorted through the thick lenses. "You're that girl that William kidnapped, ain't you? The one that testified against him?"

Lisa nodded, and Brad clenched his hands by his side. "We recently learned you were married to White's brother. Do you know where he is?"

"Sure do," Zizi said. "Over at the cemetery."

Brad arched a brow. "He's visiting his brother's grave?"

"Hell, no, Clyde never visited that sorry piece of shit. Not after what William did to their mama."

"What do you mean?" Brad asked.

"Clyde said he beat her up one too many times."

"He killed his mother?" Lisa asked.

Zizi nodded. "Don't think anyone knew, though. William blamed her death on his old man. Old man was found dead the next day. Got drunk and ran his car off the Chattahoochee Bridge."

Brad wasn't surprised William White had killed either of his parents, especially his mother. It fit with his profile.

And if Clyde had known and had protected him, would he do it a second time? Maybe Clyde had been with William when he'd abducted Lisa....

"You said Clyde was at the cemetery?" Brad asked.

She folded her arms and smirked. "Been there ten years now."

"You mean he's buried there?" Lisa asked.

"That's right."

Brad took a second to assimilate that information. "What happened to him?"

Zizi blew out a tired breath. "Died just like his old man."

Suspicious sounding, Brad thought. "Did anyone look into their deaths?"

Zizi shrugged. "Naw, they were both drunks. Everyone figured they had too much liquor in 'em and lost control."

But what if their deaths hadn't been accidental? If

William White had killed his mother, then his father, maybe he'd killed his brother as well. Then the police could have added three more murder charges to his file.

Not that it mattered now.

But White's brother obviously wasn't their man.

Still, someone had visited William and pretended to be Clyde White. Who had used his name to impersonate him, and why use a disguise?

THE BRIGHT REDS and oranges faded to a grayish hue over the lake as Vernon slipped on gloves, then jimmied the bedroom window where Lisa had slept. His craving for her mounted with every second. He hesitated as his feet hit the floor, inhaled deeply to absorb her scent, then studied the room, remembering how she'd looked asleep on the double bed, with her beautiful silky hair fanned across the pillow. He had been so close. Had touched that hair. Had wanted her so badly he'd nearly creamed his pants.

Shame heated his neck at the thought. He had to learn control. When he finally got the chance to be with her, he didn't want to disappoint her.

Evening shadows fell across the room, the heat lifting slightly as a breeze from the lake floated into the room. The bed had been carefully made, a last ray of light dappling an old-fashioned chenille bedspread similar to the one his mother had draped over her own iron bed at home. When he was a child, it had reminded him of his sweet little grandmother. She'd baked pies, cleaned the house until it smelled like lemon polish and always had a soft spot for him.

But his mother had been a slut. A good-for-nothing, two-timing, big-haired whore who'd had a different man every night. She hadn't cared what the man looked like, only that he laid his money on the scarred end table beside that bed before she spread her legs for him. And that chenille bedspread had been stained with her ugliness. So much that Vernon had hated the sight of the yellowed, frayed fabric. The thready knots that had once been pretty had been picked to death, the fringe around the bottom ragged and uneven where she and her men friends had defaced it.

That spread symbolized every vile and dirty thing about her.

A hiss of disgust escaped him, and he ripped the chenille spread from Lisa's bed.

His beloved Lisa deserved better.

He carefully retrieved the satin comforter from outside the window, then unfolded it across the bed, smiling at the crisp white material. He imagined Lisa's long legs stretched out on the shiny, slick bedding. White for virginal. Purity. Innocence.

Yes, Lisa was the opposite of his mother.

She was a teacher now. He liked that about her. Liked the fact that she had a homey little place in the mountains. That she took care of little children. That she picked apples in the orchards and baked pies and canned jelly.

She was the marrying kind.

Exhilarated again by the scent of her lingering in the room, he moved toward the suitcase she'd left open on the wooden chair in the corner. A pair of jeans lay on top, neatly folded, then two T-shirts and a soft nightshirt in lilac.

His fingers trembled as he picked it up and pressed it to his cheek. Closing his eyes, he inhaled the fragrance, imagined touching her skin. He wanted her to wear this lingerie for him. When he finally opened his eyes, he glimpsed a pair of black panties. A red pair lay folded beside it, a pink thong tucked below. His blood ran hot, the air around him growing more humid as sweat beaded on his lip.

He clutched the garments in his hands, then, mindless of the danger, slipped off his gloves so he could feel the delicate material between his fingers. Unable to help himself, he lifted them and smelled the slinky, forbidden underwear, smiling at the fresh clean scent. Then he rubbed them across his cheek, his body hardening as if he held Lisa in his arms and could feel her tender kisses.

Lisa had stolen his heart four years ago. It had always belonged to her.

And it was time that he showed his face and told her.

Then he'd thank agent Booker for leading him to her.

And if Booker interfered, he'd take Lisa and run away.

She would be his forever.

And Booker couldn't stop him.

TIME WAS RUNNING OUT for Darcy Mae Richards.

Fear vibrated in every bone in Lisa's body, just as it had four years ago when she first realized William had kidnapped those other women.

His face flashed into Lisa's mind as they'd driven

around the town, searching for old abandoned buildings and houses, hunting for anyplace a killer might have stashed Darcy Mae. While Brad phoned in a request for the prison security camera photos of the inmates' visitors, Lisa once again contemplated how she could have been so naive. The psychiatrist had assured her that William was a sociopath, a pathological liar who had fooled others before, too. That he had no conscience, so much so that he could have probably passed a polygraph test without even blinking twice.

Knowing that on a logical level didn't alleviate her sense of responsibility or her distrust of men.

Except she did trust Brad.

She'd known he would save her, and he had.

Of course, she'd felt like a fool for not believing him the first time he'd hinted that William might be dangerous...but she'd quickly learned he was right.

She studied the tight set to his jaw now, the fine lines around his eyes. The first time she'd met him he'd acted cold. Insensitive. Intimidating. A man who could care for no one.

Now she saw beneath that surface. He'd had a difficult youth. He wanted to save all these women. Maybe that drive had something to do with his childhood, maybe not. She didn't know the details yet, but she wanted him to open up to her, to share his painful past.

He was hurting now. Blaming himself for Mindy Faulkner's death. Worrying about her. And struggling with his guilt.

God, she understood about guilt.

"I also want a warrant for medical records on a Vernon Hanks," Brad said into the phone. "He might have had plastic surgery. I need his doctor's name and any other information about him, an address and phone number if you can find it. And a photo of his face after plastic surgery. Thanks."

He hung up and turned to her. "Are you all right?"

Lisa nodded. "If Vernon had surgery in the Atlanta area, my father might be able to help you. Maybe he could pull some strings. He knows most of the physicians on staff at all the major hospitals, and some at the teaching ones, as well."

Brad hesitated. He and her father had a strained relationship during the trial. She'd felt the tension, although she hadn't quite understood it.

"You're right," Brad hissed. "He may refuse to talk to me."

"No. He'll want to help find this killer." Lisa punched in her father's number, then, seconds later, informed his assistant that the two of them would stop by.

It took over half an hour in the blistering heat and traffic to reach First Peachtree Hospital. On the drive, Brad had phoned to find out if Darcy Mae had ever worked at First Peachtree, but she hadn't. Grasping at straws, he also checked to see if Joann Worthy might have worked in one of the offices. Surprisingly, he learned she hadn't, but that she had volunteered at a small private hospital in Buckhead. Hmm, the three of them had been associated with hospitals. But what did that mean?

Irritable drivers honked and cursed at two fender benders that blocked the right-hand lanes of I-85. Brad took advantage of his siren to bypass the worst, then swerved into the hospital parking lot and cut the engine.

Lisa hadn't seen her father in months, and her nerves zinged as they entered the main lobby. Brad's hand went to her back, gently coaxing her into the elevator, as if he sensed her anxiety level rising.

Seconds later, she greeted Gioni Kerr, her father's longtime assistant. Lisa was almost certain they'd been having an affair, and wondered why her dad had never married the woman. It was obvious Gioni would do anything for him.

"Gioni, this is Special Agent Brad Booker."

"Yes, I remember him from the trial."

Lisa nodded. She'd forgotten Gioni had been there, holding up her father, supporting him while he'd grown more distant from Lisa herself.

"Your father's waiting on you," Gioni said. "Would you like some coffee?"

"No, it's too hot," Brad said.

"How about some water or a soda," Gioni offered.

Brad declined again. Lisa craved a glass of cold water, but her hands were suddenly shaking too much to handle a glass. She entered her father's office, gauging his reaction. He sat behind his desk, looking austere in his pin-striped suit and a tie, his computer screen blinking with a screen saver. He must have had consultations or appointments today instead of surgery.

"Dad."

"Lisa." He gave Brad a withering look of disdain. "Agent Booker, what are you doing here?"

Lisa started to explain, but Brad spoke up and quickly brought him up to date on the investigation. "Someone visited White in jail and impersonated White's brother. I've requested the prison security files to compare faces and get a name."

"You think this man Vernon Hanks might be the copycat killer?" her father asked.

"It's possible," Brad said. "He was infatuated with White and Lisa."

Her father's gaze darted to her, questioning. "Have you seen him lately?"

"No." Lisa licked her dry lips. "But he might have had plastic surgery. That's why we're here."

"So, you wouldn't necessarily recognize him?"

"That's right," she replied.

"I've already requested a warrant for his medical files," Brad said, "but we have another woman missing and the clock is ticking, Dr. Langley. If there's any way you can help us cut through some red tape and find out about Hanks's surgery, it might help. We need a picture, too, if you can obtain one."

Her father studied Brad for a long moment. "Let me make some calls. If this will help find the killer, I'll do everything I can."

"Thanks, Dr. Langley." Brad stood and shook his hand. "We're still trying to figure out the connection between the victims. I thought Darcy Mae Richards might have worked at First Peachtree, but that wasn't the case. But I just learned that Joann Worthy volunteered at a small private hospital in Buckhead."

Frown lines creased Langley's face. "You think he's choosing all hospital staff, even volunteers now?"

"I don't know. But two of the victims have been nurses, and Joann was a volunteer. There has to be some significance to that."

Her dad's jaw went rigid, his gaze level with Brad's. Lisa stood silently by, aching for him to hug her. But he simply gave her an odd look, then turned and went back to his work, his dismissal a reminder of the distance between them. She had disappointed him when she'd become a victim. It was as if he'd shut down his heart and written her out of his life.

And she had no idea how to make things right.

LIAM CLOSED HIS EYES, squeezing them tightly shut as the door closed and Lisa walked out with Agent Brad Booker. A mixture of anger and pain knifed through him. Brad Booker was not good enough for his darling daughter.

Of course, no man was.

But there was something between them. He'd sensed it at the trial four years ago, but had hoped it had ended when Lisa moved away.

Dark shadows of the approaching night deepened his sour mood, threatening to take him back to that depressed time of the trial.

But he forced them aside, letting an instant replay of Lisa's childhood float through his crazed mind. Lisa as a baby with her mother rocking her in the cradle. Her first birthday party, when she'd dug her fingers into the chocolate cake and smeared it all over her pretty face. They'd laughed and videotaped the scene, then played it year after year on her birthday. And then that adorable Little Miss Magnolia pageant. Right before her mother had died.

He'd wanted so badly for Lisa to continue those pageants. Had always encouraged her to seek the limelight.

But she had been so shy.

And so damn trusting.

Now the dark shadowy memories gripped him. The humiliation of watching Lisa in that courtroom, describing the vile things White had done to her. He hadn't wanted her to testify. To have to endure that pain and suffering.

For other people to stare and look at her in horror.

But White hadn't been horrified. No, he'd been smug. Proud of his sadistic accomplishments. During the trial, he'd gawked at Lisa as if he intended to come back and finish what he'd started.

But he hadn't.

Liam had seen to that.

Fuck William White's memory.

He wouldn't waste a minute feeling guilty for that sick son of a bitch.

Especially seeing Lisa now. She'd changed since the kidnapping. Had withdrawn into a shell even more. Given up dreams of beauty pageants. Of a medical career. Run off to the mountains to hide.

He hated what White had done to her.

Knowing that another killer was out there using

White's MO made Liam feel as if a scalpel had been dug into his skin, tearing and rooting away layers of blood vessels and tissue, ripping through cartilage and severing bone. He had been so helpless to do anything when she'd been abducted. So damn helpless.

For a man who'd saved hundreds of lives, brought people back from the brink of death so many times and given them hope for life, it was torture standing idly by while his own daughter had been trapped in a five-foot-four-inch coffin.

He would never forgive himself.

The only momentary reprieve from guilt had come the day White had died. The instant Liam had felt the life drain from the man, a peace had washed over him.

But now the kidnappings were happening all over again. The Grave Digger had returned from the dead.

But why? And who was it?

What if Liam couldn't keep Lisa safe this time?

Perspiration poured down his back, and he lifted his head, wiped his face with a handkerchief, then went and flicked the air conditioner down another notch, again contemplating the way Booker looked at his daughter. The man had it bad.

But Liam knew things about Brad Booker that would shock his little girl.

His own indiscretions suddenly charged back. Who was he to judge?

He'd crossed the line more than once since her abduction.

But he'd had good reason.

William White's disgusting face flashed into his mind. Again, Liam saw the photos of Lisa taken from that goddamned burial spot, and he spat out a curse. Hell, he'd do it all over again if he had to.

Fueled with vengeance and anger, he picked up the phone to find out everything he could on Vernon Hanks, his supposed accident and plastic surgery. Liam also knew a judge who owed him big time. He might be able to unlock sealed records if there were any to find.

The name Darcy Mae Richards echoed in his ears as he made the phone call, and his chest tightened, his heartbeat accelerating. He had to learn more about her job at St. Jude's and Joann Worthy's volunteer work. If it was possible…

No. He squashed the disturbing thought. Surely, he hadn't set the wheels in motion for the copycat killer to resume White's crimes.

God wouldn't be so cruel and punish him that way a second time….

BRAD STEELED HIMSELF against any emotion as he strode into the interrogation room holding Dennis Hooper, Darcy Mae Richards's fiancé. The police had questioned the man twice, but Brad didn't have total faith in the locals, so he'd finally decided to interrogate Hooper himself.

He scrutinized the man's slumped posture and body language, his anguished expression, the nervous way he kept pressing a finger to his temple.

Brad was usually a pretty good judge of character. Sometimes he could tell if a perp was innocent or guilty just by studying him through the two-way mirror before he even spoke to him.

This man wasn't acting. He really loved his fiancée.

But Brad couldn't let emotions affect his interrogation. What if he was wrong? If there was one copycat, there was always the chance there might be two.

"Mr. Hooper, I'm Special Agent Brad Booker."

The wiry-haired man looked up, his eyes red, his skin blotchy. "I've already told the police everything I know."

"Suppose you tell me again."

Frustration washed over his bony features. He was gangly, in his early twenties, with a choppy haircut, close-set eyes and a cleft chin. He was also missing the tip of his third finger on his right hand.

His prints would be unique. Not that the investigators had found any at the crime scenes so far.

Brad flipped a wooden chair around and straddled it. "When was the last time you saw Darcy Mae Richards?"

Dennis heaved a breath. "Like I told the other cops, we had lunch the other day."

"You're a student?"

He nodded. "I'm in grad school. Bioengineering."

A medical background would definitely give him an advantage if he wanted to commit a crime. Then again, Hooper didn't seem like a misfit, so he didn't exactly fit the profile. "How long have you been engaged to Darcy Mae?"

"About six weeks." He choked up for a second, then cleared his throat. "I gave her a diamond on her twenty-fourth birthday. That was two weeks ago."

Brad's jaw tightened. "And how was your relation-ship since?"

Dennis worked his mouth side to side, then stared down at his hands. "It was good. We were planning the wedding. She…was so excited. She wanted a church service."

"And you?"

"I just wanted to make her happy." He bowed his head against his folded hands, emotions overcoming him.

Brad stood and pivoted for a second, giving him time to compose himself, more certain every second that he wasn't guilty.

"We have estimated that Darcy Mae disappeared sometime between 8:00 p.m. and 9:00 p.m. Where were you?"

"In my lab," Dennis said. "I was supposed to meet her, but the class r…ran over."

Again he choked up, and Brad moved toward the door. He had to verify the man's story.

"Do you think she was kidnapped by that Grave Digger?" Dennis asked.

Brad squared his shoulders, the man's emotions stirring up his own. He was almost convinced this guy was innocent now. And he knew exactly how it felt to be sitting in his place, imagining the worst, seeing images of the woman he loved in trouble.

Brad couldn't allow the man to see that he sympa-thized, though.

The same way he couldn't reveal his feelings to Lisa.

Especially after seeing her father again. Lisa's relationship with her dad needed mending. She was hurting. And more than anything, he wanted her to be happy.

And Brad would only stand in the way of that reconciliation.

Dennis caught him by the arm before he could exit. "Please, Agent Booker, you have to find her. Darcy Mae's everything to me. I d-don't want her to die...."

DARCY MAE DID NOT WANT to die.

She had been begging God all day to save her. But as each hour passed, her courage and faith waned. It was so quiet and isolated in this box. Her arms and legs had gone numb from attempting to maneuver sideways, and her body had sweated so much that she knew she must be dehydrated. She'd even tried to wiggle enough to lift her hand and lick the sweat off her fingers, hoping the salty dampness might soothe her dry, parched throat. But just as she'd read in the paper, he'd built the coffin to fit her shape, giving her no room to move.

If only she could convince him to release her for just a few minutes, maybe she could find some way to escape.

She'd lost track of time, but figured he'd been gone now for hours. How much longer would he leave her here? She tried to remember how long he'd kept the other victims. Had it been two days? Three?

The door suddenly screeched open, and a shudder rippled through her as footsteps thundered across the wooden floor. Her stomach clenched as the box began to move. He was dragging it outside.

That could only mean one thing. He was taking her

to the woods to bury her. She'd seen the photos of the other mounds of dirt where the women had been left.

Horror swept through her. She couldn't go like this. She had a wedding to plan, babies to have and take care of. And poor Dennis…what would he do without her?

Although she thought she'd cried all her tears, a sob welled in her throat, and she screamed holy terror. But somewhere in the distance, a train chugged and blew its warning call, drowning out the sound.

And when she heard a car door open and felt herself being lifted, her hope for being rescued died.

Resigned to her fate, she closed her eyes and began to whisper the Lord's Prayer, begging him to take her quickly up to heaven, where the angels would welcome her home.

CHAPTER FOURTEEN

THROUGH THE TWO-WAY mirror, Lisa studied Dennis Hooper's behavior during the interrogation. She wasn't an expert on romance by any means, but she recognized true love when she saw it, and this man loved his fiancée. Loved her so much he was broken up inside and barely holding together. If Darcy Mae survived, would the two of them be able to recover from the trauma of her ordeal and move on with their lives?

Then again, Lisa hadn't been that good of a judge of character where William was concerned….

Dennis Hooper dropped his head into his hands and began to cry—heartfelt, soulful sobs that wrenched his body. Yes, he did love Darcy Mae.

A sliver of envy wormed its way inside Lisa's heart.

What would it be like for a man to care for her like that? So unconditionally…

Not like her father, who approved of her only when she did everything his way. When she was beautiful. But she couldn't be that beauty-queen child. And she'd had to stand up to William.

Because his so-called love had been about total possession and power.

Not a real love, filled with respect and longing and hunger.

Brad appeared in front of her and her pulse kicked up, a tingle of desire and yearning igniting within her. He looked haggard and exhausted from the long hours that accompanied his job; riddled with worry. She sensed a loneliness that she'd never recognized before, a depth of sadness that shook her to the core.

He was an honorable man, a protector. One who put his life on the line to save others. A man who had rescued her and held her, comforting her and giving her hope during the darkest hours of her life.

She was falling deeper in love with him. So deep there was no turning back. Maybe there never had been. But she couldn't fight her feelings.

She didn't even want to. She wanted to reach out, gently move the hair back from his eyes, soothe the tension from his brow and hold him all night. She wanted to lie naked with him and whisper sweet nothings until dawn, and forget that the rest of the world existed for just a little while.

But did Brad want her? Would she be making a fool out of herself if she proclaimed her love?

Maybe she should just show him….

"Let's go." Brad's pace picked up as he stalked toward the car.

Lisa practically jogged to keep up with him, but didn't complain. Outside, the steamy night scalded her instantly, the lack of a breeze draining the air from her lungs. Poor Darcy Mae. Was she struggling for her last breath now?

Shaking with fury at the image of another innocent woman in the ground fighting for her life, she slid into Brad's car. The ride to his cabin was filled with cloying heat and a strained silence.

Finally, she couldn't stand it any longer. She had to break the tension, get him to talk and open up. He seemed to be falling deeper and deeper into the well of guilt. "What do you think about Dennis Hooper?"

Brad raked a hand over the back of his neck. "I don't think he's the killer." He hesitated. "Besides, his alibi checks out."

She nodded. So her instincts had been right. Maybe she was learning to read people better.

The lake seemed eerily quiet as they drove the winding road to Brad's cabin. The sun had disappeared, taking with it the relentlessly pounding heat, but the air still carried the scents of dry earth and sweaty skin. A small fishing craft had settled in a cove nearby; the sound of a boat motor rumbled in the distance. During the day, water-skiers, fishermen and vacationers raced to the lake for relief and recreation, but tonight, the body of water looked like a deserted mirage of colors and light. The mutt ran to her side of the car, and Lisa climbed out and petted him, then followed Brad inside the cabin. She ached to talk to him, but he quickly checked the rooms, then changed into a pair of running shorts and a T-shirt, left food and water out for Beauregard, grabbed his boxing gloves and headed down to the tree where she'd watched him punch out his frustrations the other night.

Knowing he needed time alone, she watched him go, struggling over whether to join him by the lake or go to bed. But if she lay down, images of Darcy Mae in that wooden coffin would haunt her.

Needing something to calm her, she found a bottle of wine open in the refrigerator, poured herself a small amount in a goblet from the cabinet, then stepped outside in the sultry heat to listen to the night sounds. Once again she was struck by the quiet outside tonight. Even the animals seemed to be asleep. Either that or they were so exhausted from the heat they didn't have the energy to move or come out into the night.

"What do you think, Beauregard?" Lisa asked as she sat down on the porch with the wine. She scratched his head, and he stretched out beside her, content. "Do you think Brad has room in his life for both of us?"

The dog looked up at her with big, sad eyes, and she laughed and sipped the wine. As he slumped down to sleep beside her, she stared through the trees at the water, the temptation to take off her clothes and jump in, to feel the refreshing coolness of it lapping against her body, almost irresistible. When she'd been lying inside that box with the heat engulfing her, the sweat coating her arms and thighs, she'd closed her eyes and imagined being able to sink herself into a pond or mountain stream, had imagined what the cool water would feel like tingling her skin, giving her renewed life.

The sound of Brad grunting as he punched the bag drifted through the darkness. The raw pain and frustration echoed in the air as he slammed his fists into the bag over and over. In her mind, she saw the anguish on his face. The blood dripping from his hands as they had the time before.

Unable to fight her need any longer, she retrieved a towel from the kitchen, then walked down the embankment toward him. Brad had taken care of her once, just as he took care of others and that homeless dog.

Tonight he needed someone to take care of him.

BRAD SENSED LISA BEHIND him before she actually appeared. He'd been a bastard for not talking to her on the way home, but he'd reached the end of his patience with this case. And the temptation to take Lisa in his arms, make love to her until reality disappeared, at least temporarily, had been almost too strong for him to resist.

So, just as he'd done for the last four years, he'd resorted to pounding out his anger and adrenaline on the punching bag. He swiped the back of his arm over his forehead to stop the sweat from rolling into his eyes, and slammed his fist into the center of the bag again. And again. And again. Each time a myriad of women's faces flashed in his mind. Joann Worthy's. Mindy Faulkner's. Darcy Mae Richards's.

Lisa's.

God, he couldn't stand it if this psycho got his hands on her. He'd lived through it once.

He couldn't survive it a second time.

Blood began to seep through the edge of his boxing gloves and trickle down his arm. He ignored it and punched the bag harder, every breath he took a reminder that he still lived on, while a psycho brutally murdered women around him. And there was nothing he could do about it.

Just as there hadn't been when he was a teen.

The image of his foster sister's face materialized, and he nearly choked on the bile. She'd survived the beating the old man had given her. And Brad had decided to pay him back.

He'd almost killed the girl's father. Had known then that he possessed an animal instinct that he couldn't control. He'd been removed from that foster family because of it. Later, he learned the old man had beaten the girl again.

That time, she hadn't made it.

He'd been filled with hatred and anger. Had lived on the streets afterward because, after all, no one wanted a volatile kid around.

And Liam Langley certainly wouldn't have a man like that for his daughter.

Not that Brad could blame him. Lisa deserved so much better.

Pain knifed through his hands, and he staggered, the heat draining his already exhausted body as he slammed into the bag again.

"Brad."

He hesitated, let the bag swing back and whack him in the thigh, then hugged it to him, heaving for air and wishing he had the energy to keep going. But he didn't. Not anymore.

Lisa walked toward him, her angelic face like a light

in the midst of the darkness. "Let me see your hands," she said softly.

He shook his head, then turned away and ripped the gloves off, pressing his bruised knuckles to his shorts to stop the bleeding. Her shoes crunched the brittle grass as she approached him. He stiffened, knowing he should just show her his hands, his ugliness, then she wouldn't see him as this false kind of savior.

Instead, the air left his lungs as she gently lifted his right hand, pressed a towel around it and dried the blood. He tried to yank it away, but she held on, turned it over and kissed his palm, then gently did the same with the other hand. This time she pressed it between both her own until he relaxed, although a different kind of heat pulsed between them. His body hardened in response, a sexual fire burning through him. He wanted her more than he'd ever wanted another woman in his life.

"Talk to me, Brad." Her blue eyes met his, imploring. "I know you're hurting, and I'm here for you."

Her sweetness never ceased to amaze him. "It's just the case, Lisa. My job is my life."

She lifted their joined hands and pressed them to her cheek. "It doesn't have to be."

He swallowed hard. What was she saying? That she wanted something from him?

Jesus, he wasn't the man she thought he was.

"I'm sorry, I don't have room for anything else." He pulled his hand away. "I don't know how to be anything but who I am."

"I'm not asking for you to be anything different."

He balled his fist over his chest. "Lisa, you don't know the real me. I'm not just an FBI agent, I've killed people before. Taken lives."

"I know that."

"But what you don't know is that I didn't mind." He saw the faint flair of shock darken her eyes. "I didn't feel guilt or remorse because they deserved it." His voice rose an octave. "Don't you see? They call me a man without mercy because I'm as bad as the men I've taken down. I started when I was a teen, and I haven't stopped. There's evil in my soul."

Unable to bear the disappointment he knew he'd see in her eyes, he turned around, strode to the edge of the lake, shucked off every scrap of his clothing and dived into the water.

Pounding the punching bag hadn't done anything to purge the desire spreading through his body, the constant hunger and need for Lisa that was driving him wild. Maybe the cool lake water would.

Because he couldn't take Lisa to bed, couldn't sate his own selfish lust and feel the pleasure her body would give him, while Darcy Mae Richards lay in a coffin in the ground waiting to die.

LISA WATCHED AS Brad dived into the water, her heart racing. She'd practically thrown herself at him, but he had turned her down.

Because he didn't want her, or because of his job?

No, he *did* want her. She'd seen the need in his eyes, felt the heat and hunger rippling between them, seen the evidence of his desire in the hard rigid length of his sex just before he'd jumped into the lake.

So why had he turned away? It was almost as if he was running from her.

Or running from something else...

Did he think she'd expect commitment?

And why had he said he was evil, when he was a hero in her eyes?

A slight breeze rustled the trees, lifting her hair and making it easier to breathe. The sound of water churning as Brad cut through it echoed around her, each stroke smooth and even, pulling him farther away from her.

But she wouldn't let him shut her out.

He swam until his head was only a dot in the distance, then finally rolled over and backstroked his way toward the shore. Over and over, his arms glided through the water. A few stars twinkled above, fighting their way through the grayness, and a sliver of moonlight shone off his hair, surrounding him like a halo.

Her pulse kicked in, the surge of longing deepening in her chest. She'd never been bold with a man before. Never asked for what she wanted.

Because her ordeal with William had changed her. Had forced her to be even more cautious.

But she was through hiding out. She wanted to be with Brad, and she had to gather her courage to go to him, or William would have tainted her forever.

Another woman might die tonight. The thought came unbidden.

It also served to remind her that time was short, that

death happened in a heartbeat. That she had to embrace life while she could. And she wanted to be with Brad.

He rolled over, switching to a breaststroke. His gaze caught hers, fastened to her as he repeated the stroke.

Emboldened by her growing thirst for him, she slid her jeans down her legs, then slipped her T-shirt over her head. Hot air bathed her body, along with freedom.

She wanted to be totally free. Free of the fear. Of the rigid control she'd created for herself. Of the ties to William.

Swallowing hard, she slid her bra off next, then her panties, and tossed them onto the pile of clothes she'd discarded already. When she looked up, Brad had stopped swimming. He was treading water. Staring at her in the moonlight.

Her naked body tingled.

She licked her dry lips, forced her hands to remain by her sides, and let him look her over. She knew her body wasn't great or perfect. But her nipples hardened as his smoky gaze rested on them. She still bore a few scars from William's brutal beatings, but they had faded, and now seemed unimportant.

Time seemed to stand still, the tension between them palpable. She ached for Brad to swim toward her. But he remained frozen in the lake, his arms gently moving beside him as he maintained his distance.

Still the hungry look in his eyes beckoned her.

Knowing he might push her away again, but burning with intense desire, she slowly stepped into the water. It felt cool to the touch, lapped up against her scalding hot skin, made her arms and legs sing with feeling. She moved deeper and deeper into the lake, smiling as the water sloshed against her feminine curls, rose to her waist, then brushed her nipples. Pinpoints of pleasure stung her nerve endings, spiking her hunger even more as Brad's eyes darkened. He still watched her, as if he felt the magnetic draw of her body to his.

Finally he began to move toward her.

The soft sound of his arms splashing through the water mingled with the night sounds of the crickets chirping. Her heart pounded, her breathing becoming more erratic as he closed the distance. Finally he stopped in front of her, his gaze glued to hers.

"Lisa?"

"Shh."

"You don't know what you're doing, who I am."

"I know everything I need to know." She took his hand, floated backward until they could stand in the water.

His jaw tightened. "I told you, I'm a killer. No better than—"

She pressed a finger to his lips, let him taste her skin and the water. "You don't have the heart of a killer, Brad," she whispered. "And I want to be close to you. Right here, tonight."

He started to shake his head, but she slid her hand against his cheek, then into his hair.

One moment his mouth hardened as if he intended to push her away, the next his eyes flickered with such longing that she glided toward him, then closed her mouth over his.

His lips were firm yet tender, and he parted them and delved his tongue inside her mouth. His hands cupped her face, angling it sideways to give him better access, and he deepened the kiss, molding and shaping her to his touch. She made a throaty little moan, and her legs buckled, but he caught her, sliding one arm around her waist while the other hand stroked her hair and then skated down her back. She wrapped her legs around him, clinging to his arms, savoring the kiss. Her body churned to life for the first time in years as he spread kisses along her jaw, then down the sensitive skin of her throat and lower. Lisa whispered his name, hoping he wouldn't stop until he joined them together and made love to her in the moonlight.

BRAD HAD TRIED TO SAY NO, but watching Lisa undress, seeing her standing naked with the moonlight dappling her body in pure gold, had completely shattered his resistance. He'd known she was beautiful clothed, and had seen her naked once, but he shook away that tragic memory and focused on the heavenly one before him now.

Lisa offering herself to him. Lisa with her lips pressed against him, her slender legs wrapping themselves around his rough, hair-dusted ones, her breasts swaying and bobbing in the lake water, begging for his touch.

His entire body erupted into one big hard-on, the force of his need a reminder that he had to tread slowly. Lisa wasn't some two-bit hooker or even a one-night-stand kind of girl. She was sweet. Vulnerable.

And so damn sexy that he felt lucky as hell.

Her breath rasped out as he lowered his head and tugged one nipple into his mouth. He licked the rigid peak, swirling his tongue around it until she arched her back, then he closed his lips around her and suckled her until she moaned his name. His own body throbbing, he slid a hand down to play with her curls while his mouth inched its way to her other breast, loving and suckling her the same way. She stroked the back of his calf with her foot, clinging to his arms as if she might melt into a puddle if he released her. As sexy as he found the lake water lapping around their hot bodies, brushing nerve endings and rippling against his thighs, he didn't want to take her there, not this first time. So he gently lifted her in his arms and carried her to the shore. Then he lowered her to the ground and spread their clothes out as a makeshift blanket. Stars twinkled above them, lighting the sky, and moonlight slashed across her cheeks, giving him a glimpse of the desire on her face.

"You're so beautiful, Lisa." His voice cracked. "I don't deserve to be with you."

She shook her head and let her gaze roam over his face, then lower. Her lips parted as if in invitation as she looked at his length, then she slid her hand down to close around him. White-hot fire surged through his loins.

He groaned, then claimed her mouth again. One kiss led to another and another, each time his tongue delving deeper inside as he trapped her with his body. Her breasts teased his chest, her heat cradled his thighs. Then he was suckling her again, teasing her nipples and dipping his fingers lower to spread her legs wider and push a finger inside her tight sheath. She arched and gripped his arms, and he hesitated, then looked into her eyes. He'd expected to see fear, but the pure radiant glow of a woman on the brink of sexual pleasure shone instead. Deeper, deeper, he thrust his finger, stroking her folds and stretching her open, as the urge to taste her nearly sent him over the edge. He lowered his head, settled his lips where his hands had been, then drank in the sweet juices of her release as she climaxed below him.

Her body jerked in response, and she reached for him, but he continued to kiss her and love her until the tremors rocking through her subsided. She whimpered and pulled at his arms, and he rose above her, then gazed into her eyes. The sated, sleepy look of a well-loved woman stared back, giving him more joy than anything he'd felt in years.

And he hadn't climaxed yet himself.

Slowly, though, he realized that he couldn't, not tonight.

"Brad?" Her husky, sated voice skated over his raw senses, but he moved off her and cradled her by his side.

"What's wrong?" Lisa whispered against his neck.

He threaded his fingers into her hair. "I...don't have protection," he murmured in a husky voice.

"But—"

He pressed a finger to her lips. "No, Lisa. I promised to take care of you, and I intend to keep that promise. That means protecting you in every way."

She sighed as if frustrated, then slid her hand down, closing it over him. "Then let me love you like this."

Stunned by her suggestion, he started to comply. But

he didn't want Lisa making sacrifices for him. He'd already taken too much.

So he pushed her hand away and sat up. "Not tonight."

After all, the realization that another woman might die while he was having pleasure was something he couldn't live with.

"Go back to the cabin, Lisa." He grabbed her clothes, shoved them into her hands, then turned away from her, yanking on his own.

She touched his shoulder. "Brad, please—"

"Go," he barked. "I'll be up in a minute."

Lisa dragged on her clothes, then the sound of her footsteps trampling grass and gravel cut through the night as she did as he said.

But seconds later, Lisa screamed his name.

He took off running, his heart clamoring in his chest.

CHAPTER FIFTEEN

VERNON DIDN'T CONSIDER himself a violent man, but he'd watched Lisa strip off her clothes and climb into the lake with Booker, and every cell in his body had nearly exploded with rage. Lisa was supposed to be his now.

He had survived White. Had even gotten revenge in the end.

And he had healed. Had changed his face. Had started over.

Just for her.

But she'd let Booker touch her and do things to her that no man but her husband should do. Just like his trampy mama.

Booker raced toward the house the minute Lisa yelled his name. She must have seen the new comforter, noticed that he'd touched her underwear and had spread it across the bed, and been frightened. He hadn't meant to scare her…

But he had to keep Booker away from her.

Vernon grabbed a tree limb and slunk down low to hide behind the bushes. His breath rattled out as he waited. Booker might have his gun with him. Vernon had to time it just right.

Just as the agent approached the front porch, Vernon lurched out from behind the tree and slammed the branch into his head. A second whack sent him falling into the dirt. Blood seeped from his scalp and trickled down his neck. His body lay limp.

Vernon dragged him to the side of the porch and kicked his legs. But Booker didn't move.

He was a goner.

Sweat pooled on Vernon's lip and forehead, then zigzagged across his jaw as he climbed the steps to the porch. The wood floor creaked. Lisa came running toward him and nearly slammed into him.

"Whoa." He grabbed her arms, elated to finally touch her. She was so close now he could feel her breath on his skin. The mere scent of her soothed the burning heat roaring through him.

But her eyes widened in shock, and she instantly tried to jerk away. He gripped her harder, staring at her with pleading eyes. But she was frightened. She tensed, her lip quivering.

"Who are you?" she whispered in a ragged tone.

He smiled. "Don't you recognize me, Lisa?"

"N-no…." She shivered, her blond hair tumbling wildly around her shoulders as she tried to pull away again. A flashing image of her naked in Booker's arms drifted back, sparking Vernon's anger, and he gripped her tighter, refusing to release her. He wanted her naked with him. Pure. Perfect.

A whimper tore from her throat. "Y-you're the man who came to Ellijay. My…my new neighbor."

He grinned, smiling widely to show off the new caps on his teeth. "That's right."

Again she tried to back away, but he tightened his hold. Now that he had her, he never wanted to let her go.

"Please," she whispered. "Don't hurt me."

He shook his head, then stroked her arms with his fingers. "I won't hurt you, Lisa. I love you."

Her expression became pinched. "You put that comforter on my bed...went through my things."

"Oh, Lisa, I've wanted you for so long. I had to feel your silky panties on my skin," he said in a low voice. "I closed my eyes and pretended it was you touching me."

"Why?" Lisa asked. "What do you want?"

"I told you, I love you. I've always loved you. Only you." He paused, his breathing growing more erratic. "I want to make you happy, make you mine."

"But you're Aiden Henderson. I just met you," she said, her voice breaking.

"No, it's me, Vernon. Remember me from school? Vernon Hanks." He lowered his voice, hoping to calm her. "I used a fake name because I wanted to get to know you so you wouldn't be scared, but then you ran off with Booker."

Lisa's gaze flew to the lake, her chest heaving as she struggled for a breath. "Where's Brad? What did you do to him?"

He shrugged, his white dress shirt stretching over his shoulders. "He was in the way, Lisa. Don't you see? You belong with me, not him. You always have, but that William ruined everything."

Lisa's eyes flared with panic. "You…killed those women." Her voice rose, hysterical. "And now you did something to Brad, and you want to do the same thing to me."

Vernon staggered back a step, her accusations stunning him. "No…no, you don't understand."

"You always followed along behind William. You tried to emulate him back in college and now you're doing it again by copying his crimes."

"No, that's a lie. Back in college when I disappeared, you don't know what happened."

Lisa heaved a breath, glanced past him again as if searching for the agent. "If you love me, then let me go," she whispered. "Let me see Brad."

He shook her gently. He had to made her see that they belonged together. "You have to listen. It's all William's fault…he caused my accident four years ago, a car wreck that almost killed me. That's why I disappeared from school. He ran me off the road and left me to die, or we would have been together back then." He sighed, then rushing on. "It took me a long time to recover. I was in the hospital, in rehab therapy, even had plastic surgery because I didn't want to see you again until I could face you like a man." The old familiar low esteem ate at him, gnawing its way to the surface. He heard his mother's voice telling him he was no good.

But he wasn't that same old Vernon Hanks. He was different. Better. God had given him a second chance with Lisa. He couldn't lose her.

"Please, Lisa, I took care of White for you, so you'd never have to worry about him again."

"What do you mean, you took care of him?" Lisa asked in a trembling voice.

BRAD GROANED AND DRAGGED a hand over the back of his head. Something sticky and pasty coated his hair. He lifted his hand and saw the blood.

Shit.

His memory crashed back. Lisa had screamed his name. He'd gone running toward the house.

And then someone had clobbered the hell out of him. His head throbbed, and he was drenched in cold sweat. The world spun in a dizzying motion as he forced himself to his knees. Struggling to breathe, he exhaled sharply, trying to orient himself and steady his legs so he could stand.

Pulse pounding, he forced his feet to move, and crossed the distance to the porch. He grabbed the rail, hoisted himself up and automatically reached for his gun. But he'd left it by the lake. Damn it. No time to go back for it now.

Adrenaline surged through him. He tiptoed up the steps and inside, cocking one ear to listen for sounds. A man's reedy voice. Then Lisa's broken whisper. She was begging the man to let her go. Calling him Vernon.

It was Hanks.

Brad inched to the door and peered inside just as she swung her knee up to attack. Brad catapulted into motion, then leaped onto Hanks's back.

The man was surprisingly strong, and his blow to the head had weakened Brad, but Brad was fighting for Lisa's life. Spurred on by fury, he pounded his fists into the man's face, his bruised knuckles bleeding as he knocked him to the floor.

Lisa screamed and jumped backward, horror in her eyes, but he couldn't stop.

He'd told Lisa he was a killer but she didn't believe him. Now she saw the truth.

Hanks groaned and went limp, but Brad pounded him again until the whites of his eyes bulged. Each time he thought of Lisa. The other victims.

"Brad, stop." Lisa tugged at his arm.

Finally he glanced up. Tears streaked her face. His chest clenched, and he released his grip on Hanks's neck.

But he wasn't sure Lisa had stopped him in time, if the man would survive long enough to give a confession.

A HALF HOUR LATER, Lisa watched in abject shock as the paramedics lifted Vernon Hanks into the ambulance. Blunt force trauma to the head had caused him to slip into unconsciousness.

Brad had retreated into his sullen shell, using a clipped tone to deliver his account of the attack. Captain Rosberg had spoken with her, and she'd answered the questions as best she could, trying to recall Vernon's rantings word for word.

"He admitted putting the new comforter on the bed and going through your clothing?" Brad asked.

Lisa nodded. "He didn't explain the bedspread, but

he said he liked touching my clothes. And he admitted renting the cabin next to mine in Ellijay so he could be close to me. But he told me there his name was Aiden Henderson."

"Typical stalker behavior." Captain Rosberg consulted his notepad. "You said he claimed White caused his accident?"

She glanced at Brad and wrapped her arms around herself. Earlier she'd felt so close to him. Now she felt as if he was a million miles away. Untouchable. "Yes, he said he'd been in the hospital, then rehab, that he had to have plastic surgery."

"His sister mentioned that he'd been in an accident, too," Brad confirmed.

Captain Rosberg shot Brad a dark look. Lisa sensed he was upset with him for beating Vernon so badly.

But he had been protecting her...hadn't he?

The ambulance spun away, siren blaring, its lights twirling in the darkness.

"We'll have someone stationed at his door," Captain Rosberg said. "When he wakes up, we'll question him."

If he wakes up. Would he? The question lingered in the ensuing silence.

Then Brad's phone trilled from inside the house, and he stalked up the steps to answer it.

"Miss Langley, did Vernon Hanks admit that he's the copycat Grave Digger?"

Lisa shook her head, Vernon's wild-eyed look flashing back to her.

"Did he mention the other girls at all? Give you any

indication that he was involved or that he'd kidnapped and buried them?"

Lisa massaged her temple, her lungs tight. Everything had happened so quickly. And she had been so afraid. But Vernon…he'd actually looked upset when she'd accused him of the murders.

"Miss Langley?"

"No," Lisa said quietly. "He denied being the killer. And he claimed that he wouldn't hurt me, that he loved me."

Rosberg frowned, but the screen door slapped open, and Brad stalked outside, his look feral. "That was Nettleton."

Lisa clenched the porch railing for support, fearing his next words.

"He knows where Darcy Mae Richards is?" Captain Rosberg asked.

Brad nodded, and the horror continued.

IT WAS ANOTHER all-nighter. A night of tracking through the woods, of facing the possibility of failure, a night of finding another woman who had been buried alive in the infernal heat.

Brad grimaced as the M.E. examined Darcy Mae Richards's body. The crime scene techs that had been at the other sites had arrived just as Brad had. This time Dunbar was leading the crew.

Darcy Mae hadn't been dead that long. Hadn't fought with the box like the others. Must have realized it was no use.

Either that or perhaps she'd suffered heatstroke, and her heart had expired before the air had.

He hung his head, sweat soaking his shirt and back, the realization that he'd missed Nettleton's first call intensifying his guilt. Apparently Nettleton had left a message on his cell phone while Brad had been swimming in the lake. Then he'd been so busy making love to Lisa that he'd forgotten to check it immediately.

Would it have made a difference for Darcy Mae if he'd received the call thirty minutes earlier?

God, what if it had? What if he could have rescued this woman in time…?

Nettleton approached, his smarmy face almost pious. The tail had confirmed that Nettleton had been at home the night before, but Brad still wondered if he could have slipped out.

Brad had ordered Lisa to stay in the car, and had left Officer Surges waiting beside her as a guard dog. Through the bushes, he saw Wayne Nettleton charging toward the vehicle and Lisa. Brad sprinted after him. The last thing Lisa needed was to have her picture in the *Atlanta Daily* or on the news. But Nettleton didn't give a rat's ass about her safety.

Before Brad could reach him, the man's camera flashed. Lisa ducked behind her hands, and Brad tore into Nettleton.

"Take your hands off of me," the reporter shouted.

Brad spun him around by the collar. "You'd better not print that picture, Nettleton. You could be putting Lisa's life in danger."

"The public has a right to know what's going on," Nettleton argued. "They want to see what happened to Langley's princess daughter, how she made it these last four years, what she thinks about this second Grave Digger."

"The public will have to wait," Brad barked. "You're not going to put her life in jeopardy just to make a story."

"Don't you think her life already is in jeopardy?" Nettleton asked snidely. "Isn't that the reason you have her staying with you? Or is it because you want her for yourself?"

Brad slammed his fist into the man's mouth.

Nettleton cursed and coughed blood. Officer Surges stepped forward as if to temper things. "Agent Booker, maybe you'd better take a walk."

Brad glared at him. "You think I should listen to a cop who pukes at every crime scene?"

Surges's face turned crimson, and he backed away.

Lisa tried to open the door, but Brad waved for her to remain inside. This fight was between him and Nettleton.

"You're a hothead, Booker," Nettleton said. "You're out of control. I heard you nearly beat that man Hanks to death."

"He attacked Lisa Langley," Brad said. "End of story." And he didn't regret one second of the beating.

Nettleton arched a brow. "Do you really think he's the copycat Grave Digger?"

"I'm not at liberty to say. Now get out of here."

"Lisa knew this man Hanks before, didn't she? Just like she knew William White."

Brad jerked Nettleton away from the car. "I told you to leave."

But Nettleton refused to be deterred. "Did Hanks confess?"

"I'm not going to discuss this investigation with you."

"You're forgetting that I'm the one calling you with information on the bodies. That I'm the one the killer is talking to."

"Which makes you a prime suspect," Brad snapped.

Nettleton chuckled. "I've already given Captain Rosberg my alibi."

"Alibis can be faked," Brad said. "And if I find out yours was, I'll personally haul you in."

"Then you don't think Vernon Hanks is the Grave Digger?"

"Leave now, and stay away from Lisa Langley." Brad gave him a shove, then waited until Nettleton climbed into his SUV and drove away before he returned to the crime scene.

An hour later, he and Lisa were at the precinct. Running on twenty-four hours without sleep, he chugged a cup of coffee while Lisa sat slumped in a chair in the corner, looking pale and exhausted. Lisa had begged him to have his head checked but Brad assured her he was fine.

Rosberg had already chewed him out in his office, threatened to call Brad's superior at the bureau, and had phoned the hospital several times, but Hanks hadn't yet regained consciousness.

The estimated time of death for Darcy Mae Richards had been 11:00 p.m. Nettleton had supposedly received the call around 11:30.

Hanks had attacked Lisa around midnight.

It was still possible that he was the killer.

Rosberg handed Brad a fax that had just come in. "This is from the prison."

"White's visitors." Brad studied the series of shots. Two visitors. Wayne Nettleton a few weeks before White's death. The other man, Vernon Hanks, aka Aiden Henderson, had visited White on two occasions. The last was the day White had died.

So Hanks had impersonated White's brother. But why?

Lisa moved up beside him. "What are those?"

He showed her the photos. "That's Vernon," Lisa said. "He pretended to be White's brother."

Lisa gasped, then pressed her hand over her mouth.

"What is it?" Brad asked.

"Vernon...there was something he said. I didn't understand it at the time." She lifted her face, met his eyes. "He said that he took care of William, that he did it for me so William would never bother me again."

Brad's mouth went dry. What had he meant?

White had died from a fight, and Vernon hadn't been present. Still...other possibilities came to mind.

What if Hanks had paid someone to kill White, then decided to replace him by mimicking his crimes?

Brad punched in the chief coroner's number. "This is Special Agent Booker. Have you confirmed White's identity?"

"Yes," Zaxberg said. "The man who was buried is definitely William White."

Brad had known it all along, but still sighed in relief. "Did you check for drugs in White's system? Something that might have caused his death, or caused him to be weakened so that he couldn't defend himself in case of an attack?"

"No organ-damaging drugs," the coroner said. "If he had, he wouldn't have been able to donate them."

Right. Brad scratched his head. He still didn't understand why a sadistic killer would have given his organs for transplant. Then again, White had probably done so thinking he'd live on through the recipients.

But if Vernon hadn't drugged White and caused his death, he must have paid someone in the pen to kill him.

LIAM LANGLEY STARED at his daughter's picture in the early edition of the morning paper and nearly choked on his coffee. She had been attacked last night by that man named Vernon Hanks. Booker had come to the rescue.

And Darcy Mae Richards had been found dead. Another victim of the copycat Grave Digger.

Son of a bitch.

His heart pounding, he picked up the phone and dialed Lisa's cell. He let it ring and ring, but she didn't answer, so he called Booker.

"Special Agent Booker."

"Liam Langley. Is my daughter with you?"

"Yes."

"Is she all right?"

The agent hesitated. "Yes. She's exhausted. We just returned from the precinct a few minutes ago. I'm trying to get her to lie down."

"Let me speak to her."

Booker grunted, then must have handed Lisa the phone. "Dad?"

"Good God, Lisa, I saw the news. Why the hell didn't you call me last night?"

"Because there was nothing you could do. Brad caught Vernon Hanks and…he's in custody."

"According to the paper, he's unconscious."

"Yes."

"Good, then he can't hurt you again." He hesitated, knowing he had to see the man for himself. "Why don't you have Booker bring you here. I have state-of-the-art security. You can rest in your old room. Let the house-keeper pamper you."

"I'm fine here, Dad."

Liam paced the room. "Listen, tell Booker that I talked to a friend of mine about Hanks's medical records. He was in an accident four years ago. Went to rehab and had plastic surgery. The doctors said he claimed that someone had run him off the road, but then nothing ever came of it. He was on so much medication that the police thought he'd been hallucinating."

"Vernon said that William ran him off the road."

"What difference does that make?" Liam bellowed. "He was still stalking you, and killing these women."

Lisa sighed, her voice low. "He never confessed, Dad. And he told me he didn't kill them."

"You really think he would have admitted to murder?"

"I don't know. For some reason…" Lisa hesitated, then continued, "I just don't know if he has the heart of a killer."

Liam paused in front of his desk, stared at his daughter's picture. Remembered her in that pink frilly dress when she was crowned Little Miss Magnolia. The way she'd squealed when her mother had given her that amethyst. Then at her mother's funeral.

And all those Christmas photos with her dolls and toys afterward. When she'd looked so sad and lonely.

The photo from four years ago at the trial flashed back in his mind. And now another this morning. Why couldn't all these crazies and that damn reporter leave her alone? Hadn't she suffered enough?

"Don't tell me you feel sorry for this lunatic," Liam said between gritted teeth. "My God, Lisa, didn't you learn anything from what happened with White?"

"I'm sure Brad will find out the truth when Vernon wakes up," Lisa said stiffly.

If he wakes up, Liam thought, already stuffing his wallet into his slacks. And he didn't intend to wait on Booker. He intended to pay Vernon Hanks a visit himself.

The man wasn't going to attack his little girl and get away with it, not without dealing with him.

A half hour later, he'd convinced the officer stationed at Hanks's hospital room door to let him in. Liam's stomach churned as he approached the bed.

Vernon Hanks was a pitiful looking man. Thin. Wiry hair. Pale freckled skin. A man who looked as if he'd tried to work out and build muscles, but the rail-thin angular features had never quite filled out as he'd wanted. Liam had read the man's medical files.

Vernon had an irregular heartbeat.

All it would take was a simple shock, maybe even a

little shot of the wrong drug or a miscalculated dosage, and he would go into cardiac arrest.

After all, Liam had crossed the line once, with William White. Would this be any different?

HE WAS SO WEARY. He tried to move his hand to press it to his chest, but he couldn't lift it. Fatigue weighed him down. He needed sleep. Needed to climb into that dark hole where his mind allowed him to forget what he'd done. Forget that his second chance at living had turned into a nightmare from which he had to run.

Darcy Mae Richards had been one of the women who'd carved out his heart.

Just like Joann Worthy. And Mindy Faulkner.

And Lisa.

Everything came back to Lisa. Lisa tattling to that special agent Booker. Lisa taking the stand against him. Lisa turning him away and looking at him like he was a monster.

In the haze of gray murky light enveloping him, he saw Dr. Langley. First condemning him. Then hovering above him. His surgical mask in place. His eyes peering at him as if he was looking into his soul. His hand poised and ready to kill him or save his life.

But he'd carved him open just as the women had.

Then the third day he'd risen from the dead.

The new soul drove him forward.

And he'd come back for them all. Only they hadn't recognized him. No one had. But he had frozen images of each of them in his mind.

Joann, Mindy, Darcy Mae. Lisa.

It always came back to Lisa.

He had wanted her way back when.

He had never stopped loving her.

He had come back from the grave to get her.

And she *would* be his.

CHAPTER SIXTEEN

LIAM LANGLEY'S HANDS shook with the effort not to choke Vernon Hanks, the temptation to end the man's life warring with his conscience. Booker had done a number on the man, beaten him until his face was swollen and discolored.

Begrudgingly, Liam realized he owed the agent thanks. Too bad Booker hadn't finished off Hanks. From what he knew, Booker could be a pretty cold killer. Until White had come into his life and destroyed his daughter, Liam had never understood the pleasure in the kill.

Now he did.

Seven days and nights of pure torture while he'd waited on the cops to find Lisa, agonizing minutes of not knowing, of wondering what kinds of things that sick man was doing to her. Of imagining her helpless, hurting, lying in that homemade grave, dying of thirst and lack of oxygen. Of being terrified that she was dead and gone forever.

White should have died the same way. But White had had it easy.

And Liam had known then that White's life had to count for something. That he deserved to die.

Just like Vernon Hanks did now.

The machinery keeping him alive droned in the deafening silence, the steady drip of the IV a reminder that it would be so easy to feed Hanks a death serum. Liam unknotted his fists, then shoved his right hand into his pocket to remove a hypodermic just as Hanks's eyelids fluttered. A cold sweat exploded on Liam's neck. If he was going to do this, now was the time.

Hanks's eyes were opened at half mast, mere slits between the swollen purple-and-blue bags cradling his irises.

"You tried to kill my daughter," Liam said coldly.

Hanks narrowed the slits, obviously disoriented.

"Give me one reason I should let you live."

"I…I wouldn't hurt Lisa." He paused, wheezing for a breath. "I love her…."

Liam's hand moved, gripping the hypodermic tighter, but the door squeaked open.

"Liam?"

He froze, Gioni's silky, worried voice washing over him. "I knew I'd find you here." Her footsteps padded toward him, and she pressed one hand to his back. "What are you doing?"

He lifted his shoulders slightly, his gaze locking with Hanks's as the man struggled to stay conscious.

"He attacked my daughter last night." Liam slid the hypodermic back inside his pocket. "The police think he's the Grave Digger."

Hanks shook his head from side to side, his eyes rolling up in his head, then closing as if he couldn't fight the battle any longer.

"Leave me for a minute," Liam said quietly.

"No." Gioni stepped around to face him, then captured his hands in hers. "You have to let the police handle this, Liam. Let them do their jobs."

"But you don't understand." His voice cracked with emotions. "This man tried to hurt my daughter, and I didn't protect her. He doesn't deserve to live—"

"That's not your decision," Gioni said in a low voice. "Don't let him destroy who you are, Liam. You're a healer, a saver of lives."

"It's too late," he replied, his chest swelling. "I crossed the line with White, and I can't go back."

"That was different," Gioni said. "Just think about it, Liam. What would Lisa want you to do?"

CURTIS THIGS LOPED from the bathroom into Chartrese's bedroom, buck naked and feeling randy. He had punished Chartrese for threatening to phone the police.

And now he had her right where he wanted her.

She'd recanted her accusations. Pleaded and begged for him to forgive her. And spread her legs for him time and time again.

It was funny how a man got used to jerking off in prison. But when he had a prime, juicy piece of woman to sink himself into, the hand job held no appeal.

Maybe this time he'd make Chartrese use her mouth.

Deny her the satisfaction of holding his cock inside her until she pleasured him.

Teach her that he should always come first....

A laugh rumbled from his chest at the double meaning.

He rubbed at the scar on his chest, then watched Chartrese push the tangle of hair from her eyes as she studied him from the unmade bed. The top sheet lay on the floor, a quilt dangling from the foot of the bed where he'd kicked it off in his haste to drag her beneath him.

Her big eyes looked up at him, terrified. She was wondering if he was the Grave Digger. His dick twitched and grew thicker. He liked that fear in her eyes. That respect she gave him.

Not like that pansy-ass, White. He hadn't been able to get it up with the women.

Curtis Thigs didn't have that problem. At least not with Chartrese.

Granted, he'd lost it a few times in his life. And those women had suffered for it.

Just as White had made them pay for not being able to please him.

He stalked toward Chartrese, then stopped in front of the bed.

She twirled a strand of that fire-engine-red hair around a finger. "You want to go again, honey?"

He grinned. Chartrese might have considered leaving him while he was in the joint. But he was back now. And she was a quick study.

"Yeah, baby." He threaded his fingers in her hair,

then dragged her head down toward him. She made a whimpering sound, then crawled to her hands and knees and closed her mouth around his length.

Seconds later, a pounding at the door jarred him, and he froze, his hand still pressed to Chartrese's head. He ignored the sound, closed his eyes and tried to concentrate, willing the noise to stop. But the pounding grew louder.

He cursed, pushed Chartrese back on the bed and ordered her to stay. Then he grabbed his jeans, shucked them on and strode toward the door to get rid of the intruder. When he opened the door, he realized he'd made a mistake.

"Curtis Thigs?"

He muttered another curse. This guy had FBI written all over him.

"Special Agent Manning." The fed flashed his badge. "You're under arrest for violation of parole."

"What?"

"You failed to show up for your parole meeting. I'm taking you in."

"Since when does the goddamn FBI care about me and my parole officer?"

"Since you became a suspect in the copycat Grave Digger killings."

"Curtis?"

He glanced back and saw Chartrese standing in the doorway, belting a robe.

"This is bullshit, baby." He gestured toward the bedroom. "Stay right there. I'll be back soon."

He grabbed a shirt off the edge of the chair, then went with the agent, planning his story in his head. Chartrese would give him an alibi for the past week, he was sure of that.

In fact, if she knew what was good for her, she'd lie for him without him even having to ask.

BRAD TRIED TO PERSUADE Lisa to rest, but the conversation with her father had upset her, and she'd been pacing the small den ever since. Her strained relationship with Liam Langley disturbed her more than she wanted to admit. He wished her father could see that and make things right.

Brad would help her if he could.

But Liam Langley would never accept him. Just as his parents and those foster parents never had.

The fresh bruises he'd gotten from beating Hanks mocked him with the realization that Lisa's father was right about him. His hands were too dirty to touch Lisa again.

His phone rang, and he rushed to answer it, hoping it was the hospital, that Hanks had awakened and confessed. Then he could put this case to rest.

Ethan's voice echoed over on the line. "I heard you caught Vernon Hanks."

"Yeah." Brad scrubbed a hand over the rough stubble on his jaw. "He attacked Lisa."

"No confession?"

"Not yet."

"I lucked out tonight, too. Curtis Thigs is in custody."

"You're shittin' me?"

"No. He's at the precinct right now being booked for parole violation."

"Did you get a chance to question him?"

"Yeah, but no confession either. Claims he has an alibi for the nights the women were killed, that his wife will verify his statement."

"Damn it. At least hold him twenty-four hours."

"Done." Ethan hesitated. "Listen, Rosberg said something about Hanks maybe setting up White's death."

"Yeah, it looks that way."

"Thigs admitted that a couple of the brothers in the joint had been buying drugs from Hanks. Apparently he gave them prescription painkillers he'd received after his surgeries, and they were getting high."

"And the trade-off?" Brad asked.

"According to Thigs, they were supposed to take care of White."

Brad whistled. "So, it's looking more and more like Hanks is our perp."

"Either way, at least both our prime suspects are in custody. Sooner or later, one of them will confess."

Brad hung up and glanced at Lisa. He hoped to hell they did have the killer. Or Lisa still wasn't safe.

LISA COULDN'T SLEEP. Long after she'd hung up the phone, her father's comment gnawed at her. *Hadn't she learned anything from William?*

Yes, she'd learned not to trust men. She'd hidden away from life. She'd shut herself off from a future.

But she was still alive. She'd been lucky. Given another chance. The other victims hadn't.

And she couldn't let them down—she had to make that chance count.

"Lisa, are you all right?"

Brad's husky voice skated over her raw nerve endings. Soothing. Sultry. Evoking desire.

But she felt so dirty from Vernon's touch. And then the stifling heat and stench of Darcy Mae's grave site.

"Lisa, please lie down for a while. You need some rest."

"So do you."

Brad merely shrugged. She ached for him to come to her, hold her, make love to her, but he made no move.

"I'd like to shower first," she said softly, wishing he would join her.

He simply nodded and turned away, busying himself making coffee. She couldn't push him now, not with Darcy Mae's death so fresh. But she wouldn't give up on Brad Booker, either.

Resigned to give him time, she ducked inside the bedroom, but the sight of her clothes still strewn across the white comforter sent a shudder through her. She couldn't wear those things, not after Vernon had touched them.

She stripped and stepped into the shower, letting the warm water and soap cleanse her of the stench of death, then she shampooed her hair and rinsed it, scrubbing her scalp to ease the tension. Finally, she towel dried her hair and wrapped another towel around her. After combing through the wet strands, she went into the den, where Brad stood at the French doors, breathing in the fresh air. Lisa could hear waves rippling against the shore from a boater who had headed out to fish.

She strode forward, hesitating a fraction of a second when he stiffened, then reached up and placed her hand on his back. "Brad?"

"Go to bed, Lisa."

She closed her eyes, willed her courage to remain. "I...can't sleep in that room. Not now."

His head jerked toward her. Anguish darkened his eyes, but understanding filled them, too.

"Take my bed," he said in a husky voice.

"Lie down with me," Lisa whispered. "You need some rest, too."

He swallowed, his eyes slanting downward, lingering a second on the towel around her. She felt her nipples tighten, the familiar stir of desire bubbling in her stomach.

"I have to clean up first." His voice sounded harsh, but she understood the need to wash away the dirtiness of the night. He lifted a finger to the damp ends of her hair, brushed them away from her cheek. Her breath hitched in her throat.

But he pulled back, then turned and strode into the bathroom. Lisa leaned against the open doorway, inhaling the sultry air as the sun rose in its glory. Today would be another scorching one. The blistering heat would kill more grass, cause more flowers to die.

But if Vernon was the copycat killer, then maybe this streak of violence would end and no more women would lose their lives.

Still, she couldn't shake her gut feeling that Vernon wasn't the killer, that he had been sincere in his denial of the crimes. But as her father had reminded her with William, she hadn't believed he was a killer at first, either.

Not until she'd found those clippings of the women's fingernails, and he'd taken her as one of his victims....

SOMETHING WAS BOTHERING Liam about the victims.

He'd accessed all of Vernon Hanks's medical files, which had made him start thinking about Lisa's comment.

Hanks didn't have the heart of a killer.

Liam had read some research on the criminal mind in med school, had always been fascinated by the discussion of whether criminal behavior was inherited or learned. When White had gone to trial, he'd studied the man's medical records as well as his psychological profile. For some morbid reason, he'd wanted to try to understand why the man had murdered four women and almost killed his own daughter.

White had been traumatized and abused as a child. If he had genetic problems, they hadn't shown up. A severe injury, trauma to his head, had caused his bipolar disorder. Coupled with that and the abuse he'd suffered, he'd become a full-fledged sociopath.

But what if the tests had been wrong or inconclusive? What if White had some genetic abnormality that had predisposed him to become a serial killer? Liam had heard various views on the possibilities, seen data supporting the theory....

He stared at the photo of Darcy Mae Richards in the

paper, tapping his memory banks. Darcy Mae had worked at St. Jude's…was it possible?

With a sense of foreboding tightening his chest, he picked up the phone and dialed a colleague of his at St. Jude's.

As the questions formed in his mind, he shuddered. They couldn't be true.

Because if they were, then he had not only crossed the line with White, but he had set the wheels in motion for him to be reborn and kill again….

CHAPTER SEVENTEEN

VERNON WAS IN the hospital. Curtis Thigs was in custody.

And Lisa was lying in Brad's bed, where she felt safe for the first time in years. Safe, free and full of hope.

Brad emerged from the shower, a towel knotted at his waist. Lisa had thrown on one of his shirts to sleep in, and rolled the sleeves up, but the shirt still swallowed her whole.

"I hope you don't mind. I borrowed it from your closet."

He stared at her, his dark eyes hooded, then hunger flared. "You look good in it."

She rubbed her hand along the open neckline. "It smells like you."

He closed his eyes for a brief moment as if exerting control. "God, Lisa."

She pushed the covers aside, waited for him to open his eyes, then patted the bed beside her.

Droplets of water glistened on the dark mat covering his bronzed chest, and his damp hair had fallen over one eye, giving him a rakish look. He pushed it back, then seemed to lose the battle with his ironclad control and walked toward her. Her breath caught in her throat as he lowered himself on the bed beside her. But instead of lying down, he simply reached out and stroked her hair from her cheek, then traced a finger down her arm. "Go to sleep, Lisa. You have to be exhausted."

"So do you."

"I'm used to it. It's my job."

Lisa pressed her palm over his hand. "Even FBI agents have to rest once in a while."

"Just rest," he said in a thick voice. "We're both too wrung out to know what we want."

She opened her mouth to argue, but he shook his head, and she accepted his comment, but only because she refused to beg. And he was right. Her limbs and body ached from fatigue. She was exhausted. Maybe they'd sleep, then talk about the future.

If there was going to be one between them.

He surprised her then by sliding down beside her. Then he took her in his arms. She cuddled against him, the throes of sleep tugging at her. Brad pressed a kiss to her temple, then rubbed slow circles on her back, his breathing deep and heavy. She needed more, to have him naked and sliding against her skin, but her eyes refused to stay open. She savored the feel of his hands on her back, of his leg as he wrapped it over hers, of the way he turned her spoon-style against him and hugged her close as she fell asleep in his arms.

BRAD LAY FOR A LONG TIME simply looking at Lisa as she drifted to sleep. He inhaled the scent of her freshly washed hair spread across his pillow, smiled at the small movements she made as she cuddled next to him, enjoyed the tingle of desire that ripped through him as the shirt she wore slid up and her bare butt brushed his thigh.

God, he wanted her—so badly he could hardly stand it. Ached to caress her silky skin and kiss every inch of her, tease her until she cried out his name and begged for more.

And then sink himself inside her until he reached her core, a place where he could erase the dark shadows that had dogged him forever.

Was this what it felt like to love someone?

He honestly didn't know. Had never felt this way for a woman. Had no idea what being in a long-term relationship meant.

Had no intention of forcing her to live in constant danger just by association with him.

She whimpered and moved closer to him, and he tightened his arms around her, resigned to the fact that this delicious moment would have to last him for the rest of his life.

Finally he fell asleep, dreaming of Lisa and a life that didn't exist, of babies and laughter and a real home, one that he'd never known and never would.

DUSK WAS SETTING when Brad awakened. Beside him, Lisa lay looking up at him, that beautiful innocence in her eyes shining like a star.

"Brad?"

She smiled, then lifted a hand and brushed it along

his beard stubble. He hadn't bothered to shave before he'd showered, had been too tired to think straight, and his coarse face hair rasped across her delicate skin.

He turned to get up, but she caught him and traced a finger along his chest, teasing his nipple with her finger. Then her hand slid lower, lower until she contacted the skin on his thigh. He sucked in a sharp breath and moved to pull away, but she pressed him back on the bed with one hand, then leaned on her elbow and looked down at him.

"Why do you keep pushing me away?"

"I don't want to take advantage of you," he said gruffly.

She laughed, a soft throaty sound that was so utterly feminine it only heightened his desire.

Then her expression turned serious. "Are you sure? Or do you just not want me?"

He froze, wondering why in the hell she'd think something like that.

"Lisa—"

"We're both rested now, so I'm thinking clearly," she whispered, gesturing toward the soft light filtering in through the window. "Now, tell me the truth, Brad. After everything we've been through together, you owe me that."

He stared into her eyes, read naked longing, but a vulnerability that cut him to the bone. Except for the time she'd been with Brad by the lake, she hadn't made love with anyone since her failed attempts with William. Had never had a man really make love to her. She'd admitted that after the trial. She had to have dug for courage to ask him this now.

And he desperately wanted to give her the satisfaction of knowing just how much he did want her.

If that was all she was asking.

"A man would be a fool not to want you, Lisa."

She feathered back his hair. "I'm not talking about any man, Brad. I'm talking about you."

God help him but he had to admit the truth. "I've wanted you from the first moment I met you," he said in a husky voice. "And I've wanted you every day for the past four years." He licked his lips, saw a spark of surprise light her eyes. "In fact, I've wanted you every night and day since you've been back in my life."

She flattened her palm over his chest again, playing in his chest hair. "Then make love to me, Brad."

He caught her hand, then brought it to his lips and kissed it before looking into her eyes. His sex throbbed, bolder, harder now, and his breathing had turned erratic. He wasn't ashamed of the strength of his desire. Didn't care now if she knew it. "I'm no good for you, Lisa. You—" his voice cracked "—deserve so much more."

She stared at him for so long he thought he'd crossed the line, jaunted into unknown territory. After all, what did he know about women?

He was on the brink of apologizing when she finally whispered, "Why don't you let me decide that?"

He grabbed her other hand before she could close it around his sex. "Just know that I want you, but I can't promise you more than tonight," he said in a gruff voice. "That's not who I am, Lisa. I…don't want to hurt you."

Sadness tinged her eyes for a brief second, then she

blinked and it disappeared, the undeniable ripple of desire and heat flaring again. Without hesitating, this time he threaded his hands in her hair and brought her face down to his, claiming her mouth with his kisses as his resistance shattered.

LISA MELTED INTO Brad's arms, grateful he'd finally abandoned whatever reservations had been holding him back. The two of them were meant to be together.

Didn't he feel it when he held her?

She pushed all fears of rejection and insecurities aside, relying on her instincts. He plunged his tongue into her mouth and she parted her lips, inviting him to take her however he wanted. Fast. Hard. Passionate.

She wanted it all. Wanted to know what it felt like to be thoroughly loved and sated.

Brad didn't disappoint her.

He flipped her to her back, then rose above her. From there, he trailed kisses along her neck and the sensitive skin of her earlobe, made light sucking sounds along her collarbone, then dipped his head and flicked her nipple with the tip of his wet tongue.

She arched her back, aching for more. Praying he wouldn't stop this time until he'd filled her completely.

He teased her nipple to a hard peak, then grasped it in his mouth and held it between his teeth until she cried out and begged for him to hurry. His hands stroked her sensitive places, the rise of her hip, the indentation of her spine, the insides of her thighs until she thought she would die from the pleasure. Then he switched to the other breast and continued the torturous ministrations.

"Brad, please…" She clung to the muscles in his arms, felt them bunch and his body grow slick with heat. His hands were bold, big, tender, hungry as his fingers gripped her hips, then he buried his leg in between her thighs, the raspy hair stroking her sensitive flesh as he moved above her. She clawed his back, then slid one hand down to find his erection, a flash of satisfaction filling her at the look on his face. His eyes went wild, his breathing tormented as he tried to pull away.

But this time she refused to let him. She liked the feel of his sex in her hand. Felt moisture wet her legs as he pulsed between her fingers. Felt heady knowing that she could make this strong, courageous man quiver this way.

He groaned her name, then grabbed her hands, pushed them above her, pinning them down. His breath rasped out while he nipped at her flesh and licked his way down her belly. She cried out his name, wanting him inside her.

He placed his tongue there instead.

Licking. Teasing. Tasting. Smiling up at her as if he enjoyed the pure essence of her response.

She nearly came at the erotic feeling.

"Brad, please, I need you," she whispered raggedly.

He shook his head, dipped his head lower. His hair brushed her legs, his tongue lapped her juices and she bucked upward, her hands digging into his hair as sensations spiraled through her. In a heartbeat, he rose above her, rolled on a condom and thrust inside her.

She grabbed his arms, clung to him as fire shot through her. Moaning his name, she wrapped her legs around his hips, and thrust upward as he rammed inside her, over and over, deeper and deeper, his guttural groan of pleasure triggering an even longer, more intense orgasm to rip through her as he spilled himself inside her.

INTENSE EMOTIONS ROCKETED through Brad, the feeling of euphoria mind-numbing. But even as the tidal wave of his orgasm slowly passed, he wanted Lisa again.

He always would.

For him, it had always been Lisa.

But he couldn't confess his feelings.

He pressed her into the curve of his embrace, closing his eyes and memorizing each tender moment they shared. The way she clung to his arms. The throaty moans she made in the aftermath of love. The sweet way she kissed his neck and traced a fingernail down his spine.

God, he never wanted to let her go.

But he'd promised himself and her father that he'd protect her. And he had done so by keeping her with him.

Now he would do so by setting her free.

Only he'd never expected the sharp pang that knifed through his chest at the thought.

But he could endure any amount of pain if it meant Lisa was safe and alive.

"Brad?"

He closed his eyes, his body pulsing with pleasure at the sultry sound of her voice. Laden with the sweet

bliss of satisfaction, it sounded like a cat's purr, beck-
oning him to make love to her again.

"Yeah?"

She slid her hand beneath his arm and scraped her
fingernails down his back. "Make love to me again. All
through the night."

Unable to resist her, he lowered his head and kissed
her, delving into the recesses of her mouth to taste her.
He was so hungry. Starving for this woman.

One taste led to another and another until he joined
their bodies again, taking her over and over through
the rest of the night, stopping only long enough to
sleep, eat and shower together. Then they'd made love
once more, until she quivered and cried beneath him.
He had to sate himself, memorizing every inch of her
body and imprinting her voice and her touch into his
mind forever.

As LISA AWAKENED, muscles that she'd never used
before ached. But the heavenly euphoria of being with
Brad negated any discomfort. He had made love to her
until she'd thought she had melded with his body, until
she was nothing but a puddle of satisfaction. Yet the
longing still persisted, a constant craving that would
never go away.

She had been empty without Brad. A broken shell of
a woman who had never known joy.

Now, she wanted to lie here in his arms, drowning in
desire, forever.

He rolled over and opened his eyes. Looked at her

with a longing that spoke of the hot sultry night they'd just spent together. Whispered memories of the decadent things they'd done together in the heat of the night.

Things she'd never forget.

Things she desperately wanted to do again.

And other things she'd yet to try...

"Lisa, I need to go to the precinct and question Curtis Thigs."

She nodded, settling back on his arm, using it as her pillow.

"And I want to see if Hanks has regained consciousness. As soon as I get a confession, I'll drive you back to Ellijay."

The elation she'd felt moments earlier dissipated into fear. A long silence stretched between them.

"Lisa?"

She licked her dry mouth. "I don't know if I can go back there now."

He sat up, dislodging his arm from behind her. "You love the town and the mountains, Lisa. Your job, your friends, they'll all be waiting."

"My picture, the story about this Grave Digger killer—it's all over the papers and news now. I can't go back there as Lisa Long."

Brad sighed, standing and rubbing his hand over his chest. She reached up, captured his hand and clung to it. She couldn't go back to Ellijay yet, not when they'd just made love. There was so much more she wanted with Brad. More lovemaking. Talking. She wanted to find out everything about the man, his favorite color, the types of food he liked, what he enjoyed doing for pleasure.

"You can explain to them what happened," Brad said, oblivious to her thoughts. "And in a few weeks, the talk will die down." He caressed her arm with his finger. "Don't worry. It'll be fine."

"You don't understand," Lisa whispered. "I want to be with you."

He suddenly turned away from her, grabbed his jeans and shucked them on, and she felt utterly alone. Brad hadn't made any promises. Had warned her he couldn't.

But how could she return to Ellijay when home meant being in his arms? When her heart would always belong here with him?

WAYNE NETTLETON YANKED surgical scrubs over his clothes, pulled on a lab coat he'd found in one of the doctor's lounges, then tied a surgical mask around his neck. Next came a stethoscope and a pair of square glasses with nonprescription lenses. A perfect disguise.

Oh, and he couldn't forget the name tag.

Dr. Wickerbottom. He chuckled. The name was as good as any. After all, he would only be Dr. Wickerbottom for a short while.

Jutting his chin up to emulate the air of a doctor, he strode down the hall, smiling at a few of the nurses who turned his way. Hmm. Not a bad disguise. Might earn him a night with the ladies. He might have to try it after hours.

But tonight was about work.

Of course, he could talk to a few of the nurses later, see what information he could glean. After he spoke with Vernon Hanks.

Determined to complete his act, he grabbed a chart from the vacant nurses' station, then sauntered to Hanks's room. The cop on duty, some chubby guy who was half asleep at the switch, grunted as he approached.

"Dr. Wickerbottom. I'm here to check Vernon Hanks's condition."

The man gave him a once-over and a half-witted smile, then nodded and stepped aside. Nettleton nearly chuckled out loud at the man's ineptitude, but bit the inside of his cheek instead and slipped into the room.

Vernon Hanks lay in a hospital bed with stark white sheets, making his pale but bruised face and body look purple beneath the fluorescent hospital lights. Tubes were hooked up to his arms, machines monitoring his condition whirred and worked in the eerie quiet.

Nettleton had never liked hospitals. His recent stay had made him even more paranoid of the health care field.

The guard cop's incompetence only heightened that fear.

Hanks still lay unconscious, but his eyelids flickered sporadically. Nettleton was on a time clock. Booker had refused to talk to him, and so had the locals. He couldn't afford to let another press member outscoop this story before he did. He had to know if they'd gotten Hanks to make a confession.

Knowing his career depended on it, he removed his

pocket camera and snapped a couple of photos, then shook the patient's arm. "Wake up, Hanks. Talk to me."

He jerked, an almost inhuman response. His eyes twitched, and machines bleeped as if his blood pressure had risen.

Nettleton shook him again. "Listen to me, you puny shit. I might be your only defense. If you want to get out of this alive, you'd better wake up and talk to me."

The man's eyes fluttered open, then shut, and a screeching sound ripped from his lips. Nettleton slammed a hand over his mouth, afraid the cop would wake up and charge in.

Hanks's eyes blinked open again, terror registering.

"I'm from the press," Nettleton said. "Now, tell me what happened, and I'll print your version of the story."

Hanks coughed and sputtered, his voice rasping out, "Dr. Langley…he tried to k…kill me."

Nettleton's eyebrows arched in surprise. "What the hell are you talking about?"

Hanks choked, trying to yank out the oxygen tube. "He was going to k-kill me…."

"You attacked his daughter, you sick son of a bitch, that's why." Nettleton spat out a curse. "Now tell me, did you confess to murdering those other women?"

"No…I love Lisa, would never hurt her…" The heart monitor suddenly went wild. Shit. Hanks was going into cardiac arrest.

Knowing the staff would rush in any minute, he turned and fled. The cop outside the door must have been half-dead, either that or he was asleep again, because he blinked and jerked up as if he'd nodded off, mindless of the catastrophe inside.

Good. Nettleton could get away without being spotted. If Hanks died, he didn't want questions turning to him.

He sneaked down the hall and ducked inside a linen closet to rid himself of the disguise.

He'd heard that Booker had beaten the man into unconsciousness. But Hanks claimed Langley tried to kill him—maybe at the hospital?

Other pieces of the case that he hadn't connected started gelling in his mind. Booker had requested an exhumation of White's body. Langley worked at the same hospital where White had died.

Was it possible that Langley had killed William White?

HE HAD A LIST OF WOMEN who had wronged him.

One by one he was making them pay.

He had wanted to do so much more with his life. Had tried to make a success. Had struggled through classes and tests. Wanted to be a federal agent, but hadn't made it. And a cop, too. He was there at the crime scenes now. Had seen the police and feds chasing their tails, and laughed. They deserved it for not letting him in.

The women's faces came to mind…he'd struggled there, too. How many times had they laughed at him, rejected him, turned him away?

But that was way back when.

When he was weak. Scrawny. When he'd lacked the strength and courage to take control.

Not anymore. None of the women laughed now.

He pressed his hand to his chest, the jittery thump of his heart a reminder of the new life he'd been given. The new person he'd become.

A chuckle bubbled in his throat, heady and full of self-deprecating humor.

He'd never imagined the surgery would do this to him.

Had fought it at first. Hadn't wanted to accept that it was true.

But he couldn't fight it anymore. He was a different man.

At night, he could feel them carving out his organs. Feel the scalpel slicing through bones and tissue. See the blood dripping from open skin. Taste the beauty of living on and the stench of dying.

Now they must pay.

Plunged in shadows, he let himself into Gioni Kerr's apartment through the second bedroom window, slipping soundlessly down the hall toward her room. He'd been in her complex earlier. Knew the layout of the place. Knew exactly where her bed was and how many steps it took for her to reach the door to escape.

She'd never make it in time.

Grinning in the dark, he flexed his gloved hands. He was an expert, knew how to cover his tracks. His past self and the new one blended well together, grew into one more clearly each day. Into a new man who took what he wanted and never felt defeat.

The whistle of the air conditioner helped to camou-flage his breathing as he stepped inside Gioni's bedroom. She lay curled on her side asleep, her hair disheveled, her slender leg poking out from beneath the dark green bedding.

One step. Two. Three.

He hovered over her. Waiting for her to wake. To feel his presence. To see him clearly.

Just as he'd seen her the day she'd written his death certificate by helping Liam Langley cut into his body.

His breathing grew more erratic as she rolled over. Her gown slipped open, revealing breasts that Liam Langley had touched. Ones that would give him pleasure, if he wanted. But Langley's darling daughter would be so much better.

It would serve Langley right to see both the women he cared for suffer.

Gioni suddenly twitched and opened her eyes. The realization was immediate.

She tried to scream, but he laughed and clamped his hand over her lips, then jerked her head back so hard her eyes bulged.

Cold terror and confusion mingled in her expression. She had no idea who he was.

But he knew her.

And it was payback time for her and Langley.

CHAPTER EIGHTEEN

NETTLETON HID in the corner hallway of the hospital, listening to the nurses discuss Vernon Hanks.

Apparently they hadn't been able to revive him from the heart attack.

He silently whistled a sigh of relief as he shed his garb. Thankfully, no one had seen him exiting the man's room.

And now he had enough suppositions on Booker and Dr. Liam Langley to spice up his story. Had Langley given White something to make him go into cardiac arrest?

And if so, had Langley crossed the line with other patients?

Nettleton's heart accelerated at the mere thought of such smut on a prestigious doctor like Langley. It was too good to be true.

Obviously he wasn't as clean and pristine as the image he portrayed to the public. Ironic how, when Daddy's little princess had fallen from grace, she'd dragged Daddy down with her.

Nettleton slicked back his hair, waited until the small

group of gossipers disbanded, then picked out a bland young nurse in her early thirties, deciding she wasn't so pretty she would snub him or so geekish she'd turn her nose up at an advance.

He made it a point to read her nametag before he approached and introduced himself. A few minutes and several compliments later, he had her eating out of the palm of his hand.

"Tell me about Dr. Langley. It must have been hard for him after his daughter was kidnapped."

"It was." Tina flicked her brown bob with her fingers. "I heard he hasn't been the same since his wife died. But there's a rumor that he and his assistant, Gioni Kerr, are an item."

"A hospital romance," Nettleton said with a smile.

"Yes, Gioni would do anything for him. A lot of people around here are very loyal to him."

"And this guy, Hanks—when he attacked Dr. Langley's daughter, the doc must have been really upset."

"Of course." Tina's small eyes scrunched together. "I mean, Hanks is that creepy copycat killer, isn't he?"

Nettleton almost laughed at the panic on her young face, but shrugged, noncommittal. "Were you here when William White was brought in for treatment?"

Tina hesitated, then picked at a piece of lint on her bright pink nurse's pants. "I...no. Not exactly."

"What do you mean?"

"I was still in training, but I did a shift in the E.R."

"So you heard talk about the night White was brought in?"

For the first time since he'd spoken to the woman, she fidgeted, looked uncomfortable.

"I really can't say, Mr. Nettleton. I'd better get back to work."

He caught her hand, rubbed his thumb along her palm, saw her shiver. Then she looked into his eyes and he knew he had her. "What happened that night, Tina?"

She chewed her bottom lip, then motioned for him to follow her into the lounge. He did, excitement mounting. She was going to spill all Liam Langley's dirty little secrets.

LIAM HAD TO TALK TO Gioni.

She was the only one who saw the entire picture. She would tell him what to do.

And she would stand by him all the way. Because she knew his secrets. And she hadn't judged him for what he'd done. No, she'd understood.

But what would Lisa say if she found out the truth?

Would she hate him more than she did already? Despise him for not protecting her again?

Cut him out of her life entirely?

He flattened his clammy hands on his face, scrubbing downward in frustration, then grabbed some coffee. He hadn't slept a wink all night. Had convinced himself that he had nothing to do with these women's deaths.

But the eerie premonition that he was wrong had latched on to his conscience and wouldn't let go.

Exhaling to calm himself, he picked up the phone and dialed Gioni. The phone trilled and rang, over and over.

He checked his watch. It was early. But Gioni was a morning person.

Maybe she was in the shower.

He'd stop by her apartment. Maybe she could alleviate his worries. And maybe they'd get a quickie in before they went to his office.

"I'LL DRIVE YOU BACK to Ellijay, Lisa," Brad said. "But I want to stop and see if Hanks has regained consciousness first. And then I'll go to the station and see Thigs."

"I told you, Brad, I'm not ready to return to Ellijay."

Brad cradled her elbows in his hands and forced her to look at him. "Lisa, I saw how happy you were in the mountains. You had friends, a job you like, those pictures of the kids on the wall." He braced himself for a goodbye. "You're a born teacher. You were meant to find someone who can love you, someone who'll settle down with you, have a family."

Lisa hesitated, looked into his eyes. He sensed an unspoken question, one she already knew the answer to.

He wasn't the man to give her all that.

Still, she waited a fraction of a second longer. In her eyes, he saw hurt when he didn't reply. Acceptance. Maybe even understanding. Something he didn't deserve, not after the way he'd taken her all night.

"I should get dressed then," she finally said.

He simply nodded.

The shower water kicked on, and he imagined her body slick with soap and water, saw himself climbing into the spray with her and running his fingers and lips over every inch of that beautiful skin. The skin he'd memorized. The body he knew so well.

The woman he thought he couldn't live without.

The woman he'd protect by letting her go back to her safe life.

Convinced he was doing the right thing for her, for both of them, he dressed quickly, made a pot of coffee, then left food and water on the back stoop for the dog. When Lisa reappeared, dressed in jeans and a V-necked blue T-shirt, he handed her a cup of coffee, and they headed outside. He was starving, so he pulled into a drive-thru and ordered a couple of sausage biscuits. Lisa merely nibbled on hers while he downed his in three bites. The sex had made him hungry.

The woman beside him made him hungrier.

But he'd have to settle for breakfast.

Lisa was quiet, looking out the window, and although he wanted to be ecstatic that they'd caught the right man, a bad feeling settled in his gut. Hanks hadn't confessed to the murders.

HANKS WAS DEAD. A heart attack in the night. He had to tell Lisa. The facts of the case rolled through Brad's head again, and he had the distinct feeling that if the man was guilty, he'd want to brag about his crimes. The profiler's comments rushed back—how he was socially inept. Had probably tried to make it as a cop or doctor or some other high profile job but failed.

On a hunch, Brad called Ethan from the car. "Listen,

did you ever look at that list of applicants for the police force or the Bureau, the ones who didn't make it?"

"I just received it, haven't had time to look at it yet."

"Scroll down," Brad said, "and see if there are any names you recognize. Anyone local."

Brad glanced at Lisa and saw her watching him, but he turned back to the road, waiting on his partner.

"Booker?"

"Yeah?"

"Shit, you aren't going to believe this."

"What?"

"You know that guy Surges who got sick at the crime scenes."

Brad swallowed, the bad feeling in his stomach growing. "Yeah?"

"Four years ago, he applied to the academy, but they turned him down. He barely slid in by the skin of his teeth last year."

"Jesus." Brad muttered a curse. "Call Rosberg and have him get Surges in for questioning."

"Will do."

Brad hung up, scrubbing a hand through his hair. Surges appeared to be a weakling emotionally, yet physically he might be strong. He could be frustrated because he wanted to be a cop but didn't have the stomach for it. And Brad had felt sorry for the guy. Hell, Brad had even stationed him beside Lisa at the last scene to protect her.

"What was that about?" she asked.

He explained about Hanks's death and his suspicions about Surges, hating the renewed look of fear on her face.

"So if this cop's the killer, then he was at the crime scenes. He could have altered the evidence."

Brad nodded. "And he found the note at the cabin that day."

"He could have put it there."

Brad nodded again. But his cell phone rang before he could elaborate. "Booker here."

"Agent Booker?"

"Yes. Who is this?"

"Dr. Langley's assistant, Gioni." The woman's voice sounded muffled. Or maybe they had a bad connection. "Is Lisa Langley with you?"

"Yes."

"May I speak to her, please?"

He gave a clipped yes, then handed Lisa the phone. "It's your father's assistant, Gioni."

Lisa frowned. "Hello." She hesitated. "Yes, Gioni, I'll have Brad drop me off."

Lisa hung up, looking puzzled.

"What's going on?"

"She wants me to come to her place. She said my dad's going to meet us there, that he has something to tell me."

"I'll drop you off, and pick you up after I check on Surges."

Lisa gave him directions to a condominium complex near the hospital, and he maneuvered through traffic, finding it with no problem. He parked and Lisa reached for the door.

"I'm walking you in."

"Brad, that's not necessary."

"Indulge me. I'm not taking any chances until I know for sure that Hanks or Thigs is the Grave Digger."

She nodded and climbed out, and he escorted her up the sidewalk. Lisa rang the doorbell, but no one answered. Brad tried the knob, and the door swung open. Instantly alert, he reached for his gun, pushed Lisa behind him and slipped inside.

Seconds later, something hard slammed against his head. His legs buckled and his gun went skittering across the floor. He tried to crawl toward it, but the intruder grabbed it first and fired. A bullet pierced Brad's shoulder and tossed his body backward.

Lisa screamed and reached for him, but the man grabbed her, then fired the gun again. The second bullet zinged through Brad, ripping into his chest.

He coughed up blood, then the world went black.

LIAM TRIED GIONI on his cell phone as he drove toward her apartment, cursing when she didn't answer. He dialed the hospital to see if she'd arrived early, but the receptionist hadn't seen her.

His chest tightened. Something was wrong. He could feel it in his gut.

The things he'd learned about Darcy Mae Richards the night before taunted him with what-ifs. He'd spent half the night doing research, the other half telling himself he was losing his mind to even contemplate such a possibility, that if he went to Booker with his theory the agent would not only think he was crazy, but

Liam would be putting his career on the line. Maybe for nothing.

His tires screeched as he steered his Lexus into the parking lot, then a siren wailed behind him. He cursed, assuming a policeman had caught him speeding, but glanced in his rearview window. An ambulance raced behind the police car, fast on its tail.

His pulse kicked into overdrive.

The next second he spotted Booker's black sedan, and panic rolled through him. He slammed on his brakes, threw the car into Park and bolted out of it. The two officers in the police car beat him to Gioni's door. The paramedics jumped from the ambulance and rushed up behind them.

"Wait, sir," a heavyset officer ordered Langley. "Someone called it in, there was gunfire. The shooter may still be inside."

"But I'm a doctor," Langley said. "This condo belongs to my assistant."

"We'll let you know when it's clear."

The officers removed their weapons and checked the apartment. Seconds later, one of them ran out and motioned toward the paramedics. "Get a stretcher in here now!" He glanced at Langley. "We have a cop down, and an injured woman."

"Gioni." Liam ran inside, his heart thundering. Booker lay on the floor in a puddle of blood, while Gioni had been tied and gagged near the sofa. He stopped to check for a pulse on Booker. "He's alive."

Then he ran to Gioni. The other cop was untying her.

She was unconscious, had been beaten badly, but he thought she would survive. That is, unless she had internal injuries.

His heart pounding, Langley began barking orders left and right while the paramedics lifted Booker onto the stretcher.

Gioni roused and tried to speak, dried blood crusting her lip. "He took…Lisa," she whispered.

"What?" He clutched her hand, hating the sight of her swollen, bruised face, the black-and-blue marks on her arms. "Who?"

"Grave Digger," she said with a raggedy cry. "So sorry, Liam…had to call."

"Jesus." He yelled at the cop to phone in Lisa's disappearance, then swallowed back bile. Gioni had called Lisa, and she and Booker had walked into a trap.

Booker didn't look good. Liam wasn't sure if he'd even make it.

And if they didn't find Lisa, she wouldn't, either.

LISA DID NOT WANT TO DIE. Not now. She had too much to live for.

She'd just found Brad. Had discovered the sweet, wonderful feeling of being in love. Of having a sexual relationship. Of feeling whole and having hope for a future.

Brad.

Tears streamed down her face as she struggled with the bindings around her arms and ankles. He'd been shot trying to save her. The blood…it had been everywhere.

Was he still alive?

Grief swelled inside her, an ache so deep and horrible that she brought her knees up to her chest and rocked herself back and forth, the sound of her sobs filling the still, dank air.

And Gioni—poor Gioni. Her father's assistant had been beaten so severely she'd been unconscious. Would she survive?

Her father's face flashed into her mind. He'd lost her mother and had been devastated. What would it do to him to lose Gioni?

And now her....

More tears streamed down her face and into her hair, the cold terror gripping her.

She had no idea where she was. Or how long she'd been here. But she wasn't in the box. Not yet. If so, she wouldn't be able to move.

Maybe there was time.

The dark shadows of the room clawed at her with the realization that she was helpless, though, taking her back to another time. To four years ago, when she'd almost lost her life.

Anger suddenly surfaced, battling its way through the terror, and she tried to roll sideways to study the room.

Then she saw his eyes. Dark, evil, piercing orbs shining like two black pieces of coal suspended in a surreal world where a predator stalked his captive before the kill.

She refused to show him her fear.

"Who are you?" she whispered.

He smiled, crooked teeth flashing in the night. "Don't you know, Lisa?"

She squinted, but it was so dark all she could see was the faint outline of a man's face. Smell the stench of a sour odor that probably existed only in her mind, it was so evil. His voice didn't sound familiar, either.

"Tell me," she said, at least wanting a name to use when she addressed him.

"William."

She frowned, shaking her head. She had seen this man somewhere. At the crime scenes, maybe. "William is dead."

"No... Your father gave him new life. And now he lives in me." His voice sounded hollow, rough like sandpaper. He reached out, ran a blunt fingernail across her brow. She shuddered, recoiling as her stomach convulsed. "I was weak before, but he made me strong. And he wants me to have you."

Swallowing back the bile in her throat, she licked her dry lips. It was so hot, a million degrees in the room. The air was stifling, sticky and filled with an acrid odor.

The shadow of his movements caught in a tiny stream of light. Sweat trickled along his jaw, and he wiped it away, then turned a bottle of water up and drank greedily. His Adam's apple bobbed up and down as he filled his mouth with more. Water leaked from the bottle, spilling from his lips and running down his neck.

Her mouth clenched, the dry insides sticking together.

Instead of offering her a drink, he wiped a tear from her cheek, then lifted his finger to her mouth. "Are you thirsty, Lisa?"

She bit down on her lip, refusing to lick his finger.

Maybe if she stalled, Brad would find her.

Only he had been bleeding so badly… What if he didn't make it? Grief consumed her again, powerful and all-consuming. A sob escaped, from deep within her soul.

But his laughter brought it to a halt.

She had to hold on to hope, do something, find out why he was doing this. "I don't understand," she finally whispered.

He suddenly gripped his head, shaking it back and forth, then stood and moved across the dark room like an animal that had been caged. "Neither did I. Not at first. All I wanted was a chance to live, to be someone, to make it as a cop."

His voice had changed, become lower, softer. More ominous.

"All my life, I dreamed of being a detective or an FBI agent." He halted, ripped open his shirt. She stared at the long jagged scar, the puckered flesh where he'd had heart surgery, and horror dawned.

"But my heart was too damn weak before," he said in a feeble voice.

"You couldn't pass the physical," Lisa whispered.

He shook his head again, a wild, strange look in his eyes as he approached her, his voice rising with agitation, "Don't you see? They wouldn't let me in the Bureau. It was all I ever wanted to do, and they refused me. But after the transplant I was stronger. White gave me life. I'm a new man."

He had been at all of the crime scenes. And he'd

probably found and hidden any trace evidence. No wonder they hadn't been able to identify him.

And they probably never would.

Lisa squelched the panic that realization brought. She couldn't give up. Maybe Gioni or Brad had figured out the truth. Maybe they were on their way to find her now. And this time they'd save her before he put her in the ground.

Oh, God, they had to. She couldn't go there, not again....

He threw up his hands and waved them near his head, ranting and pacing just as William had.

"You received a second chance," Lisa said. "So why hurt people?"

"White is in control now." A flat tone replaced the feeble one.

"You're not White."

"I...didn't know what was happening at first, didn't understand. I'd wake up in a strange place, be somewhere I didn't remember going to at all." He paced again, his heels clicking on the floor as he picked up speed. "I'd have blood and dirt on my hands. My head would be spinning." He raked his hand down his chest. "I'd have scratches on my body."

"You were blacking out," Lisa said.

"I thought I was crazy," he said in a shrill tone. "I started hearing voices, dark whispers telling me what to do."

"You don't have to listen to them," Lisa said, desperate to stall. "You're stronger than William. Think about your career."

A harsh laugh echoed in the air. "No, *he's* stronger than me. The minute I discovered my donor's identity, I realized what was happening. He was speaking to me, ordering me to get revenge on the people who'd carved him up."

A shudder coursed through Lisa. This man honestly thought that having William's heart had turned him into a killer.

"You don't have to be like him," she pleaded. "That's not who you are."

"But it is now." His voice sounded crazed again. "I have memories, I see the faces of the women. Joann Worthy, Mindy Faulkner, Darcy Mae Richards—they all helped carve out my organs, and gave them away to someone else."

"So you could have a better life…." Lisa cried, terrified at the look on his face.

The stench of his sweaty body odor sizzled in the still air around him. "You shouldn't have told on William," he murmured. "He loved you so much, Lisa."

"He didn't know anything about love," she argued. "When you love someone, you don't hurt them."

"He did love you." He stopped in front of her, his voice angry. "But you turned on him. Turned to that fucking agent Booker. And now you have to be punished."

He jerked her head sideways so hard her neck cracked and she grunted in pain, more tears streaming down her face as he angled her head sideways.

Then she saw the box.

CHAPTER NINETEEN

THE NEXT TWENTY-FOUR hours were torture for Liam Langley. Booker hadn't yet regained consciousness, but he'd survive. Gioni had faded in and out, but she'd been too weak to speak. When they'd arrived at the hospital, they'd discovered she had internal bleeding, so they'd rushed her to surgery to remove her spleen. He'd been out of his mind, afraid he'd lose her.

Afraid that it was all his fault.

They still had no leads as to where the Grave Digger had taken Lisa. Liam was ill, thinking about what she must be going through. The unbearable heat. The brutality. The knowledge that the man intended to bury her alive.

How would she survive a second time?

Shaking with fury and terror, he paced beside Gioni's bed, praying she'd wake up. Maybe if she did, she could identify the killer. Liam had been on the phone constantly, badgering the police to hurry. They'd assured him they were doing everything they could, but they'd promised that before.

So, he had taken matters into his own hands. Had

decided to pursue the possibility that he'd been contemplating all night.

That the organ transplant surgery he'd performed might have something to do with this copycat's appearance.

He'd finally reached his friend at St. Jude's. Darcy Mae Richards had been on the team that had performed two of the transplant surgeries at St. Jude's.

His own lies haunted him.

Mindy Faulkner had been on duty the night White had died. In fact, Mindy had assisted him in the surgical procedure to remove White's organs. Later, Liam had covered his tracks and hers by faking the paperwork and paying off a couple of nurses to lie for him. The other woman, Joann Worthy, had been more puzzling, but he'd finally discovered her connection. It hadn't been the jury duty; instead, she had volunteered at the Buckhead hospital, had handled the paperwork with the transfer of organs.

Liam had confiscated all the medical files on the recipients—liver, kidney, corneas, lungs and heart—and was debating whether to tell the police. Would they believe such a ludicrous possibility, or think he was crazy?

Gioni moaned, and Liam darted back to her bedside, then clasped her hand in his, his chest tight. He'd been frantic with worry all night, for her and Lisa. "Gioni?"

Her eyelids fluttered open, then closed, and she whimpered.

He lowered his head against his hands, trying to compose himself. He hated to see her suffer. Wished he'd been better to her over the years. Had vowed a thousand times during the night that if she woke up and forgave him, he would.

Finally calmer, he said in a low voice, "I know you're in pain, sweetheart, but please open your eyes. We have to find Lisa."

"L...isa," she whispered in a weak voice.

He stroked her hand gently, cognizant of the fact that she must be sore and tender. Her wrists and feet were raw from rope burns, her eyes and jaw swollen, her flesh discolored. This woman had done so much for him over the years, yet he'd held himself at a distance from her. Had been too afraid to love because he feared the pain of loss.

But last night as he'd waited during surgery, he'd realized he loved her, that he had for a long time. That he'd simply been denying his feelings. That he didn't want her to die, either.

"So sorry," she whispered. Her eyes fluttered open again, this time tears streaming down her battered cheeks. "Don't...hate me, Liam. So scared..."

Emotions welled in his throat. She looked so pale, and she was suffering. And it was his fault. "I don't hate you, Gioni, I never could." He pressed a kiss to her hand, then laid it on his cheek. "I'm so sorry you were hurt. It's my fault, Gioni. My fault. Every woman I've ever cared for gets hurt. Mindy argued with me about White, but I didn't listen and she's dead."

"No...shh, Liam." She shook her head, but guilt mushroomed in his chest. He hadn't protected Lisa four years ago. And now two women he loved had been hurt again.

All because he had wanted revenge.

And oh, God, if what he suspected was true, other women had suffered and died because of him….

"Gioni, I've been thinking," he choked out. "The night we performed surgery on White—"

Her eyes widened as if to protest, but he continued. "No, listen. We both know White hadn't agreed to be an organ donor, that I falsified those papers because of my own need for revenge. I—" His voice broke. "I wanted to hurt him, to make him suffer the way Lisa had."

Another tear dribbled down her cheek. "It's okay, Liam, I understand."

"You saw the man who attacked you, didn't you?"

She nodded, her chin trembling.

"Do you know his name?"

"No." She flinched as if remembering the beating. "He stuck a knife to my head and made me call Lisa. I…shouldn't have done it. I should have just let him kill me…but I was s-scared…."

"Shh, it's okay, we'll find her." Liam kissed her forehead tenderly, then grabbed the files he'd gathered. "But you have to help me, sweetheart. Look at these pictures, and tell me if you recognize any of these men."

Two of the organ recipients had been women, so he held up the other photos. One, a black man named Clarence Walls, the next a white man in his mid-forties, named Teddy Lamar, and the last, a young man in his mid-twenties named Dale Dunbar.

Gioni gasped and began to wail in terror. "That's him."

Liam's heart clenched. So he had been right. He had created a monster when he'd taken those organs without White's permission.

"I have to tell the police."

She grabbed his hand. "Liam, don't tell them that you forged the papers. It'll ruin your career."

He hesitated, stroked her hair gently from her face. "My career means nothing without you and Lisa."

He kissed her on the lips, then hurried to Booker's room to see if he was awake.

THROUGH THE NIGHTMARISH fog of pain and drugs, Brad opened his eyes. His body felt as if it weighed a thousand pounds, his mind was a blur and his side and shoulder hurt like hell.

Captain Rosberg stood by the window, his hands jammed in his pockets.

The reality of what had happened crashed in on him. "Lisa?" He clutched his chest and tried to sit up, but Ethan coaxed him back down.

"We're doing everything we can to find her," Ethan said.

Which wouldn't be enough. They had missed something....

"How long have I been here?" Brad asked in a husky voice.

"Since yesterday."

God no. He nearly choked on the anguish knifing through him.

"Jesus." Brad pushed at the covers. "I have to get out of here."

"The doctors says you're not going anywhere," the captain stated. "We'll take it from here."

"Have you found Surges?"

Rosberg frowned. "He was dismissed from the department two days ago. No one's seen him since, but we're looking for him. And we've got a tail on Nettleton."

"Good."

"About the first victim volunteering at that small private hospital in Buckhead. We're wondering if that's the connection instead of the jury duty."

Brad's mind raced as he cut his eyes toward the captain. Three people associated with three different hospitals had been victims. Mindy had worked at the one where White died. White hadn't faked his death, but still something bothered Brad about that night... The fact that White had been an organ donor.

The organ transplants...

"I want to speak with Dr. Langley," Brad said.

Rosberg's sympathetic look twisted the knife deeper in his chest. He knew Brad was weak. Knew he'd fallen for Lisa.

Knew that time was running out.

"Whoa, Booker. Let Manning handle it."

"I need to find this killer and save Lisa."

Liam Langley suddenly burst into the room. "It's urgent I talk to you, Booker."

Brad's gaze met Langley's, his earlier suspicions mounting.

"He's through investigating this case, Dr. Langley," Rosberg said. "You can talk to me."

Langley moved toward the bed. "No, it's Booker I want to speak to. Alone."

Brad sat up, his chest heaving. "Leave us for a minute."

The men traded curious looks but finally Rosberg stepped outside, fuming.

Brad braced himself for a confrontation. He deserved it. Langley could say or do whatever he wanted to him, and Brad wouldn't blame him. If they didn't find Lisa, he didn't want to live himself.

Then again, he wanted to ask about those transplants... "Langley, Rosberg reminded me that Joann Worthy volunteered at a small private hospital in Buckhead. What's going on? This case has something to do with the night White died, doesn't it?"

"Listen, Booker, that's why I'm here." Langley hesitated, his breathing labored. "It has everything to do with that night, and it's all my fault."

"What?"

Langley jerked a photo from inside his jacket. "This is the man who kidnapped Lisa. Gioni identified him."

"Dunbar." Brad's chest felt as if a cannon had exploded inside. "Where did you get this? How do you know he's our perp?"

Langley's voice trembled as he confessed about the night White had come into the E.R. "I thought White had taken so many lives that his organs should be used to save someone else. But I didn't know the names of the recipients." Langley rubbed his forehead. "But then I got a hunch, so I checked at St. Jude's. Darcy Mae Richards was on the team that performed the heart transplant."

"I didn't think recipients knew the donor's names," Brad said.

"It's not standard policy to tell them, no. But Dunbar must have found out…" Langley's voice broke. "I…it's all my fault. He must have adopted White's MO to get revenge because White hadn't agreed to be a donor."

"I'm not sure I follow," Brad argued. "It seems he'd be glad you gave him the heart so he would live."

"That's just it," Langley said. "Some research about heart transplant patients suggests their recipients are different after surgery. They have different personalities, suffer depression. And if White's psychosis was in some way genetic, well…I gave this man the heart of a killer."

The pieces fell together in Brad's mind. "Dunbar was a CSI techie, so he could cover up evidence," Brad said. "In fact, he was at each of the crime scenes." Just as Surges had been.

He'd probably been laughing his ass off that the FBI hadn't caught on.

Damn it! "You have to help me out of here," Brad said. "And call my partner, Ethan. We'll need his help."

Brad yanked the IV from his arm and threw his legs over the side of the bed. Time was of the essence. He'd almost lost Lisa once.

He couldn't lose her a second time.

He had locked her in the box.

Lisa closed her eyes, the infernal drip, drip, drip of the faucet in the neighboring room a constant reminder that she was slowly becoming dehydrated. She had perspired so much she was sure her sweat glands were empty. Her throat was so dry that when she tried to scream, her voice came out a croak. And every muscle in her body was sore from where he'd beaten her.

Details of the case kept floating back as the minutes and seconds ticked by. The similarities between this killer and William. The differences. This latest copycat killer left a cross on the victims—because he believed he had risen from the dead.

He had also tried to sexually assault his victims. So far, he had spared her that hellish experience, but she had no idea what he would do next, or if that atrocity was still to come.

Determined not to spend her final hours agonizing over what horrors she faced, she closed her eyes and lapsed into a surreal state where she let her mind drift away. She'd done the same thing the first time she'd been abducted.

This time she would, too. And she wouldn't give up hope.

At least, not until the very end.

An image of Brad floated through her mind. The blood...

No, she banished that image. Couldn't stand the fear that knotted her chest at the thought. Brad was strong, tough. He'd somehow manage to pull through. And he'd lead the police to find her.

He *would*.

She couldn't allow herself to believe anything different.

Her breathing became more shallow. She'd rest. Conserve air. Save her energy so if he opened the box when he returned, she'd have the strength to fight.

She forced her mind back to the happy times.

When she was little and her mother was still alive, they'd both sit on the bed, Lisa tucked between her mom's legs, and her mother would drag the brush through her hair, counting as she did. Later, she'd sing pretty songs while she turned out the light and tucked Lisa into bed. There were days when her parents would hold hands and walk beside her in the park. Rare days when her father would lift her up on his shoulders or take her for a piggyback ride across the yard. Nights when she'd sneak into the den late in the evening and see her parents dancing like two lovers in the twilight.

The day her mother had given her the amethyst. Lisa had held it up to the light and watched the shades of purple glitter.

Then her mother had died.

Lisa knotted her fists by her side. No, she wouldn't think about that day or the life that came after. Only the happy times. The pony ride on her fourth birthday. The toys that magically appeared under the Christmas tree. Her father dressed as Santa Claus for the kids at the hospital.

Although she thought she'd cried all her tears, moisture pooled in her eyes. She wanted kids of her own, wanted to dance with her own lover in the twilight, wanted to have babies and play Santa for them.

Images of Brad's face and the past few days flashed back.

Brad at her school in Ellijay. Eating dinner with her in the cabin. The anguish in his eyes that night by the lake when he'd been pounding the punching bag. The tender passionate way he'd held her and pressed his lips to hers.

The sight of him dripping wet with that towel around his waist. Water glistening off the dark hair on his chest. The look of rapture on his face when he'd risen above her and thrust inside.

The image of him holding a baby. Their baby. A son, maybe. Or a little girl with his whiskey-colored eyes.

The door in the room screeched open, and Lisa tensed, the images receding as the well of fear dragged her into its dark abyss. He was coming toward her, his footsteps thundering.

She'd seen the devil in his eyes as he'd shot Brad, then dragged her to the floor and knocked her out. He pulled at the top of the box now, opening it, and she shrank back.

But there was no place to hide.

Damn it, where had the killer hidden Lisa?

Brad tugged his shirt on and fumbled with the buttons. He had to get out of the hospital.

Ethan frowned at him. "What the hell do you think you're doing?"

"What does it look like I'm doing?" he asked. "I'm going after Lisa."

Ethan gestured toward the bandages across Brad's shoulder and chest. "You're not in any shape to hunt down a killer."

Langley cleared his throat. "He's right, Booker. As a doctor—"

"Consider yourself and the hospital free of any responsibility." Brad gripped Ethan by the collar. "Listen, Langley thinks this lunatic is Dunbar. And I'm not lying in bed while Lisa's suffering."

Ethan glared at him. "Tell me what you know, and I'll get a team on it."

Brad heaved himself to a standing position and tucked the shirt into his pants. "I promised Lisa I'd protect her, and I'm not breaking that promise. Now, you drive, and Dr. Langley and I'll fill you in on the way."

Brad started walking, swayed slightly, then hesitated and started again, refusing Langley's assistance. Five minutes later, they settled in the car.

"Now, what?" Ethan asked.

"Radio in and find out where Dunbar lives."

"The CSI guy?" Ethan asked.

"Yeah. And get a search warrant." Brad explained Langley's theory, omitting the part about him falsifying White's donor forms. Langley cleared his throat, obviously willing to come clean, but Brad shook his head, cutting him off. They'd deal with that indiscretion later. He didn't want any issues muddying the case.

Ethan cranked up the air conditioner while they waited on the dispatch officer to give him the address. Perspiration coated Brad's face and arms, and his hands trembled, the pain in his chest like a knife blade twisting inside his body.

"Do you need something for the pain?" Langley asked. "I can give you—"

"No." Medication would only slow him down. It sure as hell wouldn't do him any good now or cure what really hurt him.

Only finding Lisa alive could do that.

"He lives near Lake Lanier," Ethan said.

Shit. Not too far from his own house.

No wonder the killer had been able to sneak into the woods by the lake to bury the bodies. He could have hauled the boxes over in a boat. Another reason they hadn't found tire tracks.

Ethan flipped on the siren, spun onto I-285, then sped toward Peachtree Industrial Boulevard. Ten minutes later, he maneuvered through traffic, taking the right shoulder when necessary. It still took fifteen more minutes before they'd reached the turnoff for the road that led to the lake.

Dark clouds obliterated any remaining light and threatened rain, although the drought continued. Brad tried to banish thoughts of how hot it would be in that box. Langley clenched the back of Brad's seat in a white-knuckled grip, his breathing labored as they bumped over the ruts in the dirt road.

Brad had prayed only once in his life. Now he was making it twice—both times, that they would find Lisa alive.

Ethan screeched to a stop, and all three men jumped

out. Ethan unholstered his gun, then reached inside his pant leg, removed a smaller pistol and handed it to Brad. Brad nodded in thanks, then gestured for Langley to get behind them as they darted toward the house.

Moving together with practiced ease, he and Ethan ducked down low, then slipped up to the side windows. The lights were off. The house seemed unusually quiet. Eerie.

Damn it. No! It hadn't been three days yet.

The man couldn't have already taken Lisa to her grave....

CHAPTER TWENTY

SECONDS LATER, Brad and Ethan stormed Dunbar's house. Another team was supposed to search Surges's place. A worn plaid couch and chair faced a big-screen TV, while newspapers littered an oak coffee table. An empty scotch bottle lay overturned on the floor next to a pair of dusty boots.

Brad paused and listened for sounds. Nothing.

Ethan ducked to the left, into the tiny kitchen, and Brad veered to the right to check the bedroom. It was empty.

"Kitchen's clean," Ethan said behind him.

Disappointment bolted through Brad. Lisa wasn't here, and neither was Dunbar.

Langley was supposed to be waiting outside, but he rushed into the room, pale and shaking. "Did you find her?"

"No." Brad glanced at the unmade bed, the tangle of sheets, the discarded jeans and T-shirts lying in a pile on the floor, and grimaced. Details of what the Grave Digger did to his victims before he killed them raced through his mind.

"I'll search the kitchen again," Ethan said, jerking

him from the thoughts. "See if there's anything there to tell us where he might have gone."

Brad did the same in the bedroom, first checking the desk drawer, then the closet. In the back, tucked inside a shoe box, he found four bags holding nail clippings.

Four. Joann Worthy. Mindy Faulkner. Darcy Mae Richards.

Lisa.

God. He grabbed the wall for support, nausea building. Dunbar was their man. And he'd been right under their noses. Brad should have seen it sooner. The man was cool, unemotional, had the expertise to cover the crimes.

"Booker?"

"Evidence," he said without elaborating. "You were right, it's Dunbar." No reason for Langley to know that the sicko had already clipped her nails.

What else had he done to her?

Trembling, he scrounged through the closet again, but found nothing. Remembering that White had kept Lisa in the box beneath his bed for the first few days, he dropped to his knees and looked under it, hoping she was there.

There was no box. But there were track marks where Dunbar had dragged a long, rectangular-shaped object across the faded carpet.

"I should have put it together sooner," Langley said. "Sometimes with the surgery, patients go into depression. Some men are even afraid of sex, afraid they'll have a heart attack. Sometimes the medication affects them. Makes them impotent."

Brad grimaced. He'd tried not to believe all the crap about genetics making a killer, but now he wasn't so sure.

Langley paced the bedroom, a chalky pallor to his skin. "Where the hell is he keeping her?"

Brad strode to the front of the house to find his partner. "Call Rosberg. Tell him to organize several teams to search the areas near where the other victims were buried. And get some dogs here to see if they can trace Dunbar's scent or Lisa's."

Ethan nodded, then gestured behind him. "I found his workroom."

Brad opened the door to the attached garage and grimaced. There was enough wood there to build several more coffins.

THE MOTION OF THE VEHICLE rocked Lisa back and forth, back and forth, making her already rumbling stomach queasy. She fought not to throw up, knowing she couldn't lose more water. Suffocating heat enveloped her, robbing her of air, and the smell of gasoline rose to add to the nasty scent of her own sweaty, naked body.

He was driving her to her burial spot. But where was it?

And how would Brad find her?

Brad... If only she knew he'd survived the gunshot wound. That he had talked to Gioni....

The reality that he might not have survived yanked at her frayed nerves. Blinding terror over her own destiny dredged up the horror she'd tried so hard to forget the past four years. She had to tap into the man's conscience.

William didn't have one.

But she sensed this man did. That he was conflicted about what he was doing. That he thought he had no power to stop it.

Maybe she could convince him that if William lived inside him, he could fight him and win.

Her thoughts raced, images of the other three women being pulled from the grave playing on her mind.

Forget them. Don't think about it or it'll paralyze you.

Yes, she had to focus on the sounds around her. Maybe then she could figure out where he was taking her.

But what then? How would her location help her if she couldn't escape this damn box?

The car hit a bump, the gears grinding. She froze and listened as gravel spewed and pinged off the sides of the vehicle. Bells clamored and he slowed, braked, then sat waiting. For what?

The shrill of a train whistle echoed in the distance, and she realized he had stopped at the tracks. She closed her eyes, hating the darkness, and tried to discern if the train was a freight train or a passenger one. Probably freight. They were definitely driving in the country; she could tell that from the winding, bumpy roads.

Finally, the train rolled past, the metal bars screeched upward and he gunned the engine, bouncing over the tracks. Then he made a sharp turn to the right, and Lisa's breath caught as memory dawned. William had made a sharp turn four years ago after crossing the railroad tracks.

This man must be taking her to the same place where White had left her.

BRAD, ETHAN AND LANGLEY met the rest of the task force members, along with a group of local officers, detectives and rangers who'd come forward to help with the search. Rosberg had argued with Brad, but Brad refused to leave.

Ethan organized them into groups, assigning maps and various segments of the area for the teams to focus upon. Choppers had also been called in to help expedite the search. Everyone was armed with water, emergency supplies, flashlights and phones, and a team of dogs led by a specialist was combing the area along the lake on foot. But if Dunbar had used a boat, the dogs might not be able to locate and track his scent.

And if Dunbar had buried her, what time had he done so? How much oxygen would she have? How much heat could she stand without water?

His shoulder pinched, the stitches pulling, the incessant throbbing in his chest gnawing at his endurance as he and Langley combed the woods nearest Brad's cabin. If the psycho wanted to torture Brad, why not do it as close to his place as possible? An in-your-face move?

Brad was counting on that.

Having come up empty, they met to regroup. Exhausted faces and strained looks were all they had to show for their work.

"She's not here," Ethan said. "We've searched every inch of the lake property within a fifteen-mile radius."

"She has to be," Brad said, refusing to give up.

Langley leaned against a tree, his face haggard. "I can't believe this is happening a second time. God, why?"

"The dogs didn't come up with anything?" Brad asked.

Officer Gunther shook his head. "I'm afraid not. We picked up other scents, presumably of the first three victims, but not Lisa Langley's."

"Maybe Dunbar didn't bring her here at all," Ethan said.

Brad's mind raced. "Then where did he take her?" He glanced at Langley and saw the ill expression on his face. The search had been tense, Langley's guilt palpable. Brad still didn't know whether or not he believed the doctor's theory. Neither had he decided what to do about Langley's unethical conduct.

Nothing mattered but finding Lisa.

Then it hit him. They'd assumed the Grave Digger would bury her near the other victims. But maybe not... "If he's thinking like White..."

"What?" Langley croaked.

"Then he might have taken Lisa to the same place White did. Death Valley."

LISA CRAVED THE LIGHT. Light and water. And air. But it was becoming harder and harder to breathe. She could almost feel her heart slowing down. The energy it took to pump blood through her system was waning. Her body felt scorched, on fire, dry as if flames had fried the skin, as if the fire had settled in to eat away the next layer, then the next.

Soon her body would just shut down and die.

A tremor rocked through her at the thought.

The truck gears ground and the vehicle slowed to a crawl, then stopped. A sob of relief mingled with panic tugged at her nerves. Stopping meant they had reached their destination. That soon it would be over.

That time was almost up.

She closed her eyes and prayed to lapse into unconsciousness before he put her underground this time. She didn't think she could stand the sound of dirt and rocks pinging off the box again. Of imagining herself sinking deeper and deeper underground as the mound of dirt grew higher.

The sound of a car door opening cut through the night. The box scraped the bottom of the vehicle bed, then she felt jarred as he hoisted it down. Brush snapped and broke beneath the weight as he dragged it across the ground. Her head slammed against the wooden top, her sore body bouncing inside. She clawed the side, grappling for control, but it seemed like an eternity before he stopped again.

A sob welled in her throat and came out, a screeching, tortured sound like that of a sick animal. He jiggled the top. He was opening the box.

She had to fight and get out.

The top lifted slightly, cool air brushed her skin, and she dragged in a breath, almost choking with relief. Limbs and leaves cast shadows all around her, and the eerie outline of his hand holding a gun was silhouetted in the faint glow of moonlight shimmering through the trees. Then he dangled a gold cross in front of her, swinging it back and forth in the murky night. His final preparations. The necklace. Then he'd chop off her hair. And it would be over.

"You have to wear the cross while we make love. Then to your grave," he said in a voice that sounded faraway. Detached. As if it didn't belong to the man in front of her.

She summoned every ounce of strength she had, thrust her body upward and tore at his face. Her broken nails contacted his eyes and she jabbed hard, punching with all her might. He bellowed, dropped the weapon and swung his fists at her, but she pushed his chest so hard he fell backward. His hands covered his eyes for a minute, his cry wild, and she threw herself out of the box and into the dirt. She scrambled for a tree limb, anything to help her stand, but she was so weak her knees buckled. He lunged for her, and she crawled on her hands and knees, grabbed rocks, dirt, leaves—anything she could find—and threw it at his face. He coughed and sputtered, fighting to see, blocking the debris with his splayed fingers, and cursing madly. She pushed up and finally stood, swaying and wobbling as she ran through the woods.

He caught her seconds later, slapped her so hard she slammed against a tree. Her bare back stung as the bark scraped her, and the jolt sent a bolt of pain through her lungs. But she fought back. Brought her knee up and connected with his groin. Reached for a stick and swung it at his face, poking at his eyes as if she was jabbing at a fire.

"Lisa! Goddamn it, stop fighting!" He lunged again, shouting, cursing and spitting her name.

She rammed the stick at his chest, gasping for air as he wailed and staggered back. Taking advantage of that second, she turned and ran again. She needed to reach the car, but he was blocking the way, so she ran into the bowels of the forest, stumbling and tripping, grabbing at trees and bushes and weeds to steady herself. Her foot hit a huge rock, and she tripped and went rolling downhill. Down. Down. Down to the bottom of Death Valley.

Her head slammed against a boulder, and she tasted blood and dirt. Still, she tried to scramble up. She had to keep going. Get away. Save herself.

Seconds later, she screamed as he gripped her hair, yanked her head backward and dragged her toward the grave.

SIRENS BLARED through the night, car lights flashing, as Ethan managed to reach "Death Valley" in record time. Langley had kept his head bowed in his hands the entire ride, muttering mindlessly.

Brad prayed and held his chest, because the pain had begun to explode, ripping down his arms and sides, splintering up toward his head so that he had to grip it once or twice and inhale sharply to keep from passing out.

Ethan screeched to a stop. The other officers from the search team were following at a distance, but Brad, Ethan and Langley didn't wait. They jumped out, Brad a little unsteadily, but he managed to find the ground with his feet and hold on for dear life.

Lisa's. Not his own. As long as he saved her, he didn't

care what happened to him. Let death claim him if it wanted him that badly.

The men ran through the trees, Brad leading as he remembered the trail that led to the part of the valley where they'd found Lisa the first time. The woods were thick with brush and briars, buzzing insects, sweltering heat.

Then a sound splintered the night.

"No!"

Lisa. She was screaming.

She was alive.

"That way!" Brad pointed toward a thicket of pines and darted toward it, picking up his pace although blood seeped from his chest wound and his head swam. Ethan followed, with Langley trailing them, their breath rattling out as they raced toward the clearing.

"No! Help! Somebody please help me!"

Brad gritted his teeth, wielding the gun as he burst through the clearing. Dunbar had Lisa by the hair and was shoving her into a hole in the ground. She was naked and fighting, clawing wildly at his arms.

"Hold it! FBI!" Ethan yelled.

Brad didn't wait. The sight of Dunbar hurting Lisa sent him rocketing toward the man. He pounced on his back and tore him away from her, pressing the gun to his temple. "Move and I'll blow your head off."

Langley ran toward his daughter, quickly covering her with his jacket. Brad glanced sideways to see if she was okay, but Dunbar took advantage, swung his arm up and knocked the gun to the ground. The two men rolled in the dirt, trading punches and blows while Ethan circled with his gun drawn, looking for a chance to fire.

Brad slammed his fist into Dunbar's head, then his face, blood spurting as he pummeled him over and over. Dunbar fought back, but adrenaline surged through Brad, and he jerked Dunbar up by the neck, then slammed his head against a rock. The man's skull cracked and his eyes rolled back in his head.

Brad slammed him again, but Ethan grabbed his arm. "He's out, man. Let's call it in."

Brad ignored him, but his partner dragged him off. "See about the girl."

Ethan's words registered, and he shoved away from Dunbar's limp body, grabbed his gun, then staggered toward Lisa. His chest was bleeding heavily, but he didn't care. Ethan unpocketed his cell phone to tell the others their location, and to call for an ambulance.

Lisa was sobbing and hanging on to her father, but as Brad approached, she looked up into his eyes. The sight of her swollen and puffy face sent fresh fury and anguish through him.

"Brad! He has a gun!" She pushed at her father's arms to reach Brad, but Dunbar found his gun. Suddenly a gunshot blasted the air.

The bullet ripped through Brad's lower back, and he fell to his knees. Lisa screamed again, her eyes widening in horror. He twisted slightly, just enough to fire a bullet into Dunbar's chest. Ethan's bullet hit the man next. Dunbar fell backward, blood spilling from his chest and mouth.

Brad collapsed onto the dirt, the world spinning. Numbness seeped into his limbs, replacing the pain.

He was going to die.

But Lisa was safe. Safe and alive.

And he could die a happy man.

Because for a heartbeat in time, she had been his.

CHAPTER TWENTY-ONE

"No!" LISA LUNGED TOWARD Brad. She had to get to him. Touch him. See if he was all right.

Her father grabbed her, trying to hold her back, but she shoved him away. "Daddy! Help him!" She crawled across the ground to Brad, sobbing with panic. Blood gushed from his chest and back. He was so still. His eyes were closed.

Was he breathing?

Her father rushed to help her, but she waved him toward Brad. "I'm okay. Help him, Daddy! Please… p-please help Brad!"

Her father dropped to his side and checked for a pulse. Lisa cradled Brad's hand in hers and pressed it to her chest, rocking back and forth. "Please don't leave me, Brad, you can't die." Sobs wrenched from her, but she was so dehydrated, she started to heave.

"Get her some water!" her father barked.

Brad's partner knelt beside her, patted her back, then stuck a water bottle to her lips. She drank greedily, the cool water flowing down her throat and spilling onto her chin.

"Shh, slow down," Ethan murmured.

She coughed and choked, then swiped at her mouth with the back of her hand. "Daddy, is he alive?"

"He has a pulse." Her father gave her a grim look, then removed his handkerchief and applied pressure to the wound. "But it's low and thready. We have to get him to a hospital fast."

Ethan punched in the number for the others. "Where the hell are you? We have an officer down! Get an ambulance in here now!"

Lisa gulped another sip of water, then hugged Brad's hand to her again, her eyes glued to the blood oozing from him. He couldn't leave her now. They'd gone through too much to have things end this way.

He had saved her once. No, twice. And he'd taken a bullet for her. Three to be exact.

He just couldn't die.

A group of men burst through the opening, and the next half hour erupted into chaos as they strapped Brad to a stretcher. Her father wrapped a blanket around her and cradled her in his arms. "Shh, baby, it's going to be all right."

"I have to ride with him," Lisa whispered.

"Okay. But I'm going to check you over, get you some fluids."

Lisa nodded and collapsed against him, terror for Brad zapping her last remaining strength. "Please, Dad," she whispered. "Please keep him alive."

"I'll do everything I can, princess. I promise."

She nodded again, then her father carried her to the ambulance and settled her inside. The paramedic started an IV while her father gave the orders to begin treating Brad, then the ambulance tore off into the night.

Two days later

BRAD WAS DYING. He saw a light so bright it beckoned him to float toward it. He welcomed the peace and quiet, then almost laughed, wondering why he'd expect peace and quiet.

If he'd died, he sure as hell wouldn't be going to heaven. No, the devil would take him home where he belonged. He wasn't a saint, but a sinner.

But at least Lisa was alive.

Her father would take care of her. Brad had seen the tears in her eyes before he'd passed out, though. Heard her cries of terror. And he'd seen the bruises on her face. The bruises she'd sustained because he hadn't done his job right.

Pain knifed through his chest, his shoulder and his lower back. His legs felt like dead weights. But the pain—wasn't death supposed to be free of pain?

Not in hell. You burned there for eternity.

Yes, he was in hell. His body was on fire. Pinpoints of fire burning through the muscle and tissue. Flashes of light flickered behind his eyes.

Wait—there was light. But no fire.

He knew because he'd opened his eyes.

"Welcome back to the land of the living."

He grunted, then blinked to bring the world into focus. Nope. He wasn't in hell. Not technically. But in a hospital bed with a zillion machines bleeping and tubes attached to his body like battery wires keeping him alive.

He tried to speak, but a croak came out instead.

"You've been here two days," Ethan said. "About time you woke up."

"L…isa?"

"Is fine. They treated her for contusions and dehydration, and she's resting on the floor below you."

He closed his eyes, thanked God for the first time in his life.

The door squeaked open, and Dr. Langley appeared, his expression grim, but better than the last time he'd seen him. "I'm sure you're in pain now," Langley said. "But you're going to be fine, Booker. You need time to heal."

Brad remained silent. He really didn't care now if he lived or died.

Ethan stepped away, looked out the window as if to offer them privacy while Langley moved up beside him.

"Thank you for saving my daughter," the doctor stated.

"She…she's really all right?" he said in a gruff whisper.

Langley's mouth tightened. "She will be. She's a tough girl. Woman."

Brad tried to smile, but it hurt too damn bad.

Wayne Nettleton burst into the room. "So you are awake, Agent Booker. And you're in here, too, Dr. Langley. Just the two men I wanted to see."

Ethan grabbed the man's arm. "What the hell are you doing here?"

Langley froze and looked at Brad, unsettled issues lingering between them.

Brad shook his head, and Langley's eyes narrowed.

"Dr. Langley, is it true that the Grave Digger was the recipient of William White's heart?"

Lisa's father nodded.

"And is it true that White did not give legal permission to be a transplant donor?"

Langley's pale face turned gray, but Brad cleared his throat. "I don't know where you got that information, but you're wrong."

Langley gave him an odd look, but Brad continued. "In fact, Dr. Langley was the first one to suspect that the killer might be a recipient."

"That's because he took his organs illegally," Nettleton said.

"You can't print that," Brad barked.

"Get out of here, Nettleton," Ethan snapped. "Agent Booker has had surgery and needs his rest."

"But the public deserves the truth," the reporter argued.

"Then we'll tell them how you were in Vernon Hanks's room right before he died," Ethan said. "That you upset him and caused him to go into arrhythmia, then you ran from the room like a coward without calling for help. That if you had, you might have saved the man's life."

Nettleton visibly paled and staggered back. "But you can't—"

"The hospital security has you on tape, and I have two witnesses," Ethan said in an icy tone. "Just think what will happen to your career at the *Atlanta Daily* when you're arrested."

"I didn't know he was going to die," Nettleton whined. He glanced at Brad and Langley in a panic. "Please, we'll make a deal here. I'll keep quiet about any suspicions over the organ transplants if you don't press charges."

Brad lifted a weak hand to rub at his chest. "I told you your information is wrong."

"Yes, yes, it must be." Nettleton backed away, pleading with Ethan for a deal. Ethan escorted him out, the man still sputtering.

Langley's mouth was set in a tight line. "Why did you do that, Booker? I was prepared to come forward with the truth."

Brad swallowed. God, his mouth was so dry. And he wanted to see Lisa one more time.

"Because we're more alike than you want to think, Langley." He paused, tried to moisten his mouth, then muttered, "And we both did what we did for Lisa."

LISA HAD THOUGHT THE TIME she'd spent in that box had been long, but the past forty-eight hours waiting to find out if Brad would survive were excruciating.

She'd lain in bed and rested, slept the first twenty-four hours, sucked down water and IV fluids, and had finally gotten a bath. One of her father's nurses had filed her chopped-off nails so they were smooth again—all things to make her feel better.

Gioni had visited, the two of them hugging and crying like children as they'd talked about their close brush with death, and compared the bruises, which had turned a rainbow of purples, yellows and oranges. Gioni had apologized a thousand times, but Lisa had forgiven her instantly. She only hoped her father came to his senses and made things right with Gioni. He needed a wife. And Gioni loved him dearly.

Lisa had seen more emotion in him the past two days than she had for the last four years. And she had hopes that the two of them would be close again.

After all, he had saved Brad. She owed him for that.

The door creaked open, and he poked his head in. "How's my little princess feeling?"

"Dad?"

His face colored. "I'm sorry, I know you're all grown up, but you'll always be my baby." He walked toward her, his eyes glimmering with emotions she didn't understand. "Are you feeling stronger today?"

"Yes. Dad, tell me about Brad." She clutched his hand. "Is he out of intensive care? Can I see him?"

"Yes, and yes," her father said. "But first there's something I have to tell you."

"Can't it wait, Dad? I need to see Brad."

He scraped a hand over the back of his neck, then looked at her and nodded. "I'll get a wheelchair."

"I can walk."

She threw the covers aside and reached for the robe he'd brought her the day before. She slipped her arms in the sleeves, then stepped up to the mirror, nearly gasping at how horrible she looked. "I wish I had some makeup," she said softly, touching her battered cheek.

Her father turned her toward him, then cupped her face in his hands. "My God, Lisa, you are so beautiful."

"No, Dad, I...I know I've disappointed you—"

"Lisa, shh. You are beautiful inside and out. I finally realize my mistakes. That's what's important. All I want is for you to be happy."

She hugged him, tears filling her eyes as he embraced her back.

"I'm so sorry about all this, baby. So sorry."

"Shh, Daddy, it's okay. I'm all right and so is Gioni. We're both strong women."

He nodded against her hair, and when she looked up, she saw tears in his eyes.

"Daddy, we're going to be okay. I hope you will."

"I thought I'd lost both of you," he said in a broken voice. "I...don't know what I would have done."

Lisa's throat closed. "You're not losing either one of us, so stop thinking like that." They hugged for another long moment, then she pulled away and pressed a hand to his cheek. "Please, Dad, I have to see Brad now."

He nodded and walked her into the hall, then helped her onto the elevator. Her mind whirled with possibilities for the future. Brad had survived, but he'd need time to recover. She wanted to take care of him. Stay with him when he went home until he felt better. Until they could make love again and figure out their future.

But Brad had planned to drive her back to Ellijay. Would he change his mind now if he knew she loved him?

BRAD GRIPPED THE ENDS of the sheet, bracing himself, as Lisa walked into his room. He'd done nothing but think about her since he'd woken up. Hell, he'd done nothing but dream about her while he'd been unconscious. Crazy, ridiculous dreams of holding her forever, of marrying her and having babies and picking apples on Sundays so she could bake him a damn pie.

But between those dreams, unbidden memories of Dunbar yanking her hair, twisting her neck back, of that shovel stuck in the ground, assaulted him. He saw Lisa naked and injured, knew that as long as she was with him, she wouldn't be safe.

"Brad?"

He faced her, his heart wrenching at the sight of the bruises on her face and her swollen eye. He wanted to reach out and touch the wounds, soothe her with kisses, promise her he'd never let anyone hurt her again.

But he'd done that before. Twice. And he'd failed both times.

A man who did that to a woman didn't deserve a third chance.

She inched to the bedside, a long white, silky robe knotted at her waist, her hair spilling over her shoulders in silken threads that looked like spun gold beneath the hospital lights. A soft smile formed on her mouth, although the movement accentuated a tiny cut at the corner of her upper lip.

His hands fisted by his side. Damn Dunbar. The hate swelled inside Brad, clenching his insides in a viselike grip.

"I...had to see you." She reached out, laid her hand over his, and damned if his body didn't betray him. He curled his fingers up to latch on to her hand, though he was too weak to raise his arm. The last bullet had come damn close to hitting his spine. He still wasn't sure what kind of nerve damage he'd have. It might take months of rehab before he could walk, and Langley had warned him he might need a cane.

An FBI agent with a cane. Hell, he couldn't handle desk duty.

"How do you feel?" she asked.

Like a crippled failure. "Fine," he said instead. He squeezed her hand, decided he had to be a man and apologize. "I'm sorry he got you, Lisa—"

"Shh." Tears glistened in her eyes, then she dropped her head forward and pressed a tender kiss to his lips. "I'm just glad we both survived."

He licked his lips, memorized her taste. "He can't ever hurt you again."

She nodded. "I know. It's finally over."

Brad's throat grew thick. Yes, it was. But he wasn't ready for it to be over between them.

Although it had to be. Dragging it out would only hurt more.

He had to let her go. Lisa belonged in the mountains with the fresh air, the kids she taught, those apple trees and her pies.

"I…I wanted to die when I saw you take that bullet," Lisa admitted in a shaky voice. "And waiting through surgery… I thought it would never end."

"Shh, it's over now, Lisa. You can return to Ellijay, to your life."

Her mouth twisted slightly. "I...I love you, Brad."

Three words he'd never heard before. Three words he didn't know how to deal with.

"Get out of here, Lisa. Go back to the mountains."

She placed her hand over his jaw, and he tensed. "No, Brad...we have something special here, between us—"

He gritted his teeth, planting his mask back on his face. "I was just doing my job, Lisa."

"I don't believe that. I...felt something between us." Hurt tinged her voice. "When we made love—"

"We had sex, Lisa. Men and women do it all the time." He adopted his poker face. Easier to be a bastard than try to be something he wasn't. A family man. That was what Lisa wanted, and he had no idea how to be that. "I told you, no promises."

"But—"

"I can't even let that damn dog in my house, Lisa. How the hell do you think I'd deal with a woman all the time?"

Her face crumpled, all the love he'd seen shining there turning to pain. Her breath quivered out, and she slowly released his hand. "Thank you for saving my life."

Then she turned and fled, the sound of a muffled sob breaking his heart as the door shut behind her. His fate was sealed. Now Lisa would return to her life. She'd find someone else to love, move on, have that future she deserved.

And he'd go back to his. His cabin by the lake. His job. The dog he kept outside.

He faced the window again, the first tear he'd ever shed slipping from his eye.

LISA TRIED TO MUFFLE her cries as she ran from Brad's room, but she felt as if her heart had been ripped to shreds. She had to leave the hospital. Get away from Atlanta. Go back to Ellijay and forget everything that had happened. That she'd been attacked and kidnapped again and almost died.

That she'd fallen in love for the second time in her life, and that both times it had been with Brad.

Blinded by tears, she stumbled toward the elevator, but suddenly two hands gripped her arms. She shrieked and looked up, ready to fight, but her father stared down at her with worry in his eyes. "Good Lord, Lisa, what's wrong?"

She crumpled against him, let him take her in his arms. "Daddy, take me home. Please, please get me out of here and take me home."

He pressed her head against his chest and stroked her hair. "What happened, princess? I thought you were going to see Booker."

"I did," she whispered. "But he doesn't want me, Daddy. I...I told him I love him, but he doesn't love me back."

CHAPTER TWENTY-TWO

Two months later

THE DROUGHT HAD FINALLY ended, and it had rained nonstop for the past few weeks, but Lisa welcomed the storms. She didn't know if she'd ever tire of the rain cooling her skin, watering the earth and turning things green again. She'd spent hours walking in the frequent showers, thinking about things, healing, sometimes throwing her head back and letting the rainwater sluice down her throat. In some ways, the constant storms mirrored the storm of emotions she'd dealt with daily, the tears she'd shed over Brad that had fallen like raindrops. She'd also felt badly for Vernon Hanks. She'd sensed he wasn't a killer, yet he'd died anyway. But the counselor at the hospital had assured her that he had died of natural causes, that with his obsessive behavior, he might have turned violent any minute. After all, he had bartered to hire someone to kill William White.

The new school year had begun, too. Ruby had been surprised but understanding when she'd learned Lisa's true identity. She'd also been slightly hurt that Lisa hadn't trusted her with the truth, but Lisa had sworn she'd kept her identity a secret to protect her. And Ruby had landed a job as her assistant at school this year, too. Even the principal and families of Lisa's former students had been supportive.

Lisa had a new class, a darling bunch of curious kindergartners who were eager to learn, precocious and loving. Even the mischievous ones had already stolen her heart.

Yet part of it would always belong to Brad.

A soul-deep ache stirred within her as she looked out at the apples growing plump and round on the trees. Some had already dropped to the ground; some were being harvested now. She'd made applesauce and apple butter but she hadn't yet made a pie, the memory of the one she'd shared with Brad too fresh on her mind.

Halloween had passed and Thanksgiving would be here soon. She glanced at the hand-drawn turkeys the children had painted, each tail feather of the bird describing something they were thankful for. She still thanked God that she was alive. That she'd been blessed with a few moments in time with the love of her life.

Ruby poked her head into the classroom where Lisa was busy straightening up for the day. "Lisa, there's someone here to see you."

Her heart fluttered for a moment, then her father walked into the room.

"You look disappointed, princess."

Lisa smiled and shook her head, then stood and kissed her father's cheek. "No, Dad, you know I love seeing you." One good thing had come out of the ordeal with the copycat killer. She and her father were getting close again. Talking about what went wrong, all the misunderstandings they'd had. The guilt that he'd wrestled with after her first abduction.

The guilt he still wrestled with now.

He'd finally admitted that he'd falsified William's donor forms and removed the organs himself. At the time, he'd thought that by doing so, that at least White's death would account for something, that he would be giving life instead of taking it. But his logic had backfired and three innocent women had died because Dunbar believed White had taken over his body.

Her father had wanted to come forward publicly, but Lisa encouraged him not to. She didn't want his career ruined. He didn't deserve that. And he didn't deserve the guilt....

To her surprise, he'd announced that he was giving up his practice, retiring to open a free clinic for the needy. She supposed he felt he had to atone for his unethical behavior.

But she'd been shocked even more that Brad had kept quiet. One day maybe she could ask him why. Knowing the two men didn't get along, she would have thought it the perfect opportunity for Brad to wield his power.

"How's school going?" her father asked.

"Good. The kids keep me on my toes."

Liam laughed. "You used to keep me on mine, too."

They laughed together as he shared another memory from the scrapbook of her youth. He'd been doing a lot of that lately. Telling her more about her mother, too.

Finally, he paused and glanced into her eyes. "Lisa… are you really okay? You still seem so sad. Aren't you sleeping well? Still having nightmares?"

"Some, but the therapy helps. You worry too much." She forced a smile. How could she tell her father she couldn't sleep for dreaming of Brad? "I'm really fine. I love being here, teaching the children. Besides, Thanksgiving's coming up, and we'll be together as a family this year."

Her father shuffled, suddenly looking nervous.

"Dad, what is it?"

"There's something I wanted to talk to you about. It's about Thanksgiving."

Disappointment ballooned in her chest. He was going away, just as he had when she was little. She and Gioni had both thought they were slowly chiseling away the protective walls he'd erected, but maybe they were wrong.

"I've asked Gioni to marry me," he blurted, a sheepish look coloring his face. "The wedding is the day before Thanksgiving, and we want you to be there."

Lisa stared at her father in surprise. "You're getting married?"

He took her hand in his. "Lisa, honey, I know it may be hard for you, and I hope you don't blame Gioni for calling you that night—"

"Dad," Lisa said, cutting him off. "I like Gioni. I don't blame her at all." She stood on tiptoe and threw her arms around his neck. "I'm so happy for you. It's about time you married her!"

He hugged her back, and for the first time in years,

she saw peace and happiness light his eyes. At least one of them would marry this fall, she thought as he drove away later. She tried not to think about the fact that she'd hoped it would be her.

BRAD TOSSED A ROCK into the lake and watched it zip across the surface. With the constant rain they'd had, the lake was full, finally recovering from the endless summer drought.

Ethan slumped onto a tree stump beside him. "How's it going?"

"Fine."

"Heard you graduated from the cane."

"Yeah, a few months and maybe I'll be able to jog around the lake." Brad grunted. "Did you find out what happened to Surges?"

"He decided to quit. Hear he's applied to firefighters' school." Ethan laughed. "Have you decided what you're going to do about the Bureau?"

Brad shrugged. "I'll be back." After all, what else did he know to do? His job was waiting. But he couldn't muster any enthusiasm for rushing his recovery.

"Have you talked to Lisa?"

He shot Ethan a lethal look. His partner had badgered him constantly to call her. To see her.

"No. She's better off."

"And what about you?"

"I told you I'm fine."

"You're not fine, Booker. You're a goddamn mess." Ethan stood, picked up a handful of rocks himself and plunked one into the water. "You've shut yourself off up here like you're some kind of recluse, feeling sorry for yourself."

Brad glared at him. "I'm not doing that. Lisa deserves to feel safe. She can't do that with me in her life."

"Look, Booker, I know what you're afraid of. I lived that nightmare." Ethan's voice cracked. "I watched my wife and kid get blown up, but you know what? Even though it kills me, and sometimes I wished I had walked away from them earlier, I know I'm better off for having had them in my life."

Shocked at his admission, Brad watched as Ethan turned and strode off. What the hell kind of logic was that? Selfish, that's what it was.

He stood, his lower back throbbing, but yanked on his boxing gloves and began to punch the bag. Over and over and over. One for the mother who'd thrown him away. One for the father who'd never claimed him. One for the foster parents who hadn't wanted him. Another for all the crazy lunatic killers.

And one more for the fact that he couldn't have Lisa.

Beauregard loped up and parked his ass beside him, and Brad gave him a foul look. "What? I let you in the house last night. What more do you want?"

The dog whined. "I know you miss her, too."

Memories flooded him. Lisa climbing from the car, bending to pet his mangy dog. Lisa climbing into his bed. Lisa naked and writhing below him.

Lisa whispering that she loved him.

A car engine cut through his inner diatribe, and he

paused, then glanced up the trail, figuring Ethan was back to badger him some more. But a white Cadillac glimmered through the trees. Liam Langley's.

His heart skipped a beat. God, something was wrong. Lisa.

He tossed the gloves to the ground and stalked up the path through the woods, running and limping. His breath wheezed out, and he leaned against the trunk of an oak, bracing himself as Langley exited his car.

The older man stood and folded his arms. "We have to talk, Booker."

"What's wrong?" Brad asked.

A thundercloud clapped above, threatening more rain, and Langley moved to the porch. Brad followed.

"What the hell is it? Is Lisa okay? Has something happened?"

Langley paced the porch. "She's okay. I guess."

Brad was sweating. "What kind of answer is that?"

Her father paused, stared him in the eye. "She misses you, Booker."

Brad's lungs tightened, exploding on a breath. "What?"

"I said she misses you." Langley jammed his hands in his pockets. "I...I owe you a lot. You took a bullet for her. Three, that is."

"I don't want your gratitude. I did that for Lisa." And he'd do it again, in a heartbeat.

"Well, you've got it and my respect. You covered my ass, and saved my reputation."

"I did that for Lisa, too."

"I know." The doctor lifted his steady gaze, scrutinizing. Brad felt as if he was under the knife. "At the hospital, you said that we're alike."

Brad nodded.

"You're right. We would both do anything for Lisa." Langley pressed his hand to his chest. "I know why I feel that way. She's my daughter, and I love her."

I love her, too. Brad almost said the words out loud but caught himself.

Langley waited, then shocked him by saying them for him. "You love her, too."

Brad remained silent. He'd only recently admitted it to himself. He wasn't ready to admit that to her father, not and face his wrath.

"As you pointed out four years ago," Brad finally said, "I'm no good for Lisa. She deserves someone better."

Langley whirled around, stared down the path, dropped his head forward as if struggling with something. "I did say that, and I meant it at the time. But I was dealing with my own guilt over not protecting Lisa." He hesitated again, then glanced up, a grave expression on his face. "We're both just men, Booker. If there's anything I've learned lately, it's that we're human. We make mistakes."

Brad swallowed, emotions battling their way to the surface. "Do you think she'll ever forgive us?"

A wry smile lit Langley's eyes. "That's the amazing thing about Lisa, Booker. She already has. And you know what else?"

Brad shook his head.

"She loves us anyway."

Unconditional love? He'd heard of the concept but didn't believe it existed.

"I did some checking into your past," Langley continued.

Damn. He knew Langley had to have an ulterior motive. "I know why you were arrested as a teen. Why you tried to kill your foster father."

"What does it matter?" Brad asked. "I left Lisa. You don't have to worry—"

"It does matter," Langley said, his voice commanding. "You were protecting your foster sister. That makes a helluva difference."

Brad opened his mouth to argue but couldn't. He saw the face of the little girl as if the incident had happened yesterday. "I didn't, though. She died."

"I know, and I'm sorry." Langley cleared his throat. "And you blame yourself because you couldn't save her."

"How do you know that?"

"Like you said, you and I are alike. I blamed myself for not being able to save Lisa's mother. And then I shut myself off from Lisa after the first attack, because I blamed myself for not keeping her safe." Langley stalked toward him. "I nearly lost it all. Lisa. Gioni. Just like you're going to do if you don't stop being a coward."

Brad had no idea what to say. Where Langley was going.

"When I'm wrong about someone, I say it. You're a fine upstanding man, Booker." Langley paused. "And my daughter would be lucky to have you." He removed an envelope from his pocket and dropped it onto the cane-back chair on the porch. "This is an invitation to Gioni's and my wedding. Lisa will be there. And I want you to be my best man." He started down the porch, not bothering to wait for a reply. "Don't be a fool and let your past keep you from having a future."

Brad watched the man stalk away in silence. Was Langley right? Was he really protecting Lisa by staying away from her?

Or was he simply too afraid of losing again to try?

"THANK YOU FOR BEING my maid of honor." Gioni hugged Lisa, her veil tangling as they pulled away.

Lisa laughed and fluffed the lace, her chest tight with happiness for her father and this woman. "I'm thrilled to have you in the family."

The bridal march started and Gioni smiled, her white tea-length, strapless satin dress molded to her figure as she stepped aside. Lisa moved to the church entrance and glanced down the aisle. The place was filled with her father's friends and coworkers, as well as Gioni's friends. Her father stood in a black tux, looking regal, with a grin on his face that made tears come to her eyes. She was so happy for him, her heart swelled.

Yet a sharp pang also ran through her.

But she squared her chin, determined not to allow thoughts of Brad and her own heartsick loneliness to ruin her father's day. She held the bouquet of roses in front of her, then stepped forward, glancing at the best man. Her dad hadn't told her who he'd asked, but she'd assumed it was one of his colleagues. For a minute, her vision must have blurred, though, because she thought Brad was standing beside him.

Her footsteps faltered.

No, she was seeing things. Willing Brad to be here in her mind. Having fantasies about the wedding she had wanted.

She blinked, then took another step, but the man raised his chin, and she faltered again.

He was tall. Broad shouldered. Muscular. Dark hair that had been trimmed brushed a black suit jacket. A chiseled face with wide cheekbones wore an emotionless mask.

But a pair of whiskey-colored eyes met hers. Searched her face.

Wariness filled his irises. Then unease. Then…desire.

Someone cleared his throat, and she realized it was her father. Out of the corner of her eye, she saw him motion her forward.

The rest of the wedding passed in a blur. Her dad and Gioni exchanged their vows and rings, but Lisa couldn't take her eyes off Brad.

Then suddenly the bridal couple rushed down the aisle, the guests cheered and Brad extended his arm for her. Lisa accepted it, a tingle traveling through her as his muscles tightened beneath her hand. Like a thirst she couldn't quench, one touch only wetted her need for more.

Brad ushered her into the reception area, where flowers, food and white-linen-covered tables laden with gifts and wedding cake beckoned. A band was already playing big band music. Her father and Gioni moved to the dance floor for their first celebratory dance as husband and wife.

It felt so good to be near Brad again that Lisa didn't want to release his arm, but she had so many questions. Why was he here? Had he missed her?

Her nerves ping-ponged back and forth from hope to fear as she turned to face him. She couldn't stand putting her heart out there again. What if he said no, that he had moved on with his life?

But God, he looked so handsome. She'd lain in bed so many nights wanting him.

"What are you doing here?" she whispered.

"Your father came to see me," he said in a low voice. "He asked me to be his best man."

Lisa frowned. Was that the only reason?

"He told me about the volunteer work."

Her heart was shattering.

He shifted, shoved his hand through his hair, sighed and looked down. "I...I moved the dog inside."

She twisted her fingers together, confused. Why was he talking about Beauregard?

Then it hit her. And hope flickered.

A smile twitched at one corner of his mouth as their gazes met. "He sleeps by the bed now."

She licked her lips, ached to reach out and kiss him. "I'm sure he likes that."

Brad nodded and studied his feet again.

Lisa saw him struggling and took pity. "Would you

like to dance, Brad?" Maybe he could relax then. Loosen up. Maybe then he'd kiss her.

"I don't know how," he said in a gruff voice.

"You don't know how to dance?" she asked, her breath raspy.

He shook his head, met her gaze, hunger flaring.

She took his hand. "I could teach you."

"No…"

Hope faded to a burning ember. He didn't love her.

"I don't know how to do this, either." He reached inside his pocket, removed a ring and held it up to her. Tears pooled in her eyes and spilled over. It was a beautiful amethyst in a white gold setting. Almost identical to the one her mother had given her, only larger.

"I don't know how to be in a relationship, to be a…husband," he said gruffly. "But I want to try."

Lisa's heart twisted. "I can teach you that, too."

"I know it's not the same ring—"

"Shh." She pressed her finger to his lips. "It's beautiful, Brad. I…love it. And I love you."

For a heartbeat, they simply stared into each other's eyes. Seeking. Yearning.

Then he slipped the ring on her finger, held out his arms, and she went into them.

WHILE THEY DANCED, their bodies gliding together, Brad imagined it as a prelude to making love, although Lisa had to lead and he kept stepping on her toes. He had wanted so badly to have Lisa back in his arms. And she had accepted his ring, had told him she loved him.

But he hadn't said the words back. Maybe he didn't have to. Maybe it was enough he was there with her. Maybe the ring said it all.

Or maybe he was afraid of saying it.

At midnight, they said goodbye to Gioni and her father, drove to the lake and picked up his dog, then went to Ellijay. The ride was practically silent, but Lisa curled up against him, and he savored the contact. Fantasized about what the long night ahead would hold. Bodies touching. Loving. Kissing. Joining.

He was hot simply from the thoughts.

Rain splattered the roof and ground as they climbed out and ran up to her porch. Beauregard barked, then loped inside and sprawled on the braided rug as if he owned the place.

Moisture glistened off Lisa's face, dripping from her hair as it did his. He twined a finger around a strand, then his gaze met hers for a long second before it fell to her breasts. The white silk halter top she wore was soaked, plastered to her skin, her nipples tight and puckering, pushing at the thin damp fabric.

"You are the most beautiful woman in the world," he whispered.

Lisa smiled, held out her hand, then led him to the bedroom. She lit a candle, flipped on an Alicia Keys CD, then turned and grasped for his hand just as the singer belted out, "I keep on falling in love again...."

In silent invitation, she placed his hand on her breast. He felt her heart beating beneath his fingers, felt her nipples tighten, her breath catch, and knew he'd never forget the sight of her, so sweet, so sexy, so unselfish, offering herself to him in the candlelight.

Without asking for anything.

She was so courageous, much more so than him.

"God, Lisa." He slid his hand to the tie at the top of her neck, wiggled it loose, then watched, his body hardening, as the sheer fabric slithered down, revealing her bare breasts. He swallowed, looking his fill, wishing he could be the man she deserved.

"I…I don't know how to be what you want," he said gruffly. "I'm so afraid I'll disappoint you."

Lisa cupped his face in her hands. "You already are the man I want, Brad, just the way you are." She pressed her lips to his and unfastened the buttons of his shirt, her fingers tangling in his chest hair, her touch igniting the flame of desire burning within him. "And you could never disappoint me."

He quivered with the need to believe her.

She thought he had saved her, but in reality, she had been the one to save him.

Emotions crowded his throat at the realization. He eased her down on the bed, stripped the skirt from her legs, ran his fingers and tongue over her body, loving every inch of her as she writhed in his arms. And when he sank inside her, and she cried out her love, every shred of doubt and fear shattered within him.

He rose above her, the two of them still connected in the deepest way possible, then whispered for her to open her eyes. "Look at us together, Lisa."

She glanced down at their bodies entwined, a sultry look darkening her irises. "I love you so much, Brad."

"I love you, too, Lisa."

With every ounce of emotion he possessed, he thrust inside her one more time, bringing them both to a mind-shattering climax that rocked his soul as they came together.

As they lay in each other's arms, rain softly splattered the roof and music floated through the air. Through the open window, the fresh scents of grass, of cinnamon and apples, and of hope drifted toward him. He imagined Lisa picking apples, making pies, rocking his babies and being his wife.

He hugged her to him, planted a kiss in her hair, then ran a finger along her cheek, stunned that he was with her now, that he had gotten so lucky.

In a heartbeat, he had almost lost Lisa. But a heartbeat later, she was back.

And she was his forever.

* * * * *

Don't miss Rita Herron's next gripping romantic suspense when LAST KISS GOODBYE debuts later this year!